FREEDOM
LAND

FREEDOM LAND

MARTIN L. MARCUS

A TOM DOHERTY ASSOCIATES BOOK

NEW YORK

FREEDOM LAND

Book design by Mark Abrams.

A Forge Book
Published by Tom Doherty Associates, LLC
175 Fifth Avenue
New York, NY 10010

www.tor.com

Forge® is a registered trademark of Tom Doherty Associates, LLC.

ISBN 0-765-30482-1

First Edition: January 2003

Printed in the United States of America

0 9 8 7 6 5 4 3 2 1

FOR *THE PUSS*,
CAROL DURBIN

ACKNOWLEDGMENTS

First and foremost, I wish to acknowledge Carol Durbin. Without her support, contributions, inspiration, imagination, and encouragement, this novel would not have been possible. Second, I wish to acknowledge Lionel Goldstein for giving me the characters, Amelia Herbert Hampton, Larrs Van Luys and Abraham. I also wish to acknowledge Keith Williams for his suggestions and edits on *Freedom Land*.

My editor, Michaela Hamilton, suggested the structure for the novel, and did a yeoman's job of helping me flesh out the characters. John Paine's line edit brought the story I was telling to the forefront. Ruth Sloviter's edit removed the malapropisms and improved my grammar. Finally, thank you to Tony Seidl. Without his belief in my novel, *Freedom Land* would not have found a publisher.

FREEDOM
LAND

PROLOGUE

The distinctive sound of a high C note, made by a silver knife tapping against fine crystal, rang out three times. The guests, twenty-five members of the South Georgia Cotton Planters Association and their wives, seated on both sides of a formal dining table, quieted. They looked toward their host, General Duncan Clinch.

Both his body and head were large. His prominent, protruding jowls were covered with white whiskers that stuck straight out. The remainder of his three-hundred-pound bulk was stuffed into a customized blue uniform, laced with gaudy gold braids and large epaulets.

A formally dressed house slave poured the 1812 Napoleon Brandy into the general's glass. He held it up for the toast.

"Ladies and gentlemen," said Clinch as he rose out of his chair, "let us open our tenth annual meeting with a toast to a real son of Georgia, Congressman Thomas Reilly."

There was polite applause. Clinch had founded the organization in 1825 to promote laws favoring cotton, in both the Georgia legislature and the United States Congress.

The general took a sip, savoring the nectar. He looked at his guests, and in response to his glance they followed suit.

"Congressman Reilly," continued Clinch, "played an important part in the treaty which will move the Seminole out of the lands south of here and into the territory west of the Mississippi, where their style of living will be more suited to the terrain."

Sitting on the general's left was the vivacious Amelia Herbert Hampton. She wore a fuchsia silk gown most recently of Charleston, but designed in and imported from Paris. Her plantation, five miles to the south, made her his closest neighbor. At forty-four years of age she looked a decade younger and was easily the most desirable woman in the room. She was the widow of the late General Oliver Herbert Hampton, a real general, as Amelia liked to say, unlike General Clinch, whose commission was in the Georgia militia.

Clinch took another sip of the brandy as the guests politely applauded. "And now, to celebrate our tenth anniversary, I have a special surprise," he announced, intentionally saving the best for last. "Under the terms of the treaty, the Seminoles have agreed that, when they move, they will deliver our runaway slaves back to us!"

The room lit up with applause from all except Amelia, who instead gave the general a polite nod. The general held up his hands, summoning the audience to quiet down. The room became still, anticipating his next announcement.

"This is finally the end of Abraham and that so-called Freedom Land!" said Clinch, not disguising his contempt. It brought an even louder ovation from his guests.

"That's right. No more sanctuary for nigras!" shouted Clinch over the applause. He nodded at his guests in response to the tribute, then sat down.

Clinch felt invincible. He turned to Amelia and whispered, "Marry me."

"Oh, General, that's the brandy speaking," said Amelia, politely putting off her host.

Before Clinch could respond he noticed his overseer, Larrs Van Luys, standing by the door, holding his hat in his hand. Van Luys was a gruff man in dress and manner, completely out of place at this function. Clinch thought to himself, "This had better be good." He'd lectured the man on several occasions about interrupting when he was entertaining. Clinch excused himself.

As the general approached, Van Luys retreated farther into the hall and began twisting his hat as if wringing the water out of it.

"Apologies for interrupting, sir," said Van Luys before the general could speak.

"What is it?" asked Clinch, being very short.

"Runaways," whispered Van Luys, so as not to alert the guests to this embarrassment.

"How many?" asked Clinch.

"Two, and they took their brat," answered Van Luys.

"Why are you telling me? Didn't I make it clear? Any more runaways and it comes out of your pocket."

"Yes sir, but—"

The general turned his back on the overseer in mid-sentence and walked toward his guests.

"We'll get em, General," called out the overseer.

PART ONE

BILLY,
ABRAHAM
& JIM

1

Dark clouds on the far horizon obscured the late-afternoon sun. The coming storm threatened to engorge the swollen stream racing through the center of the village. Unseasonably warm temperatures had caused the snow to melt. The adjacent fields of corn and beans had already flooded, forcing the farmers to dig emergency ditches to siphon off the water.

The red mud seeped into their houses, made of wooden posts with palmetto frond roofs. Some of these residences were without wood-planked floors, forcing the inhabitants to eat and sleep in the muck.

In a muddy hollow, inside the wall that surrounded the village, close to the front gate, a dozen boys took time out from their ditch-digging duties for a bit of sport. They surrounded the smallest boy and bound his wrists behind him with a leather tie. Yelling insults, they took turns racing up to him, taunting him with light punches and kicks. Their captive was fair-haired and blue-eyed.

It wasn't the first time eleven-year-old Billy Powell had been tied up, spit on, kicked, or insulted. To his playmates, Billy looked white. So who better to play the white man in their game?

Most of the other boys, older and stronger, ranging in age from twelve to fifteen, pulled their punches as they struck Billy. They did not intend to physically hurt him, merely to remind him that to them he was white.

He didn't protest when the bigger boys lifted him up and tethered him to the post. He remained quiet as they danced by, each boy landing a glancing blow. Billy prided himself in being able to take punishment. He might have inherited his father's fair coloring, but in his heart he longed to be accepted by his mother's people. He would show these young warriors he had the courage to endure.

For one of the players this exercise was more than a game. John MacIntosh, the sturdy younger son of Chief William MacIntosh, suddenly raced in and delivered a strong kick to the back of Billy's thigh, sending him face-first into the mud. Unable to use his hands, Billy struggled to his knees. He coughed the red earth from his mouth, then wiped his eyes on each of his shoulders.

With a start Billy realized the other boys had stopped their dancing and became silent. Then they parted, allowing a clear path to the post. Billy looked up. Standing before him was his father. In Billy's eyes he seemed a giant of a man. Just then the sun broke through the black cloud, making his father's wavy auburn hair and bristling copper whiskers appear aglow. His face was pale white and freckled, and he wore a bright red British major's tunic with shiny brass buttons.

The other boys stood silently watching as the major untied Billy. "Come laddie," he said as he took Billy's hand. "Let's go home." Billy smiled up at his father. He couldn't be more proud. Major

William Powell, of His Majesty's Ninth Regiment of Foot, was feared by his enemies and respected by the elders.

Father and son walked by two newly planted fields of corn and potatoes, past the rows of square huts with frond roofs, toward the livestock pens containing horses, cattle and pigs. There they stopped.

"How's your mother, lad?" asked the major.

"We both missed you," answered Billy, who spoke in the same Scottish brogue as his father. He tried to emulate his father in everything—dress, speech and manners. Billy resisted the urge to run home and alert his mother. Instead he pointed to the small pen in front of them where a well-groomed hog was segregated.

"Yon's the baby pig you gave me," said Billy, proudly.

The major nodded his approval of the animal's appearance.

Billy beamed up at his father as they continued walking toward their log cabin, located at the far corner of the walled village. Beyond the fence, the major could see a broader expanse of cleared land than when he had left in the spring.

Father and son saw their closest neighbor, Birdtail, whose dwelling of traditional Creek construction was leaking badly. His family, all related through his wife, inhabited each of the four residences built in a square around a courtyard and granary.

Birdtail was busy giving directions to his sixteen-year-old son, Little Crow, who was on the roof replacing the dwarf palmetto fronds. His wife and her three sisters, their husbands and three toddlers, stood nearby.

Dressed for the crisp damp weather, Birdtail wore his Creek finery: turban, feathers, braids, metal jewelry and a leg-of-mutton-sleeved coat. Except for his dark red skin and prominent nose, Birdtail looked more like a Gypsy pirate than a forty-year-old Indian.

Birdtail grudgingly acknowledged the major and Billy with a nod of his head and a grunt. Then he quickly turned away and continued supervising the roof repairs.

Billy and the major reached their cabin just as the sun cast its final rays across the valley. The cabin was made of oak timbers with a red brick chimney. It was built on a wood-beam foundation raising the oak-paneled floor eighteen inches above the ground. This kept the cabin dry in the rainy season when the stream running through the village rose. Outside the cabin, Billy's mother had planted a small vegetable garden. The beans, lettuce and potatoes were all sprouting.

"Let me surprise your mother," said the major in a hushed tone, bringing his finger to his lips.

Billy remained outside as his father opened the oak door and strode inside, calling out a hearty, "Hello, Jasmine me darlin'."

Jasmine looked up from cleaning a freshwater snapping turtle Billy had snared out of the swollen stream. She was wearing a red cotton turban similar to the one worn by all well-dressed members of the tribe. Her wool jacket and shirt would have been acceptable to any frontiersman's wife, for they had been acquired by the major at the general store in Terminus. Her necklaces set her apart from any white settler's woman. One was made of a strip of leather fastened to a circular flattened copper strip brought to a polish, the other was a strand of multicolored beads.

She was startled to see the major enter. Then she laid aside the pot containing the skinned and cleaned turtle, placed her hands on her hips and drew herself up to her full height. The fact that she barely came up to the major's chin made her no less imposing.

"Six months I don't know if you're dead or alive," scolded Jasmine in her brand of English, featuring a slight Scottish brogue. "And now you expect me to resume the marriage?"

"Aye," said Major William Powell with a grin that lit up his pale blue eyes.

"You better," said Jasmine, breaking into a smile. She fell into his arms. Their hungry kiss would have lasted much longer had Jasmine not noticed her son watching from the doorway.

"Billy, go to the stream and catch dinner," said Jasmine.

"I already did," answered Billy, not wanting to leave.

"Then go and wash. You're filthy," chided Jasmine.

"Aye, mother," said Billy. He understood they wanted to be alone.

Since he had first encountered the Creeks, William Powell had seen them adapt many of the white man's ways. The name "Creek" came from the shortening of "Ocheese Creek Indians"—a name given by the English to the native people living along that creek. Any tribe in the southeastern United States that lived beside a creek became "Creeks." Actually, they were part of the Muskogean Confederacy, consisting of two dozen loosely related tribes sharing a common language. Until the early eighteenth century, they controlled all of Georgia and parts of Alabama and Florida.

Several men in the tribe had abandoned their thatched huts and copied the log home with the brick chimney that Major William Powell had built for himself and his Creek wife, Jasmine. Still others used the white man's plow to turn the earth before planting crops. Perhaps most tellingly, an increasing number of Creeks had forsaken tribal names for Christian names, and spoke passable English. The ascension to Chief of William MacIntosh, the son of a Scottish trader, was a capstone of the changing times. To earlier generations, the idea of following a man with white blood in his veins would have been unthinkable.

Major William Powell had been on an extended mission among the tribes in the southeastern United States, doing his best to stir them up and bring them into England's war against the Americans. Powell, who'd shown a proficiency in language as a child, said in a half dozen native tongues: "The Americans will steal all of the native people's lands." He promised them guns, the friendship of the crown and their land in perpetuity, if they would fight against the Americans.

Though Powell had some success inciting the Chickasaws and Choctaws, he was unsuccessful in convincing his own wife's tribe,

the Northern Creeks, to go on the offensive. Nevertheless, he respected their decision.

William Powell was glad to be back with his family. He lay spent
in his wife's arms. For more than half a year he had anticipated this
reunion. It had been just as passionate as ever. Relaxing in their
carved four-poster bed with the white scalloped-silk canopy, the
major remembered when he had seen the bed in a catalog in the
general store in Terminus, and knew he had to have it. He'd visited
the thriving little community in the guise of a settler purchasing
supplies. Six months later, he picked it up and surprised Jasmine
with it.

The major stroked her long black hair, partially obscuring her
supple breasts. He brushed the hair aside and studied her large dark
nipples. She was as beautiful, perhaps even more so, as when he
first laid eyes upon her.

"Jasmine," he said softly. "D'you remember what I told you when
I brought home this bed?"

"That you like to make love to me in it," answered Jasmine.

"No!" protested the major.

"No? You don't like to make love to me in it?" said Jasmine,
playfully acting as if she was hurt by that statement. Of course she
wasn't. She couldn't keep her face sad very long and broke into a
wide grin.

"What else did I tell you?" asked the major.

"You told me that this was the kind of bed European royalty slept
in and that I was your queen," she answered with a kiss.

"That's right," said the major. "And I'll tell you something else.
I've got big plans for that boy of ours. He's special."

"Does that mean we're going to be seeing more of you?" asked
Jasmine.

"Yes," said the major. "When this war is over, I'm going to come
back here and we'll be a proper family."

Then he proceeded to show her just how much he did like making love to her in that bed.

Jasmine's Creek name was Tough Child because she had survived on two occasions when the medicine man had declared her condition hopeless. Her own mother had died in childbirth.

When she was seven years old, her father had been killed in a border skirmish with the Cherokees, who were attempting to invade the Creek lands. Now the Cherokees were gone, forced west by the white interlopers, and it seemed the Creeks were about to suffer the same fate.

Jasmine Powell had learned to be resourceful. She was adopted by the tribe as a community child, and several women, her aunts as she called them, had taken her under their wing, educating and caring for her.

Jasmine was sixteen years old the first summer Major William Powell took up with the tribe. She had been assigned by the Chief to familiarize him with tribal life. She changed her name to Jasmine because Major Powell took to calling her that. He said her scent reminded him of the fragrance.

The major stayed eight months the first time. When he returned from the Caribbean, where his assignment was to subvert French interests, Jasmine was in her seventh month carrying his child, whom he would christen Billy Powell. Ever since then, he'd been spending between six and eight months each year with Jasmine and their son.

That night, as the reunited family sat by the fire, Billy displayed his father's musket.

"Father, what do you think?" asked Billy, proudly holding up the oiled and polished musket for him to inspect. The major had taught Billy what seemed to him to be the entire British field manual, and Billy took great pride in demonstrating his proficiency with firearms.

"You did a fine job. Do you want to go hunting with me?" asked the major.

Billy became so excited that all he could do was to nod his head yes.

The next morning before dawn, Billy and the major set out. William forsook his officer's tunic for a buckskin jacket more suitable to the task at hand. They walked through the forest toward a spot where the major knew deer congregated. Billy carried his father's musket, though the weapon was almost as big as him.

"What stronger breastplate than a heart untainted," said the major in a theatrical voice.

Billy looked up at his father and smiled. How he loved to listen to him recite poetry.

"Thrice is he armed that hath his quarrel just, and he but naked, though locked up in steel, whose conscience with injustice is corrupted," continued the major.

"Teach me your words, Father," pleaded Billy.

"Those are William Shakespeare's words."

"Is he in your regiment?"

"No, son, he lived two hundred years ago. What do you think the words mean?"

"I don't know."

"What stronger breastplate than a heart untainted?" repeated the major.

"What is un, unpay—"

"Untainted. It means pure."

"What does that mean, Father?" asked Billy.

"What stronger armor than a pure heart?" asked the major.

"None, father."

"Now you say it."

Suddenly twigs snapped in the bushes to their right. Father and son froze.

A stag pranced out of the bush, crossed their path and bounded off. Billy raised the musket and fired, shattering the buck's shoulder with his one shot at over fifty yards. The animal tripped, cartwheeling forward. It broke its neck and was dead before it came to rest on the ground.

Father and son trotted to the animal. The major tied a rope around the antlers. He tossed the other end over a branch of the nearest tree. Father and son pulled on the rope, hoisting the stag until only the tips of its hind legs were touching the ground. The major then proceeded to gut the animal, draining its blood and removing its organs.

While he butchered the deer, he again recited the passage and had Billy repeat it several times, correcting his pronunciation until he was satisfied Billy had mastered the phrase and its meaning. Then he cut off each leg at the knee. Last, he cut the animal's neck at the shoulder. The butchered carcass separated and dropped to the ground, leaving the head and antlers swinging in the breeze.

That night, while dining on the fresh venison, Billy and the major retold the event to Jasmine. The major concluded by remarking, "Billy is a better shot than any man in my regiment."

After dinner Billy brought out the sack containing the chess pieces and board his father had brought him the previous year. The set was a gift to the major from his regimental sergeant, who'd whittled and then painted the pieces during a long boat ride to America.

Billy set up the chessmen exactly as his father had taught him. Billy sat behind the white pieces, his father behind the black.

Billy moved his queen's pawn two squares forward. His father gave him a discreet nod, then moved his own queen's pawn the same. Billy took his queen's knight and moved it diagonally behind the pawn. The major moved his queen's bishop's pawn two squares forward. Billy took his queen's bishop and brought it out four squares. He looked up at his father, who discreetly shook his head. Billy put the piece in its original position.

"What are you going to do three moves from now?" asked the major.

"I don't know. Does it not depend on what you do?" answered Billy, trying to grasp the concept.

"Aye and nay," explained his father. "Aye, you need a move for whatever I do, but you need to decide in advance what you want to accomplish."

The major moved his king's bishop, threatening Billy's knight. "Your knight," said the major, alerting Billy.

Billy responded by moving the piece. Then the major brought out his queen, again menacing Billy's knight. When Billy moved the knight, the major brought his bishop over, threatening Billy's king. "Check," he said.

Billy was frantic. He couldn't believe that he didn't see the threat to his king coming. He moved his king forward into the only space available. His father moved his knight and cut off Billy's king. "Checkmate," said the major. Billy stared, disappointed at the turn of events.

"That's a diversion," explained the major. "When an enemy's actions are too obvious, you'd be wise to look elsewhere. Conversely, when you're going to strike, make the enemy think you're attacking elsewhere."

Billy loved when his father talked to him like a soldier.

2

The company of Georgia militia, two hundred men, accompanied by volunteers from Alabama, was commanded by 260-pound Captain Duncan Clinch. They'd marched west from the captain's extensive South Georgia plantation. They were wearing newly issued blue wool tunics that protected them against the moist wind and forty-degree temperature.

Initially the terrain along the well-traveled road consisted of broad, sweeping hills dotted with trees. Then the road ended and the militia entered a hardwood forest following an ancient Indian trail. In places it was too muddy or not wide enough to accommodate the horse-drawn five-pound cannon or Duncan Clinch's deluxe carriage. In those places, the militiamen were forced to make a detour or physically lift a carriage wheel out of the mud or over a tree stump or boulder, all the while trying their best not to disturb the sleeping passenger.

Despite their best efforts, on two occasions during the night Clinch was forced to alight from the carriage so the wheels could be lifted. Clinch had planned an overnight march and dawn attack. The trip, slowed by a soggy trail, took thirty-six hours longer than planned. The army didn't arrive until the following evening.

"A preemptive strike will take the Creeks out of the war," had been Clinch's argument to the Georgia legislature when he met with them in a secret session to secure funding for his scheme. He did not mention the fact that the Northern Creeks had no intention of joining the Red Sticks, a warring faction of Creeks fighting on the side of the British in the ongoing War of 1812. Nor that the attack would afford Clinch the opportunity for increasing his own land holdings.

Rain was falling as the militia assembled a mile from the Creek village. The village was surrounded by an eight-foot wooden fence that ran over one mile in perimeter. There was a large wooden gate at the entrance. Two streams converged into one and ran under the fence near the front of the gate and continued out the rear.

Two groups of militia, fifty men in each, would enter the village. One would turn left, the other right, and proceed along each perimeter. Clinch's plan was to herd the Indians toward the center and encourage them to flee out the gate. One hundred and sixty Kentucky long rifles in the hands of expert marksmen would be pointing at the gate, waiting to finish the job. To ensure the riflemen's accuracy, Clinch promised a five-dollar bounty on male scalps.

Before leaving on his most recent mission, Major Powell had repeatedly warned Chief MacIntosh of the possibility that his village would be assaulted. Though the Creeks were reluctant to attack the Americans, they had accepted Major Powell's supply of British-made muskets and his plan for their defense. Powell had organized the Indians into forty-man squads. Each squad would protect a preassigned area: the well, the grain depository, and the front gate.

When the attack did not come, the Chief believed his declarations of friendship and refusal to partake in the hostilities had insulated the village from the war. Despite that, the approach of the militia had caused tempers to fray.

"This is your fault," shouted Birdtail at Chief William MacIntosh in Muskegon. "If you hadn't let the Redcoat stay with us, the Americans wouldn't be here."

Standing before the chief were Birdtail; Little Crow; Ed McBain, the medicine man; and James MacIntosh, the chief's fifteen-year-old son, who had reported the nearing Georgia militia.

"What are we going to do?" asked McBain.

"I say we give them the Redcoat," said Birdtail. "I say we tie him up, march him outside and hand him over."

"Maybe we should just hang him from the front gate," suggested MacIntosh sarcastically.

"Give them the Redcoat," insisted Birdtail.

Chief MacIntosh raised his hand, calling for silence. "How many are they?" he asked his son James.

"Over two hundred, Father, and they have a big gun."

"Where are they?"

"Only a mile from the gate."

"Shall we forget Major Powell has married into our family? Shall we give back the Redcoat's muskets?" asked the Chief rhetorically.

Birdtail knew that the weapons he and his son were holding were a gift from the King of England.

"And the advice and friendship Powell has shown us? Shall we forsake all that?" asked the Chief. No one answered.

"I will speak with them," announced the Chief.

"Shall I sound the alarm, Father?" asked James.

"No. You accompany me along with McBain and Birdtail. Little Crow and my son John will quietly alert the men to take up the defensive positions Major Powell has assigned."

———

A half mile from the village, the militia was surprised to see four unarmed Indians approaching them waving white cloths.

Clinch got out of his carriage. A soldier held an umbrella over him to keep him dry, as fifty militiamen pointed their Kentucky long rifles at the Indians.

"Let me welcome you," began Chief MacIntosh. He stood just over six feet tall. His chin-length black hair, parted in the middle, was held in place by a thin white cotton headband that also held a solitary eagle's feather. He knew of Clinch but had never met the man. "This is my son James and two of the men from the village," continued the Chief.

Captain Clinch just stood silently, staring at the Chief.

"Every man in the village is glad you are here," continued MacIntosh, breaking the silence. "You know we have rejected the Red Sticks and their war on you. Not a man belonging to our village has ever stolen a horse from or has done injury to a white man. We are your friends."

Clinch removed his gold pocketwatch and checked the time. Then he looked at William MacIntosh.

"Chief, I will give you twenty minutes to have all the men in the village lay their weapons in a pile outside the gate."

"We cannot do this, Clinch. The Red Sticks have threatened us for not joining them. Suppose they attack us?" asked the Chief.

"You have nineteen minutes, Chief," said Clinch, before turning to his second in command. "Bring up the cannon," he ordered.

"Please, Clinch, we are your friends," implored the Chief.

Again Clinch consulted his watch. "We attack in eighteen minutes!"

Chief MacIntosh, James, Birdtail and Ed McBain hurried back into the village and closed the gate behind them.

"They do not even know the Redcoat is here," the Chief chided Birdtail. "Powell was right, they're here to steal our land. Sound the alarm, son. I will stand with the forty men guarding the entrance."

The Chief pointed to the granary. "Birdtail, stand with the men protecting the well and granary. We will fall back to your position and then counterattack."

Twelve-year-old John ran up to his father and tugged on his sleeve. MacIntosh looked down at the boy. "I want to fight with you, Father," said John.

"Stand with your brother," said the Chief.

James began ringing the chime installed at the behest of Major William Powell.

Every family in the village came out of their homes, muskets, tomahawks and knives in hand.

Just then the cannon roared. The ball hit the gate, splintering it into dozens of pieces. When the second round hit, what remained of the large doors fell off the hinges, leaving a twenty-foot gap in the fence. A hundred men screamed at the top of their lungs as they ran through the opening.

William MacIntosh and his Creek warriors knelt behind piles of firewood, muskets pointed at the advancing militia. As the major had preached, each of the Indians marked a target, holding their fire as the enemy came closer.

Chief MacIntosh fired first, hitting a young militiaman squarely in the chest, sending him to his maker. The other thirty-nine Creeks fired, hitting twenty more of the charging soldiers. Despite the losses, the militiamen kept coming. The Indians had no opportunity to reload. Instead they rose up and met the onrushing soldiers with tomahawks and knives.

Chief MacIntosh wielded his war club, knocking down and killing the first two soldiers who reached his position. Then he felt a blow to the back of his head. He fell to his knees.

James and John were crouched next to one another behind the granary, muskets in hand, watching the battle. They saw their father fall. "Come on, John," shouted James to his younger brother as he rose to rescue his father. John froze. "Come on," implored James.

John backed away, then turned and ran in the other direction.

James rushed across the battlefield and plunged his knife into the soldier who was about to bayonet his father. Then he dragged his stunned father back toward the granary, where Birdtail and the second line of defense were waiting.

Seeing James dragging the chief, Birdtail ran out to help. A bullet struck his forehead. He fell dead instantly. Two soldiers anxious to cash in on the bounty hustled over. One grabbed his necklaces and continued on. The other soldier proceeded to scalp him. Little Crow watched helplessly from behind the granary as his father's body was mutilated.

"I shot him, the scalp's mine," screamed another militiaman as he stopped his charge and bent over the soldier taking Birdtail's scalp.

"Seeins how I got it in my hand, it's hardly yours," answered the soldier, looking up.

The militiaman pushed the soldier away from the prize. They looked at one another, then simultaneously grabbed the bloody scalp dangling from Birdtail's head, held only by a thin layer of flesh. They ripped the prize free, and a tug of war ensued.

"Stop it," shouted an officer at the two men fighting over the scalp. When the men ignored him, the officer swung his sword between them, barely missing the men's hands, but splitting the scalp. Each of the militiamen fell backward with a portion of the bloodied scalp in his hand. They both looked up at the officer.

"Continue the attack," ordered the officer, "or I'll kill you both."

The men just stared at him as he held his sword in front of their faces.

"There's more scalps to be had." Both men rose up, stuffed the trophies in their pouches and continued on.

"Knight to queen's bishop three, checkmate!" announced Billy. His opening gambit mated his father in eight moves. Of course, the major had deliberately allowed Billy to mate him. At that moment they heard the alarm. A few seconds later the cannon roared, and the gates to the Creek village were blown open.

Jasmine helped the major into his tunic. Billy quickly loaded his father's musket and handed it to him. The major gave Billy a hug. Then he peered outside the door. The firing and shouting were very close. The major motioned, and Billy and Jasmine followed him out, alongside their cabin, to the fence and the little door he had cut into it for just such an occasion. That's when Billy remembered the chess set. He ran back through the fence and into the cabin.

"Billy! No!" screamed his mother.

In the cabin Billy hastily gathered the pieces into a small sack. As he fled the cabin, the two militiamen who had fought over Birdtail's scalp rushed toward him.

"Kill'm," shouted the first to his compatriot. Billy ducked as they both fired. Two bullets tore into the wall just above his head. The soldiers converged on Billy. One blocked his retreat through the fence; the other came at him with fixed bayonet. Billy frantically sidestepped, avoiding his thrust.

Stepping back through the fence, the major caved in the back of the first soldier's head with his musket butt. Then he came at the other.

"Make war on children, do ye?" he yelled. "Let's see how ye handle someone your size."

The soldier turned his bayonet on the major, who easily parried his thrust, then fired point-blank into the soldier's stomach. The man toppled in excruciating pain.

"Let's go, mister, double time!" barked the major. Billy ran through the fence into his mother's waiting arms. When his father joined them, he was carrying a tunic belonging to one of the soldiers he'd just killed. He pointed to the sack with the chess set Billy carried.

"You disobeyed orders!" said the major angrily. "In a battle, each soldier must be counted on to do his part!"

The major removed his own tunic and handed it to Jasmine. "Go into the woods to the meeting place." The village had a designated location to regroup after just such an emergency. "I've got to try to stop this."

"Sir, take me with you," said Billy, standing at attention.

His father smiled at him, but he said, "Nay, you're a soldier now. Soldiers obey orders. Go with your mother, protect her. . . . You have your orders now."

The major put on the militiaman's uniform. He gave Jasmine a hug and a kiss, then stood up straight and saluted Billy, who stood at attention and saluted back.

When he saw they were safely hidden in the woods, the major circled through the woods to the front of the village, where he saw Clinch's carriage.

"Urgent message for the commander," he shouted to the sentry in his best American accent.

Then he walked past the man and stepped toward the lavish carriage. Custom-made at Fischer Carriage Works in Philadelphia, it featured an oak panel that folded down into a dinner table, seating four guests comfortably. Beneath the front window, which slid open for the captain to give the driver instructions, was a bar containing several bottles of the finest Kentucky whiskey, imported French wines and crystal glasses used when entertaining. The interior was upholstered in glossy black leather.

The captain's domestic staff had sent along several picnic baskets containing six fried capons, an entire rack of baby lamb, corn bread, and mashed potatoes for the overnight trip. The captain had a powerful appetite.

Major Powell entered the carriage. Clinch didn't so much as look up from the fried chicken he was devouring. Only when Powell stuck his pistol barrel against Clinch's cheek did he stop chewing and stare incredulously at the major.

"Tell the bugler to sound retreat."

With a pistol pointed at his head, Clinch stuck his head out the carriage door window, spat the chicken from his mouth and bellowed to the bugler as the major commanded.

Then Powell tied Clinch's hands behind his back with the red ribbon from the picnic basket. He picked up one of the embroidered linen napkins and stuffed it into the captain's mouth.

Finally he opened the bar and selected a bottle of brandy. He put it under his left arm and gave Clinch a mock salute with his right. "His Majesty's compliments."

Leaving the carriage, he encountered the same sentry. "The captain is not to be disturbed," said the major, grandly.

In the village, the outnumbered Creeks were putting up a spirited but futile defense in hand-to-hand combat when the bugle called the retreat. No one was sure why it was sounded, but the militiamen disengaged and withdrew from the village, allowing the Creeks to flee deep into the woods to their prearranged meeting place.

When they were sure the militia was gone, the Creeks came out of the woods and moved back into their village. Billy noticed the gate was a splintered shambles. Half of the thatched huts were burned to the ground. The grain supplies were looted. His pig and all the rest of the livestock were gone. Fifty-three of the women, and a hundred of the children, were now without husbands and fathers who had been killed in the attack.

Chief MacIntosh led the tribe to the ancient mounds located outside the village. There he conducted a Green Corn Ceremony so that the dead might join their ancestors in the spirit world.

When several tribal members suggested establishing themselves elsewhere, the Chief argued that they'd weathered the storm. Then he reminded them of the bond they had with this land and those who came before them.

Billy and his mother moved back into what was left of the house the major had built. The brick chimney and the adjacent room still stood, but the two rooms around it were destroyed.

Billy kept waiting for his father to return but, with the war against the United States over, the major, despite his protests, was assigned to India.

3

When Major Powell had been gone for one year, Chief MacIntosh decided to pay Jasmine Powell a visit.

"It has been many months since your father saved our people," began Chief MacIntosh. He addressed Billy and his mother, who sat by the fireplace listening. He was accompanied on this visit by his sons, John and James, who stood by his side. John was not happy. He stood fidgeting, doing his best to contain his hatred for Billy, who got the praise he never received and was respected by all, whereas John was respected by none. Now John was supposed to embrace this interloper as his brother.

"Since he has not returned, we can only assume he gave his life for our cause," said Chief MacIntosh.

"He's no' dead. I know so!" argued Billy.

"Billy!" chided his mother.

"Allow me to show our people's appreciation by adopting you

into my family as a son," said the Chief to Billy. "From now on, these are your brothers."

"No!" said thirteen-year-old John and stormed out of the cabin. James followed.

"I apologize for my son," said the Chief.

"This is a great honor, Billy," said Jasmine.

"I want my own father," insisted Billy.

"So do I, dear, but this is for the best," said Jasmine.

"Billy," said the Chief, "the tribe's survival depends on becoming like the whites. I want you to be the first among us to get a white man's education." Chief MacIntosh believed that the best strategy to keep their land was to assimilate. Billy would make an excellent ambassador for his tribe. He looked and spoke like a white man.

On the first day of school Billy walked the five miles from his village. He was wearing a white man's cotton shirt that his mother had purchased at Clinch's company store.

In the schoolhouse, the teacher assigned Billy a desk. As he sat down, the boy seated on his left stood.

"My pa says I don't have to have no truck with savages."

"There are no savages in my school," retorted the teacher. Yet after school was over, the other boys surrounded Billy, chanting, "Savage, savage!" Billy threw the first punch, knocking the tallest boy down. The other five boys around him converged. They knocked Billy down and began kicking him.

Luckily for him, a man on a seventeen-hand gelding was riding through the center of Clinchville. When he reached the schoolhouse, he saw the gang of youths beating Billy.

"Stop that!" Everyone knew of Clinch. They immediately obeyed his command.

"Get off that boy!" ordered Clinch. The boys moved away from Billy.

"He's Creek," explained the leader of the gang.

"Come here, boy," ordered Clinch.

Billy managed to get to his feet. He was badly bruised about the head and body.

"Do you speak English, boy?"

Billy nodded.

"Come here then, I won't hurt you."

Clinch reached down from his tall horse. "Take my arm, boy. I'll take you home."

Clinch hoisted Billy up onto the gelding. Billy sat behind the fat soldier. Unable to put his arms around Clinch's waist, he held onto the sides of his uniform as the gelding trotted off in the direction of the Creek village.

"What are you called, boy?"

"Billy."

"What kind of Indian name is that?"

Billy didn't answer.

"Did they abduct you from a white family?"

"My father is a Scotsman," said Billy proudly.

There was something familiar to Clinch about the boy's accent. Then Clinch remembered the British officer with the Scottish accent who had so badly embarrassed him outside the Creek village.

"Where is your father, son?" asked Clinch, hoping to be able to surprise the rogue and pay him back.

"He's with His Majesty's Ninth Regiment of Foot, sir," answered Billy proudly.

Clinch gave a thought to killing the boy and stomping out this line of vermin, but he had a more important task at hand and the boy would be useful.

As they arrived at the Creek village, several warriors greeted the newly promoted Major Duncan Clinch with muskets aimed and cocked. Billy pointed the way to Chief MacIntosh's hut. Inside, Clinch and Billy sat down opposite the Chief.

"Brave boy," said Clinch, referring to Billy.

"What happened?" asked the Chief.

"He took on five of his schoolmates single-handed."

"He is my adopted son," explained the Chief proudly.

John stood in the background, seething. He couldn't stand it when his father admired Billy.

"Chief, I have an important matter to discuss with you, in private," said Clinch.

"James, take John and Billy and wait outside," instructed the Chief. James led the boys out of the hut. As soon as they were out the door, John pushed Billy, knocking him to the ground. James jumped between him and Billy, preventing John from inflicting more blows.

"Why?" asked Billy, looking up.

"I wish they had killed you," said John.

Already bruised and battered, Billy slowly raised himself off the ground and ran home.

"You hate him because you're a coward and he's not," said James, not disguising the contempt he felt for his younger brother.

"No," screamed John. "It's because he's white."

"We're as white as him," reminded James.

Back inside, Clinch got down to business. "Chief, would you like to have this land in perpetuity?"

"What is that, Clinch?"

"Your warriors are very brave and accomplished soldiers. Would you be willing to fight for your new country in return for this land forever?"

"You took most of our land; will you give it back?" MacIntosh asked.

"Your people backed the wrong side in the war," reminded Clinch, annoyed at the question. "Do you want to stay on this land or not?" As the Chief thought about it, Clinch continued. "A band of escaped slaves has taken up residence in an abandoned fort. These slaves are my property. They are aided by the Seminole. Dislodge these interlopers and the Georgia legislature will deed you the land you are living on, and I will give you half the slaves we capture."

"And if we don't fight?" asked the Chief.

"You will have to move to the Indian Territories . . . Arkansas," said Clinch.

The War of 1812 had cost the Creeks twenty-two million acres of land in Georgia and Alabama. Chief MacIntosh was aware that several Creek tribes had negotiated treaties that exchanged their ancestral lands for land in the west. Up to this point, Indian emigration had been voluntary, and only a small number of Creeks actually moved. Now, however, Clinch was threatening to force his people west if they didn't do his bidding.

"Clinch," said Chief MacIntosh, "we will fight."

"Turn your face toward the fire," said Jasmine. It was very warm, and sitting on the floor this close to the brick fireplace was uncomfortable for Billy. Nevertheless he did as his mother instructed. The light from the fire enabled her to find and, using a wet cotton cloth, gently remove the last specks of dirt from the wound above Billy's eye. Then she wrung out the cloth in a dish of water. The crackle of burning wood was the only other noise.

Next she tended to Billy's scraped and bloodied elbow. Though visibly upset, Billy was doing his best to remain stoic by looking away.

"Look at me, Billy," said his mother. He turned his head and looked her in the eye, doing his best not to cry.

"You are not a savage."

She saw that Billy wasn't convinced.

"You think the whites are civilized?"

Billy didn't answer.

"They lie all the time," explained Jasmine.

Billy thought about this. He knew of the dishonor associated with lying, and couldn't imagine that was true. He looked at his mother, unbelieving.

"They lock their doors at night," continued Jasmine, "so their own white brothers won't steal from them."

Billy knew that if anyone lied or stole, they'd be shunned and driven out of Creek society. He tried to imagine a place where everyone lied and stole and he couldn't.

"They hoard food while their brothers starve. Is that civilized?" asked Jasmine.

Billy answered by shaking his head.

Then Billy realized that all white men weren't like that.

"My father did no' lie and steal."

"He was not like them," said Jasmine softly. "He was different, and so are you. You are Scottish and Creek, and both peoples have their own proud traditions."

"I'll not go back. If the Chief wants me to have a white man's education, my real father'll have to come back and give it to me," announced Billy. He pulled his arm away from his mother, emphasizing his protest.

"You don't have to go if you don't want to," said Jasmine as she lovingly stroked her son's hair. As she did this, Billy thought to himself that the white armies that had forced his people into submission didn't seem very formidable. Surely his father, leading his regiment, could beat the whole lot of them. Then Billy daydreamed about himself, leading his father's regiment to victory over the Americans.

4

HAITI 1806

Three soldiers walked down a mountain trail lined with lush tropical vegetation. They wore neither shoes nor shirts. Their black skin, wet from sweat, shimmered in the noonday sun. One carried an outdated French-made flintlock. The other two brandished machetes previously used to slice sugar cane, now more often than not used to lop off fingers, hands, arms and heads. They led their captives, whose hands were bound, by pulling on the rope tied around the necks of the man and the two little boys.

Abraham sat upon his horse, watching the procession come toward him. He was impeccably dressed, wearing an expropriated blue French general's uniform and polished patent leather boots.

"What crime did this man commit?" shouted Abraham in Creole, a bastardization of French and native African words formed by the slave population of Haiti.

The soldiers did not answer. Instead they led their captives over to Abraham.

"Please, sir, we have committed no crime," pleaded the prisoner in French.

"Shut up," said the soldier carrying the musket. He struck the man with the butt of the weapon, knocking him down.

"He sold rum to Henri Christophe's followers," explained the second soldier in Creole.

"Please, sir, spare my boys," pleaded the man from the ground. "They are only five and six years old."

"What is the punishment for his crime?" asked Abraham. As he spoke, he kept his rifle pointed vaguely in the direction of the three soldiers.

"Emperor Dessalines has ordered them boiled in oil," answered the soldier, as nonchalantly as he would describe boiling a potato. Abraham was shocked, but kept his outward composure.

"The boys too?" asked Abraham.

"The whole family," said the soldier.

"Tell the emperor that they escaped," he instructed.

The soldiers became very frightened at even the suggestion of disobeying the emperor. They'd witnessed the consequences.

"We cannot, sir, he will boil us."

"Perhaps you should not serve such a man," said Abraham.

"If we desert, sir, he will kill our families."

"Do you know who I am?"

"Oh yes, sir, you are General Abraham."

"Then say that General Abraham ordered their release."

"We cannot, sir," said the soldier, pulling back the hammer and raising his musket in Abraham's direction. The other two soldiers raised their machetes and moved toward Abraham.

Abraham spurred his horse, driving between the two machete-wielding soldiers. He hit the first with his rifle butt, sending the man sprawling to the ground. The second took off at a dead run back up the trail. The soldier holding the musket fired, sending Abraham's blue-and-gold general's hat flying off his head. Having missed his opportunity, the soldier threw down his flintlock and ran into the bush.

Abraham trotted his horse over to the captives. Dismounting, he took a knife and cut the rope. "You are free," he said in perfect French.

"Allow me to introduce myself," said the grateful man as he rose off the ground. "Henri LeBofe, master brewer, at your service, sir. These are my sons, Henri junior and Jean. We are forever in your debt, sir."

Abraham was part of what his former owner and mentor, General Oliver Herbert Hampton, called the grand experiment. He had doubts about the basis for slavery, that the Negro was an inferior being and needed caring for. The general decided to test the assumption by educating Abraham, an orphaned slave living on his plantation. Under his tutelage, Abraham quickly learned to read and write, and then taught himself the classics. The general taught him military history and strategy.

Abraham believed that Negroes could have their own country and freedom by following the pattern of the American Revolution. When he heard about the revolution in Haiti, it was his opportunity to put his beliefs into action. The general gave Abraham one thousand dollars and arranged passage from Savannah, Georgia, to a small town in the north of Haiti, Cap Haitien. There he was discreetly put ashore.

"Koupe tet, boule kay," chanted the machete-wielding mob of ex-slaves as they chased a French bureaucrat and his wife along the road that led down to the docks. The French army, under General

Leclerc, had withdrawn south in the middle of the night, leaving the French population there unprotected.

Abraham watched as the irate mob caught up with the couple. They had already burned down the couple's house. Now they hacked off their heads. Abraham learned that the chant, in Creole, meant, "Cut off their heads, burn their houses." It struck terror in the hearts of the French.

Abraham sought out and found the leader of the resistance against the French, General Dessalines. He presented the general with a cache of arms he had purchased from a British agent. Dessalines appreciated the gift, as well as Abraham's advice on organizing his army of ex-slaves and attacking the French.

Abraham deplored the waste. Burning residences that homeless Haitians could live in made no sense to him. He pleaded with Dessalines to have his followers curtail the destruction, but Dessalines would have no part of anything French.

After he helped defeat the French, Abraham stayed on and worked for Dessalines, hoping to bring about the utopia he'd dreamed of.

The palace was made from imported French marble, designed to look like the palace at Versailles, but on a much smaller scale. The approach to the edifice was a narrow cobblestone street lined with carts full of vegetables. Women sold sweet corn, sugar cane and beans to all who passed. Squads of soldiers led prisoners, arms and legs bound by hemp, into the palace for the emperor's judgment.

In the cavernous rooms of the palace other soldiers had already begun to carry out the emperor's judgments. Screams echoed throughout as men pleaded for their lives. Others begged to be put to death and out of their misery.

"How could I ever have fought for such a man?" was Abraham's thought as he walked through the palace.

Jean-Jacques Dessalines, self-appointed emperor and protector of the Haitian people's rights, slouched on his hand-carved mahogany throne. In his right hand was the bottle of rum he'd been drinking from since shortly after he'd awakened. The white French admiral's jacket he wore was unbuttoned exposing his massive chest. At forty-seven years of age, the six foot, five inch Dessalines still possessed a formidable physical presence. When the emperor saw Abraham, he motioned with his left hand for his general to approach.

"Sir, I agreed to help you rid this island of the French and establish the world's first independent Negro republic," began Abraham.

"These people are not ready for self-government," interrupted Dessalines. "Furthermore, my soldiers tell me you interfered with justice."

"Justice? Killing innocent boys because a father plied his trade is not justice," said Abraham emphatically.

"I will not tolerate those who give comfort to my rival," stated Dessalines.

"Selling rum is not aiding your enemies," insisted Abraham. Then he changed the subject. "Sir, I am no longer needed here in Haiti," said Abraham softly, careful not to anger the potentate.

Dessalines took a long pull from the bottle of rum. Then he looked down and scowled at Abraham. "Who told you that? Did I tell you that?" asked the emperor.

"No, you didn't, sir," said Abraham very calmly.

"Well, then where did you get that idea from? Henri Christophe?"

"Oh no, sir, I only serve you, sir. Haven't I served you faithfully?" reminded Abraham.

"Yes, you have until now. What will you do? Where will you go?" asked Dessalines.

"Return to the United States."

"And be a slave to the white man? Please reconsider. You are my best general."

"I cannot, sir. I beg your leave," said Abraham, bowing.

The emperor flicked his wrist, indicating Abraham was dismissed.

Abraham turned and walked out of the inner chamber.

Dessalines took another long pull from the bottle and then motioned with his finger for his personal guards to come closer.

Walking back through the large marble hall, Abraham heard a man who was being tortured in a corner, pleading to be put to death. Instead, the soldiers put a red-hot poker in his other eye. His scream could be heard throughout the palace.

Abraham walked over, drew his pistol and fired, putting the man out of his misery. The soldiers looked up at the general, disappointed that he had ruined their sport. Then Abraham walked out of the palace.

In his chamber, the emperor spoke to his palace guard. "Suppose General Abraham allies with Henri Christophe?" he asked.

Fearful of giving the wrong answer, no one in the room spoke.

"We cannot allow that, can we?" said the emperor, answering his own question.

Abraham arrived home to his four-room cottage on a hill overlooking the harbor in Port-au-Prince. It was one of the few residences saved from the torch. Painted white, it had real glass windows and a ceramic tile roof imported from Paris. The house's architect and former occupier was a French businessman who had exported Haitian sugar throughout the Caribbean.

Entering, Abraham hugged his wife, widely considered to be the most beautiful woman on the island.

"What's wrong?" inquired Antoinette, surprised to see Abraham home at midday.

"I'm concerned for our safety," said Abraham in his native English. "We need to leave immediately."

"And go where?" asked Antoinette.

"To the United States."

"United States?" she repeated. "How will we live there?"

Five-year-old Maria walked into the room, still in her pajamas. Abraham lifted her into his arms.

"Give Daddy a kiss." The child had her mother's light skin and chiseled features. She gave Abraham a peck on the cheek.

"How's my girl today?" asked Abraham, still holding his child.

"I love you, Daddy."

Abraham couldn't resist and gave her a noisy smooch on the cheek. Then he put her down and turned to his wife.

"There are places in America where we can live, free, away from all of this brutality. I am going down to the dock to arrange passage. Don't leave the house."

"I can't leave without saying good-bye to my mother," said Antoinette.

"When I return we will go into Port-au-Prince and make our farewell," ordered Abraham.

Antoinette fondly watched him leave. She was a second-generation mulatto. Her own mother had been the product of a mixed coupling, Antoinette's grandfather having been a French administrator who had spotted her grandmother as a twelve-year-old child, and kept her in luxury as his private concubine. He'd long since gone back to Paris, leaving the mother and daughter with a house, a small income and the social status that came from having lighter skin than ninety-nine percent of the population. Antoinette herself was the result of a similar arrangement, making her three quarters white.

Shortly after arriving in Haiti, Abraham had met Antoinette, was taken with her beauty, and went about charming her in her native French as well as English. He introduced her to poetry and literature. In turn she taught him to speak Creole. They married a year later. It was both the first formal marriage and the first black man involved with the family in three generations.

The five-man squad of soldiers arrived soon after Abraham left for the port. When their knock was not answered, they broke down the front door and walked into the house.

"Where is General Abraham? The emperor demands his presence," announced the leader.

"How dare you come into my home uninvited?" said Antoinette, not disguising her indignation. The soldiers all knew of Antoinette. She had always been unapproachable to the dark-skinned peasants who made up the revolutionary army of General, and now Emperor, Dessalines. They had driven out the French, but this vestige of French rule held her ground before them.

"I will have you whipped for this," threatened Antoinette.

Under the old regime, the soldier would have begged Antoinette for forgiveness. Now, however, her husband, General Abraham, was an enemy of the state, and the soldiers knew it. Rather than grovel, the soldier gently stroked Antoinette's cheek in anticipation of taking his pleasure with the condemned man's property.

"How dare you!" she said as she slapped the soldier hard across the face.

"Leave my mother alone," mimicked little Marie as she boldly gave a child's slap to the intruder's leg. The soldier raised his machete and struck the child. She collapsed in a bloody heap.

"My baby!" screamed Antoinette, falling to the floor. She was cradling her child when they peeled her arms away from the child and took their pleasure. When they were done, they hacked her to death with their machetes.

When Abraham returned home, he saw the broken-down front door, and his heart sank. Inside, mother and daughter lay in a bloody, unrecognizable heap. Abraham saw the two bloodied bodies and refused to believe his eyes. He dropped to the floor. Tears streamed down his cheeks as he gently wiped the blood away from the faces of his wife and daughter. "Why did I leave them alone? Why didn't I take them with me?" thought Abraham. He knew what

Dessalines was capable of. Then a rage came over him. He would not rest until Dessalines and his followers paid.

A wave broke against the rocks, sending white spray up into the air before retreating back into the sea. Standing on a sheer cliff fifty feet above the rocks, with his back to the ocean, Henri Christophe exhorted two hundred of his followers.

"With our help, Dessalines has driven out the white man, but now he has betrayed us by taking the white man's place. He has made us his slaves," Christophe boomed, in order to be heard above the crashing surf.

Standing nearby, Abraham watched Christophe pacing back and forth along the edge of the cliff. Abraham looked down at the turbulent ocean and noticed that, even standing this far above the surf, his boots were wet from the rising sea mist. The pain from the death of his wife and daughter was so strong that he had to resist the urge to throw himself off the cliff and onto the rocks below. Only his burning desire for revenge kept him focused on the job at hand.

"No man is better than another. We are all equal in God's eyes."

Abraham heard Christophe's words and he looked up and saw Christophe waving a red, blue and black flag.

"This will be our flag," shouted Christophe, "the French tricolor with black instead of white, symbolizing that there will be no whites in my regime." His followers cheered. "No black man has any more right than another," he continued when the cheers abated. "We all came here as slaves, making us all brothers," said Christophe. "Liberty, Equality, Fraternity."

He spoke the words in French, as they were first spoken, and his audience was enthralled. Christophe held up his hands, motioning for silence from his followers. "General Abraham, do you have news for us?"

Abraham looked out at Christophe's army. Like himself, many of them had previously fought for Dessalines before disillusionment with the corruption and brutality of his regime set in.

"We attack at six o'clock," announced Abraham to Christophe's followers, igniting a loud cheer. "The guards around the palace will be in no condition to resist."

Abraham was barefoot, shirtless, and had a rifle slung over each shoulder, with two pistols tucked into his belt. As part of his disguise, he wore a frayed straw hat and a patch over one eye, partially obscuring his face. He slowly drove a one-horse cart loaded with jugs of rum. Tied behind the cart on a loose rein was Henri LeBofe.

As he approached the palace gates, in full view of the guards, he grasped Henri LeBofe's arms and shoved him to the ground. Then he lifted him to his feet and pushed him toward the palace.

"Come and get it!" Abraham shouted as he entered the gates waving a machete that marked him as a follower of Emperor Dessalines.

The palace guard gathered round. "Help yourselves, men," said Abraham, pointing to the jugs of rum.

The guards immediately unloaded the jugs and began drinking as Abraham entered the palace with Henri LeBofe in tow. Abraham knew that very soon the guards would be rendered helpless by the poison laced into the brew.

At that moment the soldier he'd rescued Henri from exited the emperor's inner chamber. He saw Abraham with Henri standing before him. He raised his musket and pointed it at Abraham. "You have brought the prisoner back, General Abraham? I don't believe it. This is a trick," said the soldier.

Abraham looked down the barrel of the man's weapon. "You are correct. I have come to kill the emperor and free the people," said Abraham.

The guard looked at him incredulously, cocking his flintlock. Then he heard the screams of his compatriots. He turned and saw them writhing on the floor in pain. Henri freed his hands from the sham knot, drew one of the two pistols from Abraham's belt and fired. The guard fell dead. Around them the guards were in too much pain to pay attention to the intruders.

Dessalines heard the commotion and dispatched his two personal guards to see what was going on. When they opened the door, they saw soldiers, some on their knees, others rolling around the floor, all in pain. Afraid for their lives, they dropped their muskets and ran out of the chamber, hoping to flee. Dessalines screamed for them to halt, but they paid him no mind. Then he saw Abraham and fled out of the rear entrance.

Abraham and his soldiers caught up with Dessalines just north of Port-au-Prince as he was crossing the Pont-Rouge, the stone bridge constructed by French engineers a decade earlier. When it was obvious to Dessalines that there was no escape, he dropped to his knees and begged.

"Please, Abraham. I'll give you more money than you've ever seen," he pleaded. He saw Abraham was unmoved. "I'll make you my partner. We'll govern together."

Abraham took a rifle from his shoulder and pointed at Dessalines.

"Emperor. I'll make you emperor. Just let me live," pleaded Dessalines.

Abraham could think only of his murdered family. "For high crimes against the people, I sentence you to suffer."

Abraham fired, hitting Dessalines in the left thigh, shattering his leg. Then he drew his pistol and fired it, blowing a hole in his other leg. Dessalines lay before him, writhing in pain, helpless to move, whimpering for mercy.

Abraham stepped closer. Dessalines raised his arms in a defensive posture, and Abraham swung the machete, slicing off several of Dessalines' fingers. He swung the machete again, slicing off his arm, then his other arm. He then hacked at both his legs. Abraham was still swinging the machete into the bloody pulp that was Emperor Dessalines when Christophe's soldiers pulled him away.

———

The boat rocked up and back as it traversed the five-foot waves. Of the passengers, only Henri's two boys weren't seasick. Abraham stood in the bow, leaning against the rail, when the urge hit him to throw up his breakfast. Beside him stood Henri LeBofe, barely containing his own food at the sight of Abraham retching. All the while his boys played pirate on the schooner deck.

"Part of me hates to leave our island," said Henri.

Abraham was silent as he reflected on the series of events that had led up to Dessalines' execution. "I sense that the oppression of the people is not over."

"How do you know all of this?" asked Henri.

"I have read history and studied its lessons," answered Abraham.

LeBofe was very impressed, though that was not Abraham's intent. "Will you teach me to read?"

"Yes, and also to speak English," said Abraham.

"How can I ever repay you?"

"I'm going to need hard currency to carry out my plans to establish a free community of Negroes in Florida. What better way than quenching the white man's thirst with your rum?" answered Abraham. Then he put his arm around Henri's shoulder and squeezed it in an obvious display of affection.

Abraham was returning to an area not very far from his roots in Georgia. He had a bold idea. He would establish in Florida a free Negro community where escaped slaves could find sanctuary.

5

FLORIDA 1807

Abraham strolled up the road that led to the Seminole village. He was wearing a six-button knee-length jacket flared at the waist, a ruffled white silk shirt and knee-high polished leather boots. He whistled "Raise a Ruckus Tonight" as he walked. A six-foot-two-inch, thirty-year-old native-born Negro, dressed in buckskin, stepped out of the bush into Abraham's path. He held a rifle in his hands and had another slung over his left shoulder.

Abraham stood still as the man walked around him, looking him over from top to bottom. "What are you?"

"Good morning, sir," said Abraham, bowing and tipping his broad-brimmed hat. "I am a man not unlike yourself."

"You some kinda glorified house nigger?" asked the man.

"No," said Abraham.

Then he touched Abraham's cheek and rubbed his skin.

"What are you doing?" inquired Abraham.

"I want to see if the color come off. No black man sound like that."

Both men laughed.

"Appearances are often deceiving," counseled Abraham.

"What you say?"

"I apologize if my speech confuses you, mister—" Abraham searched for the man's moniker.

"Gar-cia," said the young hunter.

"Garcia," repeated Abraham. "Pleased to make your acquaintance. I am Abraham."

"You do not confuse me," said Garcia.

"Offend?" asked Abraham.

"Maybe," said Garcia. "The white man is the devil. If you sound like the devil you may be him."

"You should not judge a man by his speech," said Abraham, "but by his deeds."

"Here it only matters how you shoot," said Garcia. "You don't shoot, you don't eat." Garcia took the musket off his left shoulder. "You ever use one of these?" he asked.

"I know the butt from the barrel," answered Abraham.

Garcia handed it to Abraham.

They walked together into the high grass. Soon a flock of quail took flight in front of them. Garcia quickly raised his weapon and fired. A bird fluttered to earth. An instant later Abraham's musket discharged, bringing down a second small bird. Garcia looked at him, surprised he could make such a shot.

"I should know that any man dressed like you better be able to shoot," said Garcia. The two laughed again.

"I left Haiti in a hurry," explained Abraham. "I borrowed these clothes. They belonged to a French nobleman who owned a sugar plantation."

"This white man, he don't mind you take his clothes?"

"No, he didn't mind. He and every other white person in Haiti are dead."

"They kill every white man?" asked Garcia, delighted.

"Every single white: men, women, children. Put to death. None were spared," explained Abraham.

Garcia slung his weapon back over his shoulder. He stepped into the high grass and picked up the quail.

"Do you know a chief called Micanopy?" asked Abraham, changing the subject.

Garcia nodded, then gestured with his arm for Abraham to follow.

Leaving the high grass, they entered a large cultivated field. At the far end of the field a black man was tilling the soil.

"That's Tom. He's an escaped slave," said Garcia. "The Seminole let him stay. In return he farms for them."

"Are you an escaped slave?" asked Abraham.

"No. The Seminole find me when I was a baby."

"Floating in a cradle among the reeds?" asked Abraham.

"Why you ask that?" said Garcia.

"Long ago an abandoned baby of an oppressed people, not unlike ourselves, returned and led his people out of slavery," answered Abraham.

"What was he called?" asked Garcia.

"Moses," answered Abraham.

"He led an army and freed all the slaves?" asked Garcia.

"No, he was just one man."

"One man?" repeated Garcia incredulously.

"He had God with him," said Abraham.

"But he wasn't fighting the United States," pointed out Garcia.

"No, a much more powerful empire, Egypt," said Abraham.

"I will go to the American leader—" said Garcia.

"The President," informed Abraham.

"I will go to the President and demand he free the slaves," joked Garcia.

"That's the spirit," said Abraham.

They arrived at a stream that ran about the perimeter of the Seminole village. Garcia intentionally waded into the shallow water, expecting Abraham to follow and ruin his suit. On the opposite bank Garcia looked back for Abraham and saw him crossing downstream by stepping on the rocks in the water. Abraham, still dry, rejoined Garcia and they entered the village.

"Will you teach me the Seminole language and customs?" requested Abraham. Garcia smiled and nodded.

As they entered the village, their first greeting was from a mongrel dog. It trotted up to Garcia wagging its tail.

"E-fee," said Garcia, patting it on the head. Garcia saw the confusion on Abraham's face

"All dogs are e-fee," he explained.

"E-fee," repeated Abraham, as the dog sniffed the dead birds tied to a string that Garcia was carrying. Reaching into his pocket, Garcia took out a piece of dried meat and fed it to the animal. Satisfied, the dog trotted off.

"Chic-kee," said Garcia. He was broadly pointing to the hundred dwellings made of cypress logs with woven palm thatch roofs.

"Chic-kee," repeated Abraham, mimicking Garcia's pronunciation

"For cooking," said Garcia, pointing to a cluster of chickees that had fires burning on the ground and holes in the roof where the smoke escaped.

"For sleeping." He broadly gestured to the other ninety structures that made up the village. They had no side walls, and the roofs extended down to the ground on both sides.

Abraham accompanied Garcia as he walked over to a woman and two teenage girls standing over a large wooden pail, pounding the contents with sticks. The woman wore a hand-sewn, multicolored, striped, long skirt with an amply cut long-sleeved top. Strings of beads layered one upon another covered her entire neck. Only her face and hands were exposed.

Sitting on the ground beside the woman was a trio of little girls similarly dressed, but without the beads. Two girls, about six years old, were sewing different ends of a multicolored cloth with hand needles. The third, a child no more than three, sat holding a hand-sewn rag doll.

The girls looked up and smiled at Garcia, but paid no mind to the strangely dressed black man accompanying him. Abraham winked at the young girls as Garcia handed the quail to the woman. She took the birds as the girls giggled and stared at the handsome stranger accompanying Garcia.

Abraham smiled and tipped his hat.

"She's a widow," whispered Garcia, "in case you are interested in marriage." The woman turned away, resuming her work.

"What are they doing?" asked Abraham.

"They are making sofkee by pounding the corn into meal," explained Garcia. "It's very good."

Garcia and Abraham continued walking. At the east end of the village the stream emptied into a lake. A dozen dugout canoes made from hollowed-out cypress logs lined the bank. Abraham saw two Seminole men wearing multicolored patchwork shirts, paddling a canoe toward shore. Between them, tied upside down on a stick, was a freshly killed deer. When they saw Garcia standing on the bank they lifted their kill for him to see.

Garcia acknowledged their feat by raising his clenched fist in the air and smiling. Paddling ashore, the men were greeted by two boys who relieved them of their kill, taking it to one of the cooking chickees. Then the men shoved off again.

On the lake Abraham saw two teenage boys glide by in another canoe. One stood in the bow holding a small spear with a rope attached. The boy flung the spear into the water, then reeled in the rope and removed a large bass impaled through its gills.

Garcia tapped Abraham's shoulder and they continued the tour. He brought Abraham to a chickee located adjacent to the bank of the lake. Standing in front of the chickee, with his suntanned arms crossed in front of his chest, was Chief Micanopy. He wore a kiltlike striped skirt, a multicolored patchwork shirt, a red headband and an alligator-tooth necklace. He was thirty years old and stood six feet tall.

Garcia had a quick word with the Chief, and then Micanopy invited him and the well-dressed stranger into his chickee. Micanopy motioned for Abraham to sit down. Abraham sat on the finished wooden plank floor opposite the Chief, who made himself comfortable on a cotton cushion. Garcia remained standing behind Abraham. Micanopy motioned for Abraham to speak.

"I want to establish a place where escaped slaves can live free," were the first words Abraham said.

Micanopy regarded the tall, strangely dressed black man sitting opposite him.

"When the Spanish came fifteen generations ago, those before me were plentiful," said Micanopy in very good English. "Our tribes, the Yamasee, Timugua, Alabachi, Euchee, Tequesta and others lived throughout all Florida." As he spoke, Micanopy made a wide, sweeping gesture with his arms, indicating that his ancestors were everywhere. "We were like the saw grass—all free people. The Spanish brought the white man's disease, and it killed almost everyone. Not even one man in one hundred survived. Still, the Spanish could not conquer us. What was left of our people came together here in this part of Florida. Because we referred to ourselves as *Isti Siminoli*, free people, the Spanish called us Seminoles," explained Micanopy.

"Allow me to bring my people here and you will be strong again," said Abraham. "We will raise crops and pay you one quarter of the harvest forever."

"I fear that if your people come in large numbers, the white man will follow," said Micanopy.

"The white man is coming no matter what," said Abraham. "Sooner or later he will want your land and will make slaves of your people."

Micanopy did not reply while digesting Abraham's words.

"Chief, allow me to bring my people here," implored Abraham, breaking the silence. "I will equip and train an army. Your enemy shall be our enemy. When the white man comes, you will be strong."

"How will your people know to come here?" asked Micanopy.

"I will go into the fields where they toil and tell them they have a sanctuary where they can be free."

Before Micanopy could respond, Abraham opened his shirt and took a pouch of gold coins from a money belt. He handed the pouch to Micanopy. "Please accept this gift as our gesture of gratitude."

Micanopy was overwhelmed. He directed Abraham to a site three miles from his village. In that location Abraham could build a village, he said, and farm all of the land south of there.

Garcia was breathless. The man had been here less than one day, and already he had organized a new community. A free community made up of free black people. A community that would be a beacon for escaping slaves. With Garcia's help, Abraham pounded a stake with a sign attached to it into the ground. It read, *Freedom Land*.

6

Garcia was leading forty-five soldiers on a five-mile run. They were circling a field just over a half mile in circumference. The closest man to him was twenty yards behind. Each carried their own musket, alternating hands as it became too heavy.

Abraham insisted his soldiers be able to run five miles. Abraham said it could be the difference between freedom and slavery. After four years of training with Abraham, Garcia prided himself on being the fastest runner and best soldier.

The seventh time around, Garcia saw a newcomer standing at the north edge of the field. At five feet, ten inches tall, with long, flowing hair and beautiful facial features, she was a sight to behold even in the tattered rags she wore. He sped up to finish the run. Garcia easily outdistanced the soldiers behind him, even lapping a few of the stragglers.

He stopped in front of the woman, gasping for breath. "What a woman," thought Garcia. He was at a loss for words.

The woman just stared at the handsome man, halted with his hands on his knees, leaning forward, trying to catch his breath. Garcia regained his breath and composure simultaneously.

"Who are you?" asked Garcia, still puffing hard.

She smiled at Garcia. "My name is Jamima Joseph. The overseer ask me to go into the woods with him," she said. "I tell him I would go ahead to find a nice place to lay, and just kept going. I swam the river and run away south. I lived in the woods for seven days, hiding during the day, and traveling at night. I hear bears, wildcats and came across all kinds of snakes, but wasn't scared of nothing. I slept on logs with moss for a pillow."

"You telling me that you just escaped from slavery?" asked Garcia.

"Yes," she answered proudly.

"I am Garcia. I put you up until we build you a home," he volunteered.

The soldiers still running noticed the newest member of the community walking away with Garcia.

Jamima followed him to his chickee. He brought her inside. "This is your bed. It was my father's. You wash in the stream behind the chickee." Garcia handed her a cotton shirt from Cuba and a pair of buckskin pants that had belonged to his late father.

"Don't look," instructed Jamima. Garcia obeyed and turned away. She quickly peeled off her rags and tried on her new outfit. Jamima was pleased by the way the clothes fit and looked. She'd never worn a cotton shirt or leather pants.

The soldiers had completed the run and were milling about when Abraham arrived.

"Where is your commander?" he asked.

"A beautiful woman come out of the woods, and he left with her," said a trainee, with a touch of envy in his voice.

Abraham was instantly livid, though he did his best to disguise his anger. A commander abandoning his troops in the middle of drilling was unacceptable.

Just then Garcia returned with Jamima in tow. All eyes were on her.

"Attention," barked Abraham, and the troops fell into five rows of nine soldiers, one behind the other, all standing perfectly straight.

When Jamima and Garcia reached the troops, Abraham stepped forward. "On behalf of the entire community, welcome to Freedom Land, mademoiselle," he said, bowing as if addressing royalty. Clearly he was not at a loss for words. Even wearing Garcia's father's clothes, Jamima was statuesque.

Jamima stared at Abraham. She had never experienced such manners in a man. Fond as he was of his friend, at that particular moment Garcia wished the much more articulate Abraham would get lost.

Abraham turned back to his troops. "Right shoulder arms," he said, and the soldiers reacted smartly.

"Present arms," said Abraham, and the soldiers thrust their weapons forward in this close-order drill staged for Jamima's benefit.

While the drill was in progress, Jamima whispered in Garcia's ear, "Abraham got him a wife?" She saw a sad look come over the face of the handsome boy next to her.

Garcia walked up to Abraham. "You're showing off for the lady," he accused.

"No, I'm doing your job. Remember, you're the commander," said Abraham, not hiding his anger. "What kind of an example is that, leaving your troops in the middle of an exercise? I have to seriously question your ability to lead these men."

"That's not what this is about. This is about Jamima," said Garcia, raising his voice.

Now all of the recruits were watching the drama.

"Stay away from her," threatened Garcia.

"You saw her first so she's yours?" asked Abraham rhetorically.

His purpose was to point out to Garcia his mistake as a leader rather than making a play for Jamima. Garcia didn't take it that way.

"Company dismissed," shouted Garcia, as if to prove he was still in charge. The men relaxed but stood nearby waiting for the drama to play out.

Abraham made the next move. Calling to Jamima, he said, "You do not have to stay with Garcia."

Jamima looked at Abraham seductively. "Can I stay with you?" she asked. Garcia's heart sank.

"No," said Abraham. Much as he was tempted, he didn't want to anger Garcia.

Jamima was shocked. In her young life no man had ever been able to resist her.

"I stay with Garcia," said Jamima seductively, letting Abraham know what he'd be missing.

That night as Garcia was lying in bed, unable to sleep, Jamima climbed out of her bed.

"Either get into it or stay out," said Garcia in a sharp tone. Jamima climbed into his bed and they made passionate love.

The next day, Don Pasquel Baca, personal envoy from the Spanish court of King Ferdinand VII, arrived at Freedom Land and requested an audience with Abraham. They met in the village meeting place, a wooden platform in the center of the houses.

Abraham and Garcia sat upon a bench. Opposite them sat Baca and his two lieutenants. Most of the six hundred members of the community sat on the ground around the platform.

"How do you know of us?" asked Abraham.

"Everyone in Cuba knows about the great Abraham," said Baca in perfect English.

"What do they say?"

"That your soldiers control Florida."

"And that is why you are here?" asked Abraham.

"Spain is faced with encroachment from the Americans. I am authorized to offer Spanish citizenship and land grants in return for military service," stated Baca.

"What does that mean?" asked Garcia.

"That you can travel and live as free men throughout the Spanish empire. Cuba, Mexico, Spain itself, and, of course, here in Florida," answered Baca.

"We live here free," said Abraham.

"You are escaped slaves," reminded Baca. "As citizens of Spain you would be legally free."

Baca saw that Abraham was unmoved.

"The leaders would also hold the rank of general in the Spanish army."

"What is it you request of us?" asked Garcia, interested in this idea.

"We built a fort in northwest Florida to discourage the French and British from invading," explained Baca. "Whoever controls the fort controls Florida. I ask you to garrison that fort for one year or until the Spanish army arrives, which could be any day."

Neither Abraham nor Garcia said a word. Their silence was an indication to Baca that they were not swayed.

"It will also be your duty to prohibit slavery in Florida. There are two large sugar plantations along the Apalachicola just north of the Gulf of Mexico. The owners have petitioned the United States government to annex Florida. Seize the plantations and free the slaves."

Garcia had a vision of ex-slaves owning and sharing equally in the land and the crops. Better yet, he saw an entire territory, farmed and owned by ex-slaves, protected by his army and backed by Spain.

"If the plantation owners did petition for annexation, and then were massacred, it would bring down the Americans even faster," said Abraham.

"How can you not march to free your brothers?" asked Baca. "I understand your reluctance to strike north into Georgia, but this is

Florida and we Spanish are blessing this action. I have a suggestion. Send half your army. I am told you have over six hundred men under arms, with more arriving daily."

"And when the Americans send an army," retorted Abraham, "we'll be six hundred against twenty thousand and the Spanish will be powerless to help."

"I would be a general in the Spanish army?" asked Garcia, paying no heed to Abraham's warning.

"Is that what is important to you?" asked Abraham. "I will make you a general in our army."

"And my soldiers?" asked Garcia.

"You will designate which are to be officers and all will be paid in gold, with the first three months in advance." Baca motioned for his lieutenant, who stepped forward. He opened a small box containing gold coins. He ran his hand through them, lifting the coins up and letting them drop through his fingers.

Garcia was wide-eyed at the sight of all that gold.

"Don't do this," implored Abraham. "These people are counting on your judgment."

"You told me of the man Moses who freed the people. I will do the same," said Garcia to Abraham. "Who will go with me to free our brothers and become Spanish citizens?" shouted Garcia to everyone gathered.

"People of Freedom Land," shouted Abraham in reply, "you are free to make your own choice. If you leave this sanctuary to do Spain's bidding, you will probably end up dead or worse. You could become slaves again."

"Abraham is trying to scare you," answered Garcia. "Who's to say the Americans won't come here?"

Then he plunged his hands into the box, lifting out the coins and allowing them to cascade down before the crowd. "Step forward now," he urged, "receive your gold and citizenship." Then, raising his voice to a shout, "Let us march against the plantations!"

A cheer rang out from half of the populace. The others, taking Abraham's lead, stood silent.

The next day, the cheers were absent as the villagers who chose to remain made their good-byes to those leaving. Many in the crowd hugged their former friends and neighbors. There was a sense that they might be seeing each other for the last time.

Jamima stood beside Garcia. She didn't want to leave, but she had thrown her lot in with him. She realized that she was partly responsible for these events. If she hadn't shown interest in Abraham, Garcia might not have become jealous and used this excuse to take her away.

She walked over to Abraham and extended her arms for a hug. She wanted reassurance from him that she was not to blame for this fissure in the community.

"Please forgive me," she whispered as she put her arms around him.

Abraham stood stiff, refusing to return the embrace. Instead, he removed her arms and turned to his remaining followers. "Let us all wish them Godspeed in their journey."

Jamima was at Garcia's side as he led 284 men and women, fully armed and provisioned courtesy of Spain, out of Freedom Land.

Members of the community didn't understand why Abraham did nothing to stop the exodus. Though he desperately wanted to stop them from leaving, his memories of the despot Dessalines wouldn't allow him to inhibit the free will of these former slaves. For to stop them he'd have to become what he despised the most and fought against: a dictator with absolute power.

7

Garcia pulled up his last line. As he did he felt the nibble and then the hit. He thought by the tension that he'd hooked a red fish. He'd baited the hook with a live shrimp and let it out a hundred feet. In the six months he'd been at the fort he'd hooked a lot of fish and every species had its own feel. He prided himself on being an accomplished fisherman, although he wasn't fishing to feed the compound. He had a crew of twenty who did that. This was relaxation— sitting on the observation deck in the moonlight, fishing the Gulf of Mexico. That night he'd already pulled up four sea trout, two grouper and a sand shark.

Garcia had taken his position as Spanish general very seriously. His army liberated both plantations and 146 slaves. In a show of mercy, he allowed the owners and their families to leave the plantations unharmed. Garcia gave the former slaves the option of working the land and sharing equally with the other workers, or joining his army at the fort he had named Fort Negro, in a demonstration of defiance and racial pride.

Now, the trickiest part was hauling the fish the last twenty feet up the wall. He'd lost more than one prize this close. There it was, a red fish! He was right. The fish dangled, swinging back and forth, desperate to free itself. Garcia was especially careful. He didn't want to lose this delicacy. He thought of his adopted father, Etobe, a great hunter and fisherman, the man who had imparted all of his considerable skills to him. How he missed him and the hours they'd spent together fishing! Etobe was a storyteller. Garcia's favorite story was about himself, and Etobe had told it to him many times.

"I sat in the thicket waiting on mister deer. I see a slave running—carrying a baby. She place the baby in the bush. She rather the baby die than be a slave. Then I see the men tracking her. I watch them rape her. I should have done something. Then she grab a knife and plunge it in her own heart. She rather die. Then I take the baby from the bush and promise Breathmaker to care for him. You were that baby."

Etobe always finished the story by asking young Garcia's forgiveness for not intervening and trying to save his mother. Garcia would say he forgave him. Etobe's own wife and infant son had died in childbirth the previous year. For Etobe, young Garcia was his son reborn.

As Etobe's son he was accepted by the Seminole as one of their own. When he grew up, young Garcia became the best hunter, and was considered a prize by all the eligible women, both Seminole and among the small community of escaped slaves living amidst them.

He had the prize he wanted, though. Jamima came up behind Garcia, draped her arms over his shoulders and pulled him to her. She put her head next to his and kissed his cheek.

The moonlight accentuated her beauty. He lifted the line and showed her his catch. "Dinner, Jamima." Jamima could whip up quite a dish with a red fish.

They sat there in the moonlight. She took his hand. "Do you ever think that maybe you should have stayed with Abraham?" asked Garcia.

"Garcia, listen to me. When I was twelve, the Arabs surround my village, set it ablaze. They led the people—one hundred thirty-eight—off in chains. They kill twenty-one old men, women and babies. Eleven months later I am branded and laboring in the white man's fields. For three years I learn the language and the land before I could escape. Three years in the fields. But you know what, Garcia? I'm happy. It means I be with you!"

"The first time I saw you I knew that I loved you," said Garcia. That's when they heard the dogs barking.

Garcia was relieved. The noise outside the fort signified to him that the Americans and their Indian mercenary army had arrived. The worst part for Garcia had been the waiting. He knew his soldiers would be tested and was confident they'd be up to the task. The possibility of defeat never entered his mind. He even toyed with the idea of taking his soldiers out of the fort and annihilating the invaders in an open battle. He outnumbered and out-gunned his opposition. But there'd be casualties in a battle, and Garcia did not want to risk losing even one of his followers needlessly.

Built in 1756 to deter the other colonial powers from seizing Florida, the triangular bastion was constructed on a fifty-acre site at the end of a peninsula. One side commanded the mouth of the Apalachicola River, deterring intruders from coming upstream. The other side was a sheer sea wall, looking out over the Gulf of Mexico. The third side faced the swamp. That approach was under six inches of water at high tide. Fifteen-foot timbers made of a combination of oak and cypress rose from an earth embankment five feet above ground level, creating a formidable palisade. Inside the walls, a ten-foot-wide observation deck accessible by ladders ran the length of the fort. On it, one of the two cannons was positioned. It could be aimed at the swamp approach, or wheeled along the deck and pointed out to sea by the ten-man crew. A second cannon was located on the ground, pointed at the front gate.

A three-story barracks, located adjacent to and running the length of the sea wall, housed Garcia's army. The garrison was on alert. Garcia's scouts had reported the approach of two hundred Creek Indians led by American officers.

Garcia had ordered his cannon crew on the deck to touch off an occasional round over the landward approach to the fort. He hoped that the fireworks display would strike terror in the hearts of the invaders.

Men on the wall converged on the landward side, rifles ready. The cannon crew sprang to life. They wheeled back the cannon, loaded it with a ball and then wheeled it forward. Sentries scoured the terrain in front of the walls but could see no one in the unforgiving swamp. The captain of the watch ordered two men to throw hand bombs into the jungle on both sides of the road. Garcia heard the two explosions. Then Garcia and Jamima walked around the deck to the swamp side. The enemy was upon them.

Dragonflies filled the air, chasing the swarming mosquitoes. Water moccasins slithered about looking to feast on tadpoles and young frogs. A sea trout carried in with the tide was feeding on the young shrimp that hid among the mangroves. An alligator glided in behind it, catching the trout with a quick snap of its jaws.

A black cloud drifted over the swamp, bringing a brief torrential downpour and the briefest respite from the 105-degree heat and oppressive humidity. By the end of the afternoon the receding tide drained the brackish water out of the marsh back into the Apalachicola River and then out into the Gulf of Mexico. Steam rose as the remaining puddles of warm water evaporated into the cooler night air, giving the muddy road through the center of the marsh a ghostly appearance.

Billy watched as James MacIntosh covered his face and arms with mud so he'd blend in with the swamp. The sixteen-year-old stood as his father, William MacIntosh, gave his oldest son final instructions. James was to lead the scouting sortie.

"Determine where to attack the walls and gate, and remember, no contact with the defenders! There'll be time enough for that. Understand?"

James nodded his head. Billy Powell stood next to him listening. He was to accompany James.

"Please take me," implored John, joining his brothers.

"No," said James emphatically.

"Please, Father, make him take me. I can help," said John.

All the members of the tribe were aware of John's cowardice when the Americans had attacked their village. Though he was extremely embarrassed by his son's behavior, Chief MacIntosh never admonished him. Instead he encouraged the boy by telling him that he would do better next time. Secretly, however, he questioned his son's courage.

"All right," said the Chief. "Go with your brothers. Watch out for one another, protect one another, and return together." He was not only a veteran talking to three novices. He was a father talking to his three sons.

Thirteen-year-old John saw this as his opportunity for redemption. He wanted to prove himself and show the tribe's warriors that he could be brave. John and Billy both reached down for a handful of mud and camouflaged their arms and faces. Billy was wearing only a loincloth and the headband holding his long blond hair. He was twelve years old, not big for his age but strong, well coordinated and a very fast runner.

From the swamp a white puff of smoke and faint thunder announced that the fort's defenders had touched off a cannon round. The Indians watched the artillery shell's arching trajectory, listened to the ever-closer piercing whistle, and waited. High above the marsh the cannon ball exploded into hundreds of fragments, each its own shade of orange. The hot shrapnel rained down onto the marsh, giving the observers a visual feast as well as a reminder that it would be suicide to attack. Because the tribe's warriors refused to approach the fort, Chief William MacIntosh sent his own sons to scout out the objective.

The Chief looked up nervously at the fireworks display. "How could he send his sons on such a mission?" was his thought.

"We'll be fine, father," said James, as if he could read his father's mind.

John, James and Billy stepped stealthily through the ankle-deep bog, doing their best to avoid detection by both the defenders and the deadly inhabitants of the swamp. They were armed only with knives so they could run unencumbered.

Reaching the fort, they looked up at the walls and the gate. From their perspective, the triangular fort, situated at the end of the reptile-infested promontory, appeared impregnable.

Billy didn't understand what they were doing there and why they were fighting the black Indians inside the fort, at the behest of the Americans. The arrangement that allied the Creeks to their sworn enemy, to fight against strangers they had no quarrel with, was alien to him. His father had never explained the inconceivable alliances that politics and war create.

Nevertheless, Billy liked the tension and excitement. It was similar to what he had felt when his village was attacked by the same Americans. He had played at soldier countless times. Now he would have the opportunity to test and display his courage.

The other Creek warriors did not feel that way. When Chief MacIntosh announced to the tribe his plan to fight for the Americans, there were screams of protest. It was only after his people understood what refusal meant that the men of the village took their weapons and followed their Chief to Florida.

———

When the dogs inside the fort started barking, the boys dropped to the ground and crawled into the thick mangroves that lined the road.

Peering out over the walls, the defenders couldn't see the intruders. Having no target for their muskets, they lit the fuses on two hand bombs and tossed them over the wall.

One exploded harmlessly. The other bomb burst in the air just above the boys. Pieces of hot metal tore into James' back and John's arm, leaving only Billy unscathed.

Billy and John got to their feet and quickly moved through the mangroves away from the fort. James tried to get up but couldn't move.

"Help me," he cried.

Billy and John stopped running and looked back. They saw James on the ground, covered in his own blood, trying to crawl toward them.

Then they saw hungry alligators all around James, moving slowly, deliberately toward him. Billy hurried back and quickly positioned himself between James and the nearest alligator. He pulled out his knife, then stomped his right foot. The beast hesitated.

Another alligator moved in.

"John, help me!" screamed James.

John stood trembling, holding his bloody arm, unable to muster his courage.

James looked into the eyes of a hungry reptile. He brandished his knife at the beast. Suddenly it lunged. With a snap of its jaws, it bit off James' hand. Another alligator moved in and bit into James' leg, twisting and pulling.

Billy attacked the alligator holding James' leg by stabbing it behind the head with his knife. The blade stuck in the alligator's hide, which merely served to anger the beast. It whipped its deadly tail, barely missing Billy, who jumped out of the way. All Billy could do was watch helplessly as the alligator swam off with his knife stuck

in its head, and James' leg in its mouth. Billy was suddenly nause-
ated. He gagged and threw up as the horror of the situation sunk
in.

John came limping out of the swamp to his father. "A bomb, alligators," he said searching for words. He was barely able to speak
before he began crying. His father slapped him hard.

"How did you get out? Did you abandon your brothers?" asked
the Chief.

"No!" John said through his tears. "There was nothing I could
do."

MacIntosh looked at his son with contempt. Then he turned his
back on him.

"I'm not a coward," shouted John as he walked away.

Then Billy came staggering out. He was carrying James' lifeless
torso, stripped of both arms and one leg. He laid the dead warrior
at the Chief's feet.

Chief MacIntosh looked down. His oldest son, his pride and joy,
lay mutilated before him. He knelt beside the body. Tears streamed
down his cheeks. Not only was his firstborn gone, but he'd be forced
to bury him in this terrible place. His son's spirit might never find
its way home.

For the members of the tribe watching, their belief in the futility
of attacking the fort was reinforced.

The Chief wrapped James' body in his blanket. Then he carried
him to a clearing fifty yards from the entrance to the swamp. Everyone watched from afar, respecting his privacy as he laid the body
down on the soft ground.

Kneeling, he used his knife and bare hands to dig a shallow grave.
He placed his son's shrouded body into the earth and covered him
with dirt, twigs and palm fronds.

"Forgive me, son," choked out the Chief between sobs. Then he
stood up, spread his arms and looked up at the sky.

"Breathmaker, guide my son's spirit that he may find his way home and join his ancestors."

Meanwhile, Ed McBain saw young John MacIntosh heading into the swamp. He hurried in after him.

"Come back. It's not your fault," he called to John.

John stopped but didn't turn around. He didn't want the medicine man to see his tears.

Catching up with John, McBain gently examined and dressed his wounded arm. Then, without another word, he led John out of the swamp.

"Now go make peace with your brother's spirit," advised Ed McBain.

Reluctantly, John walked over and stood by his father. The Chief did not acknowledge him. Separately they paid their last respects.

Billy had not moved from where he had laid his brother. He stood there dazed as Ed McBain took a damp cloth and washed the blood off his arms and legs.

"There was nothing we could do," mumbled Billy through his tears.

"You did fine, Billy," comforted the medicine man.

On the peninsula above the swamp, Major Clinch was as comfortable as possible in the heat. He sat under an umbrella, looking at the fort through his spyglass as a slave stood fanning him. Two other slaves, his cooks, were preparing a rabbit stew for breakfast. Nearby were his sleeping quarters: a tent, covered with mosquito netting, that housed his military cot and a dresser. On the dresser were a hand-held mirror, a straight razor and a pitcher of fresh water for washing and shaving. In the drawers were a half dozen fresh outfits. Two slaves had fanned him all night as he slept.

Nearby, sitting outside his own tent, shotgun across his lap, was Clinch's second in command, Lieutenant Simon McFarland. The man had no military experience. He had accepted the commission at Clinch's behest. The sole purpose for his presence was to discourage Clinch's personal slaves from fleeing to the enemy.

Chief MacIntosh requested that Billy accompany him up the hill to report to Major Clinch. They walked together in silence. Billy's body was unharmed from the harrowing experience, but the events kept running over and over again in his mind. He didn't understand why his brother had died there fighting for the white man.

Billy stood beside Chief William MacIntosh, waiting for their audience with the "fat soldier." Clinch was at that moment preoccupied. Galloping up to his position was the hero of New Orleans, the individual many said would be the next President, General Andrew Jackson.

Billy sensed the man in the buckskin was an important general. He had a prominent nose and wore his long silver hair combed back. He had the look of a hawk. Dismounting, leaving his two aides on horseback, Jackson walked over to Clinch.

"Good afternoon, General. Would you care for refreshments?" uttered Clinch nervously as he motioned toward his luxurious carriage.

"I was informed, sir, that you are a man we can count on," said Jackson in his deep southern drawl.

"Absolutely, General," said Clinch.

"Damn it, then, get those savages to attack! There's a frigate going to sail by here and fire its cannons at the fort."

"Sir, they're reluctant to advance through the swamp," said Clinch apologetically. "Perhaps after the navy bombards the fort—"

"Damn it!" interrupted Jackson. "The fort is garrisoned by nigras and savages. Take the fort and Florida's ours."

"We're invading Florida, General?" asked Clinch.

"No!" bellowed Jackson. "I can't declare war. Only Congress can declare war."

"Then having the savages attack is a brilliant idea. If the Spanish protest, it wasn't us," concluded Clinch, laying his praise on thick.

"I believe, sir," said Jackson, "you'll make a fine diplomat, and an even better general, if you can get those savages to attack."

"Maybe if you spoke to them, General."

"I can't do that," explained Jackson. "I'm not supposed to be here. Damn it, Madison himself sent me on this mission and I assure you, sir, I will not go back to Washington having failed."

"Perhaps if we offer them terms," suggested Clinch.

"Terms," repeated Jackson. "You want to offer nigras terms?"

"What difference does it make what we promise?" suggested Clinch. "Once we get them outside the fort—"

"Do whatever is necessary," said Jackson. Then he rejoined his aides and rode off.

An hour later, Billy accompanied Chief William MacIntosh as he walked down the road through the swamp carrying a white flag of truce. The defenders manning the walls held their fire.

Outside the gate Billy pointed to where James had fallen. Only one moccasin and fragments of his shirt marked the spot. The chief picked up the moccasin and wiped off the mud. He gave it to Billy to hold. Then, fighting back his emotions, he hardened himself for the job at hand.

The huge wooden gate at the end of the road opened, and MacIntosh and Billy entered. Inside they were greeted by the fort's commander.

"Welcome to Fort Negro. I am Garcia." Standing behind him were twenty black men, each pointing a musket at the intruders. Garcia waved his arm, and the soldiers lowered their rifles.

"I am William MacIntosh, Chief of the Northern Creek."

Garcia nodded his head in a gesture of respect.

"You are surrounded," began Chief MacIntosh. "There is no escape." He spoke weakly, for his heart wasn't in it. "Abandon the fort and we will allow you to retreat into Florida."

Billy could tell by his confident demeanor that Garcia didn't take MacIntosh's assessment of his situation seriously.

"Why you fighting for the white man?" asked Garcia. "No matter what he promise, he cheat you."

MacIntosh didn't answer, but thought to himself, "What choice do I have?"

"Join us!" suggested Garcia. "The Spanish gave us citizenship, land. We defend Florida against the Americans."

Billy wanted to express his desire to join Garcia, but knew better. Instead he silently hoped MacIntosh would accept Garcia's offer.

"How can I switch sides?" thought the Chief. "The Americans would surely attack our village and kill the women and children left behind."

Looking about the fort, Billy noticed at least three hundred defenders, mostly men with some women and children. All were well armed and in excellent spirits. He saw two cannon crews of ten men each. One crew manned the cannon on the deck pointed at the road down the middle of the swamp. The other was at ground level, pointed at the huge wooden gates. "Anyone attacking up the road would be annihilated," thought Billy.

Crates of gunpowder, hand bombs and cannonballs were stored under a canopy. Salted food hung under another. Near the barracks was a freshwater well. Then they heard a familiar sound, the grunt cattle make when they're hungry. In the far corner of the fort, two of the defenders were shoveling hay into a pen containing half a dozen steers. Billy realized that the defenders could hold out indefinitely.

Garcia saw Billy looking at the cattle. "Join us for dinner, Chief. We have more than enough food." MacIntosh nodded and accepted the invitation.

———

Five women placed a table and chairs in the middle of the fort. Garcia motioned for MacIntosh and Billy to sit down. Chief MacIntosh saw his dilemma clearly. The fort was on high, dry ground and had an ocean breeze. He would be fighting in a swamp that felt like the inside of an oven. He was a farmer. His people were farmers. Here he was, fighting for a man he loathed against a man that he instantly liked.

Two women brought out plates of sweet plantains, fresh red snapper and beefsteak. "Look at you, William MacIntosh," said Garcia, interrupting the Chief's thoughts, "fighting for the white man."

MacIntosh knew Garcia's point was well taken. "But what can I do?" he thought.

"Tell the white man to come and get us himself," said Garcia, as if he was reading MacIntosh's thoughts.

Out in the Gulf, the frigate *Betsy Ross* appeared as a speck on the horizon. Captained by Eli Watson, the ship had been patrolling the Florida Straits for smugglers bringing contraband out of Cuba. The captain didn't understand why he had been ordered miles off course to take gunnery practice on an old fort where the Apalachicola River ran into the Gulf of Mexico. The *Betsy Ross* had been ordered to take one run and fire her starboard guns, turn, come back across the fort and fire the port guns, then break off.

As the *Betsy Ross* approached, those inside the fort proudly raised the Spanish flag. When it rose from the fort, Watson realized this was more than gunnery practice. He also knew that they were not at war with Spain. Still, this was his first command and he wasn't about to disobey orders.

Watson signaled, and the starboard guns fired in rapid succession at the fort. The first three shots hit the sea wall, barely making a dent. On the walls a dozen defenders wheeled the cannon along the deck from the land side around to the seaward side to get a shot at the frigate.

Garcia, sitting with his guests, remained impassive and outwardly unconcerned as cannon balls struck the sea wall. Billy was certain his time had come, but bravely sat there, ramrod still.

Rounds whistled over the fort and exploded in the swamp beyond.

"You can't fight the white man," implored Chief MacIntosh. "He's got a navy, huge armies, and an endless supply of munitions. Surrender to me and I'll guarantee your safety. You can retreat into Florida."

More rounds whistled by, followed by explosions. Garcia just sat there, ignoring MacIntosh's offer.

"Don't you want to survive?" asked MacIntosh.

"Only as a free man," answered Garcia.

"What about your followers?" asked MacIntosh.

He looked about. Their skins were various shades between red and black, many being the product of intermarriage with the Seminole. Thus the term *Maroon* was coined, to describe their skin color. All were aware that in the United States they would become slaves.

"My brothers," shouted Garcia as he rose from the table. "The Chief says if we want to survive, surrender to him. What do you say?"

"Better to die than live as slaves," shouted Garcia's wife, Jamima Joseph. Another woman, standing with the soldiers, broke ranks and walked up to MacIntosh. Unable to control her contempt, she spat in his face. As MacIntosh wiped off the saliva, other women stepped forward, following suit, spitting on him and Billy. Then the women began punching them. Billy did his best to protect himself, covering his head with his arms.

"Enough!" shouted Garcia and the bludgeoning stopped. "Surrender to me and I guarantee your safety," he mimicked. "Get out before I let the women kill you!"

In the Gulf, the *Betsy Ross* tacked to come about, battling both strong winds and the incoming tide to fire the port guns. The captain gave the gunners the order to change trajectories. The fort's cannon fired and hit the forward mast, breaking it in two and dropping it onto the deck. In the fort the defenders let out a cheer and quickly wheeled back the cannon and loaded another round. Now they had her in range.

On board Captain Watson knew he was in grave danger of having his first command shot out from under him. Yet he was undaunted. He ordered his helmsman, "Bring 'er in closer, I want to ram one down their throats!"

The gunners on the wall did not expect the frigate to turn toward them and sail closer. Their next shot sailed just over the frigate and landed harmlessly in the Gulf.

Clinch was reviewing his choices for lunch. Eggs, rabbit or chicken? Standing in front of him were his cooks and manservant. The overseer, who usually sat watching with rifle cocked, ensuring everyone's obedience, went behind his tent to the latrine.

Billy and MacIntosh walked through the entourage and stopped before Major Clinch.

"Not now," he barked, annoyed by the interruption. He turned back to his attendants.

"Fried eggs, sunny-side up with a rasher of bacon," ordered the major.

"It is not possible to capture the fort," said the Chief as his own patience waned.

"We will attack!" demanded Clinch.

"We will cross the swamp and attack the fort only if you lead us, Clinch," said the Chief, suspecting the fat soldier was a coward.

"Ungrateful swine," shouted Clinch. "I promised you land and bounty on the niggers. Attack now or your tribe will be sent to Arkansas!"

MacIntosh looked at Billy. The same thought crossed their minds simultaneously. MacIntosh took his sharpened tomahawk and stepped toward Clinch. He would kill the fat soldier who had raided their village. Then they would march back, gather the women and children and join Garcia as free men fighting the white man.

The ship's gunners fired the cannon. The shot traveled five hundred yards into the air before it reached its apex and came down. It landed on top of the canopy protecting the gunpowder from rain and tore through it.

The explosion that immediately followed killed everyone within fifty feet. It blasted open the wooden gate, imploded the walls and sent a ball of fire hundreds of feet in the air. Two hundred ninety of the defenders, including all twelve children, were killed in the inferno.

Clinch stared at MacIntosh striding toward him, tomahawk in hand, rage in his eyes. He'd pushed the savage too far. Clinch tried to rise out of his chair, yet he was paralyzed by fear. "Where is the overseer?" he thought. MacIntosh was about to strike him when he felt a blast, so powerful it shook the ground he was standing on. MacIntosh turned and saw the huge wall of flame shoot into the sky.

"We've done it!" shouted Clinch, recovering his voice. "We've destroyed the fort."

MacIntosh stared at the once formidable fort in the distance, torn apart by the explosion and burning. "What should I do?" he thought. There was no choice really. He lowered his arm. His people would be able to remain on their land. There would even be slaves to sell.

Clinch came out of the chair and dropped to his knees. Placing his palms together, he pointed his hands up to the heavens.

"Thank you, Lord, for delivering me from the savage. I know now that I am your messenger." He rose and turned back to Chief MacIntosh, one of God's lesser creatures.

"What are you waiting for? Track down the survivors and hang their leader."

Billy accompanied the Chief as he led his warriors back through the swamp. He saw large black birds pecking at and fighting over body parts that were scattered among the mangroves. As he got closer to the shattered fort, he heard the groans and pleas of dying men. Stepping inside the crumbled walls of the still-smoldering fort, Billy saw torsos with arms, legs, and heads blown off from the force of the explosion. Defenders were burned beyond recognition. The severely wounded survivors begged to die.

The Chief and Billy searched among the few survivors for Garcia. Billy hoped that he might have somehow miraculously escaped.

Then they saw him. He was lying in the dirt away from the burning debris. Jamima was cuddling his broken body in her arms. Pieces of shrapnel had torn into his back, severing his spine and puncturing his lungs. Blood oozed from his mouth.

Billy watched as Jamima leaned over and kissed his bloody lips, trying to infuse life into him. Garcia regained consciousness briefly. He smiled at her and then fell back into his delirium.

Chief MacIntosh pried the mortally wounded Garcia out of his wife's arms. With the help of several warriors, he hoisted Garcia's limp body up and hung him from one of the remaining gate timbers. He would remain there until he rotted away, reminding all that to defy the United States meant death.

Billy was glad the man was more dead than alive. The Creeks had been part of the triumph, and yet Billy felt no joy. He was ashamed of the tribe for being soldiers for the white man. At that moment he would rather have died honorably alongside Garcia than achieved victory for this corrupt cause.

Billy had seen killing before but nothing like this. Looking about at the devastation, he wondered why the white man always won. Then it came to him. The various tribes were fragmented and often hated each other. A united effort was necessary to combat this evil.

Jamima Joseph was among the twenty-seven survivors of Fort Negro who marched in single file away from the fort to Clinch's command post for inspection. Though many were wounded, they were bound together by ropes around each of their necks and ankles.

All of them stared up at Garcia's limp, bloody body. They all wished they had heeded Abraham's advice and remained at Freedom Land. It was the end of their hopes and dreams and a return to the nightmare of slavery.

Standing in front of his command post, Clinch watched as his over-seer and second in command, Simon McFarland, counted out twelve of the defenders.

"Chief," said Clinch, "you can return home now, proud to have served your country."

Clinch saw Billy standing near the Chief and smiled at the boy. After all, he was half white, and having met his father, Clinch knew him to be well bred. He also knew that he was not lacking in courage. Perhaps he could groom this boy to become leader of the tribe and do his bidding.

"Billy," called out Clinch. "Come here, boy." Billy was surprised to hear his name. He looked at Clinch but didn't move. "Billy, come here," Clinch called out and motioned with his arm in a friendly manner.

Billy saw the big smile on his face and couldn't imagine how anyone could be happy at this moment. Chief MacIntosh thought, here was another opportunity. Major Duncan Clinch liked his adopted son. This could go a long way toward his tribe's acceptance by the white community, reasoned Chief MacIntosh. He unfolded his arms and gave Billy a gentle push on the back to move him forward.

Billy stopped in front of Clinch.

"Lieutenant," ordered Clinch, "present the Chief's son his share."

McFarland handed the end of the rope holding the twelve slaves to Billy. The boy looked at the black Indians tied together, stripped down to their undergarments. He was anything but proud. He dropped the rope in disgust.

"Billy," called out Chief MacIntosh. Billy knew that the Chief wanted him to pick up the rope, but he didn't move. Instead, John MacIntosh came forward. He looked at his father for approval. His father nodded and John picked up the rope. When he tugged the rope forward the first slave fell. Billy could see an open, festering wound on the man's leg.

"Niggers are lazy by nature," said Clinch. "You can't show them any kindness. He's your nigger now, get him up."

John kicked the man hard in the ribs. The man grunted and began to moan.

McFarland stepped forward and stood over the captive, his bullwhip in hand. "Get up now or else, nigger," he threatened.

When the man didn't budge, McFarland cracked the whip. Billy shuddered as he watched the bullwhip tear open the man's shoulder. The other captives took him by the arms and helped him up to his feet.

"Leave him be," ordered McFarland. He picked up his rifle and aimed it at the wounded man. "He walks himself or he dies."

"Then kill me," said the captive defiantly as he promptly sat down on the ground.

"Stop!" shouted Chief MacIntosh. "There has been enough killing. He is my slave. I say let him live."

McFarland looked at Clinch.

"He is correct. It is his slave to do with as he pleases," instructed Clinch.

McFarland lowered his rifle.

John led the slaves over to his father.

Clinch had his men pass out jugs of corn liquor to the Creeks to celebrate his triumph.

McFarland had selected all of the stout, healthy-looking slaves for Clinch. He had noticed Jamima and made sure to include her. As overseer, he was accustomed to having his way with the female slaves, and none had ever looked as good as Jamima.

McFarland couldn't wait to take his pleasure. He untied her from the others and led her into his tent. "Take your clothes off," he said. Jamima ignored his order.

"Take your clothes off, bitch!" reiterated McFarland, raising his voice.

As he put his hand on her bloodied cotton shirt, Jamima released her pent-up rage and punched McFarland in the face, sending him through the tent's opening onto the ground in full view of the Indians and Clinch. Everyone laughed.

McFarland got up, dusted himself off and immediately went over to his employer. "Sir, I would like to buy that one," he requested, with one hand holding his swollen eye. Usually that meant he would torture and kill his new possession. But in this case he wanted to use her hard.

"She's not for sale," answered Clinch. Chuckling, he added, "But you can use her anytime—anytime you want to take your life in your hands."

Determined, McFarland reentered his tent.

"Kill me," taunted Jamima.

McFarland would have beaten any other slave, but she wasn't his property and his vision of raping her reappeared. He knew that she would be his once they arrived at Auld Lang Syne, Clinch's burgeoning Georgia plantation. So McFarland called outside for assistance. Three soldiers came in and took hold of Jamima, then dragged her out and tied her to the other fourteen slaves.

They broke down the tent, gathered their gear and started the trek back to Georgia. The slaves walked between the dual columns of twenty soldiers on horseback, riding behind Clinch's horse-drawn carriage.

The Creeks, who were drinking as they walked, were soon outdistanced by Clinch and his men. Billy fell in step alongside the Chief.

"Why do we need slaves?" asked Billy.

"It's the white man's way," answered the Chief.

"Why do we have to be like the white man?" asked Billy.

"We have no choice," answered Chief MacIntosh.

"The fat soldier has gone up ahead. Let's free the black Indians," implored Billy.

"No," said the Chief. "Clinch would find out and that would displease him."

Late that night, as the fires burned down and everyone slept, Billy lay awake. "What would my father do?" Billy thought. He remembered his father telling him, "It's difficult to stand alone against evil." Then he heard the words, "To your own self be true." There was more to the phrase his father had him repeat all those years ago, but these six words captured the essence of his father's philosophy. Billy had his answer.

Careful not to awaken anyone, Billy crawled on his stomach, using his elbows and knees to propel himself forward. Soon he reached the slaves, tethered to a post in the ground.

He put his hand over the mouth of the first one, the wounded and beaten slave. He motioned for the man and his compatriots, several of whom were now awake, to keep quiet. Then Billy quickly cut the ropes.

Seeing the look of hope in the captives' eyes was worth the risk. He pointed south. One by one they slinked out of the camp into the dark and freedom.

The next morning, John sounded the alarm.

"Shall we track them, Father?" he asked, hoping to incur his father's favor. "They won't be hard to catch. They are wounded. Please, Father."

The Chief looked at his warriors, hung over from the corn liquor. Then he looked at Billy, standing proud and erect. He knew that Billy was the culprit, but all he said was, "Let them go."

8

Alabossa was a happy man. He was twenty-five years of age and lived in a village in east Africa, close to the Indian Ocean. He had two wives and counted among his possessions forty goats and thirty milk cows. He sold milk to his poorer neighbors who did not own any livestock. Then he reinvested his profits by buying more livestock.

He bought a small piece of prime land to farm. Almost immediately he realized that it was cheaper to hire one of his neighbors to work the land in return for a measure of milk and a percentage of the crops. This gave Alabossa the opportunity to expand his business to a village ten miles to the north.

The first day there he noticed Latasha, a fourteen-year-old girl, tending her family's sheep at the well. Alabossa made inquiries and found out that her family was of modest means and that she was in love with a poor shepherd boy.

Alabossa decided Latasha would be his third wife. Her family knew that she loved the shepherd, but he had nothing to offer for her. Alabossa offered them ten goats and five cows. Latasha tried her best to persuade her parents not to sell her to this man. She reasoned that they had enough livestock. When that didn't work she promised them she'd go to work and earn more than the cost of the goats. When that didn't work, she got down on her knees and begged. It was of no use. Finally, she refused to go to her new husband's residence. Alabossa was forced to come and fetch her.

"I don't love you," said Latasha, very matter-of-factly, to Alabossa as they walked together toward his village.

"I didn't expect you to love me, yet. We just met," pointed out Alabossa. "But you will."

"No. I will never love you," said Latasha with emotion resonating in her voice. "I love someone else."

"Childhood infatuation," said Alabossa, summing up his view of her attachment to the young shepherd. "You will get used to being a rich man's wife, and then you'll appreciate me."

That night Alabossa went to her to consummate the marriage. When he took Latasha in his arms, she pushed him away. Breaking free of his grasp, she taunted her husband, "I'm not a virgin."

Alabossa became enraged. He grabbed his young wife and threw her down onto the bed. He ripped off her clothes. All the while, Latasha continued mocking him. "You'll never have me willingly," she said as Alabossa forced her legs apart.

"Go ahead," she said, as Alabossa entered her. "This is the only way you'll ever have me." That's when he punched her in the face with his fist, bloodying her nose.

"I will have what is mine," ranted Alabossa, as he hit her again and again. Battered and bruised, Latasha slipped into unconsciousness. When she awoke, Alabossa was at her again, as if to prove his ownership.

Unlike his other two wives, Latasha was forced to work. Because of her previous experience, she became responsible for tending her husband's goats. This was what Latasha wanted. During her shepherding, she began secretly meeting her lover. Frustrated with the beatings, Latasha came up with a solution. "We could be with each other all of the time, and you could be rich," were her words to her lover.

"How?" asked the boy.

"Get rid of my husband," said Latasha.

"Kill him?" asked the boy, horrified.

"No," she said to her lover's relief. "We will do to him what he did to me. Sell him into slavery."

"How?" he asked.

"We will hire two men," she said.

"How will we pay them?" he asked.

"With his own goats," she said.

Early one morning, Latasha came to Alabossa, screaming, "A lion is eating the goats. Hurry if you want to save the herd." Alabossa took his musket and followed Latasha. He was the only man in the village who owned a firearm.

When they reached the herd, a dozen goats were missing. They followed a trail of blood to a nearby cave. Just inside the cave, Alabossa could see a dead goat. He cocked the rifle and walked closer. There was no sign of a lion. When Alabossa entered the cave, two men came up behind him, knocked him down, and shackled his arms and legs with iron chains.

The last thing Alabossa saw, as his abductors put a sack over his head, was his new wife smiling and kissing her lover. "I will come back and kill you both," he screamed.

His captors led Alabossa fifty miles to the west, where they sold him to a caravan of Arab slavers. His kidnappers divided up the twenty dollars worth of trinkets paid for him. When they returned to Alabossa's village, Latasha paid them to get rid of the other two wives, leaving her sole owner of Alabossa's land and livestock.

Arriving in America, Alabossa was part of a wholesale lot sold to Duncan Clinch to work the new cotton fields at his recently expanded plantation. Simon McFarland noticed Alabossa's bruised face as he stood in line, chained hand and foot to the other slaves. Twice during his captivity he'd tried unsuccessfully to escape and been beaten. "A troublemaker," thought McFarland.

Slaves off the boat didn't understand English, so McFarland taught by example. He motioned for Alabossa to step forward. When Alabossa hesitated, McFarland attacked him with his bullwhip, lashing him across his shoulder. The blow knocked Alabossa down and tore open his flesh.

"That'll teach you to come when I call," said McFarland. "Now get up," demanded the overseer. Alabossa sat on the ground, the open wound on his shoulder oozing blood. McFarland brought the whip down hard across Alabossa's back.

Leering at him, McFarland said, "Get up." Alabossa looked up. When he saw McFarland raise the whip again, he scurried to his feet.

"Maybe you're not so stupid, boy," said the overseer. "Let's see, what am I going to call you?" Simon McFarland refused to acknowledge African names, so he simply renamed all his slaves. "Jim, that's your name," decided the overseer.

Pointing to himself, McFarland said, "Master." Then, pointing at Alabossa, he said, "Jim." Alabossa understood that the overseer was calling him a name other than his own. He merely meant to correct McFarland, and not show defiance, when he pointed to himself and said, "Alabossa."

McFarland cracked the whip across Alabossa's thigh, sending him to the ground, reeling in pain. "Jim," screamed the overseer, pointing at Alabossa. "You savez?" asked the overseer as he raised the whip again, ready to give Alabossa another lesson.

"Jim," repeated Alabossa, referring to himself. His first English lesson was completed.

In his conversations with the other slaves, Jim referred to himself as Alabossa. They got to calling him Alabossa Jim, which was soon bastardized into Alabama Jim.

Tawna was nineteen years old when she arrived at Auld Lang Syne. She stood five feet eight inches tall, had dark brown skin, a broad nose and dark eyes that exuded the hatred she felt for her white masters. Tawna's previous owner thought her too stupid to perform even the simplest of tasks because she went about the labors very slowly, often doing the opposite of her instructions.

Clinch, though, considered himself something of a geneticist. His idea was to breed for speed and intelligence in horses, and size and stupidity in niggers. Clinch's standing offer to his fellow planters to purchase large, feeble-minded niggers had brought Tawna to Auld Lang Syne to work in the cotton fields and procreate.

At ten one Sunday morning, Jim had already been in the field for five hours. His hands were raw from picking cotton. As he bent over, extracting the cotton from the boll, the sun beat down on his unprotected back and neck, drenching him in his own sweat.

Tawna was the slave working closest to him when the church wagon arrived.

"Church!" called out McFarland.

Slaves throughout the field gravitated toward the wagon.

"Come on," urged Tawna when Jim didn't move. He had no interest in worshiping the white god, especially when he hadn't met his quota. To finish the day without picking enough cotton could mean a beating.

"Come to church," repeated Tawna, imploring Jim to join her.

"Will the white god set me free?" asked Jim.

"No, but the preacher might."

"How's he going to help?" answered Jim, making light of her suggestion.

"You'll just have to come along and find out," answered Tawna. Jim didn't move. "Okay, you stay and pick cotton and let the white man see your anger. You'll never get within a mile of freedom. Jim, you've got to play their game," said Tawna. Then she walked slowly toward the wagon.

At that instant, Jim had an epiphany. He would become a model slave and earn the trust of the whites. In this way, he reasoned, his opportunity to escape would come. Jim hurried over to the wagon as it was leaving. "Masser, let me go to church, please," pleaded Jim, as he trotted alongside the wagon.

"I don't know that you earned the right to worship our Lord Jesus," said the overseer.

"Please, masser," implored Jim,

"You been a good nigger?" asked McFarland.

"I been good, masser," said Jim. He opened his burlap sack and showed it to the overseer.

"You got a long way to go, Jim."

"Please, Masser," begged Jim.

Tawna watched along with the other slaves as Jim groveled. Finally McFarland nodded his head and stopped the wagon. Jim climbed aboard. Tawna moved over, making room for him.

"You ain't foolin' me with that 'please, masser' talk, but you fooled him," whispered Tawna to Alabama Jim. "You'd like to cut his throat and I'd like to help."

Jim looked at Tawna. He saw her inner rancor, and it reflected his own burning hatred.

The church was a dilapidated one-room building with a large cross affixed to the door. The three steps leading up to the entrance creaked as Jim followed Tawna and the other slaves in. The overseer stood in the back, leaning against the wall.

"Welcome, my children, Jesus loves you all," began Brother Jacob from the pulpit in the front. The preacher, a former slave raised and trained by a Baptist minister, had been freed by the man to spread God's message among his lesser creatures, the Negroes.

"Marriage is a sacred institution blessed by our lord Jesus," instructed Brother Jacob. "We should all have children for the greater glory of Jesus."

Satisfied that the slave population was being taught the heavenly rewards of redemption for service to the white man, McFarland stepped outside to smoke his pipe. A slave in the rear stood watch by the door, monitoring the overseer's whereabouts. When he gave the all-clear signal by waving his arm, Brother Jacob's message changed.

"We are God's chosen people. Believe in the Bible, and believe in Jesus and he will deliver us from this bondage," said Brother Jacob with a new urgency in his tone.

"Amen," shouted the congregation.

"While we await our exodus from this bondage, you must keep the faith, and teach your children and their children, for the lord Jesus will not forsake us."

"Amen," shouted the congregation.

"Just as Jesus turned water into wine."

"Jesus is Lord," shouted the congregation.

"Just as he raised the dead."

"Praise Jesus!" shouted the congregation.

"If we believe with all our heart and soul, he will send a deliverer to end our bondage. Hallelujah!" hailed Brother Jacob.

"Hallelujah!" shouted the congregation.

"South of here, there is a place called Freedom Land, where escaped slaves are given sanctuary by a man called Abraham," said the preacher in a hushed tone.

"Praise Jesus," shouted the slave in the rear keeping watch. That was the signal to change messages. The overseer entered the building.

"May the Lord bless you and keep you," said Brother Jacob, as he closed the service with a benediction.

After the church service was over, Jim approached the overseer. He waited while the man counted heads, making sure he was returning with all the slaves.

"Masser, I wants to marry Tawna," said Jim, taking Tawna's hand. Outwardly, Tawna kept the same vacant look on her face that she always wore around McFarland. Inwardly, though, she was overjoyed.

McFarland looked at them standing there, together. He was satisfied that Jim was a broken nigger.

"You do that," said McFarland. "Make us some strappin' young niggers."

"Thank you, Masser."

Jamima wasn't sure when it happened—when she decided she wanted to live. She knew she'd made a mistake attacking the overseer. Now she'd have to wait years, maybe even a decade, to get the overseer's confidence so she could effect her escape. Jamima was obsessed with getting back to Freedom Land.

Previously when she'd plotted her escape she needed to learn the English language and the terrain. Now she was faced with what seemed to her a more difficult challenge. Simon McFarland made sure she was chained at all times. Jamima realized what she had to do.

The other slaves at Auld Lang Syne knew of the defiant women the overseer kept chained in solitary confinement. They passed by her prison, an eight-by-eight-foot slave shack with a wooden shutter for a window that was kept bolted closed. A potbelly stove in the middle of the dirt floor doubled as her heater on cold nights. Her only contacts were the discreet words of encouragement, "Hold on girl, we with you," and other phrases the other slaves would call out as they walked by her shack.

"I be your whore," Jamima said to McFarland as she loosened her dress and dropped it over her shoulder, exposing her breasts. McFarland didn't trust her. Nevertheless he mounted her and had sex with her every way he'd imagined. He particularly relished taking her from behind, reaching around and cupping her large breasts and nipples, and riding her hard.

McFarland was at her two and three times a day for months. Sex had never before been so exhilarating for him. Jamima, for her part, played along. She gave McFarland the impression that she couldn't wait for the next time.

Three months later Jamima was pregnant with McFarland's child. Finally, when Jamima was in the eighth month of her pregnancy, McFarland unchained her.

9

After two years of sharing a bed with Jim, Tawna conceived Delores. Coincidentally, that same week, Jim got his opportunity. Detailed to pick up supplies, he accompanied Willie, a hulking, stuttering half-wit house nigger, to travel with the overseer to Valdosta.

"Take me with you," pleaded Jamima to McFarland when he told her he'd be gone several days. She didn't know Jim, but she knew Willie very well. He brought her meals to her dark prison shack. He was particularly keen on Jamima's baby boy. She in turn liked to hear Willie call out, "Garcia." The baby always smiled whenever he heard Willie call his name.

Jamima saw a chance to escape and begged McFarland to take her. Then, holding the baby still milking at her breast, she got down on her knees and serviced him orally. At that moment McFarland agreed she deserved a holiday, but the baby would have to stay at the plantation.

"If you get any ideas about running away, I'll kill the baby when I get back." McFarland thought about it some more and decided that he would put her in chains.

Like every other slave at Auld Lang Syne, Jim had heard about Jamima, but had not previously seen her. Climbing into the wagon, he took a good hard look and was immediately taken with her bewitchingly good looks.

"What are you looking at, nigger?" growled McFarland when he noticed Jim staring back at Jamima.

"I ain't looking, masser, please don't hit me," said Jim, cowering. He wasn't afraid of being hit. He just wanted to wait until the time was right to confront the man who stood between him and freedom.

On the return trip, Jim drove the wagon with Willie sitting alongside him. They were chained together at the ankle, for McFarland was taking no chances. Jamima sat in the back alongside the overseer. He was armed with a loaded pistol, a shotgun and a carving knife. He also carried a whip that he kept fastened to his belt.

Jamima put her arm around McFarland and asked, "Could we stop in that peach grove up ahead and lie down together?" He was always interested in lying with Jamima.

When McFarland ordered Jim to stop the wagon, Jamima quickly threw her arms over McFarland's head and brought her chains down around his neck.

McFarland was caught off guard. One of his hands pulled at the chain cutting off his air, as the other felt around for his pistol.

"Willie, help me," called out Jamima.

McFarland found the pistol and pointed it at Jamima. Before he could pull the trigger, Jim, yanking Willie with him, jumped in the back and knocked the pistol away. With his bare hands he tightened Jamima's chains until McFarland's face turned blue. As Jim squeezed the life out of him, he repeatedly chanted "Alabossa! Alabossa!" with particular satisfaction.

Aghast, Willie watched as McFarland slumped over dead. Jamima went through McFarland's pockets and found the keys to the chains. Quickly she unchained herself, and then Jim and Willie. Jim took the rifle, pistol and whip from McFarland. He climbed from the wagon and cut loose two of the horses.

"Let's go!" shouted Jim, pointing north.

"No, we should go south," said Jamima. "Follow me."

Willie just sat in the wagon, shaking. Strangling McFarland had made Jim fierce with anger. Seeing that Willie wasn't moving, Jim climbed up into the wagon and grabbed Willie's arm.

"You're coming, nigger!" Willie just shook his head. "You are going to stay and point—they go that way, masser. Is that what you do, Willie?"

Willie could only shake. Enraged, Jim thrust the knife into Willie's midsection. Jamima screamed, "What are you doing?"

"I'm killing this house nigger."

Jamima was numb as Willie fell from the wagon. Her friend Willie, poor helpless Willie, was dead. She couldn't think about Willie right now. Her thoughts turned to her baby. Although her baby was the result of a union with the white overseer, she longed for her baby boy, but knew she would never see and probably not think about baby Garcia ever again. She had to think about escaping. She knew the way. She'd done it before, and she had an accomplice with her to ensure they'd make it, or at least kill some white men and die trying.

They traveled all night. Before dawn they found a place in the woods to hide until dark. As she watched the sun rise, Jamima lamented, "I'll never see my son again."

"I'll never see my wife again," answered Alabama Jim in kind as he snuggled closer to her. She didn't protest at first, because he warded off the morning chill. When he began fondling her breast, though, she removed his hand and stood up.

"What, I'm not as good as the overseer?" said Alabama Jim, not hiding his annoyance at being rejected.

She feared Alabama Jim after watching him coldly kill her friend Willie, but she wasn't about to be intimidated by him.

"I need time," said Jamima softly. Tears streamed down her face. "I hate McFarland. Every time he touch me . . . I want to die." As she spoke, Jamima wrapped her arms around herself as if to protect herself from the bad memories.

Just before dawn of the sixth day, Jamima saw chickees dotting the landscape in the distance. Then she saw the sign reading FREEDOM LAND. A flood of memories washed over her. She saw Garcia standing there, smiling, the first time they met. She looked again and he was gone. Her knees felt weak, and she grasped Jim's forearm to prevent herself from falling.

"What's wrong?" asked Jim. He couldn't begin to understand the significance her previous home held for her.

In the distance she saw Abraham stride toward her. She let go of Alabama Jim's arm and stared at him. They looked at one another for a long moment. Neither had expected to see the other ever again. Abraham knew of Garcia's demise from the survivors but had no way of knowing Jamima's fate until now.

"Abraham! I come home!" shouted Jamima and she burst into tears. "I'm home! I'm home!" she cried. Then she threw her arms around Abraham, hugging him as she sobbed. Abraham hugged her back, and the two embraced for several minutes, her face buried in his shoulder.

Alabama Jim was instantly jealous. "Who is this man?" he wondered.

Though she was three years older and had been through childbirth, she hadn't lost any of her radiance, at least not in Abraham's eyes.

"This is Jim. He help me escape," said Jamima.

"You are a welcome addition to our community," said Abraham, noticing the rifle and pistol that Alabama Jim held.

"You fight the white man?" asked Jim, bristling.

"Yes," said Abraham. "Sooner or later the white man is going to come marching in here to try and take us back. With your help we will be ready."

Alabama Jim was satisfied. Then he moved over to Jamima and put an arm around her shoulder, trying to indicate to Abraham that Jamima was his.

"Thank you for bringing me here," said Jim sweetly to Jamima.

Abraham, noticing Alabama Jim's attraction to Jamima, decided he wasn't going to come between them. After all, last time she had left with Garcia.

"I'll fight too," said Jamima enthusiastically. Then she removed Jim's arm abruptly. "I want you to know, Abraham, that I'm not Jim's woman."

"We'll see about that," thought Jim.

They both joined Abraham's army. Now 212 strong, it was made up of men and women who split their time between soldiering and farming, training in groups of fifty at a time. Each group was assigned one day a week for training, and on Fridays the entire army trained together.

Abraham lectured his soldiers on the tactic of hit and run. This method of fighting was successfully employed by the "Swamp Fox," Francis Marion, against the vastly superior British army stationed in Charleston, South Carolina during the American Revolution. Marion and his men harassed the British troops by staging small surprise attacks and sabotaging communications and supply lines. Afterwards he withdrew his men into the swamp. The British commander, Banastre Tarleton, gave Marion his nickname when he complained to his superiors that it was impossible to catch the "Swamp Fox."

Part of the training consisted of making the army physically fit and disciplined so that the soldiers would be able to withstand the rigors of an all-night march, followed by a prolonged battle. During training, Abraham demanded that all his soldiers run for thirty minutes to build up endurance. Jim soon was outdistancing the other soldiers, and finishing steps behind him was Jamima. In subsequent weeks, during the runs, Jim took to encouraging, cajoling and sometimes threatening the stragglers.

All this time Jim was trying to impress Jamima, but she showed not the slightest interest. She was too busy trying to encourage Abraham's affections. Abraham noticed Alabama Jim's efforts to impress Jamima, though, even as he ignored Jamima's efforts to impress him. He had an idea.

Since Garcia's departure, Abraham had been forced to train and lead the army himself. For some time he had wanted a second in charge of training, so that he could attend to the other needs of Freedom Land. Seeing Jim's initiative and leadership, he thought he had found the right man.

Jamima was lonely. She was frustrated with her lack of progress in seducing Abraham. She thought to herself, maybe Alabama Jim isn't so bad. After all, he treated her with respect. He had rugged good looks. Then she remembered that he had killed Willie. She reasoned that being a slave to the white man could make anyone crazy.

The next day, after training, Jamima flirted with Jim. Not wanting to take the chance that she'd change her mind, he steered her to his chickee. Inside, he pulled Jamima into his arms and kissed her hard. Jamima wanted to pull back and wipe the spittle from her mouth, but knew better. She closed her eyes and prayed the passionless act would be over fast, and it was.

Jamima decided to take one last shot. She went to Abraham's chickee in the middle of the night.

Abraham was asleep but woke up as she entered. He watched her in the dark as she opened her shirt, exposing her breasts. Then she dropped her pants onto the floor and climbed into bed next to him. She began kissing him on the lips. At first he didn't return the kisses, but as she continued he found himself answering back. She kissed his neck and then his chest, making her way down to his sex. Despite his initial protest, she led him into unending passion. Jamima was confident she'd won him.

At five-thirty, as was the custom, the soldiers gathered at the training field. When Abraham didn't appear by six, Alabama Jim went to find him. He entered Abraham's chickee unannounced and was shocked to find Abraham and Jamima locked in an embrace.

"You took my woman!" yelled Alabama Jim. Before Abraham could explain, Jamima did her best to soothe Alabama Jim's feelings.

"No! I like you, Jim," said Jamima. "It's just that I love Abraham."

That only made things worse. Devastated, Jim stormed out of the chickee, believing that Abraham had used his position as leader to take her from him.

Abraham and Jamima quickly dressed and followed him out into the village. Everyone heard Abraham shout, "Jim!" Freedom Landers left whatever they were doing and gravitated to the scene being played out in the middle of their village. Abraham was reluctant to make his case in front of the entire community, but he had no choice. Jim turned and faced him with his hand on his knife.

Abraham knew that he had to either placate him or kill him. "If I could wave my hand and make her love you, I would do it," implored Abraham. "I don't love her."

Jamima began crying. It was as if all the pain of her past came gushing forth in a torrent of tears.

Jim stood knife in hand, staring at Abraham. The entire community stood still, waiting for what would come next.

"Please put your knife away," said Abraham, gently. Jim just stood there. "It's okay," reassured Abraham. "Nobody is going to hurt you."

"Freedom for our people is larger than the both of us," continued Abraham. "You're our best soldier. I want you to captain our army."

The recognition seemed to soothe Jim. He sheathed the knife.

"This is a tremendous responsibility. Are you willing to put personal feelings aside and fight for Freedom Land?" asked Abraham.

"Yes," said Alabama Jim, though he felt no less resentment toward Abraham.

"Then tell the people," said Abraham.

"I pledge, before all you, that I will fight for Freedom Land," said Jim in a booming voice.

The community stood transfixed, waiting for the next act in the drama.

Abraham started back to his chickee. Jamima fell to her knees in front of him, and draped her arms around his legs. Tears streamed down her cheeks. "Forgive me, Abraham," cried Jamima.

"Get up, girl," said Abraham as he leaned down to remove her arms and stand her up.

"Please, Abraham, please forgive me," sobbed Jamima, now standing limp in front of him. She tried to lean against his chest, but he kept her at arm's length.

All eyes were on them. This was the first time that they were seeing him as just a man, not unlike themselves. Some of the women had tears in their eyes, thinking about their own relationships. Many of the men envied him that such a beautiful woman would throw herself at his feet.

"I forgive you," said Abraham.

"Then we can be together," sobbed Jamima as she put her arms around him.

"No, we can't be together, not that way," said Abraham as he removed her arms.

"Why not? You said that you forgive me. I know you love me, and I love you," cried Jamima.

"Too much happened," said Abraham. "Going with Garcia was not wrong. Playing him against me was."

"And I paid for that evil," cried Jamima. "Believe me, I paid. Now we can be together."

"You heard me," said Abraham. "I won't." Despite his words, Abraham wanted to hold her in his arms, but he couldn't bring himself to trust her. Now, she had worked Alabama Jim to a feverish pitch.

"You'll never be with me no matter what I do?" asked Jamima, whimpering.

"No," said Abraham. He turned his back on her and went to his chickee. The rest of the community slowly dispersed.

Lying in bed in her own chickee, Jamima hated herself. She found herself thinking of Garcia. Maybe if she hadn't shown interest in Abraham, Garcia would have stayed at Freedom Land and everything would be different. She thought that if Garcia had lived she'd have a son or two with her now. She wondered about her son, baby Garcia, even though he was the white man's child.

The next morning, after training, Alabama Jim led five soldiers on patrol. They went ten miles north, and then swung east. They were looking for escaped slaves. Their job was to escort them to Freedom Land. If the slaves were being pursued, they could take the offensive and kill the slave hunters.

It was late afternoon when they saw Justin Sweet. He had just finished planting corn in a newly plowed field. He'd been a tenant farmer near Clinchville, eking out a meager existence. After the harvest, he paid Clinch half his crops. Then he repaid Clinch's company store for the seeds he planted, tools he used and food he ate. That's when he discovered that there was less than nothing left. To his great shock, he actually still owed a small debt. He fled Clinchville seeking his own land to farm.

Alabama Jim and the other members of the patrol watched as Justin Sweet planted the last of his seeds. Jim signaled for the others to wait in the brush. Then he strolled toward the farmer.

"Howdy, neighbor," called out the farmer as Alabama Jim approached.

Seeing Sweet dripping with sweat, Jim remembered working in the fields. "Aren't you afraid? They say there's Indians and renegade niggers around here," said Alabama Jim.

"Nah, what's there to be afraid of? I never owned a slave. In fact, I fled servitude myself," explained the farmer.

"What's that you planted?" asked Jim.

"Justin Sweet's the name," said the farmer, extending his right arm to shake hands with Jim. "This here will be a cornfield," he added.

Alabama Jim shook the man's hand and held it. With his left hand he reached behind him, took out his large carving knife and plunged it into Justin Sweet's midsection. Sweet's mouth dropped open, and he mumbled, "Why?" Then his legs buckled as his strength gave out. Alabama Jim held the knife, cutting Sweet open from stomach to sternum. Lying on the ground, cut wide open, Sweet stared glassy-eyed at Alabama Jim standing over him.

"Because you're a white man," said Jim as he reached down and wiped the blood off his knife using Sweet's pant leg.

The other members of the patrol came out of the bush. "No sense in killing him before he finished planting," said Jim.

When Abraham heard about the killing, he regretted his decision putting Alabama Jim in command. He viewed it as one based on expediency and not proper judgment. Then he realized he'd not given Jim enough direction. Killing innocent whites was not in Freedom Land's best interest. That kind of thing could bring the militia or, worse, the regular army marching into Freedom Land.

PART TWO

RUNAWAY
TO
FREEDOM LAND

1

SOUTH GEORGIA 1835

"Colonel," said Chief MacIntosh with a pronounced slur, "we are your friends." The Chief was sitting at a banquet table next to Duncan Clinch.

The occasion was the nineteenth anniversary of the conquest of Fort Negro. Duncan Clinch, ten pounds heavier and sporting the rank of colonel, had arranged the gala at which Chief William MacIntosh was the guest of honor.

"Yes, you are, Chief," agreed Clinch. He motioned. A slave in livery refilled MacIntosh's wineglass. "Let's drink to friendship," toasted Clinch.

"Nineteen years, Clinch, nineteen years. We pray to your god, we own your slaves, we fight in your army," said the Chief.

"That's right, Chief, and we appreciate it. Governor Trout, bring out the portrait and the Declaration of Friendship for the Chief to sign," said Clinch.

Two slaves carried out an ornately framed oil painting of Chief MacIntosh shaking hands with then-Captain Clinch. In the background Fort Negro burned.

"This portrait commemorating our triumph in Florida is a gift from the people of Georgia."

When the Chief looked at the portrait, all he could see was his dead son James looking at him with sad eyes. He quickly downed another glass of wine, trying his best to drown out the vision.

The governor then presented a document, decorated with the seal of the great state of Georgia. "Chief, this document, presented by our esteemed Governor William Trout, containing the seal of the people, will commemorate our friendship forever," said Clinch. Then he took a quill and affixed his signature to it.

Before Clinch finished speaking, Chief MacIntosh's head nodded onto the table. He had lapsed into a drunken stupor.

"What do we do now, Colonel? He hasn't signed," said the governor.

"Prop him up and put a quill in his hand," ordered Clinch.

The document was placed beside the Chief. Clinch reached and took hold of the chief's graying hair, and pulled his head up.

"Chief, you must sign or the people will be insulted."

MacIntosh just stared blurry-eyed at Clinch.

"Chief, make your mark!" demanded Clinch. He took the Chief's hand and inserted the quill between his fingers. Then he guided it across the signature line of the document, making an X. The signing completed, Clinch let go of the Chief's head. It crashed onto the dining table with a pronounced thud.

"Congratulations, Governor," said Clinch. "We have just concluded the Treaty of Indian Springs, ceding the remaining Creek land to the state government."

"And to you, Colonel, having just earned the rank of general in the state militia."

Clinch filled both their glasses with wine, and the two men toasted their ill-gotten good fortune.

One month later, shipments of corn liquor began arriving at the Creek village. Every Friday, a wagon containing jugs of the brew was left outside the front gate, a gift from General Clinch. Most of the men of the village came to look forward to the weekly delivery. By Friday night, many of them had passed out from drink.

Early one Saturday morning, one hundred members of the Georgia militia quietly entered the village just after dawn. Their rifles were loaded and cocked, with bayonets fixed. They were taking no chances, but they met no resistance, as the sentries were in a drunken stupor.

The militia commander surprised Chief MacIntosh in his bed. "What are you doing here?" demanded the Chief, as he looked up bleary-eyed at the lieutenant and his sergeant pointing their pistols at him.

"We're following orders. You signed a treaty giving General Clinch your land," said the lieutenant. "It's our job to escort you to Arkansas."

Chief MacIntosh was stunned. "There must be a mistake," said the Chief. "We have a treaty."

"There's no mistake, Chief," said the commander.

In the village, the soldiers were methodically going from hut to hut rousting the inhabitants.

When the soldiers arrived at Jasmine Powell's cabin, they were confronted by Billy, who was now just shy of thirty-one years old. He stood five foot ten inches tall and had long blond hair held in place by a headband. He wore buckskin leggings and a wool shirt. Billy was gathering firewood when he saw them.

"What are you doing here?" he asked, surprised to see soldiers in his yard.

"Moving you out of General Clinch's cabin," answered the soldier.

"Clinch's cabin? My father built this cabin twenty-five years ago. It's ours," said Billy.

"Was yours," clarified the soldier. "Now get moving."

Billy, his mother and other members of the tribe congregated in front of the Chief's hut. The Chief stepped outside his hut accompanied by the militia commander. The Chief held up his arms in a gesture for everyone to remain calm. "We're being forced to move to Arkansas. The commander has assured us that no one will be injured. All of you, go back to your homes and take whatever of your possessions that you can carry."

"How could you let this happen?" shouted Billy at the Chief.

"We are not leaving," shouted another man.

"Kill the soldiers," shouted another, as members of the tribe vented their anger.

"Form up," barked the lieutenant. The soldiers formed a line, pointing their weapons at the villagers.

"Disperse these people now or else," ordered the lieutenant.

"Please, they will shoot," said Chief MacIntosh. "Go home."

John MacIntosh and his drinking buddies, Little Crow and Ned Smith, stood nearby passing a jug of corn liquor as they watched the events.

Chief MacIntosh retreated into his hut. Billy tried to follow, but the soldiers blocked his path. "Let him in," said the Chief, referring to Billy.

Billy looked at the pathetic figure sitting on his bed.

"I tried to be a good leader and a good father," began Chief MacIntosh, "but now the young men are slaves to the bottle and I've lost my people's land."

"What happened?" asked Billy.

"The white man tricked me," moaned the Chief.

Billy noticed the painting of Fort Negro burning, against the wall of the hut. He stared at the picture.

"You should have joined Garcia," said Billy, opening an old wound.

"But I didn't," lamented the Chief. "Please, gather what you can and start the move. Don't give them an excuse to kill us."

"There must be something we can do," said Billy.

The Chief sadly shook his head, no. "There's soldiers out there who don't need much of an excuse to kill us," he said.

Billy exited and walked back to his family's cabin.

Chief MacIntosh sat alone in his hut. He could hear the wails of his people as they were dispossessed. It seemed to him that every decision he had made as Chief was wrong. His reluctance to attack the Americans, his decision to fight for them that had cost his son James his young life, his decision not to join Garcia in Florida and live as free men, and now, the final straw, allowing himself to be duped by Clinch into signing away their lands.

He picked up his knife and examined it. Then he gripped the handle with his fist, raised his right arm, and in one motion plunged the knife into the left side of his chest, piercing his heart.

Twenty minutes later John MacIntosh entered his father's hut and saw the Chief lying on his bed, with the dagger sticking in his heart. "Murder," he screamed as he exited the hut. "Billy Powell killed my father!"

He ran up to the commander of the militia. "My father's been murdered. I demand white man's justice," said John, hoping to see Billy hang. With a couple of hundred angry Indians to move, the lieutenant had no time to launch a murder investigation.

Word of the Chief's death spread among the people. Many called it the assassination of a traitor. No one in the tribe recognized it as the suicide of a heartbroken father.

Billy was carrying a sack of cornmeal to load onto his mother's mule when he heard the news. He didn't notice John MacIntosh, Little Crow and Ned Smith until he heard, "Murderer!" screamed at him by John MacIntosh.

"Murderer?" repeated Billy, as he turned to confront his accusers. He was shocked by the accusation. He'd known the Chief his entire life. The man had adopted him. Though he wasn't much of a father, at least not compared to Billy's real father, he'd shown Billy many kindnesses. "I just left him," said Billy.

"We know you just left him. That's when you killed him," accused John.

"I didn't kill him," said Billy sadly.

During the past nineteen years Billy's relationship with his contemporaries had deteriorated in direct proportion to the tribe's fortunes.

"We think you should die," said John, speaking for himself and his friends.

"I'm not going to fight with you," said Billy.

"How about this? Your mother is a white man's whore," said John, doing his best to bait Billy.

At that, Billy laid down the sack of cornmeal. Fists clenched, he strode toward MacIntosh. Little Crow ran at Billy's back, swinging his war club. Billy saw him at the last second and moved. The club missed his head, but caught him on the back and knocked him down.

Billy lay on the ground, stunned by the blow. Ned Smith stepped in and kicked him in the midsection, evoking a loud grunt. An instant later, the barrel of Jasmine Powell's rifle struck Ned across the face. He never saw it coming. The force of Jasmine's stroke broke

Ned's nose and sent blood gushing from his nostrils. He fell to his knees in a daze.

Jasmine Powell swung the rifle around and stuck it in MacIntosh's face. He gazed down the barrel and immediately threw up his hands, hoping she wouldn't pull the trigger.

Billy got to his feet. Jasmine kept the rifle trained on MacIntosh. Little Crow wanted no part of Billy Powell one on one, but before he could run, Billy attacked him. They fell to the ground and rolled around in the dirt until Billy pinned Little Crow's arms beneath his knees. He raised his right elbow and brought it down hard on Little Crow's cheek. Defiantly, Little Crow spat a bloody tooth into Billy's face, further infuriating him.

A crowd appeared. "Kill him! Kill him!" clamored the other youths of the tribe, drawn by the blood, anyone's blood. Such was the mood of the people.

Three soldiers stepped in. Two of them separated the combatants, and the other grabbed at Jasmine's rifle. She held on to the weapon, resisting the soldier's attempt to disarm her. Other soldiers hurried toward the fracas. Seeing his compatriot struggling with an Indian over possession of a rifle, a militiaman aimed his own rifle and fired. Jasmine crumpled to the ground. "I got him," shouted the soldier as he sprinted over to take credit for the shot.

Billy was stunned. His mother lay before him, bleeding profusely from a bullet hole in her back. Billy dropped to his knees and cuddled his mother. Her blood poured out all over Billy's arms.

"Billy," whispered Jasmine, mustering all of her strength. "Promise me, Billy."

"What, mother?" he asked, leaning over to hear her, as tears ran down his cheeks.

"Promise me you'll leave here, and not take revenge," said Jasmine. Her words were barely audible.

"What's going on here?" asked the lieutenant, after making his way through the mob.

"I shot him, sir," boasted the militiaman, pointing at Jasmine.

The lieutenant looked and saw Billy bent over his mother. "You idiot," he said as he slapped the soldier across the face, knocking him down. "You shot an old woman."

"I didn't know it was a woman," said the soldier as he rose to his feet.

The lieutenant walked over to where Billy was holding his mother. Looking down at him, he said, "I'm sorry. It was an accident."

Jasmine gently tugged on Billy's sleeve. Billy looked at her. "Promise me," she said.

"I promise," said Billy, choking back the tears.

Jasmine closed her eyes and died. Billy buried his head in her shoulder, his tears flowing. The soldiers and the Indians stood silently watching. Billy picked up his head, kissed his mother's cheek, and then stood up, holding her limp body in his arms. He stared at the soldier who shot his mother. He had an urge to slice the man open with his knife. He carried his mother a short distance and set her down in the shade of an oak tree. Then he strode toward the militiaman.

The officer stepped in front of him, blocking his path. "Don't do it, son," said the lieutenant. "When we get to Arkansas, I'll hold a formal inquiry into this shooting. If he's guilty he'll be punished." Turning to the soldier, the officer said, "Dig this woman's grave."

The soldier walked toward Jasmine to carry out his orders.

"No!" shouted Billy. "You keep away from her."

The soldier turned and looked at the officer, who nodded, indicating he should honor Billy's plea.

Billy returned to his mother's body. Her last request echoed in his head. Yet, he didn't feel right about it. His mother was murdered. How could he do nothing? he thought.

Billy wrapped his mother in her own blanket, dug a hole, and laid her with her head pointing toward the north. Then he covered her with the loose dirt. When he was finished, he stood up and looked at the sky. "Breathmaker, welcome your daughter," began Billy. "She was a proud member of your people, a good wife, and an excellent mother. Guide her spirit, Breathmaker, that she may join her ancestors." Billy watched the rapidly moving clouds overhead. "Breathmaker," added Billy, "give me the opportunity to avenge this evil."

The soldiers, a few on horseback, most on foot, patrolled the perimeter of the tribe. They gently prodded and, in some cases not so gently, pushed the Indians to get moving, ushering them along much as they would a herd of cattle going to market. Billy walked leading his mother's old mule.

That night the Indians made camp beside the Chatahoochie River. They would ford it in the morning. The soldiers camped around the Indians, ringing them in. A chill set in and the Indians huddled close to their fires.

Billy took Major Powell's tunic from the mule. It was the only talisman remaining from his father. He folded it up and stuffed it into a leather pouch.

The plan was simple. Billy would swim downstream, beyond the camp perimeter, then come ashore and make his way back, sneak in and steal three horses, supplies and a rifle. Before the three horses played out he'd be in Florida.

When all had fallen asleep, Billy entered the cold river, naked. He carried his possessions over his head, out of the water. The numbing cold was a shock. Only his fierce determination to get away kept him going. Two hundred yards downstream Billy climbed out of the river. Putting on his dry clothes gave him some relief, but he was shaking badly. He knew he had to control the shakes before crawling back into the soldiers' camp.

————

Charles Pearson didn't drink like the other soldiers. Consequently, many a night Charles was the only sober soldier in the camp. This night he wasn't sleeping with his rifle by his side, as there'd been no immediate danger.

Billy was taking a rifle from the stack when Charles saw him. Afraid, he just watched as Billy moved among the horses. Charles was hesitant to take on the savage himself, but he knew he had to act. Finally he shouted, "Indians! Indians stealin' the horses!" He got up and pointed at Billy, who hurriedly mounted the sorrel gelding belonging to the lieutenant.

It felt like someone knocked him down from behind with a rifle butt. He saw Billy Powell mount. He heard his cry echoed throughout the camp. He thought that he'd just close his eyes and rest a spell, at least until the commotion died down. The last thing he saw was everyone running about the camp.

When John Talbot heard Charles' cries of alarm, it took him a few seconds to get his bearings. Unlike Charles, John always slept with his weapons close at hand. When he turned toward the horses, Billy Powell had already mounted the lieutenant's horse. John raised his rifle in Billy's direction. He never saw Charlie Pearson standing up. But when he fired, he blew a silver-dollar-sized hole in Charles' back.

As Billy rode the horse out of the camp, his first thought was for his mother. How he missed her! He tried not to think about her as he rode through the darkness.

Just before daybreak he saw the morning star. It was a clear morning. Dawn came up on his left, confirming he was headed in the proper direction. He steered his horse into the woods, tied it where there was enough grass to graze, unsaddled him and bedded himself down for a day's sleep.

————

When he awoke it was late afternoon. He walked to the edge of the forest and looked north. On the far horizon were the silhouettes of six soldiers following his tracks and slowly riding his way.

Billy reviewed his choices. Wait the hour until dark and let his pursuers get dangerously close, or take a chance on being spotted and travel now.

Billy quickly mounted. Skirting the forest edge, he continued south. As it grew dark, the terrain began to change. A mist rolled in. The ground became moist and the forest turned into a marsh. He could hear his horse's feet sloshing through water, but couldn't see the ground.

Billy steered the reluctant animal over the soggy ground. Suddenly he found himself in water up to the horse's belly. He kicked the hesitant horse hard, forcing it on. Two steps farther he was on firmer ground, with water covering only the horse's ankles. There was no sense in forcing the animal farther until morning. The soldiers certainly weren't going to follow him into this bog. If they did, there'd be no way to track him. Billy dismounted and pulled himself up onto the branch of a cypress tree where he spent the night.

At dawn, the sun peaked through the marsh foliage, waking Billy out of a restless sleep. He looked about. As he dropped to the exposed root of the cypress tree, he felt a gnawing hunger.

He mounted and gingerly steered his horse through the swamp. To his left the ground became firmer. He found himself rising onto dry land, miles from where he had entered. Confident that the soldiers could not have tracked him, he dismounted, tied the horse where there was ample grazing, and lay down to sleep.

He awoke to the sound of baying hounds. "When did they have an opportunity to put dogs on my scent?" thought Billy. He quickly mounted. The gelding refused to move. He kicked it hard. The horse took a hop with its right front leg, refusing to put any weight on his left. Billy knew it was lame. He dismounted, and removed his rifle and the pouch carrying his father's uniform. He gave the animal a gentle pat on the neck, as it had served him well. He took his knife and plunged it into the horse's neck, severing his jugular vein. The horse collapsed, dead.

Then Billy heard the sound of voices and a baby's cry coming from the underbrush.

2

Larrs Van Luys was worried that the runaway niggers would reach the no-man's-land at the border of Florida, populated by renegade niggers and Indians. He was leaving nothing to chance.

Van Luys found Franklin Pane and his brothers Frederick and Ferdinand at the Whiskey Drummer, a local tavern the brothers were known to frequent. Franklin was standing at the bar hunched over a jar of bourbon.

"I got niggers for you to bring back if you can get started right away," said Van Luys, without as much as a hello. Pane looked up from his drink and stared glassy-eyed at Van Luys without speaking. "I hired Jeddadiah Barnes, so they'll be easy to track," said Van Luys nervously. Barnes was the Pane brothers' main competition. He used his hounds to track runaways and rarely returned empty-handed.

Franklin emptied the jar he was drinking from. "You're supposed to keep me from being disturbed while I'm drinking," he growled to his brothers.

"Please, I'll make it worth your while," said Van Luys.

"How?" asked Franklin Pane.

"Twenty-five dollars extra . . . when they're caught," offered Van Luys.

"Each?"

"No, not each!" said Van Luys, annoyed at the suggestion.

Still, that was good money, and the three Pane brothers agreed.

Delores and Martens, holding their infant son, ran along the side of the cotton fields. They were dripping wet from sweat and humidity, and short of breath. They needed to stop and rest, if only for five minutes. They knew they'd soon be missed. It was important to put much distance between themselves and the plantation.

The escape plan was Delores' inspiration. Martens had second thoughts from the beginning, but Delores knew she would not have her son raised a slave. Her own mother had told her repeatedly, as far back as she could remember, that they were not slaves but prisoners in a faraway land, and they must do everything possible to escape.

Martens had run once before, but north. He had been captured almost immediately. When he was returned, the overseer chained him to the post in the slave quarters and proceeded to beat him with a switch until he lost consciousness. Rather than maim him, his then owner had sold him at auction in Charleston. Three years later, he was running south.

"I'm scared. I'm scared of gettin' caught and I'm scared that this place we aim to reach ain't there," said Martens. The memory of the beating was vivid in his mind.

"It's there," said Delores, steadfast.

"Every nigger wants there to be a promised land, but I don't know. Abraham this and Abraham that. Abraham runnin' things in

Freedom Land. Sounds like Bible talk to me," said Martens.

"Well, the Bible's real," reminded Delores.

Martens took even less comfort from that remark. He had no use for any god, particularly the white man's god.

Then they heard the hounds in the far distance. They both knew that they wouldn't be able to hide from the dogs, but they sprang to their feet again. They left the path and moved through the underbrush. Martens led the way. As he pushed forward, the branches, vines and thorns tore through his shirt and pants and into his flesh, leaving bloody splotches all over. Delores held the baby wrapped in a cotton cloth against her chest, keeping the shrubs from springing back and scratching him, though her own arms were rapidly bloodied.

Thoughts raced through Martens' mind. Maybe the slave hunters would take their time. Maybe they'd stop and get drunk. More likely they'd overrun them, sic the dogs on him and repeatedly rape Delores.

The Pane brothers, Franklin, Ferdinand and Frederick, were mounted on three of the General's best imported mares, horses bred to gallop long distances. Clinch had imported an Arabian stallion and a string of ten mares from England to crossbreed with his existing stock.

They followed two hounds on fifty-foot cords. Several times, when the dogs circled trees, Franklin's brothers had to dismount to untangle them. Soon, though, the dogs had the scent of the slaves. From the sound of their baying, the slaves weren't very far ahead. The cords went taut as the hounds pulled hard, wanting to get at the prey.

"If them hounds quit their racket I daresay we could hear them niggers up ahead," said Franklin, not one to hide his displeasure.

"Them hounds is what's gonna earn you your money," reminded Barnes. He didn't take kindly to someone disparaging his dogs.

"The day I need a hound to track a nigger," quipped Franklin, "I'll cut my own throat."

Franklin resented sharing the spoils with Barnes. It was bad enough he had to take care of his idiot brothers. Truth was, in his advanced state of inebriation it was unlikely Franklin could track a herd of elephants over a flat field covered by a fresh bed of snow.

"If one of 'em's a female, I git her first," announced Ferdinand.

"Oh no!" said Frederick. "I do."

"You don't!"

"I do!"

"Shut up," said Franklin.

Jeddadiah Barnes dismounted. The dogs were baying and straining at their leashes. Jeddadiah set them loose. The hounds immediately bounded off in the direction of the runaways.

Stumbling amidst the underbrush, Delores and Martens were exhausted. They finally crashed to the ground in the high grass. Delores began to cry, certain of their imminent capture. Through it all, the baby didn't utter a sound.

Suddenly two hands reached out of the grass to help her. Delores let out a scream that Billy Powell was certain could be heard clear into the next county. Martens stood still, petrified. Billy stepped out of the brush. His face and arms were covered with his horse's blood and mud. He appeared to be the grim reaper incarnate, but he gently said, "I'm a friend. Come on, we have to hide." He gestured for Delores to come with him.

Martens looked anxiously toward the baying. The two hounds arrived, barking furiously and then growling at the runaway, as Billy, and Delores, holding her baby, retreated into the high grass. Jeddadiah dismounted and went to his dogs, hitching them back onto their leads.

Franklin dismounted, took his whip and strode over to the runaway. He lashed Martens across the shoulder, sending him to the ground.

"Where's the bitch?" growled Ferdinand as he quickly moved in, while Frederick stood holding the horses. Ferdinand kicked Martens in the stomach and asked again, "Where is she?" That's when they heard the baby's wail coming from the tall grass nearby. The men smiled at one another.

In the grass, Billy cocked his rifle, trying to make as little noise as possible. The baby cried again. Ferdinand stepped into the high grass toward the sound. He grinned from ear to ear when he saw Delores and the baby sitting there.

Billy aimed and pulled the trigger, but all he heard was the click of the hammer striking wet gunpowder. Ferdinand looked toward the sound. Billy sprang to his feet and stabbed Ferdinand in his stomach. Then he pulled back and stabbed him again and again. Ferdinand staggered backward holding his wounds and collapsed in a bloody heap at the foot of his brother, Franklin. The slave hunters froze, then dashed for cover.

Billy sprinted from his position to hide behind the closest tree. He came face-to-face with Frederick, who swung his own rifle around to shoot. Billy's free hand grabbed the barrel, pushing it down as Frederick pulled the trigger, sending the shot into the ground. Billy reached for his knife and plunged it into Frederick's midsection. The slaver cried out in agony. Billy twisted it until the man's legs gave out. Alerted by Frederick's scream, Jeddadiah got Billy in his rifle sights. Before he could pull the trigger, though, he felt a searing pain in his back and then another.

Franklin ran to his horse and mounted. He saw two arrows strike Jeddadiah. He realized he was surrounded by Indians and spurred his horse hard, taking off at a gallop.

Two men emerged from the underbrush. Wild Cat was a twenty-year-old Seminole with long black hair held in place by a bright red bandana. His skin was reddish brown, baked almost golden by the Florida sun. He was no more than five feet, five inches tall and had a nose that appeared to be too large for his face. John Horse was a nineteen-year-old black Seminole whose skin was dark with a reddish tint. He stood a foot taller than Wild Cat. Both were dressed in the eclectic garb of the Seminole: alligator moccasins, buckskin pants made from deer hides and loose-fitting cotton shirts acquired in trade with Cubans.

"Greetings," said Billy in Muskogean. He knew the Seminole language to be similar.

"Hello yourself," answered John Horse in English.

"What are you two doing here?" asked Billy, glad to be speaking English.

"We escort escaping slaves," answered John Horse.

"Well then, lucky for you two that I come along," said Billy.

"You hear that? This, ah, I don't know what he is, saved us, Horse," said Wild Cat as he looked Billy over.

"Billy Powell, great grandson of Angus McQueen and a half-blooded Creek by my mother, Jasmine, at your service."

That's when Delores emerged from the high grass, holding the infant. She was still sobbing from the harrowing experience.

"You're safe now," said John Horse, looking down at the traumatized couple as they held their baby close between them.

Soon Billy, Delores with the infant strapped to her back, and Martens were each astride one of General Clinch's steeds. John Horse rode in front of them, leading the way. Wild Cat and his newly acquired hounds brought up the rear.

An hour later the group followed John Horse up the side of a rise. Down below, riding a donkey along the bank of a river, was an older black man. He was wearing a straw hat and the rags of a tenant farmer.

"It's Abraham," shouted Wild Cat, pointing at the man below.

Delores and Martens each had their own vision of Abraham. She imagined a Moses-like character with a white beard holding the Ten Commandments. Martens pictured an immaculately dressed patriarch with a band of followers. Neither imagined a lone middle-aged black man in tatters, seated on a donkey.

Greeting Abraham, Wild Cat introduced Martens and Delores and then gave him a quick recounting of the exploits of Billy Powell. Abraham listened intently, then prodded his donkey and made his way over to Billy.

"How is it you're joining us?" Abraham asked Billy.

"I knew this territory to be populated by stout-hearted men," said Billy, thinking of brave Garcia.

"Aye, it is," said Abraham, appreciating the compliment by mimicking Billy's Scottish brogue. "And how is it you speak like a Highlander?"

"Billy Powell, son of Major William Powell, late of His Majesty's Ninth Regiment of Foot, at your service, sir," said Billy.

The fields stretched for miles: corn, wheat, beans, and more corn. Working in the fields were black men and women, Indian men and women, and children of all colors. Spontaneous cheers rang out as Abraham and the small entourage passed by. So far this was everything Billy had hoped for.

"By himself he killed three slave hunters and rescued this couple," shouted John Horse, singing Billy Powell's praises. The farmers nearby told other farmers, and by the end of the day the story was that Billy Powell had turned back a regiment of slavers.

Then, from between the seven-foot cornstalks, stepped a vision of perfection. She was seventeen, part Indian and part Negro. Her olive skin was smooth as the moon's reflection on a still lake. Billy noticed her immediately. Their eyes met and held fast, even though Billy's horse continued walking, forcing Billy to twist in the saddle to look back.

"She's promised," cautioned Wild Cat as the maiden disappeared back into the corn.

"But who is she?" demanded Billy.

"You'll want to forget her," said Wild Cat, hoping to end the conversation.

"Just tell me her name," said Billy.

"Morning Dew. She's the Chief's daughter and she's promised to the warrior Hadjo."

Two miles down the road the travelers came to a half-mile clearing filled with chickees. The population, ex-slaves who had escaped from bondage and a sprinkling of Indian women and men who married into the community, stopped their daily activities to watch the arrival of the newest members. Men, women and children gravitated toward Abraham.

Word of a slave hunter-killing warrior had already reached the village, causing much excitement. It was every ex-slave's worst nightmare to be dragged back to servitude. When one of their own killed a dreaded slaver, it was the triumph of the prey over the predator.

It seemed as though everyone was speaking at once as Abraham dismounted his donkey. He stretched out his arms for silence. He pointed at Billy. "Everyone, this is Billy Powell, the man who rescued the newest members of our family. . . . Billy Powell, we thank you. Our home is your home."

Billy had his horse take two steps forward. He bowed his head and acknowledged Abraham's accolade. Hundreds of people cheered wildly. Billy was overwhelmed, but he kept his outward composure. Still, a feeling of exhilaration shot through his entire being.

Careful to let Billy receive his due praise, Abraham remained silent until the cheers died down. Then he pointed at the other three newcomers. "This is Delores and Martens and their baby. They're also part of our family now." Another cheer went up, nowhere near as loud as the one for Billy, but still a welcoming sound.

"Tomorrow we will raise you a chickee." Abraham pointed at one of the huts. "You'll be given ten acres to farm. You'll be taxed on what you produce and you'll be trained."

"Trained for what, sir?" asked Martens in his naïveté.

Abraham knew how to work a crowd. He waited, looking about. Then, in a booming voice, he answered, "To defend this land!" The assemblage gave out a cheer, and Martens and Delores hugged each other in joy. This was truly a dream come true.

Three miles to the north was the Seminole village, almost a mirror image of Freedom Land. Chickees dotted the landscape. A meeting place with a wooden platform stood in the center of the village. Later that day, Wild Cat and his guest, Billy Powell, rode slowly in. Here no one acknowledged Billy Powell, let alone made a fuss over him.

Seeing deer meat hung out to dry reminded Billy that he hadn't eaten in almost a day. Wild Cat noticed him staring at the venison.

"Hungry?" asked Wild Cat. Billy nodded affirmatively.

Wild Cat motioned Billy to stay put as he jogged his horse over to where two Indians, Alligator and Jumper, both in their late teens, sat in front of a hut finishing several hunting arrows. One was whittling the shafts down to the proper length and width, and the other was attaching the feathers.

Alligator stood five feet eight inches tall and weighed almost two hundred pounds. His arms, shoulders and neck were mountainous. His face was pockmarked, as he had survived the ravages of smallpox. Jumper was just as tall, but slightly built. His buckskin pants and cotton shirt hung on him very loosely.

Wild Cat had a few quick words with his friends, then pointed toward Billy. The men stopped what they were doing and put their tools and arrows in the chickee. Alligator emerged, got on his horse and joined Wild Cat and Billy. The three men sat waiting as Jumper exited the chickee. He walked slowly toward his horse.

"Jumper, we invited Billy to supper, not breakfast tomorrow," quipped Wild Cat in his native tongue. Jumper paid him no mind and, if anything, moved even slower, before joining his comrades.

A short ride from the village was a large cypress tree beside a small lake partially covered with lily pads and marsh grass. Wild Cat suggested to Billy that he relax by the cypress tree while the trio went hunting.

Exhausted, Billy lay down near the tree and closed his eyes. He reflected on his mother's death, the all-night ride, the fight with the slavers, and the cheers of the Maroons. Yet all of these events paled in comparison to the vision of Morning Dew. Less than two minutes after closing his eyes, Billy was fast asleep.

"Dinner!" shouted Wild Cat.

When Billy's eyes opened, he was staring directly into the gaping mouth of an alligator. It appeared the reptile was preparing to devour him. Billy screamed and scrambled back against the tree. Wild Cat tugged the rope tied around the animal's tail and yanked it back, away from Billy. Alligator stepped forward. In one fluid motion he flipped the reptile onto its back and plunged a knife into its underbelly.

All the while Wild Cat and Jumper were laughing so hard they rolled around on the ground, pointing at Billy, trying to catch their breath. Billy quickly realized he'd been the brunt of their joke. It didn't anger him. Actually, it made him feel like he belonged.

As they sat around the fire, eating chunks of the alligator, Billy looked at Alligator and remarked, "I understand how you got your name." This caused another round of laughter, with Billy joining in and laughing the loudest.

As the day came to a close, Billy and his trio of new friends rode back into the Seminole village. Wild Cat had insisted and Billy agreed that he would bunk in Wild Cat's hut and accept a set of clean clothes.

3

The entire population of the Seminole village at Long Swamp exited their huts and walked en masse to the assembly place. The tribe sat in a half circle, men closest according to their status in the tribe. Women, even Micanopy's daughter Morning Dew, sat segregated in the rear. All had gathered to listen to their returning emissary, Chief Charlie Ematha.

The importance of this gathering reached beyond the Seminole population. A contingent of Maroons, led by Abraham, arrived shortly before the start. Abraham and his lieutenant, Alabama Jim, took seats near the front. Alabama Jim, as always armed to the teeth, was carrying a rifle and packing a pistol and a huge knife in his sash. John Horse and a dozen other Maroons took seats in the rear.

The Seminole Nation was made up of a dozen villages, each with about five hundred families and its own Chief. In the loose confederacy each Chief pledged allegiance to a single Chief of Chiefs, Micanopy.

Standing beside Micanopy in this well-orchestrated gathering was Charlie Ematha. Charlie was Chief of a village the size of Micanopy's located twenty miles to the west. He was sixty years old, and could remember when the only white men in north Florida were Spanish monks at the missions along the coast. Because of his age and dignified manner, Charlie was well respected. Micanopy had chosen him to go ahead of the tribe and inspect the land being offered to them.

Micanopy stood up and opened his arms to the assemblage. "Ematha has returned from Arkansas with news of our new home. Tell us, Chief, what did you see?" said Micanopy with a booming voice.

The audience became quiet, except for a lone baby's cry. The mother sitting in the rear quickly silenced him by putting the baby onto her breast.

"Good land, sweet water," answered Ematha.

Micanopy paused for effect, then continued the questioning.

"Trees like ours? Grass like ours?"

"No, different," said Ematha, measuring his words.

Micanopy didn't want to dwell on the differences. He knew Ematha would be honest to a fault, so he changed the subject.

"How many days' journey?" asked Micanopy.

"Two across the big sea, six along the big river they call the Mississippi, five on the trail," answered Ematha.

Micanopy adroitly changed the subject again. "All the tribes that live in Florida shall leave?" he asked.

Ematha hesitated. An astute observer could see his heart wasn't in it.

"The Miccouskees?" asked Micanopy.

"Yes," answered Ematha.

Billy, sitting in the rear with Wild Cat and Alligator, was looking through the audience and not paying attention to the theatrics being played out by the leaders. Then he saw what he was looking for. He spotted Morning Dew sitting among the women. An instant later she saw him. Their gazes met and held fast.

Hadjo sat in the front of the audience among the most privileged. Charlie Ematha's son, he owned fifty head of cattle, twenty horses, and farmed the choicest acreage. Hadjo was twenty-four years old, and had been groomed to be his father's heir. Moreover, as Micanopy didn't have a son, his daughter's husband would be a natural successor as Chief of Chiefs, and Micanopy welcomed the arranged marriage.

Hadjo, looking at his intended, couldn't help but notice she was staring at the white Indian from the north and he back at her. Micanopy and Charlie Ematha were little more than background noise for Billy Powell, Hadjo and Morning Dew.

"The Apalachicola?" asked Micanopy.

"Yes," answered Ematha.

"The Tallahassee?" asked Micanopy.

"Yes."

Abraham wasn't impressed with this orchestrated drama. His patience waning, he stood up. "And the Maroons?" he shouted, directing his question at Micanopy even though Ematha was his mouthpiece.

Ematha took a deep breath and then said, "No."

A wave of shock went through the crowd, but Micanopy had anticipated this. "Not the Maroons?" asked Micanopy, doing his best to act surprised.

"All the Negroes must be returned," said Ematha. The blacks in the crowd erupted.

Alabama Jim stormed out of the meeting. He reached his horse and galloped off toward the Maroon village.

Abraham remained impassive. As Micanopy had done earlier, Abraham raised his arms, calling for silence. A hush came over the crowd.

"Chief Micanopy," said Abraham in a booming voice. The few remaining voices became still. "Now you know for certain that the whites are not speaking the truth with their offer of new land. They know that you can never agree to these terms. We are part of the nation, part of this land, as much a part as your own people," Abraham reminded him.

Micanopy resented Abraham's intrusion into his attempt to sway his people to move. From the crowd's silence it was clear that Abraham had everyone's attention, both black and red. Still, Micanopy was prepared for the challenge.

"I witnessed the Creek nation humbled by the whites with the big guns and massive army. Now the whites are offering us good land in Arkansas and money for the return of their escaped slaves. If we resist, they will march in and kill us," said Micanopy.

Abraham was angry but kept his composure. "Are you saying that you and your people would stand aside, with bowed heads, as the white army marches in, takes your land and enslaves my people? Your own daughter, Morning Dew, is a daughter of my people."

"She was born free, from a free woman," said Micanopy.

"Only those that the whites have claims on must be returned," said Ematha, trying to explain. "They are property of the whites." This only made matters worse. In the rear of the audience sat the malcontents, those out of Micanopy's favor.

"We won't go!" shouted Alligator.

Then Wild Cat stood up. "We aren't leaving without a fight!" His friends and scattered members of the audience gave him a cheer.

Billy, sitting next to Wild Cat, was interested only in Morning Dew. He got up and walked toward her. Before he reached her, Hadjo rushed over and stood defiantly in front of Morning Dew.

"How dare you look at her. She is my woman. She is promised to me," said Hadjo.

"So?" said Billy calmly. He had loathed Hadjo from the instant he saw him. Billy recognized him as being born into privilege and considered him unworthy of Morning Dew. What had he done to deserve her?

Hadjo wasn't accustomed to being challenged. "So you have no claim here," thundered Hadjo. "I paid twenty head of cattle and ten horses to Chief Micanopy. We will marry in Arkansas."

He expected the sheer volume with which he delivered his explanation to make Billy back down. He stared at Billy hard. Yet he saw that Billy wasn't fazed. He might have intimidated a member of his tribe but not this outsider.

"What if something happens to you?" asked Billy, testing Hadjo.

Alligator and Wild Cat stepped forward and stood beside Billy. These were fighting words and their new champion was about to take on Hadjo, a man they themselves had little regard for.

Micanopy rushed from the platform and took a position next to Hadjo. In an instant all the men in attendance were split into opposing factions ready to spill blood.

Hadjo drew his knife, crouched, and began to circle Billy. Though Billy was unarmed, neither Micanopy nor Charlie Ematha made an attempt to stop Hadjo. Wild Cat took out his own knife and tossed it to Billy. He caught the knife and also went into a crouch.

Then Abraham stepped in between the combatants. "Powell, would you come to Freedom Land, accept sanctuary and then kill the Chief's son?" asked Abraham. Billy looked at Abraham, Micanopy, Ematha, and then at Morning Dew. He saw the dread on her face. He stood up straight and flipped the knife back to Wild Cat. Hadjo sheathed his knife as well.

"You keep away from my daughter," snapped Micanopy. "You have no interest here. You are not red. You're not even black. You're a white renegade. I hope to persuade the Indian agent that we had no hand in the murders you committed. You'll be lucky if I can prevent them from hanging you."

"I don't need to be protected by an old woman who does the white man's bidding," Billy replied.

Enraged by this insult, Micanopy gathered his supporters around him. Another dozen young braves gravitated to Wild Cat and Alligator. Again the village separated into two armed camps ready to attack one another.

Abraham took careful note of Billy Powell, his challenge to authority and the reaction of the other young men to his presence. Abraham caught Billy's eye.

"Powell, killing Hadjo will solve nothing," said Abraham.

Billy realized Abraham was not threatening him, but was assuming he could kill Hadjo. What was at stake here was peace among the people. He turned to Alligator and Wild Cat and motioned for them to back off. Reluctantly they took several steps backward.

Ignoring Billy, as if he were no longer of consequence, Micanopy turned back to the audience, looking to regain control. "My fellow Seminoles, let us have no more talk of killing. Let us prepare for the migration."

The population walked slowly back toward their chickees. The internal bomb, ticking since Ematha's proclamation of returning the slaves, was temporarily defused.

Alabama Jim rode hard into Freedom Land. He reined up his lathered horse in the middle of the village. He took his rifle and fired off a round. "To arms! To arms! We been sold!" he shouted. Then he took his pistol and fired again.

Stirred by the gunshots and the shouts, people rushed out of their chickees.

"The Seminoles sold us! The Seminoles sold us!" shouted Alabama Jim.

The Maroon population, men, women and children, came outdoors and gravitated to him.

"No! I won't be a slave. I won't," cried Delores. Martens stood by her side. "God help us, please, please Jesus," she pleaded.

"Get ready to fight!" called Jim to the Maroons just arriving.

Jamima walked over to Jim and stood next to his horse.

"We been sold," said Jim, looking down at her.

"I don't believe that," said Jamima, looking up. "Where is Abraham?"

"He's talking. All he ever does is talk!" said Jim, not hiding the disparagement in his tone.

"Wait for Abraham," said Jamima to the people. "We do nothing without Abraham!"

"The Seminole sold us to the white man!" insisted Jim.

"Well, I won't go," announced Martens from the crowd.

"Kill the Seminole! Kill the Seminole!" screamed Alabama Jim.

Abraham and John Horse arrived amidst the turmoil. They walked their horses to the center of the gathered crowd. Abraham saw that Alabama Jim had stirred everyone into a frenzy.

Jamima took a few steps toward Abraham. She looked up at him. "Abraham, I try."

"It's okay," said Abraham, raising his hand to let her know he would handle things.

From astride his horse Abraham met Alabama Jim's glare with his own. He looked at each face in the crowd and held his arms up, calling for silence. He waited for the last of the voices to die down. Then, in a very calm voice, he addressed his people:

"You are all aware of the situation. The Seminole have signed a treaty and soon they will be forced to move west."

"The treaty don't include us," interrupted Alabama Jim in a loud, angry tone, doing his best to incite the people. "We be slaves again, runaways, and every man here knows what that means."

In contrast to Alabama Jim, Abraham kept his composure. "Alabama Jim wants us to go on a murderous rampage. First he wants us to kill our Seminole brothers."

"I want to fight our way out of here. We are a thousand strong," interrupted Alabama Jim.

"If you plan on taking the women and children, how many miles do you plan on traveling each day?" asked Abraham, adding a touch of sarcasm.

"We could make it to Texas. It's part of Mexico and slavery is outlawed there. We could live there as free men."

Abraham smiled. "He imagines the whites will let us just walk all the way to Texas." Then, changing his voice, he mimicked an imagined conversation. "Is it okay if we go to Texas, Massah?" Changing his accent, "Fine, nigger, just keep on walking and Godspeed!"

Alabama Jim was frustrated. Never a match for Abraham with words, he said belligerently, "We can fight. We'll fight our way there."

Abraham had him now. "Fighting is one thing, and I agree with you. Choosing our battlefield is something else."

Abraham remembered what had happened at Fort Negro. Ever since, he had wished he'd been more forceful in demanding that Garcia not march off with part of the population. He would never let that happen again.

"I say we fight on our home ground, where we know the terrain and where our supply lines are short," said Abraham. "If there's a thousand-mile journey to be made for a battle to be fought, let the white army make that journey and let the battle be fought here, not on the road to Mexico!"

Frustrated, Alabama Jim answered, "We'll be trapped."

"You're confusing force and strategy," said Abraham. "Every day we welcome more runaways," he reminded the audience. "If we defend this country, we hold a flame up to every slave in the fields. They can break free, like every one of you did, because they will know they stand a chance of reaching sanctuary. . . . But if we are not here . . ."

The assemblage was silent as they digested Abraham's words and reflected on their own responsibilities. Alabama Jim's effort to stir the population into a bloodletting frenzy was over.

"Those that are for fighting their way out, raise their hands," said Abraham, breaking the silence. No one in the audience raised a hand or uttered a sound.

"Those that are for defending this land!" Sitting in the front row, Martens and Delores were the first to stand up and raise their hands. Then the entire population jumped to their feet with their arms raised high, shouting, "We'll defend our homes!"

4

In a cove off the coast of St. Augustine, Florida, the schooner *La Belle de Marseille* sat at anchor, a little higher in the water than it had been two hours previously. The sails on her three masts were trimmed, and only a skeleton crew remained aboard waiting for captain and crew to return. French-designed and -built in 1804, with the emphasis on speed, the *La Belle* delivered her cargoes and then outran every British warship of her day.

She was owned and captained by Ulysses McQueen, a Scotsman recognizable by his short red beard and the peaked captain's cap he always wore. McQueen made up for his lack of stature with a boldness necessary to command the eighteen desperate men who sailed her.

Ten members of his crew had unloaded five cases of Spanish-made breech-loading rifles from the two longboats drawn up on the beach. The rifles were the latest in firearms, with a hole at the base of the barrel where both the ball and the gunpowder were placed. In the hands of an expert, such a weapon could be fired three times a minute.

Billy Powell stood with Abraham where the forest met the beach, watching for intruders as Alligator, Wild Cat, Jumper, John Horse and a dozen Maroons carried off the five crates of rifles.

"Now's your chance," said Abraham, addressing Billy.

"And go where?" responded Billy, as he'd already given the situation much thought.

"Cuba, Brazil . . . What about Scotland?" suggested Abraham. Scotland piqued Billy's interest.

"I would like to see my father's birthplace, it's true. And I gave thought to going to England and joining his regiment. But to sail for weeks on a floating piece of wood at the whim of a stretch of canvas? I'll take my chances here," said Billy.

"And we are glad to have you," said Abraham sincerely. Abraham removed a rifle from the last case and handed it to Billy. Billy accepted it and eagerly shook Abraham's hand.

"I was wondering," Abraham continued. "Will you do me another service?" Before Billy could answer, Abraham continued. "We can't buy ammunition, but they might sell it to you."

"Who are they?" questioned Billy.

"The trading post at Fort King," said Abraham.

"I don't know," said Billy, hesitating to commit himself to go to a military installation.

"Ahoy, Abraham," shouted Captain McQueen, standing alongside his longboat, "we're shoving off." Abraham asked Billy to accompany him as he walked over to the captain.

In the longboat were two piles of alligator hides, weighing over two hundred pounds. They would be sent to England and turned into ladies' shoes and handbags. The finished product would fetch a hundred times the price the hides were bringing. Abraham handed McQueen a pouch containing gold coins, as the hides themselves did not wholly cover the cost of the arms. McQueen felt its weight in his hand and put it inside his shirt.

"This will be our last trip, I'm sorry to say," said McQueen. "The blockade's tightening."

Abraham wasn't surprised. "I understand. Here, I want you to meet Billy Powell. Billy, meet Ulysses McQueen," said Abraham.

Billy hadn't heard that name in years. "McQueen? My great-grandfather was a McQueen," said Billy.

"From Scotland?" asked McQueen in his heavy Scottish brogue, surprised to hear Billy's accent.

Billy nodded affirmatively.

"Then we're related," said McQueen. He held out his hand, and Billy shook it with gusto.

"Do you support this cause?" asked Billy, probing further.

"I can't say so. I trade anywhere there's a profit," explained McQueen.

"And we're both McQueens," said Billy, still marveling at the fact that a relative of his father's was standing here in the flesh.

"Let us toast with some Jamaican rum. It is quite a coincidence," said McQueen as he reached in the boat and brought out a jug.

"I'll tell you what. Let's drink a toast to that rogue ancestor of ours, Angus."

Smiling at this, McQueen uncorked the jug and took a long swig. Then he handed it to Billy, who had never in his life taken a drink of alcohol, but nevertheless followed suit. It burned something terrible going down, but Billy showed no outward effects. When he went to hand it back, McQueen waved him off. "You keep it. I wish you luck."

The sailors left in their longboat. Billy couldn't keep from turning his new rifle over and over. He was like a child on Christmas morning, opening and closing the breech mechanism a dozen times. Wild Cat warned him, "Remember, you can't show the rifle when we get back to the village." Billy nodded to show he understood.

Lying on the forest floor at the edge of the cove, shrouded in leaves to camouflage his presence, Hadjo kept the quintet under surveillance. Hadjo had been waiting for his opportunity for vengeance.

When Wild Cat, Alligator, Jumper and Billy entered the village, Hadjo and a dozen Seminole warriors sprang out at them, weapons pointed. No one said a thing. Billy kept his eyes fixed on Hadjo, expecting him to shoot. The group was ushered toward Micanopy's chickee. There everyone dismounted, and Wild Cat, Powell and Hadjo entered the hut. Alligator and Jumper remained outside, held at gunpoint.

Micanopy was sitting by himself. "We are forbidden to trade for arms with the Cubans," said Micanopy in harsh tones, looking at Wild Cat.

"If that displeases you, take your knife and plunge it into his heart," said Billy.

Wild Cat looked at Billy, then turned to Micanopy. "Plunge it into his heart, if you don't mind," said Wild Cat, referring to Billy.

Angered by the youth's disrespectful words, Micanopy put his hand on his knife. Hadjo hollered for help. Five members of the tribe entered the chickee, poised to do the killing for Micanopy. They stood silently, with their hands on their weapons, eyes darting back and forth, waiting for a signal.

At that instant Abraham entered the chickee. He quickly assessed the situation. "Chief Micanopy, you will surely need rifles when you take your tribe to Arkansas. There you will encounter Plains Indians and your old enemies, the Creeks and Cherokees."

Micanopy knew this was true. He stared at Abraham, considering. This was a way out of the confrontation caused by Hadjo, and he took advantage of it. He raised his arms and waved everyone out of his chickee.

———

Back in Wild Cat's chickee, the boys sat and passed around the rum, laughing and reveling in their bloodless victory.

"I wouldn't have let him kill you," said Billy to Wild Cat between pulls on the bottle. "You're my friend."

"Crazy as you are, I don't know what you'd do," answered Wild Cat as he fell over and lay on the ground laughing.

As Billy became drunk, he felt as if he had his father's approval. He heard his father's words echoing in his head: "Act boldly and unseen forces will come to your aid!" He mumbled to himself, "I did."

Early the next morning, with his head spinning and his stomach sick, Billy staggered out to the edge of the village. He threw up for the better part of twenty minutes. He remembered another piece of his father's advice, about abstaining from liquor, and told himself he'd never again take a drink. As he walked back to the chickee, feeling better with the poison out of his system, Billy saw a group of women walking toward the fields. That gave him an idea.

Billy put on his father's tunic and rode out to the cornfield where he had first seen Morning Dew. He walked his horse slowly past the rows of cornstalks being harvested by the Seminole women. Under the bright Florida sun these stalks were now almost eight feet tall. Billy dismounted and tied his horse to a stalk.

In a secluded area, hidden from the path, Morning Dew stood harvesting ears of corn. When Billy suddenly appeared, she turned her back on him.

"I was under the impression Florida was noted for the welcome offered those poor souls seeking sanctuary," said Billy.

"And which plantation did you escape from?" asked Morning Dew facetiously, without turning to look at him.

"All my born days I've been a prisoner of my mixed blood, so I have," said Billy. As he spoke he walked around and positioned himself in front of Morning Dew. He was so close to her that he could feel her body heat. She straightened up from her toil, took a deep breath, then stepped back. She found herself trembling so she brushed flecks of dust from her dress to give herself time to settle down before looking at him.

"The rumor is, you were being chased by the Georgia militia and that's what brought you here," said Morning Dew.

"True," he said, smiling warmly, hoping to evoke the same response from Morning Dew, but to no avail. "But I was headed in this direction anyway."

Billy could feel his yearning. He stared at her long and hard. He wanted to take her in his arms and kiss her, but instead he gently touched her arm. "Tell me, do you require anyone's permission to cool yourself by the river?" asked Billy.

Morning Dew raised her eyebrows and did her best to feign indignation. "I go where I please—and I was headed in that direction anyway."

Then she smiled. The smile pierced Billy's heart. It illuminated the deepest recesses of his being. He grinned back at her and they both started laughing.

Morning Dew felt lightheaded. She laid aside the basket of corn she'd husked and walked to the nearby stream. She removed her moccasins and waded in. Billy was right behind her.

"I've had the pleasure of meeting your father," said Billy with obvious sarcasm. "Tell me about your mother."

Morning Dew came a couple of steps closer and stood directly in front of Billy as the cool water ran by them. "She was from New Orleans. She died when I was fourteen."

"Was she as beautiful as you?" asked Billy.

Morning Dew smiled. "More, much more than me."

Billy couldn't imagine anyone more beautiful than Morning Dew. When she waded out of the water, Billy followed her. They sat down on the bank a few feet from one another. It was Morning Dew's turn to ask questions.

"What happened to your father?"

"My father was Major William Powell of the Ninth Regiment of Foot. I was told he died a hero's death when the Americans attacked our village, but I'm not so sure. I think he's living somewhere in Scotland, reading his Shakespeare and blowing his bagpipes."

Morning Dew smiled. She didn't have a clue who Shakespeare was or what bagpipes were, nor did she care. She found herself enjoying Billy's company.

Billy sprawled on one arm and motioned for Morning Dew to move closer.

"Is that his uniform?" asked Morning Dew without moving.

Billy nodded. "Aye, all he left my mother."

"Where is she?" asked Morning Dew.

"Dead," said Billy.

Morning Dew saw a sadness come over Billy. She smiled at him tenderly, in an effort to show Billy she understood his pain. Then she reached over and touched Billy's frayed buttons. "Some of these buttons look as though they are about to fall off," she observed.

"I've been biding my time, waiting for the right person to effect the sewing," said Billy.

With that remark Morning Dew abruptly stood up. "I cannot do that," she said in confusion.

"Because you're betrothed to that handsome buck Hadjo, him of the flashing blade?"

Morning Dew quickly walked back to the cornfield. Billy rose to his feet and joined her.

"It's what my father wants," she explained.

Billy needed clarification. "And you were headed in that direction anyway?" Morning Dew ignored the question and went back to picking.

"Why won't she answer me?" thought Billy. He recognized that he hadn't much experience with girls, but he was certain she had been flirting with him.

"Come with me. Leave this place," Billy demanded. "When the white army comes, they won't know you're free. You're half black. I know the whites. They consider only whites human."

Morning Dew maintained her composure. "My mother said all men see color. White men, red men, even black men."

"Leave this place with me. I'll protect you," he implored.

Morning Dew turned back to the stalk she was harvesting and continued to work as if Billy wasn't there. Billy didn't understand how she could ignore him. He quickly walked around the stalk so that she was facing him again.

Morning Dew looked him in the eye. "I could not love you," she said. Billy felt a pain in his stomach when he heard those words. "If you took me from my father and my mother's people," she said, finishing the statement.

"If I stay, could you love me?" asked Billy, mustering all his courage.

Morning Dew stopped cutting the corn. She realized the implication of her words. "I don't know what's going to happen, Billy," she said gently. "My mother said there is a reason for everything. I don't know why you came. I don't understand the attraction."

"Your mother was very wise. How did a slave come to know so much?" asked Billy.

"She was a free woman," answered Morning Dew with great pride.

"What was she doing here, and married to Micanopy?" asked Billy, his curiosity aroused. There was more than a hint of disparagement in his tone regarding Micanopy.

"Remember, he's my father," said Morning Dew, disarming Billy with her warm smile. Billy held up his palms in mock surrender.

"Abraham introduced her to my father and he fell in love with her," continued Morning Dew. "She was a whore in New Orleans, but gave up that life."

Billy looked at her, trying to gauge if she was comfortable with such an idea.

"I'm not ashamed of her," said Morning Dew. Then she resumed harvesting the corn ears. Billy went to the stalk next to her and joined her in harvesting. He cut free an ear, dropping it in Morning Dew's basket. She turned to him and smiled at his effort to help.

"The last thing my mother told me was to honor my father in all things."

"Powell, Powell!" From outside the cornfield, Wild Cat's voice called to him.

Billy turned toward the voice, then back to Morning Dew. He took off his father's tunic.

"Oh, no," protested Morning Dew.

Ignoring her protests, Billy gently laid the tunic on the ground next to her, then slipped between the cornstalks out of her sight. He knew exactly what he wanted, and he wouldn't be denied.

Wild Cat sat atop his horse, scanning the cornfield for a sign of Billy, whose horse was tied nearby. Billy emerged from between two stalks and sneaked under Wild Cat's horse. He pulled Wild Cat down from the blind side and pinned him on the ground.

"You call yourself an Indian?" asked Billy proudly.

Wild Cat raised his leg, and in a single motion lifted it over Billy's shoulder, then pushed it against his chest, flipping Billy off him and onto the ground. Then he pinned Billy.

"I call myself a Seminole," answered Wild Cat. "Come, ride with me to the fort."

The suggestion took Billy aback. "The fort? It's filled with soldiers."

"Abraham needs ammunition," reminded Wild Cat. "Besides, it's less dangerous than courting Morning Dew."

"That's hard to believe," said Billy.

"You don't know Hadjo," said Wild Cat.

"Do I have a choice?" asked Billy, smiling.

5

Billy and Wild Cat dismounted two hundred yards from the clearing where Fort King was being built. Construction had started even before the treaty was signed, making it a blatant intrusion onto Seminole land. It had been ordered by Congress and carried out at the urging of the Indian agent for the territory, Wiley Thompson. Now, with the coming migration, none of the natives protested.

Billy and Wild Cat watched the carpenters working on the fourth wall, which would close off the fort. As it was, from their vantage point they could still see the goings-on within. A squad of soldiers was being drilled by a Sergeant Paisley, a burly former British soldier in the War of 1812. Standing nearby was First Lieutenant Stanton Graham. Graham, a slim West Point graduate, wore an immaculately pressed uniform in contrast to the enlisted men, who wore partial uniforms with undergarments substituting for tunics, giving them a ragtag appearance.

Fort King was Graham's second posting since graduation, and his first since his promotion to first lieutenant. Graham had requested duty in the West and was initially assigned to Fort Wayne, on the Indiana frontier, where he demonstrated excellent leadership and initiative. That, combined with the dearth of experienced officers, led to his promotion and assignment to his first command in Florida.

Wild Cat and Billy led their horses through the open end of the fort. No one paid any attention to them, as there were two dozen other Seminoles there trading.

Next to the parade ground a private sat straddling a log, stripped to the waist. His arms and ankles were shackled, preventing him from moving. Red ants from the newly cut log were crawling all over his arms and onto his chest. Blood from their bites dotted his upper torso. He wore a sign around his neck reading, "intoxicated on duty."

Seeing that the man was in agony, Billy took a cup of water and splashed it over his chest and shoulders. Billy then raised the cup to the prisoner's lips. Restricted from talking while under punishment, he thanked Billy with his eyes.

"You there, what do you think you're doing?" bellowed Sergeant Paisley.

Billy and Wild Cat were already walking away from the prisoner toward the trading post. Billy had no idea Paisley was hollering at him.

Paisley left his men standing at attention and sprinted across the parade ground. He pushed Billy hard, sending him flying to the ground. Billy didn't know what hit him until he looked up at the sergeant standing over him, pointing at the private.

"That drunken swine is a serving soldier, and none of your damn business!" hollered Paisley.

Wild Cat stepped forward confronting Paisley, but Billy said, "He's mine."

Billy got to his feet, and the two men squared off, standing inches apart, eying one another. Paisley was four inches taller and sixty pounds heavier. Paisley's squad broke ranks and hurried over to watch what seemed like a certain shellacking. Indians at the trading post also joined the gathering. In an instant there was a crowd of over fifty soldiers and Indians surrounding the two combatants.

"Sergeant!" shouted Lieutenant Graham, as he moved briskly toward the combatants. Reaching the assemblage, Graham pushed his way through.

"Sergeant! Your superior is addressing you!" roared Graham. This time Paisley snapped to attention. Looking at his commanding officer, he explained, "He was interfering, sir."

"You wish to teach him manners, Sergeant?" asked Graham.

Paisley nodded.

"You there, you speak English?" asked Graham, addressing Billy.

"No, mon, Scottish," responded Billy with a smirk, laying his accent on extra thick.

"Let me teach him to mind his own business, the army way," said Paisley.

Graham turned back to Billy. "Any objections?"

Billy smiled and shook his head.

Graham knew enough to let enlisted men have their fun from time to time. Paisley was a bully, and Graham resented his continual torture of the enlisted men. But he also knew that without Paisley's rough discipline, the men might not take orders at all. Paisley peeled off his shirt. Graham turned to Billy Powell. "No knives or any other crude instruments you might be hiding in those breeches."

Billy nodded his understanding and removed his shirt and the belt containing the knife he wore behind his shoulder. Standing next to one another, naked from the waist up, the stout sergeant dwarfed Billy.

The onlookers crowded in, making a small circle for the combatants. Before the fight started a civilian pushed his way to the center and placed himself between Billy and Paisley.

The man was Robert Donnelly. He was in charge of the fort's commissary. "I'm taking three to one on the sergeant and even money on the Indian. Any takers?" the man announced.

A soldier in the crowd stepped forward and bet on Paisley. Then five more formed a line and Donnelly took bets from each of them. Billy stood there watching while Donnelly wrote each bet down in his little book. He noticed the men betting on credit; none of them handed Donnelly any money. Billy motioned to Wild Cat, who stepped into the circle. Whispering in his ear, Billy told him to bet as well.

"It's Abraham's money," protested Wild Cat. "We can't gamble with it."

"This isn't gambling," Billy assured him. Wild Cat hesitated. Forcefully Billy told him again, "Bet the money." Reluctantly Wild Cat took out the small bag of coins Abraham had entrusted to him, and handed them to Donnelly.

Within a few minutes all the punters were accommodated. Then, acting as the referee, Donnelly motioned the fighters together. The soldiers were already screaming for Paisley. The Indians were chanting, "Powell! Powell!"

Paisley immediately threw a left and then a right, but Billy ducked under the first and sidestepped the second. He responded with a blow to Paisley's kidney and then another to the side to Paisley's head. Paisley shuddered. They turned and faced each other again, cautiously moving from side to side.

Paisley hurled his huge frame directly at Billy, who fell backward and, using Paisley's momentum, flung the big sergeant over him. Paisley landed on his back, dazed from the fall. As he tried to rise, Billy landed a blow to his face and then kicked Paisley in the chin with his knee. Paisley collapsed in a heap.

The Indians whooped and hollered. The soldiers fell silent and walked away sullenly, having just lost their money. Wild Cat brought

Billy his shirt and knife. Together they approached Donnelly. He saw them coming and greeted them warmly.

"Well done! You got credit for all the liquor you two braves can drink!"

Billy wasn't satisfied. "Give me my coins back and pay me my winnings in United States currency."

"Pay them," said Lieutenant Graham, butting in. "Then pay the other Indians. I'm not going to let you start an Indian war. Perhaps you'd prefer I turn you over to them to collect?"

Donnelly quickly took out his purse and paid Billy and the other Indians. Then Donnelly walked back to the trading post. In spite of these losses he had still made a tidy profit on the fight. The soldiers had lost over three hundred dollars, payable on the fifteenth of the month out of their next pay, and Donnelly had paid out only a hundred and twenty.

Billy and Graham looked at one another, sizing each other up.

"I'm Lieutenant Graham," he said.

"Billy Powell, great-grandson of Angus McQueen, son of Major William Powell, late of the Ninth Regiment of Foot, and a half-blooded Creek Indian by way of my mother, Jasmine Powell," said Billy.

"That's quite a pedigree, but what is it your friends call you?"

"Billy," he said, anxious to get away.

Abruptly Billy and Wild Cat turned and crossed the parade ground. Neither of them was comfortable talking to American soldiers. They entered the trading post.

Wiley Thompson, the Indian agent, had watched the contest. He followed Billy and Wild Cat into the trading post. The large room inside was divided in the middle. One side had a counter with various goods, including gunpowder, knives, mirrors and kegs of whiskey. The other side was Thompson's office.

Thompson was a career bureaucrat. Previously he had worked in the Federal Land Office in Washington, in charge of disbursing appropriated Indian lands. When the entire Creek holdings wound up titled to General Clinch, there was an outcry and Thompson was forced to resign. Clinch, not one to forget his friends, recommended Thompson as Indian agent for the Seminoles, and on that basis he was appointed by Congress. His primary job was to expedite the migration.

There was no love lost between Donnelly and Thompson. The agent resented the fact that Donnelly didn't cut him in on his enterprises, and Donnelly saw Thompson as a meddler who stole from everyone he could. However, they shared the same space, and had reached an unspoken accommodation. For the most part they ignored one another.

"I warned you about gambling," Thompson told Donnelly as he entered. "One more time and I'll see you run out of here."

Donnelly wasn't at all concerned about Thompson's threat. The soldiers needed him too much. He took bets on everything: fights, horse races, even the weather. He gave the men much-needed recreation, and he sold them liquor.

Thompson turned to Billy. "Powell, is that your name?"

Billy just looked at him, not answering or even acknowledging his question.

"I haven't seen you before. How long you been in this territory?" asked Thompson.

Billy didn't like his accusatory tone and stood silently, ignoring him.

"Let me give you some advice," said Thompson. "Keep your nose out of army discipline."

Billy turned his back to conduct his business with Donnelly. This rankled Thomson, who stepped up his questioning.

"A renegade fitting your description is wanted for the murder of a soldier up in Georgia. You know anything about that?"

"My condolences to his widow," said Billy without turning around.

"What can I get for you?" interjected Donnelly, anxious to get his money back. Billy pointed to a white barrette. Donnelly removed it from the case and handed it to Billy. "You've got good taste, lad. That's genuine carved whalebone."

Billy examined the scrimshaw work, admiring the craftsmanship. "It's not cheap, mind you, but your squaw, I'm sure she'll show you her appreciation," said Donnelly with a coy smile.

"How much?" inquired Billy.

"I tell you what," answered Donnelly, "seeings how you're the new champion wrestler, only ten dollars."

Billy considered, thinking about Morning Dew. Donnelly confused his hesitation with doubt and added, "It's just a small fraction of what you just won from me."

"I'll take it," said Billy. Then, looking at Thompson, he added, "Also, as much powder and shot as this will buy." He laid Abraham's bag of coins on the table, and added to it ten dollars of his own to pay for the barrette.

Donnelly put the gunpowder and shot on the counter.

"One more thing," said Billy. "Shopkeeper, a knife, English-made if you have it. Apparently a man can't have enough knives around these parts."

Donnelly took out a selection of knives for Billy's perusal. "Let me feel the balance," requested Billy.

Thompson came around and stood in front of him. "What about the three slave hunters killed here last month? What do you know about that?"

Billy regarded Thompson blankly.

"There are witnesses to both those crimes. If someone should happen to identify you, I'll hang you."

Billy didn't take well to threats. He fixed Thompson with a cold stare. He took the knife in his hand and flipped it, sticking it into the table, close to where Thompson stood.

"If you don't mind me saying," answered Billy, "as Indian agent you ought to be more concerned with the inferior quality of goods offered in this establishment."

Billy turned back to Donnelly. He pointed to an eagle's feather on display. Donnelly handed it to Billy, who put the feather in his headband.

As Wild Cat and Billy exited the trading post, they walked past the soldier tethered to the log. Billy wondered if his father ever tortured his men.

Billy rode slowly by the cornfield, looking to retrace his previous path and find Morning Dew. Then he saw it. A scarecrow towering over the corn wearing Billy's red tunic, the still-frayed buttons dangling.

Billy stopped his horse beside the scarecrow. Then he heard her angelic voice.

"Rather becoming, isn't it?" said Morning Dew.

Billy turned in the saddle and looked down at the beauty standing beside him.

"It's the most useful thing that tunic's done since my father wore it," agreed Billy. "Don't ya think, though, it would look a wee bit better with the buttons sewed?"

"No," answered Morning Dew.

Billy positioned his horse alongside the scarecrow and removed his tunic. He dusted it off, then put it on.

"They sell needle and thread at the fort," reminded Morning Dew. "The next time you're headed in that direction . . ."

Billy dismounted. He stood facing her. He extended his arm and opened the hand containing the scrimshaw barrette. "For you."

Morning Dew put her hand out and accepted the barrette. She examined it carefully. She was overwhelmed both by the simple beauty of the gift and the thoughtfulness demonstrated by Billy. She had never before received a gift from a suitor.

Morning Dew reached out and touched Billy's hand. The gentleness of her fingers sent a chill through Billy. Then she clutched the barrette, holding it close to her heart, and disappeared into the cornfield.

6

Amelia Herbert Hampton's plantation had been passed down through three generations of her late husband's family. The main residence was built in 1753 on lands granted to Colonel William Hampton by George II, the monarch for whom the state was named. In 1742 Colonel Hampton was a hero at the Battle of Bloody Marsh, helping the outnumbered British to fight off three thousand Spanish soldiers invading from Florida in an attempt to secure Georgia for Spain.

The plantation was not the largest in the area. That distinction belonged to Duncan Clinch. What hers lacked in size, though, was made up for by its splendid appointments. Rows of oak trees lined the red brick road approach to the main residence, a three-story colonial mansion. It featured eight Corinthian-style columns, four on each side of the main entrance, supporting the overhanging shingled roof that sheltered both the second-floor terrace and the large patio abutting the front entrance. Four huge bay windows, two on each side of the front door, illuminated each of the downstairs rooms, and five brought in light and air upstairs, the additional one being above the front door. On the sides of each window were oak shutters, which could be closed in case of a storm. Two brick chimneys rose from the sides of the house, servicing eight fireplaces, four on each of the first two floors. The outside of the house was freshly painted white with red trim.

Set off to the left side were the slave quarters. Each shack had a chimney and a window covered with thin wooden slats that could be pushed out for light and air. They were made of the same red bricks, dug from a red clay pit and baked in the kiln behind the slave quarters. To the right were the pristine stables, also painted white with red trim. It was one slave's full-time job to pick up any animal dung that fell on the red brick road leading from the stables.

Amelia descended the long staircase made of polished hardwood. An imported Scottish wool carpet covered the center of the stairs from top to bottom. Area rugs from Persia dotted the floors throughout. Furniture from Paris, and life-size portraits of ancestors in various uniforms, gave the impression of visiting European royalty.

Ruth, Amelia's personal maid and longtime slave, stood at the bottom of the stairs. Amelia and Ruth had been together for twenty-five of Ruth's forty years. There was an understanding and a communication between the two that often did not require words.

This evening Amelia wore a dress featuring a calico design of dove's breast with black flowers and bows around the hem. She favored this style because it showed off her tiny waist and slender ankles. As she entered the library, the sound of her gigot brushing against the petticoat skirt announced her presence. On the wall in front of her, prominently displayed, was a life-size portrait of her late husband in his general's uniform. Looking up at it and reflecting on him, Amelia drew her shawl securely around her shoulders.

"I think if the British had kept in mind Lord George Germain's cowardly record at the Battle of Minden, Washington might have had a much harder time of it." The high-backed chair obscured the speaker, but the voice, that distinctive baritone, with perfect enunciation of each syllable, gave away the speaker's identity.

Amelia didn't miss a beat. It was as if the two of them were in the middle of a discussion they'd been having for some time. Amelia walked around the chair and looked directly at Abraham. "Oliver would say providence provided us with incompetent opposition."

Abraham closed the book he'd been reading. He stood and replaced it on a bookshelf. He was wearing an imported cotton shirt from Cuba and a coordinated cotton jacket, giving him the appearance of a man of means. Then, looking up at the general's portrait, he observed, "It's hard to keep him out of a conversation."

"It is when we're discussing military history," quipped Amelia.

When she had first met Abraham, she knew he had been the general's slave. It seemed to her that her husband treated him more like the son he never had. Raised with slaves on her own family's plantation, Abraham was the first Negro whom Amelia had met as an equal.

Twenty-five years younger then her husband, Amelia had found herself strangely attracted to Abraham. She couldn't help but notice his keen mind and muscular young body. Abraham, for his part, found himself enticed by the beautiful woman with long blond hair. They both knew that any liaison would be strictly forbidden. The general was also aware of the attraction. When Abraham was sent to Haiti, Amelia believed, at least in part, it was because of their fondness for one another.

Abraham turned to her. "He taught me most of what I know. Everything he loved, I love."

His tribute caught Amelia off guard. "Is he saying he loves me?" she wondered. She didn't know how to react and was annoyed with herself. Abraham could see the displeasure in her face, and mistakenly read it to mean she was unhappy with him.

"I forgot, us colored folk aren't capable of love," said Abraham defensively.

Now Amelia was really annoyed. He'd put words in her mouth. She didn't say that. She didn't think that, and she knew better than that. Her mood was reflected in her sharp tone. "Why are you here? If you're caught, you'll be hung!"

Abraham didn't like the way the entire conversation was going, and he brought it to a halt. "Can't we speak in the manner of old friends?" he inquired in his gentlest tone.

Amelia was all for starting over. She smiled and, looking him up and down, nodded. "Very smart clothes," she said, complimenting him.

"It's what the well-dressed Cuban is wearing these days," said Abraham, smiling. Amelia smiled as well, for she was used to seeing Abraham in the various disguises necessary for him to safely make the trek to her plantation.

Abraham quickly got down to business. "There is going to be a war. There are factions within the Seminole and my people that believe an all-out war is the only answer."

"I think not," said Amelia, brushing off his warning.

"You will lose everything: your crops, your plantation and maybe even your life. I will be powerless to help you," said Abraham.

Amelia scoffed at this prophecy. "Are you suggesting that there is something I could do to stave off this calamity?"

Abraham nodded. "Leave here now and free all of your slaves."

"That is a ridiculous suggestion," said Amelia, fiddling with one of her sleeves. Abraham gripped her arm with his hand, stilling her fidgeting, trying to get her to take him seriously. She looked at his hand and then at him.

"What do you suppose would happen if I let all the slaves go running off? They can't go back to their villages in Africa. They'd starve. And God knows what damage they'd do trying to survive," said Amelia.

Abraham was prepared for that question. "They will have me and my friends to run to."

Amelia looked Abraham in the eye. She had to tell him, she decided. "Abraham, Micanopy has been bribed. He's received cattle, horses and gold. It's sealed. They're leaving."

Abraham's face grew solemn. "Bribed? Don't you understand? If that's true, an all-out war is inevitable."

Amelia knew Abraham as a man of peace, and this sort of talk disturbed her. "You would provoke this war?" she asked.

"If the Maroons think they will have to go back to slavery, there will be a bloodletting." He reminded her, "In Haiti, every white man, woman and child was massacred."

Amelia knew that Abraham was not prone to exaggeration. "I can't afford to abandon my plantation and slaves. Besides, the slaves are well treated here, certainly by the standards the other plantations employ."

Abraham smiled at Amelia's naïveté. "They appreciate that, but they are still slaves."

Amelia nodded, acknowledging this point. "What is the alternative?" she asked.

"You harvest two more crops, then you sell your plantation and . . . free all your slaves," said Abraham.

"And you'll guarantee that no trouble will come to me when the fighting begins?"

Abraham nodded.

"Four more crops," countered Amelia.

"One more," offered Abraham.

"You just offered two," said Amelia, offended.

"You should have accepted," said Abraham.

In many respects, the deal was a relief for Amelia. She was tired of South Georgia. She yearned for Charleston and travel. She couldn't sell the slaves even if she wanted to. The general, who had had second thoughts about slavery, willed her the "help," as he referred to the slaves, in a life estate. They were to be granted their freedom upon her death or the sale of the plantation.

"Three more crops and I will free all of my slaves and leave this place," pronounced Amelia. Then she batted her eyelashes and coyly asked, "Would you come and visit me in Charleston?"

Abraham smiled. "Would I pose as your butler or your coachman?"

"Whichever," answered Amelia. "I promise that your livery would be in the latest Paris fashion."

Abraham laughed out loud at her effrontery.

Then, just as suddenly, Amelia was all business again. "Does that mean we have a deal?" she asked.

"Dismiss your overseer. You won't need him," demanded Abraham.

"Absolutely not. Who will keep the slaves here and working?"

"My word . . . and theirs," said Abraham, looking into her eyes.

They measured one another for a long moment. Amelia found this proposal inconceivable. "You're suggesting slaves will work on their own?"

"With the promise of future freedom they will," said Abraham.

Amelia looked away from Abraham. She fussed with a handkerchief in the cuff of her sleeve, then looked back into Abraham's eyes and realized how serious he was. She touched his arm. "Abraham, I'll need to think about this."

"There is no time," Abraham said. "You are with us or . . ."

"I get three more years' honest labor from every slave here. If there are no runaways, and no trouble, every slave will get their freedom," interrupted Amelia.

Abraham was unmoved. "Two more years. No more, no less."

"You drive a hard bargain."

Once again he smiled at her. "The general taught me well."

Congressman Thomas Reilly drank the remainder of his glass of bourbon and looked up as General Clinch spoke. "The fact is, Reilly, our celebration was premature, and I blame you."

Reilly slid his glass over, indicating he was ready for a refill. The house servant came immediately and filled it up. When Reilly didn't respond, the general continued. "I blame the government, and you are our government representative."

"You sit in Washington," reiterated Wiley Thompson, who was sitting across from the congressman in the general's drawing room.

"Is there an echo in here?" asked Reilly, annoyed at Thompson's remark. It was one thing to be berated by General Clinch, whose political clout extended all the way to Washington. It was something else to be admonished by this lout.

"Our patience is running thin," said Clinch, changing to a friendlier tone. "We were given every assurance the Seminoles were going to leave, and have they? They've had every excuse in creation. Their women are pregnant. Their cattle are pregnant. Their corn is pregnant."

It was August 1835, and the following year would bring a presidential election. With it would come new bureaucratic appointments, and possibly a new Indian policy. Time was of the essence.

Reilly reached for his drink, but Clinch grasped his wrist, preventing him from bringing the glass to his lips. Reilly remained calm, too calm for the general.

"I can assure you, General, pressure is being brought to bear by the various agencies to remind the Indians of their treaty obligations and to get them to move now. Micanopy has given assurances," said Reilly.

"Shit talk," barked Wiley Thompson.

"I beg your pardon, sir," said Reilly, caught off guard by the comment.

"I am the Indian agent in the territory. Force is what's called for here," demanded Thompson.

Reilly, sweating from the drink and the conversation, took a handkerchief from his breast pocket and patted his forehead. He looked at Thompson and in his most official voice said, "Force wasn't part of the treaty negotiations."

"It damn well ought to be, because that's the only language those heathen understand!" said the general.

Thompson added, "Do you know that the Indians are arming and training? Do you know they have a steady source of contraband from Cuba? Are you aware, sir, that more and more slaves are escaping to join them?"

Reilly smiled at the general, and then raised the glass to his lips.

"You've got to understand, Reilly, the Seminoles are a beacon for niggers. Let me show you," said Clinch. He stood up and walked to a table holding a rolled-up scroll. He brought it back and unfurled a map in front of Reilly. Pointing to a plot of land in South Georgia, he said, "From this area, as far north as here, the plantations are losing thirty niggers each month. The Seminole give them sanctuary. They set them up with land and weapons."

Reilly looked up at the general. "The Seminole will emigrate west very shortly."

Clinch didn't accept this. He'd heard this promise for the past eighteen months.

"Do you know how many troops I have to keep order here on the frontier, to impose the law and implement Washington's policies? Just a thousand men to control ten thousand square miles. If we are going to encourage the Seminole to get the hell out of Georgia and Florida, we'll require substantial reinforcements."

"Ever farmed cotton, Tom?" asked the general, changing his tactic to one of respect for the man and the office he held.

Reilly looked up. Having heard his first name and a kinder tone, he responded by shaking his head. "My family is—"

"Let me give you an elementary lesson," interrupted General Clinch. "Cotton fetches a dollar and twenty-five cents a bale in Liverpool. If you owned a thousand acres of virgin land for planting, capable of producing three hundred and fifty bales per acre, and worked by repatriated slaves currently being harbored by the Seminole, you'd have quite an annuity when your days of public service end. Are you following me, Tom?"

The congressman stood up. One hand grasped the side of his jacket just below the lapel. He looked the general in the eye and spoke as though he were addressing the Congress of the United States.

"What we have here is a military situation of the utmost gravity."

7

The soldiers marched in a perfect line, eleven soldiers in each of the five rows. Rifles rested on their shoulders.

"Company, halt!" barked Alabama Jim. The army stopped marching.

"Present arms!" The troops thrust their rifles forward in unison.

"Right shoulder arms!" Again the troop snapped to the command. A Prussian general would have been proud to call them his own.

Abraham watched with satisfaction as his crack company was put through its paces for the benefit of the new recruits. The company was made up mostly of men. Men outnumbered women almost three to one in their society. Still, there were ten women in this elite force who could shoot a rifle, wield a bayonet, run and ride as well as any man. Nine of them stood at attention behind their officer, thirty-five-year-old Jamima Joseph.

She cut quite a figure standing in front of her squad, her long hair flowing in the breeze. Jamima was a soldier now. She likened her appearance, particularly her hair, to a male lion's mane. As a child in the Congo she'd seen lions, and that memory burned within her.

The newest recruits, Martens and Delores, stood watching, along with several other recent arrivals, hoping to be able to imitate these soldiers one day soon. They stood with only wooden sticks on their shoulders and moccasins on their feet. They had no uniforms.

Alabama Jim came over to put the recruits through their first simple drill. "Left shoulder arms!" The trainees fumbled with the sticks. Martens confused his right with his left.

"Present arms!" Martens dropped his stick as the others presented them in a crude imitation of the soldiers they'd just watched.

Alabama Jim walked over to chastise Martens. That's when he noticed Delores standing next to him, her stick placed perfectly on her left shoulder. His icy stare turned warm. He smiled and told her, "Well done."

Jim turned his attention back to Martens, glaring in order to intimidate him. "When the white man comes to drag you back to slavery, you're gonna wish you learned to use that rifle."

Jamima had also noticed Jim's interest in Delores. She knew how brutal he was, and decided to take Delores under her wing.

"Girl, you in my company," ordered Jamima. "You do what I say. Stand up straight. You can march with me and join the woman soldiers." Delores did as Jamima instructed. She marched across the field and joined the elite group of women soldiers.

"Did you know a boy name Garcia on that plantation?" asked Jamima as Delores came close. Delores shook her head no.

Jamima would have asked more questions, but she fell silent as Abraham walked to the center of the field. He called to all of his soldiers and trainees to come to him. Alabama Jim walked up beside him. The rest of the soldiers got down on one knee, forming a semicircle looking toward him. Next to Abraham were the five cases of rifles he'd brought off the ship. The lid was pried off of one. Abraham took a rifle from the case and held it up.

"These rifles are better than those your adversaries will be using. They load faster and shoot straighter. They can be fired twice in the time the white man shoots once."

Billy Powell was watching the training from the edge of the clearing. When Abraham signaled, he came forward, holding his own rifle. He took four lead pellets in the shape of a ball from another small box and held them up for the entire army to see. Billy then put the balls into his mouth. He lifted the rifle, spat out one of the balls into his hand, and loaded the rifle by placing the ball in the hole at the base of the barrel. Then he quickly put a measure of gunpowder from the powder horn into the hole and then placed a hand crank into the hole and turned it twice.

He aimed at a dead cypress tree girdled with pumpkin vines that had grown up the trunk, using the bare branches as a trellis. Hanging from the vines were small green pumpkins, one of the staples of the Seminoles' diet. Only last evening Billy had dined on the small sweet vegetable that was fried in a pan over the open fire.

Billy fired. His shot severed a vine and a pumpkin fell to the ground. He repeated the procedure three more times in under a minute, each time cutting a pumpkin off the vine.

A cheer went up. All of the soldiers were impressed. One by one the men in the Freedom Company, as Abraham called his elite squad, stepped forward. They were each handed a rifle. There were not enough of the new rifles to go around, so the rest of the army would continue to use muskets and captured Kentucky long rifles that used traditional powder and shot rammed down the barrel.

Abraham put his arm around Billy's shoulder in an almost fatherly demonstration of affection. "Will you make another trip to the fort for me?" Billy felt a great sense of pride in being the object of Abraham's affection. "Yes, sir, I believe I will."

Billy, Jumper, Alligator and Wild Cat dismounted and tied their horses to a tree near Fort King. They walked into the fort, through the gap where the fourth wall would be.

As Billy and his friends entered the trading post, Donnelly was busily stacking goods.

"Hello, Powell. You come to fight again?" asked Donnelly, acting overly friendly.

"Not today. Today we are going to hunt. We need ammunition," said Billy, returning the solicitous greeting in kind.

Wiley Thompson leapt out of his chair and came over to Donnelly's side of the room. "You bought ammunition the other day," he said in an accusatory tone.

"Used it up," said Billy, smiling, though inwardly resenting Thompson's tone.

"Well, that's a pity," said Thompson facetiously. "I can't allow him to sell you any more."

"Why not?" asked Billy.

"Orders," said Thompson.

"Whose orders?" questioned Billy.

Thompson took umbrage at being questioned by this half-breed. "No more ammunition for Seminole until emigration, says great, white father in Washington," said Thompson, speaking in pidgin English.

"He's not my father, and I'm not Seminole," pointed out Billy.

"What exactly are you?" asked Thompson.

"I'm a half-blooded Creek by my mother, Jasmine. My father was Major William Powell of His Majesty's Ninth Regiment of Foot," said Billy proudly.

"You're a mongrel, and a mongrel wearing red is what's wanted for the killings," growled Thompson.

"I killed no one, and I'll ask you to give me the respect I am due," said Billy, remaining calm. Yet inside he wished he'd left the tunic on the scarecrow.

"You're a damn stinking liar and a murderer, and as Scottish as my boots!" roared Thompson.

Wild Cat, Alligator and Jumper all looked at Billy. He did his best to contain his anger, but the smug look on Thompson's face unleashed a torrent of resentment.

"Do you really think the Seminole are leaving? You twisted the arms of a few old men. They are not leaving," said Billy, pointing to his friends. "This is their land. You're the intruder, you and your toy soldiers!"

Thompson roared back, "They'll go of their own free will, or they'll go at the end of a bayonet."

Here was the savage temperament coming out. Thompson went back to his office. He reached into his desk drawer and took out a pistol. Coming back around, he pointed it at Billy.

"It was you the militia was chasing, and you're as good as swinging," said Thompson. "Guard!"

In a blur Billy reached for the knife he kept in his sash. He flung it in an underarm motion, and it knocked the pistol from Thompson's hand, leaving a slight cut on his index finger.

"Guards!" screamed Thompson.

Donnelly rushed out the door. He was certain that killing would start any second, and he didn't want to be among the casualties.

"You are an insurrectionist!" said Thompson, pointing at Billy while holding up his bloodied hand.

"Powell, come on," said Alligator.

"Powell!" called Jumper and Wild Cat in unison, urging Billy to leave with them. The moment they had left, Sergeant Paisley and a squad of soldiers entered. Billy was trapped. He looked at the soldiers. Nobody moved.

"Arrest the half-breed!" demanded Thompson.

The soldiers advanced warily. Billy decided he'd make a run for it and join his friends. He bolted for the door. As two soldiers grabbed him, he knocked down the first. Then something smashed him in the back of the head, sending him to his knees. When he looked up, a smiling Sergeant Paisley was holding a rifle butt. Two soldiers restrained his arms as another soldier placed chains on Billy's arms and legs.

As the soldiers were dragging Billy toward the newly finished stockade, Lieutenant Graham heard the commotion and hurried over, intercepting the party. "Stop right there, soldier!" shouted Graham. The soldiers dragging Billy let him go, and he fell to his knees.

"What's going on here?" demanded Graham.

"He threw a knife at me," said Thompson as he came running, holding up his bloody hand.

Billy looked up at Graham. "He pointed a pistol at me," said Billy.

"Release him, Sergeant," ordered Graham.

"Stay out of this, Graham. I'm the Indian agent here. An attack on me is an attack on the United States government. I'll see you court-martialed if you countermand my order," threatened Thompson. Confidently he turned to the soldiers. "Take him to the stockade!"

Graham stood there helplessly as the soldiers dragged Billy to the one-room prison.

Inside the stockade they chained Billy to a ring bolted to the wall. Then Paisley proceeded to beat him until he lost consciousness.

Wild Cat, Jumper and Alligator went to Abraham's chickee. When they entered they found Abraham relaxing, enjoying a warm bath. He was the only one in the village with an actual bathtub. He'd accepted it as a gift from Jean LaBasque after he'd negotiated a deal to free the man's slaves. It was Abraham's most prized possession, along with his books.

"Powell is in jail charged with being a renegade. They will hang him," blurted out Wild Cat.

Abraham looked at the trio. He picked up a sponge that was floating in the tub and squeezed it over his head, causing hot water to cascade down his face. "Hand me a towel," said Abraham.

Wild Cat picked up a cotton washcloth and handed it to Abraham. Abraham wiped his eyes, then looked at the Indians. "He's been here only six days, and already he's been sentenced to death."

"He was buying ammunition for you," Wild Cat said. "Use your army and break him out."

"An army is not needed for a mission like this," said Abraham. "Five men will do."

That's exactly what the three Indians wanted to hear. They looked at one another with smiles of relief.

"Please, Father, you can get him out. They will hang him!" Morning Dew stood before her father, pleading as a daughter, as a member of his tribe, and as a woman in love. She was bringing all of her considerable charm to bear.

"He should be hung," said Micanopy, thinking of the troubles Powell had already brought upon him.

"I am in love with him," pleaded Morning Dew.

"Love with him!" repeated Micanopy, immediately enraged. "Did he put a hand on you? I'll see that they hang him today."

"You do that and I'll kill myself," threatened his daughter.

They measured one another, each knowing the other meant what they said.

"You are promised to Hadjo," said Micanopy, adjusting his tone. "He is a good man. Tell me, how can I reconcile saving Powell and still fulfill your obligation to Hadjo?"

Morning Dew drew a deep breath. "I will marry Hadjo . . . if you save Powell."

"You will marry Hadjo and. . . ." instructed Micanopy.

"I will marry Hadjo and . . ." repeated Morning Dew.

"You will never see or speak to Powell again," said Micanopy.

Morning Dew couldn't bring herself to say the words her father spoke.

"Then he will hang," said Micanopy, understanding her silence.

Morning Dew began to cry uncontrollably. "Save him!" she blurted out between sobs.

"And?" demanded Micanopy.

"I will never look upon him or speak to him again," cried Morning Dew. Her words were barely intelligible.

Micanopy savored this victory over Powell. "Also, I don't want you harvesting the Maroons' corn. Gather the women, go to the fort and get some supplies. We are going to emigrate."

Private Charles Webb looked forward to guard duty, particularly since he'd couldn't afford Donnelly's corn liquor. Ever since the soldiers had arrived, an old nigger from nearby would appear and discreetly sell the sentries whiskey and rum for less than half of what Donnelly charged.

When Donnelly got wind of this, he complained to Thompson and Graham about the soldiers getting drunk on the old nigger's liquor. It was Donnelly's complaint that got Charles Webb tied to the log. When that didn't deter the competition, Donnelly began extending credit to the men. This worked out better than Donnelly imagined. Come payday most of them were forced to hand their wages over. Donnelly was getting to keep sixty soldiers' pay each month. He figured within two years he'd be able to leave there a wealthy man.

Henri appeared just after midnight. He pointed to Charles' pouch of powder and shot and offered to trade a jug of corn whiskey for it. Charles quickly complied, hoping Henri never found out what a one-sided deal this was.

A half hour later, Charles had passed out from drink when Abraham made his way past his post into the fort to the stockade. The other guards were either asleep or inebriated beyond consciousness.

"Powell. Powell," called Abraham quietly.

Billy quickly rose. "Abraham, you've come to break me out," he said jubilantly.

"No, the whites would use your escape to declare war. We need more time," explained Abraham.

"So I have to stay here?" said Billy, his anger returning.

Abraham put his finger to his lips, reminding him where they were. Billy became silent. "There is another way," said Abraham.

He called it the white man's game. "You look into their eyes and you tell the biggest lie you can while doing your very best to make them believe you."

Billy rehearsed his lines all night. Abraham threw insult after insult at him, preparing him for Thompson. Just before dawn Abraham slipped out of the fort.

Micanopy, Hadjo, Wild Cat, Alligator and Jumper filed into the Indian agent's office. Wiley Thompson, in a bad humor, stood scowling at the Indians. Billy Powell entered, pushed along by Sergeant Paisley. He was wearing his frayed red tunic. His face was battered, and he was walking with great difficulty.

Graham's contempt for the brutish sergeant was never more evident. "That will do, Sergeant. Get him a chair," ordered Graham.

Paisley slid a chair over, and Billy collapsed into it.

"Lieutenant, by what authority have you brought these people here?" asked Thompson, doing his best to cut short the proceedings.

"I am in command of this post," Graham reminded him.

"You mean, temporary command until Major Dade arrives," countered Thompson.

"I am in command," pointed out Graham.

"And I am the Indian agent for this territory. This man has committed murder."

"Not according to these witnesses," said Graham.

"Then these witnesses are lying."

Graham kept his composure. "There are five Seminoles in this room. Every one of them swears that Billy Powell was in their village when the militiaman in question was killed," said Graham.

"Chief Micanopy, what do you say?" asked Thompson.

Micanopy didn't like Billy, but he liked the whites even less and he'd given his word to his daughter. "These men speak the truth," he said.

"They're lying. Every one of them, liars!" screamed an enraged Thompson. Here was his supposed ally, Chief Micanopy, standing there, telling what he knew to be an out-and-out lie. The Indians were all lying scum, and he'd show them!

Graham remained calm. "I'm bound to take their word," he said.

"You have no authority in this. This is civilian business," said Thompson.

"You should have arrested him outside of the walls of the fort, Thompson," explained the lieutenant. "Arresting him inside the walls, and putting him in the guardhouse—that makes it army business, and I'm still in command here."

"I have orders from General Clinch," proclaimed Thompson.

Graham was sick of hearing about General Clinch. "General Clinch is Georgia militia. He has no authority inside Fort King," said Graham. He turned to Paisley. "Remove his irons."

Paisley hesitated. He looked at Thompson.

"Don't listen to him, Sergeant," said Thompson, encouraging his insubordination. "Obey that order and you go in my report."

Now it was a test of wills. Graham, the West Pointer, wasn't going to be intimidated by Thompson. "If you don't obey my order," said Graham to his sergeant, "you will find yourself shackled to the log— and I'll make it a hanging offense if anyone so much as gives you a drop of water!"

Graham meant it and Paisley knew it. He produced the key and unshackled Billy.

The Indians filed out of Thompson's office. Gladness was apparent on their faces, except for Micanopy and Hadjo. Billy was the last one out the door. He stood in front of Thompson's office, basking in the sunlight and the freedom. Wild Cat provided an arm for Billy to lean on as he walked toward the gate.

Graham joined them. "Don't come back," he said. "Thompson's sent to Valdosta for a witness to identify you as a renegade."

Powell didn't know what to think. What was this white man up to? Why was he opposing his own kind to help? Maybe Graham was the kind of officer like his father.

Billy took the feather from his headband and handed it to Graham. "When the war comes, wear it. I'll tell the others and you won't be a target."

Billy was lying on Wild Cat's bed when Morning Dew entered the chickee carrying a bowl of soup and a spoon. In pain, Billy slowly forced himself to sit upright.

"Do you have an appetite?" asked Morning Dew.

"I didn't 'afore you came," answered Billy, joking weakly.

Morning Dew sat down next to Billy and began spooning him the broth.

"If you sew as good as you cook, my coat is in good shape," said Billy between swallows.

"Billy, I'm not going to do any sewing for you," said Morning Dew.

"Aye . . . well," said Billy. He drank some more broth. He'd heard this all before.

Morning Dew put down the bowl and spoon. She looked Billy in the eye. "Ever . . . Hadjo and my father have insisted we move up the date of the wedding."

Billy was crushed. This hurt more than Paisley's beating. "Will you . . . marry him?"

"Yes, and we're leaving. Tomorrow we are getting supplies for the journey," explained Morning Dew.

"I've traveled all this way for you to break my heart?" asked Billy.

Morning Dew took the empty bowl and spoon and stood up. "The survival of my people depends on us moving to Arkansas. I am the chief's daughter. It is my responsibility to set an example. I realize it is of little comfort, but I will never forget you."

8

Bounty hunter Franklin Pane came to Fort King at Larrs Van Luys' behest. As the sole survivor of the "slave massacre," as it was termed by the locals, Pane alone could identify the perpetrator as the half-breed Billy Powell. That was what Van Luys had assured Thompson when he negotiated the deal that included a healthy finder's fee for himself.

Pane didn't particularly relish the idea of identifying the renegade. He didn't miss his brothers or even feel a need for vengeance. Van Luys' promise of twenty-five dollars and a jug of corn liquor had been the lure. Then Van Luys showed him a document, signed by General Clinch, empowering him and his agents to seize any nigger they came upon. It was common knowledge that half-breed niggers lived throughout the Floridas claiming they were Indians. Pane had been promised an additional bounty of twenty-five dollars for every nigger that he found.

When Van Luys and Pane arrived at Fort King, the last thing they expected to hear from Thompson was, "It was necessary to release him."

"I'll issue a warrant. Apprehend him and I'll consider our contract complete and pay you one hundred dollars," said Thompson. Though this made perfect sense to him, Van Luys suspected Thompson of playing him for a fool. This confirmed it.

"I paid this man twenty-five dollars," said Van Luys, pointing to Pane. "Give me back my money. Give it to me!"

Then, to compound matters, Pane figured out he was being cheated. "One hundred dollars!" shouted Pane. "You only gave me twenty-five!"

"Give me back the twenty-five, and when Thompson here pays me the one hundred, I'll give you half," shouted back Van Luys.

Pane put his hand on the large carving knife he carried in his sash. Thompson put a jug of corn liquor on the counter, hoping to defuse the situation. Pane picked it up and gulped down as much as he could. Then he pulled his knife and stepped toward Van Luys.

A sense of dread came over Morning Dew. What she had believed to be a logical decision turned out to be gut-wrenching. She couldn't get Billy out of her mind. Never before had she experienced anything like this. All she wanted was to run to Billy. In spite of that, she kept leading the women to the fort, telling herself, "Put one foot in front of the other and walk."

Arriving at the fort, Morning Dew composed herself for the job at hand. As she entered the trading post, she saw Franklin Pane, knife in hand, stalking Larrs Van Luys. Thompson was leaning against the wall behind the desk to protect himself from being dismembered. The action froze when they saw Morning Dew.

"My father sent me for rations," she announced.

Thompson became incensed. Two men were about to kill one

another and here was this half-breed, the daughter of the scum that had betrayed him, asking for rations.

"The rations are waiting for you in Arkansas," growled Thompson.

Morning Dew just stood there.

"No food! Get out!" Thompson said.

Morning Dew was angry. Never in her life had she been spoken to with such blatant disrespect. She had an urge to tell Thompson that he would pay for such insolence, but she held her tongue. Instead, she gave Thompson an icy stare, then turned and exited the office. She walked slowly toward the gates, still fuming.

Inside the store Van Luys and Pane looked at one another. Van Luys thought he'd struck gold.

"What do you think?" he asked.

"If she's not a nigger," said Pane, "I'm a Chinaman." He sheathed his knife.

Van Luys turned to Thompson. "I need three soldiers to help round up those niggers."

Thompson thought to himself that the day was saved. He stuck his head out the door and hollered for Sergeant Paisley, who was drilling his squad on the parade ground.

"Company halt!" commanded Paisley when he heard his name called. "At ease!" Then he turned, walked across the grounds and entered the office.

"Get three recruits and assist Mister Van Luys," ordered Thompson. Paisley promptly saluted him and turned to carry out the order. Thompson added a reminder, "Outside the fort."

As soon as the women walked out through the open gate, Van Luys, Pane and the soldiers surrounded them. Van Luys took out his whip and cracked it over the women's heads. Frightened, they cowered together next to Morning Dew.

"How dare you," thundered Morning Dew. "I am the daughter of Chief Micanopy."

"You're also a nigger," Franklin Pane said.

Ignoring the remark, Morning Dew turned to the women and mustered all of her courage. "Follow me," she said.

Pane's whip cracked down hard across Morning Dew's back. Screaming, she fell to her knees. Pane stood over her, whip cocked, ready to deliver another blow. As the women helped Morning Dew to her feet, she took a small knife from her sash and flung herself at Pane, aiming for his heart but slashing his arm. This time Van Luys' whip came down across Morning Dew's wrist. She dropped the knife and fell to her knees. Pane came over and kicked her hard in the stomach. She curled up in a fetal position, reeling in pain.

Lieutenant Graham rushed across the parade area and out of the fort. He fired his pistol in the air. Everyone froze. "That's enough!" he shouted.

"This is civilian business, Graham," said Thompson.

"What's my sergeant doing here, then?" asked Graham.

"He's been seconded to help these men round up renegades," explained Thompson.

"Sergeant, report to the barracks and take your men with you," ordered Graham. Paisley looked at Graham and then at Thompson. "That's an order, Sergeant!" repeated Graham. Paisley and the three recruits walked back into the fort.

"This is civilian business, Graham," countered Thompson.

Graham wasn't intimidated. "The government says let these women go."

"These women are either insurrectionists or stolen property," said Thompson.

"Courts of law make those decisions."

Van Luys took out his document. "Henceforth any niggers found in these territories are hereby considered runaways or insurrectionists and are to be confiscated. Signed General Duncan Clinch."

Van Luys handed Graham the document. He pointed to Pane, Thompson and himself. "We are authorized to confiscate them."

"But these women are Seminoles," said Graham.

"Some of them are niggers," said Thompson.

Graham looked at the frightened, cowering women. He looked at Thompson with utter contempt. "You politicians wallow in pig shit."

The women stood in line as Van Luys inspected them. Pane was by his side, his wound wrapped in his torn-off shirtsleeve. He had an uncharacteristic smile on his face. He didn't care about sex, but he liked the idea of violation. He knew what he would be able to do to Morning Dew. He felt the urge stirring within him. He couldn't wait for his opportunity.

Van Luys selected six women, including Morning Dew, with obvious Negroid features. The women were put in arm and leg chains, and were attached to each other by a separate long chain. Then the women marched, led by Van Luys on horseback, with Franklin Pane bringing up the rear.

Their wailing could be heard throughout the Seminole village, bringing the entire population out of their chickees. Wild Cat, Jumper, Alligator and Billy watched as Micanopy met with the women in the center of the village. Outwardly, Micanopy kept his composure, even though his own daughter was one of the captives. "There is nothing to be concerned about," he said in his calmest voice. "I will go to the fort and secure their freedom and arrange for the supplies for the move."

Inwardly though, he was livid. "How dare they? If they took my daughter, how can I trust them? How can anyone trust them?"

Micanopy went to the fort accompanied only by Hadjo. His reason was that he didn't want Thompson to construe their coming as a threat of violence. He would have preferred to go alone, but Hadjo insisted on accompanying him.

The two men were made to wait in front of Thompson's office for half an hour. When Thompson finally made his appearance, he stood on the landing, glaring down at them as if they'd committed a grievance.

Micanopy spoke first. "Thompson, our women came here. They were taken away as Negroes. Help me, Thompson. I have given you my word."

Thompson looked down at Micanopy. "Those women were runaway slaves. Other people's property. You people have a lot of nerve. You won't obey the treaty you signed, yet you come here expecting the government to help you."

Micanopy was stunned but he didn't show it. "My own daughter, Thompson, she is not property," he said.

Thompson ignored him. This wasn't going well at all and Micanopy knew it. He'd resorted to begging, and even that hadn't moved Thompson. The two men stared at one another.

"All right, I will intervene on your behalf," said Thompson, as though he was acquiescing. "But only when your people move! I don't mean talk about moving. I mean when you pack up your belongings and leave your villages."

Thompson was smug. He knew he had them now. He knew how to deal with savages.

"Thompson!" shouted Hadjo, rudely interrupting his daydream. "If something happens to Morning Dew, I'll kill you."

"You're threatening me? Get out before I have you hung!"

"Thompson," said Hadjo, "I'm promising you."

In sharp contrast to Micanopy's accommodation tactics, Hadjo realized, looking at Thompson, the real enemy was the encroaching white man. He had second thoughts about his support of the emigration strategy.

9

The entrance to Auld Lang Syne looked more like a fort than a cotton plantation. Sentries patrolled outside the gates. Inside, a platoon of soldiers was being put through a close-order drill by their sergeant.

General Clinch stood in front of the six women, inspecting his prizes. In his opinion, they didn't replace what he had lost, but it was a start. If Thompson was right and holding hostages made the Seminoles move, that was better yet.

Despite Morning Dew's words of encouragement, the other women were crying. All of the women had Negro blood, being the product of mixed marriages with the Seminole. Born either in Freedom Land or the Seminole village, none of them had ever experienced the cruel bindings of slavery.

Morning Dew was clearly the most desirable and youngest of the women captives. Yet as Clinch stepped closer to her, Van Luys sounded a warning. "This is a wild one, General. She near killed one of my men."

Clinch was undeterred. He found her extremely desirable, and stepped closer. Then he reached out and caressed her face, gently touching her cheek.

Instantly Morning Dew spat in the general's face. As the saliva dripped down Clinch's cheek, his initial surprise turned to anger. He smacked her across the face with the back of his hand, sending her to the ground and pulling the two women next to her down on top of her.

"Teach that one a lesson," said Clinch, turning to Van Luys.

Van Luys unshackled Morning Dew's ankle chains and separated her from the other women. For the first time in her life, Morning Dew was faced with the reality of slavery for a desirable woman. At that moment she thought of her mother and what she must have endured as a slave, and after she became a whore. She wondered how her mother was able to keep her dignity throughout.

The entire population of the village assembled to hear their Chief. Micanopy stood on the platform with Hadjo at his side. "I want everyone prepared to leave in three days' time," he said.

"Chief Micanopy, I say we take hostages to trade for the six women," shouted Wild Cat from the back of the crowd.

Others shouted in approval of Wild Cat's suggestion. Micanopy, however, was committed to his course of action.

"It would be suicide," he explained, believing this to be true. "The whites would march into our village, shooting and killing us indiscriminately. Hundreds would die and we would still not get the women back."

Again Wild Cat challenged him. "Are we men or are we cattle?" This time the majority of the assemblage shouted in approval.

"We cannot beat the whites with force," Micanopy protested. "My own daughter is among those being held. I know what is best. I am confident that she and the other women will be returned when we fulfill our commitments."

Billy had heard enough. The man was a spineless coward, too afraid to help his own daughter. Billy left the meeting, found his horse and mounted him. Though his ribs were aching from the beating he had received, particularly when he bounced in the saddle, he rode hard out of the village.

He rode the five miles directly to the fort, dismounted and tied up his horse. He put on a hat he'd borrowed from Jumper and wrapped a blanket around himself. Then he brazenly walked through the gates. From appearances, he was just another Indian coming to trade.

Inside the fort, all was still. There were no soldiers drilling on the parade grounds. Billy walked around to the rear of the barracks. Looking inside, he still didn't see what he was looking for. Then Lieutenant Graham exited the outhouse behind the barracks. Billy came up behind him.

"Lieutenant, where are the women?" he asked in a hushed voice.

Graham turned, surprised to see Billy. "Powell, are you crazy? If Thompson sees you, you'll be hung!"

"Where is Morning Dew?" demanded Billy, stepping up into the lieutenant's face.

"You can't help her," sighed Graham.

Billy didn't accept Graham's answer. "She is my woman, Graham. Tell me where she is."

"You won't be able to help her," said Graham. "The situation is hopeless."

"Are you my friend, Graham?" asked Billy. The two men stared at one another.

"The women were taken to General Clinch's plantation," said Graham.

Having gotten the information he came for, Billy started for the gate. Graham called after him. "There's a company of militia there."

Billy kept striding away toward the exit. If he had to, he was willing to take on an entire army. He would get Morning Dew back.

Martens had spent the day plowing his field so that he could plant sugar cane and corn. The former slave was proud to be toiling in his own field. Delores was working alongside him with their baby strapped to her back, papoose-style. Martens was about to begin a new row when he spotted Abraham, Alabama Jim and Billy riding toward him.

The three men dismounted at the edge of the plowed field. Leading their horses, they walked over to them. Abraham spoke first. "Martens, weren't you a slave at Auld Lang Syne?"

"Yes, sir, and so was my wife, Delores," said Martens hesitantly. Both Delores and Martens were awed in the great man's presence. Billy smiled at the baby, and seeing this, Delores told him, "We've named him Powell."

Billy was taken aback. He didn't know what to say. Abraham said it for him. "Quite an honor, Powell."

Abruptly he changed the subject to the purpose of the visit. "This is our man," Abraham told the two others.

"You know the layout of the plantation?" asked Billy.

"Worked it three years," answered Martens, not knowing why he was being asked the question.

"We need you," said Abraham.

Martens took a step backward. "You don't mean go back!" he said. Abraham slowly nodded his head. Martens' eyes widened in fright. He began to shake. "I risked everything to get away," he pleaded. "If I go back and they catch me . . ." His imagination boggled at the thought of what they'd do to him. "They'd tie me to that big oak tree in front of the house and they'd flog me. Then they'd cut off my toes so I couldn't run!" He shook his head again. "I've seen it!"

Alabama Jim regarded Martens with disdain. Then he looked at

Delores, catching her eye. Delores immediately looked away, not acknowledging the eye contact.

"Forget about him," Alabama Jim said, sneering. "Let me go. I escaped from there."

"No," said Abraham. "It's been years since you were a slave there, and I need you here."

"How long have you been working this field—your field?" asked Abraham, turning back to Martens.

"A few weeks," answered Martens.

"And before this field, you worked in other men's fields?" asked Abraham.

"Yeh sir," said Martens.

"Look around," instructed Abraham.

"Beggin' your pardon, sir," said Martens.

"Look around. Go on." Martens did as Abraham told him. He saw his own recently plowed field.

Delores stood watching Martens, but she could feel Alabama Jim's eyes on her, making her very uncomfortable.

Martens didn't know why he'd been asked to survey the surroundings. He turned his gaze back again to Abraham.

"See any man with a whip?" asked Abraham.

"No, Mr. Abraham. I had no whip on my back since I come," said Martens.

"Well, let me tell you something, Martens," said Abraham, looking him squarely in the eye. "In this life everything has a price. Freedom doesn't come without responsibility to your fellow citizens."

Martens swallowed hard and looked at Abraham, Alabama Jim and Billy.

Delores had heard enough. "I'll go. I know the plantation."

Martens had no choice. He couldn't let Delores go in his place. "That big ole oak might be waitin for me, after all, but I'll go," lamented Martens.

"You going as a man or a slave?" asked Alabama Jim.

"A man," answered Martens.

"Then act like one," said Alabama Jim, not hiding his disdain.

The rescue team gathered in Abraham's chickee. On the floor was a crude map of Auld Lang Syne drawn on a piece of parchment. Gathered around Abraham were Billy Powell, Wild Cat, Jumper, Alligator and Martens. Alabama Jim watched from the rear.

Unexpectedly, Hadjo appeared at the entrance to the chickee, rifle in hand. Alabama Jim confronted him, pointing and cocking his own rifle. "What do you want?"

Wild Cat quickly rolled up the map. Hadjo raised his open hand, letting all know he had come in peace. "I know what you're going to do," he said. "Allow me to join you."

"Allow me to kill him," said Alabama Jim fiercely, looking at Abraham.

Abraham put his hands up, indicating restraint. Then he warned Hadjo, "If you are here as Micanopy's eye and ears, I'll kill you myself."

"You mistake my intentions. Morning Dew is my bride," pleaded Hadjo. "I cannot sit by and let white men make her a slave."

Everyone in the chickee couldn't help but be convinced of Hadjo's sincerity.

Morning Dew was on her hands and knees. She was nude and a metal choker attached to a chain circled her neck. When she squirmed, Van Luys tugged on the chain, cutting off her air. Unable to breathe, she went still again. There were bruises on both her cheeks, and her broken nose dripped blood. Franklin Pane stood over her, eyes bright with the beating he'd just given her.

"Are you ready for more?" He wound up and hit her across the buttocks with his belt as hard as he could. Morning Dew screamed.

Van Luys pulled on the choker, muffling her cries. Aroused, Pane opened his pants, took out his hardened organ and penetrated her. She screamed again at the horrible pain inside her. Pane motioned to Van Luys to let her scream. Her screams heightened his satisfaction.

Morning Dew was becoming delirious. The room began to spin. She heard only the raucous laughter of Pane and Van Luys. Dimly she saw the men passing a bottle back and forth.

Outside the slave shack, three members of the militia stood drinking and listening to the rape going on within. They were waiting their turn. Van Luys exited the shack and joined the soldiers. One of them offered him the bottle they were passing back and forth. Van Luys took a long pull, wiped his mouth and smirked. "There's still life in her, boys." Seeing a patrol of six soldiers walk by, Van Luys joined them, walking with them as far as his cabin. The patrol continued walking past the main residence, the overseer's house and the slave quarters.

In the shadows, watching their progress, was Martens, trembling with fear. The blood had drained from his face. As soon as the patrol passed, Martens signaled the others and led them across the perimeter of the all-too-familiar grounds. Behind him Billy, Wild Cat, Alligator, Jumper and Hadjo followed stealthily.

Across from them were the militia's barracks. A guard was sleeping on a chair outside. Inside, thirty soldiers slept in bunks. Their rifles were stacked in the corner. As Abraham had planned, the group split into two. Each moved around the barracks in a different direction.

Inside the slave shack, Franklin Pane roused Morning Dew by yanking on the chain attached to the choker around her neck. That was the cue for the soldier who had just entered. He reached down and turned her over. He looked at her battered but otherwise perfect body. He dropped his pants and began to mount her. Morning Dew tried to close her legs, but Franklin Pane tugged on the choker. Gasping desperately for air, she stopped resisting. Then Pane, pulling on his jug of corn liquor, cheered the soldier on.

Outside the shack, the two soldiers on guard duty were passing a jug between themselves and laughing. Soon it would be their turn.

Martens watched the men from his hiding place twenty yards away. He knew what was expected of him. He rose and stepped out of the shadows. Walking deliberately, despite his growing fear, he proceeded toward the shack. He got within ten yards of the two sentries before one of them challenged him.

"Who goes there? Come forward and be recognized."

Martens took two more steps and again he was challenged.

"What'dy want here, nigger?"

Martens swallowed hard and came forward. "Boss . . . I've got something."

Martens had one arm tucked inside his shirt. He was now within reach of the two sentries. One paid him no mind and lifted the jug for another swig. The other watched Martens, hoping he had something for him to eat. Standing out in the chill night air, drinking corn liquor and waiting his turn, had stirred his appetite.

Martens whipped a long knife from his shirt. The soldier's eyes widened and he froze. Martens lunged and slashed the man's throat wide open. Blood spurted onto Martens and all over the soldier, who fell to his knees holding his gaping throat and windpipe. Horrified, the other soldier dropped the jug and tried to escape inside the shed. Jumper leapt out of the dark. Viciously he swung his tomahawk. It sliced through the back of the guard's skull, killing the man instantly.

The door to the slave shack burst open. Billy, Jumper and Hadjo rushed in. "You scum!" Jumper and Hadjo plunged their knives into the soldier on top of Morning Dew.

Franklin Pane dropped the chain and reached for his own knife. "No, you don't!" Billy grabbed his throat with both hands and squeezed. As Pane's one eye bulged out of his forehead, his left hand found his knife. He was about to plunge it into Billy when Hadjo lashed out with his tomahawk, severing Pane's left arm at the elbow. Gushing blood, his forearm, still gripping the knife, fell to the floor.

Hadjo watched as Pane's face turned blue, wishing he was the one who was choking him. Billy continued to squeeze with all his strength until he crushed the life out of him.

Jumper placed a blanket over the semiconscious Morning Dew. Dazed at the sight of the violated maiden, Hadjo tried to free her from the chain but was unable to. He placed the chain under the blanket to muffle the noise and then struck it repeatedly with his tomahawk. It was no use. Martens entered the room and saw Hadjo's problem. He said, "The overseer has a key."

Van Luys' cabin wasn't much larger than a slave shack. He had just sat down at a small table, a bottle of Scotch and a glass at his elbow, a Bible on his lap. Van Luys liked reading the Bible. It gave him comfort when he read the passages telling of the Lord's vengeance and how He smote those who opposed His will.

When the door was flung open, Van Luys looked up from the Good Book. His eyes widened in terror at the sight of an enraged Billy. He knocked over the table and backed up, into the blade of Martens, who had entered through the rear window.

"Remember me, boss?"

Hearing the words, Van Luys turned. He saw Martens standing there, knife in hand, covered with blood. Van Luys fell to his knees and began to cry for mercy. Martens put his knife to Van Luys throat. "The keys."

Van Luys crawled to a box by his door. He handed Martens a ring holding a dozen keys. Billy opened the front door, looked both ways and then exited. Martens followed with Van Luys, all the while holding the knife to his throat.

In the slave shack, Jumper knelt beside Morning Dew. Gently he told her, "Everything will be fine." Hadjo stood by the door. He was appalled by the gang rape and couldn't bring himself to look at her. All desire he had ever felt for her was dead.

Billy, Van Luys and Martens returned. Van Luys was trembling as he unlocked the chains. Billy and Jumper helped Morning Dew to her feet. Though weak, she snatched Billy's knife from his sash. In one motion she sliced through Van Luys' trousers. Jumper clamped his hands over Van Luys' mouth, muffling his scream as Morning Dew slashed off his testicles and penis. Billy picked the bloodied genitals off the floor and stuffed them into Van Luys' mouth. Then Jumper plunged his knife into the overseer's heart.

Across the grounds, Wild Cat had located and freed the other five women, locked together in one slave shack. He instructed them to be silent and keep low.

Another slave, a young man of nineteen known as Whitey, had crept out of his shack and was watching the escape. Big for his age, already standing six feet tall, he was light-skinned like his white father, the late overseer Simon McFarland, but with the striking features of his mother, Jamima Joseph.

His light, almost white skin had been the bane of his childhood. He was shunned by the other slaves. Because he was almost white, it was assumed he had more brains than the others. He was given more responsibilities, often being put in charge of the other slaves in the field, causing even more resentment.

"Take me with you," implored Whitey, as Wild Cat passed. The Seminole heard him before he saw him. He and the women froze in their tracks. Then, when Whitey rose out of the darkness, Wild Cat reached for his knife. He thought for an instant that he was a white man. Then he saw that the boy was wearing the tattered rags of a slave and sheathed his knife. "Come along," he told him.

The group squatted in the shadows waiting for the militia patrol to pass. As soon as it passed into the distance, Wild Cat and his group hurried across the grounds into the cotton fields. Waiting there for them were Billy Powell, Jumper, Hadjo, Morning Dew and Martens.

With the group united, Billy and Jumper lifted the makeshift stretcher carrying Morning Dew. Hadjo walked in front of them.

"Hadjo," said Billy.

Though he heard Billy call, Hadjo did not turn around.

"Hadjo," called out Billy again.

Hadjo turned slowly toward Billy, purposely keeping his head high, so as not to see Morning Dew. Billy saw that Hadjo was so horrified by Morning Dew's defilement that he could not even look at her.

"Thanks for your help," said Billy.

Hadjo acknowledged Billy's salutation by nodding. Then he turned back around, careful not to look down.

Billy was none too happy about the rape, but felt no less love for Morning Dew. If anything, because of the abuse that she had endured at the hands of the white men, he felt even more akin to her.

When they were two hundred yards away they could hear the alarm being sounded. Rifle shots and shouts could be heard as the raiders hurried south.

Delores was startled when Alabama Jim entered her chickee. He saw her uneasiness and did his best to reassure her. "I came to make sure you're all right—by yourself, I mean."

"I have my baby," said Delores. Baby Powell was sound asleep next to her. There was an awkward silence. "I heard you say you escaped from Auld Lang Syne," said Delores, speaking first.

"That's right, just like you," said Alabama Jim eagerly as he moved closer to her.

Delores froze.

Jim touched Delores' arm. "You need a real man to protect you, to make you feel like a woman."

She didn't know what to do. Here was one of the important men of this community making sexual advances. "Maybe this was the custom," thought Delores. "No," she reasoned. "A man like Abraham would not covet another man's wife."

As he kissed her gently on the neck, she spoke to him, trying to pretend that this wasn't happening. "Years ago my mother knew a man by the name of Alabossa. Did you know my mother? Her name was Tawna. She looked like me," said Delores.

Jim had no interest in conversation. He drew her to him and kissed her on the lips. He became excited. Delores pushed Jim, but was unable to break free of his grasp. "Didn't you like that?" asked Jim, as if that was the issue.

"Please, don't," pleaded Delores as Jim held her close.

Jim slipped his hand under her shirt and fondled her milk-swollen breast. Then he took her hand and placed it on his engorged organ. Delores pulled her hand away. Jim pushed her down, pinning her on the bed. Then he forced himself between her legs and began to take his pleasure. She closed her eyes, to avoid looking at him, but that only accentuated his hot breath and grunts in the quiet chickee. Jim pushed faster and harder. The baby awoke and began to cry as Jim finished.

He got up off of Delores. Looking down at her, he asked, "Why did you ask me about Alabossa," as if nothing had happened. Delores was sobbing as she answered, "He's my father."

Jim froze. His thoughts went back to Auld Lang Syne. "Your father? How do you know that?" he asked.

"He's the only one my mother laid with. I was born eight months after he fled," cried Delores.

Jim hastily put on his pants. "I don't believe you," said Jim.

"It's true. My mother told me. You're my father," wailed Delores.

"That bitch laid with plenty of men before me, and who knows how many after. Any one of them could be your father. So don't give me that shit."

"Take a good look," said Delores, negating Jim's statement. "This your grandson." She began crying uncontrollably. "My own father," she mumbled between sobs. "I prayed to God to find you, and you raped me!"

"You're crazy, girl," was the last thing Jim said as he left the chickee.

10

The villagers turned out of their chickees and cheered on seeing Martens. He walked into Freedom Land with his head held high. Martens looked around for Delores. He wanted to share this moment with her, but she wasn't present. He thought she must be busy with the baby.

He was accompanied by Whitey, whose reluctance to enter this strange place showed in his facial expression. "You home now, brother," said Martens, encouraging the boy. Whitey was overwhelmed by the joy on the faces of the people. He'd never seen black people this happy.

Abraham shook Martens' hand and publicly thanked him for his service.

Noticing the tall teenager standing a few paces behind Martens, Abraham asked, "Who is this?" There was something familiar about him.

"He called Whitey, sir," said Martens.

"Welcome to Freedom Land, Whitey."

The boy was speechless at these kind words. Obviously nobody here cared that he was light-skinned.

Standing, watching the events from a distance, Jamima was as happy as the rest of the community to see Martens return safely. Then she saw the boy. She noticed right away who he looked like. She began to walk toward him. As she got closer, her excitement grew. "Garcia! Garcia!" she called out.

When Abraham heard Jamima calling him that name, he recognized the boy's striking resemblance to Jamima.

"Garcia," said Jamima tenderly. Tears began streaming down her face as she stopped in front of her long-lost son. The boy didn't know her, nor did he recognize the name. Looking the boy up and down, she realized this. "You don't know me, son? I am your mother."

Whitey didn't know what to think. This woman, with tears in her eyes, was saying she was his mother? It was all too much. He'd never known his mother. He backed away several steps.

"Boy, stand fast!" ordered Abraham, grasping the situation immediately. "You are home now, and this is your mother. You will stay with her. She will teach you what you need to know to survive and contribute to our community."

Whitey stood stock-still as Jamima, with tears rolling down her cheeks, put her arms around him. Whitey remained rigid, feeling very uncomfortable. Everyone else around them, though, saw that they were truly mother and son.

Jamima led Whitey to her chickee. Along the way she pointed out the well, the training area and her neighbors. "And this is your home."

As plain as Jamima's chickee was, it was the nicest place Whitey had ever slept. She took great satisfaction in making up a bed of straw and throwing a blanket over it. She gave him her favorite pillow, made of duck, goose and chicken feathers.

"Whitey," said Jamima as she tucked in the teenager.

"Yes, ma'am," answered the boy.

"Call me Momma," instructed Jamima gently.

"Momma?" questioned Whitey.

"I am your mother," said Jamima. "Look at yourself, then look at me. Can't you see you come from me?"

"Why did you leave me?" asked Whitey.

"I had to," answered Jamima. "Slaves don't get to choose their chance to escape."

"And my father?" asked Whitey, not wanting to hear what he already suspected.

"He was the overseer," answered Jamima, ashamed. "I had no choice. I hated him but seeing you now—I was always glad I had you."

Whitey looked away. He wasn't so glad. His mother had left him behind to be tortured during his youth.

"Whitey," called Jamima, trying to get him to look up. "I'm talking to you," said Jamima, with a hint of anger.

"I hate that name," said Whitey.

"I named you Garcia after my husband, the bravest man I ever knew," explained Jamima. "From now on you shall be called by your proper name, Garcia."

That night Jamima went to bed with a smile on her face. Her son was with her at last. There was so much she could share with him. When she closed her eyes she thought of her late husband. "I named him for you," she said in the silence, "and now he is home safe with me."

It was late afternoon when the freed women walked into the Seminole village. The entire population turned out. The women rushed into the waiting arms of loved ones and family. Micanopy stood outside his chickee watching. Yet he did not see Morning Dew. Hadjo, the next to enter, rode his horse slowly. He stopped in front of Micanopy's chickee and dismounted. He avoided eye contact as he said, "I want you to return my livestock. I can no longer marry your daughter." With that, Hadjo, head down, walked off.

Micanopy had an awful feeling of foreboding. Was his daughter dead?

The rest of the raiding party arrived. Billy and Jumper were carrying Morning Dew on a stretcher. As they stopped before his chickee, Micanopy bent over his daughter, thrilled to see her still alive.

"What happened?" he asked.

"She was beaten and raped by your 'friends,'" said Billy, pinning him with his gaze.

"My little girl," muttered Micanopy, his anguish conspicuous.

The ebullience of the villagers caused by the return of the women turned to ash with the sight of Morning Dew. She was taken directly to John the Baptist, the tribal healer. John had gotten his name thirty years earlier when the village was visited by Christian missionaries. They observed John standing over a patient with his arms outstretched, asking the Great Spirit to intervene. When the patient made what the missionaries believed to be a miraculous recovery, they dubbed him John the Baptist. The Seminole were impressed he had been named after the white man's healer of souls. Thus the name stuck.

Examining Morning Dew, he was concerned with her badly bruised face, her broken nose, the fever she was running and the blood seeping from her vagina and rectum. Yet none of these were as serious as the blank expression on her face. She had received a terrible shock from which she might never recover.

Micanopy entered the healer's chickee and stood over his daughter. He was very uncomfortable and refused to look directly at her. He got down on one knee and spoke gently into her ear. "The wedding has been canceled. You are free to do as you please." He saw her deathlike state and swallowed deeply. "Please forgive me for failing you as a father."

Micanopy rose and left without speaking to Billy. At no time had the two men acknowledged one another.

Billy sat down next to Morning Dew. He took her hand and gently caressed it, kissing her fingers. He looked at John the Baptist, but the healer shook his head, indicating there was little hope. "My medicine does not work because she does not want to live."

Billy took Morning Dew's other hand. He held them both and looked into her glazed eyes. "Please don't leave me. I need you. I love you."

Seeing Billy's love, John the Baptist assured him, "All that is lacking in her is a desire to go on."

At last Morning Dew raised her head and smiled at Billy. Then she fell into a deep sleep.

Billy Powell knew that Morning Dew was his, if she lived. He left her chickee and went out into the village. He went to the platform and shouted, "My brothers! My brothers!"

His friends Jumper, Alligator and Wild Cat gravitated to him, and they took up the chant. Soon most of the villagers had assembled. Micanopy, unable to ignore the challenge, stood among his people and listened to what the young warriors had to say.

When Billy had everyone's attention, he said, "His own daughter has been ravaged by the white man." Billy pointed at Micanopy. Never before had Billy spoken with such passion. "If we do nothing, we are no better than cattle!"

Abraham arrived during this scene. He watched in fascinated silence. It was obvious to him his protégé had stepped forward.

Micanopy raised his arms. "Enough!" he shouted. "There have been abuses on both sides. Once we move to Arkansas—"

"Move?" interrupted Billy. "You speak of accommodation to the white men? Killing is what the white man understands."

These ringing words were met with shouts of encouragement among the crowd. Micanopy stepped forward.

"You would know, Powell," he said. "You speak their language. Their blood runs through your veins."

"You call me a friend of the white man?" asked Billy as he put his hand on his knife. "You're the friend of the white man," he accused. "Let the people decide who's the white man's friend."

The people instantly started moving away from Micanopy toward Billy. In less than a minute Micanopy was left with fewer than ten followers.

"You do not have a cool head, Powell. You want to lead my people to death," said Micanopy.

"My friends," interjected Abraham. It was the moment he was waiting for.

"Stay out of this," protested Micanopy. He was certain he could win back his people from Billy, but not with Abraham's eloquence behind him.

Alabama Jim and thirty members of his elite troops entered the village in five rows of six. They carried their new rifles in front of them as they marched.

"Company halt," barked Jim, and the soldiers stopped. "Formation right," he ordered, and the soldiers behind the first group formed a straight line with their rifles pointed in the air.

"This is not your land!" cried Micanopy, not intimidated by the soldiers' presence.

Alabama Jim stepped forward, and in an orchestrated show of force his troops cocked their rifles in unison. Abraham raised his arms and motioned for his troops to step back. Reluctantly, Alabama Jim signaled the troops, and they lowered their rifles. Abraham turned to the Seminole community.

"How can we stand by?" he asked. "We marry your daughters. Your enemy is our enemy. We love the land as well as any Seminole."

Everyone in the crowd, black and red, shouted their agreement.

"To try and fight the white man is useless," retorted Micanopy, trying to reassert his authority. "Our women have been returned. Powell had his revenge. It will be all I can do to prevent the white army from marching in here—"

"Let them march here. They won't return home," said Billy contemptuously.

There were shouts of agreement from the crowd. Abraham raised his voice again. "Cannons don't make the white man superior. His military planning does," he said.

He saw he had everyone's attention.

"First he turns his enemies against each other. He gets Indians to make war on Indians. He made your Creek brothers into your bitter enemies. Now he is doing it here. Can't you feel his presence? They have a saying for this strategy—divide and conquer."

Everyone was silent.

"How do they do this?" asked Billy, encouraging him to go on.

"They find someone they can bribe." Abraham turned to gaze directly at Micanopy. The chief shifted uncomfortably. The entire population was staring at him.

"What Seminole would take a bribe from a white man?" he asked indignantly.

"The Seminole who has the most to gain?" said Abraham, simply.

Micanopy's name was whispered throughout the crowd. Desperately he looked at Abraham and challenged him. "Who accuses me of taking a bribe?"

"Better, Chief Micanopy, not to place yourself in the way of temptation," advised Abraham. "I say it would be in the interest of the Seminole people if another warrior took your place."

Shouts of agreement echoed across the village. Micanopy looked around. He realized his predicament. "I am Chief and I will stay Chief," he announced.

"You may be a Chief in Arkansas, maybe," said Abraham. "Here we need a man more suited to fight the white man. And who more than a man who has white blood in his veins?" Abraham paused. When he had his audience's entire attention, he spoke the name. "Who better than Billy Powell!"

Billy was startled. This was a complete surprise. Never had he even imagined himself Chief. Everyone started cheering and shouting his name. Abraham raised his arms in the air, calling for silence.

"From now on, know this man as your War Chief," proclaimed Abraham. He took Billy's arm and thrust it aloft. "Know him as a Seminole." There were more cheers from the assemblage. "Know him as Osceola!"

Electrified by the cheering crowd, Billy grinned. Yet he asked Abraham, "Know me as who?"

"Osceola," repeated Abraham.

"If I'm going to be an Indian Chief," asked Billy, "why can't I have an Indian name like Running Bear or Cunning Fox?"

Abraham shook his head. "Trust me," he said as he smiled at Billy.

"Why me?" asked Billy.

"Fate sometimes elevates an ordinary man to accomplish extraordinary deeds in a just cause. Are you that man?"

"Yes," said Billy, with a touch of humor, "but I never thought of myself as ordinary."

Then Billy raised his arms, calling for silence. "My fellow Seminole, my first act as War Chief will be to marry Morning Dew."

The entire population became silent—he wanted to marry a woman who had just been gang raped?

Wild Cat and Jumper carried Morning Dew through the crowd on a stretcher. She was set down next to the new War Chief. Billy leaned over and kissed her. Abraham shook his hand and publicly wished him "Many years and many sons." Everyone cheered. Then Billy turned to Micanopy. "Chief Micanopy, I want you to marry us."

Chief Micanopy was astonished. Maybe, he thought, he had been wrong about Powell. He'd have to reconsider this. For now, he stepped forward and said, "I would be glad to perform the marriage ceremony."

Alabama Jim led his thirty troops as they jogged out of the Seminole village toward Freedom Land. "Company halt," said Jim, halfway home. The troop stopped. "At ease," said Jim, and the soldiers sat down and took a breather. Jim took the opportunity to address his soldiers. "Men, you all saw what a show of force can do," said Jim. "If we hadn't been there, Powell would not be Chief. Remember that."

Ten minutes later, the troops were on their feet jogging toward Freedom Land.

Delores had cried all the night before. The next day she was still weeping. The emotional pain and humiliation had lessened. Now she was filled with apprehension over the future. "If I tell Martens," she reasoned, "he'll confront Alabama Jim and will surely be killed." Then she realized that was what Alabama Jim wanted. He wanted to kill Martens so he could have her.

Martens was exhilarated when he entered the chickee. Delores hugged him. "I'm so proud of you," she told him.

"I paid back that bastard Van Luys. Watching him die felt good, especially the way he died." He related what had happened. "But poor Morning Dew. All of them, they raped and beat her."

Shuddering, he hugged Delores. "Thank God for Powell. Thank God you didn't have to go through that." That's when Delores broke down crying uncontrollably. Martens did his best to comfort her. "It's all right. I'm home, I'll protect you."

Delores wanted to tell Martens what had happened. She needed to talk to him, but how could she? If he challenged Alabama Jim, he would be killed.

When they got into bed, Martens started kissing her. She felt so dirty. She didn't make a sound, but within, her spirit screamed, "No!" She froze.

"You okay?" asked Martens.

"I'm just . . . It's Morning Dew," said Delores. "I feel terrible. It scares me to think that could have been me."

"I'll protect you," promised Martens as he pulled Delores close to him. Delores kissed him.

"I love you, Martens." Then she rolled over and pretended to go to sleep.

In the Seminole village a huge bonfire commemorated the wedding ceremony. All of the people took turns dancing around it, as they were also celebrating the rescue and return of the captive women, the ascension of a new Chief, and a renewal of the Seminole culture.

Billy sat beside Morning Dew, holding her hand, watching. She motioned for Billy to join the festivities but he protested, not wanting to leave her side. She drew him closer, and insisted he join the dancing. Reluctantly, Billy rose up and joined the tribe members dancing counterclockwise around the fire. As he danced, the drum beat faster and Billy lost himself in the fervor of celebration. He was now one of the tribe.

Just before dawn, Billy gently lifted Morning Dew from the stretcher and into his protective arms. He carried her to his chickee and laid her in his bed. He knelt beside her and took her hand. "You are the daughter of a Chief, and now you're the wife of a Chief," said Billy.

Morning Dew just lay there with her eyes open, looking at Billy. Finally a faint smile crossed her face. He smiled back. She reached out for him and they hugged.

"Did I ever tell you how I came to speak so eloquently?" he asked. Morning Dew shook her head. "My father was a British officer assisting the Creeks when he met my mother and married her. He stayed seven months before he left. He returned eight more times.

I practiced speaking like him. He once told me I spoke like a gentleman."

"What did you do when he didn't return the last time?" asked Morning Dew faintly.

"I announced to my mother that I was going to England. She explained that my father also had a proper English wife and another family and that I would not be welcome there."

Morning Dew reached out and drew Billy to her. She understood his pain and knew the rejection he must have felt. She hugged him with all her strength.

"But everything is perfect now, because I love you and you're my bride," said Billy tenderly.

Even though the wedding ceremony brought the deposition of her father as Chief, she was glad. She knew there was a reason for Billy being there. He was sent to save her people, both red and black.

PART THREE

PREPARE YOURSELVES, GENTLEMEN

1

The three riders were silhouetted by the full moon as they crossed a small stream and then headed up the embankment. Abraham cursed under his breath. After the raid on Clinch's plantation, the cavalry patrols had been increased. Furthermore, the full moon was not the time to penetrate north, but in this case he felt he had no choice. All in all, it was not a trip that Abraham relished.

Behind him on the other two horses were Henry's two sons, sixteen-year-old Elijah and fourteen-year-old Joseph. Both boys had their hands tied behind their backs and were forced to squeeze hard with their knees just to stay in the saddle.

The boys had fled Amelia's plantation, breaking the terms of the agreement between her and Abraham that there would be no runaways. As distasteful as it was for Abraham, he knew he had to take them back. The eventual freedom of all the other slaves there depended on it. Besides, he had given his word.

"Abraham the hero! You just a white man in a black man's body. You and my father both are cowards!" said Elijah, venting his anger.

Abraham reined in his horse and turned to the boys. "Call me what you like," he said, "but don't ever think that your father is anything but brave. He could have run off."

"Why didn't he?" asked Elijah.

"Because he cared too much for your mother and you."

"So why do we have to wait?" asked Joseph, changing the subject.

"Because that's the deal," said Abraham "You'll be set free if you're willing to wait."

Abraham made his way through the fields adjacent to the road. The full moon did have one advantage, he thought as he spotted a patrol while it was still half a mile away. He led the horses into a copse of trees and turned to the boys, hissing to them to "Shut up."

Henry had been a house nigger all his life. He was born on General Hampton's plantation in 1780. Pressed into service as a child, he showed intelligence and a propensity for learning. The general insisted that his "help" speak proper English, and Henry was particularly good with words. Thus he became the general's personal servant.

When the general met Amelia, Henry met her maid, Ruth. The general's courtship of Amelia paralleled Henry's courtship of Ruth. The general encouraged Henry's advances and even took a fatherly pride when Henry confided in him that he wished to marry Ruth. After his own wedding ceremony, the general attended Henry and Ruth's. They were married the same day.

Amelia was twenty-five years younger than the general. She was nineteen when they married. The general had hoped to father a son and heir, or at least a daughter, to share his vast knowledge of history, warfare, literature and philosophy. Despite a very active sex life, the general and Amelia were unable to conceive a child. Henry and Ruth's union produced two fine sons, Elijah and Joseph.

When the patrol had passed, Abraham steered the horses to Amelia's slave quarters. He helped the two boys dismount, as they still had their hands tied behind their backs. Henry was sitting in his favorite chair smoking his pipe when Abraham entered, followed by the boys. Henry got up and walked slowly around them. Without saying a word he began to untie Joseph's hands. Elijah picked up his head and looked at his father.

"He didn't have to tie us," he complained.

Henry slapped Elijah hard across the face. He turned back to Joseph and asked him if he had anything to say.

"Two years is nothing to you," said Joseph. "You been here all your life. It's different for us. Out there, there's black men doing something."

Henry slapped Joseph's face but not quite as hard. He had both boys' attention now. "What about the others here? Your mother, the children, all your kin? Abraham has bargained for our freedom. A man that only cares about himself is not a man, but some kind of animal," explained Henry.

With his business done, Abraham entered the main residence through the kitchen door. Ruth greeted him with a hug. He sat down at the table and she poured a cup of tea for him. Then he told her the news she'd been waiting for. "I brought your boys back."

Ruth closed her eyes and thanked the Lord. Her prayers had been answered. As much as she wanted freedom for her sons, the prospect of freedom for the entire slave population of Hampton Court was more important.

The kitchen door opened. Amelia stood there, watching the two talk. When Ruth noticed her, she immediately rose to her feet. Amelia turned her gaze to Abraham, who sat drinking his tea. Then he slowly rose and bowed. "My lady."

Amelia gestured with her eyes, and Abraham followed her to the drawing room.

As soon as they entered, Amelia turned on him. "We made a

deal, and they reneged on it. I'm sending for the overseer."

"I brought back Henry's boys and your horses. We're keeping our part."

"That's the second time since we began planting—"

"Young men are impatient," said Abraham, interrupting her.

"If I don't get sufficient crops in the ground—" said Amelia.

"The trouble is, they're not sure they can trust you," said Abraham, again cutting her off.

"They have no right to feel that way. I could understand it if they were badly treated," said Amelia, not hiding her offense at the suggestion that she couldn't be trusted.

"They are still slaves," Abraham protested.

"I didn't invent the system, and I don't need lectures on slavery. Not from you, of all people."

"The difference, the one and only difference, between me and the slaves in the field is the opportunity and education I was given, not the ability to use it," said Abraham.

Amelia knew she was getting nowhere. She put on her warmest smile. "Now you're being silly."

Abraham also knew he wasn't getting anywhere. He looked out over the cotton fields, illuminated by the full moon. "Are you going to honor our agreement?" asked Abraham.

"I'm shocked you would ask me that."

Abraham turned back and looked at Amelia. "Suppose in the war . . ."

"Something happens to you?" Amelia finished his sentence. She looked into his eyes. "I've kept my part of the bargain. If they want to be treated like human beings, they should keep theirs."

"We are human beings," reminded Abraham.

Amelia froze when she heard riders approaching outside. Abraham motioned with his hands for her to remain calm. Thirty troopers from Company C, led by General Clinch himself, rode up to the house, as fast as their mounts would take them. Amelia went out the front door and onto the porch.

Clinch had used the raid on his plantation to his full advantage. He went on a letter-writing campaign, pointing out, as he had predicted, niggers and Indians were attacking innocent planters in Georgia. He demanded action from Congress.

General Clinch sat atop his mount, at the head of his troops. "Amelia, thank God you're safe. May we dismount?" he asked.

Amelia gave him a bewildered look and then answered him. "Of course. Welcome to Hampton Court."

Clinch saw that Amelia didn't know what had happened. "A patrol spotted a group of niggers riding this way."

"Such talk gives me the vapors," said Amelia, playing along.

"Are you aware my plantation was raided?" said Clinch.

"My Lord, yes. Ten dead is what we heard," said Amelia.

"Completely unprovoked," said Clinch. Then he realized who was seated at his elbow. "How rude of me. You remember Congressman Reilly."

Reilly raised his hand and acknowledged Amelia. He appeared to her to be either sick or drunk, or both.

"Of course I remember our distinguished congressman. Gentlemen, may I offer you some refreshment?"

Amelia turned to Ruth, who had followed her out onto the porch. She motioned and Ruth retreated into the house. Clinch and Reilly dismounted and climbed onto the porch and took seats. Amelia sat beside the congressman. "Riding along with the cavalry at night, Congressman, I am impressed," said Amelia.

Reilly tried his best to answer but couldn't get out the words. The ride had made him pale.

"You'll feel better after you have a drink, Congressman," suggested Amelia.

Just then Reilly found his voice. "I am on a fact-finding tour," he began in a very deliberate tone. "I want to talk about your husband, or more accurately, one of his slaves, Abraham."

"Humor him," Clinch put in. "He thinks you can talk to niggers."

That got Amelia's attention. "Oh," she said, taking a deep breath.

"You did own a nigger by that name, didn't you?" asked Clinch, pressing the point.

Abraham, attired as a butler, came out of the house carrying a tray of cold drinks. He set them carefully on the table and withdrew a short distance, where he stood impassive and immobile.

"He belonged to my husband long before we were married. Oliver found him to be able and intelligent. He taught him to read and write and Abraham went on to study the classics."

"Classics?" repeated Reilly, not sure he had heard Amelia correctly.

"Yes. He also studied biology, botany and military history, particularly the Trojan War. Oliver eventually gave him his freedom," said Amelia nonchalantly.

"Why did he free him?" asked General Clinch suspiciously.

"I should go back to the beginning. Oliver had doubts about the basis of slavery, that the black race was actually inferior. So, he decided to try educating one of his young slaves to see what would happen. Abraham was selected. He accompanied my husband everywhere as part of his education. During a boar hunt Abraham had occasion to save my husband's life," explained Amelia.

Clinch looked at Amelia disdainfully. All of this sounded like a fairy tale.

Amelia saw his reaction and immediately explained, "I'm sure you would have done the same if he had saved your life, General."

"When was that?" asked Reilly, intrigued.

"That was twenty-five years ago. Abraham went to Haiti and fought in the revolution there, but the experience sickened him. You see, until that time he was of the opinion that only the white race tortured and slaughtered defenseless women and children. He learned that given power, blacks could be just as bad. His wife and child were killed, hacked to death by black men."

Amelia glanced at Abraham, hoping she hadn't brought up painful memories. He just stood there with a bland face.

"Is that when he joined the Seminoles?" asked Reilly, continuing his questions.

Amelia nodded.

"I understand that he advises them, that he went to Washington at the head of a delegation."

"It was his way of saying thank you to the Seminole," said Amelia.

Reilly gulped down the last of his drink, and Abraham quickly replaced the empty glass with another. Amelia was thoroughly enjoying the charade, and a smile crept over her face. "He's widely read, very capable and determined. If he has one real fault," said Amelia, "it is that he has been known occasionally to overstay his welcome."

Clinch and Reilly didn't know what to make of that statement. Reilly took another sip before continuing. "Would it be possible to approach Abraham," asked Reilly, between sips, "and let him know we want to parlay?"

"What would you talk about? The Seminole have been ordered to move and return the Maroons," said Amelia.

"Maroons?" repeated Reilly, not having heard that term used before.

"That is what the Negroes call themselves," explained Amelia.

"Why, the man could help us facilitate the move and avoid bloodshed," said Reilly.

"Since he is a freed slave, he could remain with the Seminoles when they move," Clinch added.

Abraham thought, "How magnanimous of this pompous blowhard."

"And sell out the others?" said Amelia, saying what she believed would have been Abraham's words. Abraham watched Amelia with keen interest as she continued this negotiation on his behalf. "Perhaps if you allowed the Maroons to migrate along with the Seminoles," recommended Amelia.

The congressman told her, "I would be glad to talk to him about these matters. How can we get word to him?"

Amelia barely contained her smile. "Word travels fast in these parts, Congressman."

Clinch was certain he was being toyed with, and in fact regarded the entire conversation as a waste of time. Erupting with frustration, his voice boomed over Amelia's and changed the mood instantly. "Enough of this talk. I've ordered two companies of artillery north from Fort Brooke, another company from St. Augustine west, and I'm sending the cavalry from Fort King south." Clinch motioned as if he was squeezing a walnut in his hand. "So much for the Seminoles and their niggers!"

The general had shouted everyone into silence, and seeing this, he stood to take his leave. Reilly, with the help of the rail, negotiated the steps down to his horse. One of the soldiers helped him mount. The general waited for Amelia to join him. Together they walked arm in arm down the steps.

"Amelia, when this is over, I'll own the largest cotton plantation in North America." He tugged her tighter to him. "Share it with me."

"I am flattered, General, but unfortunately not marriage minded at this time. In fact, I'm not certain I'm going to stay in South Georgia." That got the general's attention. "With your newly acquired lands you'll be planting north and south of me. You're not going to want my plantation dividing your vast holdings. I may consider letting you buy me out."

Clinch perked up with Amelia's announcement. He wanted Amelia, but he also wanted her plantation, Hampton Court. If he couldn't possess her, acquiring her plantation would do for now.

Amelia looked at the troops and nodded to them. Then she

turned her back on Clinch and Reilly, and ascended the stairs to her porch as the troops departed.

She entered her house and immediately searched out Abraham. She found him in the general's library, which had always been Abraham's favorite room. He was standing there perusing the books on military strategy.

"I hope you didn't learn anything. I'm not a traitor," said Amelia.

"I learned he is arrogant, opinionated, long-winded, ill-prepared and unfeeling," said Abraham.

This assessment brought a smile to her face. "And as a military leader, what is your judgment?"

Abraham smiled but didn't answer.

Amelia probed him further. "And the reinforcements from Fort Brooke?"

Abraham rolled his eyes. "There is only one road. If a mongrel dog puts his paw on it, the Seminole will know."

Fifty rifles fired within five seconds. Several bullets hit their mark, but most didn't. Martens, Delores and the other recent arrivals reloaded.

In the Maroon village preparation for war accelerated. Every member had to demonstrate proficiency with a rifle. There was to be no surrender. It was understood the entire community would fight to the death. Men, women and children had to be able to shoot and reload.

Hesitant, young Garcia hadn't fired his round. He was terrified of the noise and the recoil. Jamima came over and took him aside. She raised his musket to her shoulder. As she fired, hitting the mark dead center, Garcia put his fingers in his ears and closed his eyes. Jamima's instincts were to scold the boy, but she controlled herself. Speaking gently, she told him, "Only slavery was to be feared. If you shoot the rifle, no man can make you a slave."

Then she reloaded the rifle for her son, put her arms around his shoulders and helped him aim. "Here comes the white man. Kill him!" she shouted. Garcia fired. The ball struck the arm of the target, a silhouette of a man tacked to a large oak tree. Jamima smiled, and her son smiled back.

Martens and many of the others fired their second rounds. Delores fumbled, dropping the plunger. Alabama Jim picked up the plunger and reloaded her rifle. He smiled at her, the private smile of a man who knew her secret.

Jim believed that women would say or do anything to get what they wanted, and Delores was obviously protecting her cowardly husband with her story about being his own daughter. Then a thought crossed Jim's mind, "Maybe she is my daughter." If she was, which he seriously doubted, he certainly didn't want her married to Martens. Either way, he reasoned, she needed a real man.

Charlie Ematha was certain it was the end of everything he knew. His ally, Micanopy, had been deposed and replaced by a white renegade. War with the United States was inevitable, which meant that his people would be annihilated. In Arkansas, they would at least be able to live their lives without the constant threat of attack. Thus Ematha was moving his people west before the shooting war commenced.

Three hundred and forty-six men, women and children were carrying what they could of their belongings. They'd accepted pennies on the dollar for their land, their cattle and their crops. In return they had received, in the badlands of Arkansas, their own domain in perpetuity.

Charlie Ematha turned and looked for the last time at the empty village they had lived in all their lives. Following his example, the entire tribe looked back. That's why they did not see Billy, Alligator, Jumper and Wild Cat arriving on horseback. The four warriors stopped, deliberately blocking their path. They dismounted, holding their horses' reins with one hand, and their rifles with the other.

"Don't go west. Come join us instead," said Billy, opening his arms and appealing to the Chief.

Ematha motioned for his people to move forward, but his son Hadjo stood still. The others saw this, and no one moved. As much as they respected their Chief, they were of another mind. They yearned to stay in their village, and on their own land.

Ematha saw that his people were wavering because of Billy's offer. This brought his rage to the boiling point. Again he started walking, and he gestured to his people to follow. The populace didn't move.

"Chief Ematha, don't obey the white man," Billy urged, doing his utmost to show respect to the Chief.

Ematha didn't hide his loathing for the upstart who called himself Chief. "I have lived to see us degraded and ruined. Every season there is less land, less to eat, more trouble, more death. We will go to Arkansas," said Ematha.

"Ematha, I am the Chief, and I say you will not go," ordered Billy.

"You were made Chief because soon there will be no nation to be Chief of," said Ematha, not disguising his contempt.

Hadjo stepped forward. "Powell is right. I say we stay and kill the white man." Never before had he defied his father in public.

Ematha was momentarily stunned by his son's words. Then he composed himself. "You don't know what you're saying. The white army will march in here and enslave us all. In Arkansas—"

"No!" shouted Hadjo, interrupting his father. "I've lost everything. My bride, my dignity and my own father is a lapdog for the white man. I'm ashamed."

Ematha had heard enough. He picked up a rifle and aimed it at Billy. "You did this!" he shouted as he pulled the trigger.

Billy, standing only ten yards away, was taken by surprise. The bullet whizzed past him, tearing a hole in his loose-fitting shirt, inches from his heart, but otherwise missing him. It struck a rotting tree behind him.

Billy hadn't thought Ematha would just shoot him down, but when Ematha began to reload, Billy picked up his own rifle and pointed it. "Put the rifle down, Chief. We can resolve this peacefully."

Ignoring Billy, Ematha finished loading and aimed. Before he could pull the trigger, though, Billy fired first. The old man cried out, and toppled to the ground. The crowd was stunned into silence.

Ematha lay on the ground bleeding from a fatal wound. He looked up blankly, not sure how he had gotten there. All he heard was a ringing in his ears. All he saw was the blazing Florida sun. Then there was shade as Billy and Hadjo bent over him, blocking the sun's light. It was then he realized he'd been shot. In a barely audible whisper, he spoke to them both. "Dying here is the only reason for staying here."

Billy was heavy with remorse. He should have handled this better, but there'd been no time. There were cries and wails from many of Ematha's people.

Billy rose to his feet, not knowing if he'd have to fight Hadjo as well. He put his arm on Hadjo's shoulder in a gesture of sorrow, but Hadjo stormed off.

Billy turned to the crowd. In a sorrowful voice he cried out, "Whoever wants to go, go. I will never raise my rifle against Seminole again."

Billy stooped down and picked up Ematha's body. Holding the bloodied Chief, Billy addressed the population. "We will bury the Chief with all the honors due him. Then we will drive out the white devils who caused this tragedy. Who will join me?"

"Ho to Osceola! Ho to our new Chief!" shouted Wild Cat.

His enthusiasm was contagious. More than fifty of the young men from Ematha's village joined in. Soon the whole village was cheering for Osceola.

Yet five families elected to leave. "Let them pass," instructed Billy. Wild Cat, Jumper and Alligator moved off the road, allowing them to walk by, toward Fort King and a new life in Arkansas.

Billy was pleased. Despite the unfortunate incident, he'd been able to meld the vast majority of Ematha's tribe to the cause.

The five families that had left Ematha's tribe walked through the gates of Fort King. Word of the émigrés' arrival brought Wiley Thompson out of his office. Thompson thought smugly, "It just goes to show what I insisted all along, that a firm hand and the backbone to use it is all that is necessary in dealing with these savages." He walked across the parade ground to greet what he assumed were only the first arrivals. Yet behind them the fort's gates were shut. Thompson realized something was wrong, and his smugness evaporated. He called to an old man leading the group. "You, where is the Chief?"

The old Indian walked up to Thompson. "Chief Ematha is dead. He was killed by the new Chief, Osceola."

"Dead? Killed by Osceola?" repeated Thompson, surprised. He knew the legend of Osceola, the mythical founder of the Seminole. The great warrior and peacemaker. He laughed to himself at the desperation of these savages.

"Which Osceola is this?" asked Thompson, not hiding the cynicism in his voice. "Osceola the great god of the swamps? Osceola, lord of the spirits? Osceola, the slayer of reptiles? Well, that's a spirit to be scared of!"

Thompson laughed out loud, delighted with his own joke. Then he turned serious. "When are you people going to wake up and realize that your ancestors are not going to rise from the dead? Even if they did, the army wouldn't allow it." Thompson chuckled to himself, "Osceola, I thought I'd heard it all."

"Billy Powell is young Osceola," interrupted the old man.

His words hit like a cannonball. "Powell?" repeated Thompson, appalled. He began to shake with anger.

On the parade ground Sergeant Paisley was drilling the troops as

Lieutenant Graham looked on. Thompson stormed over to Graham and demanded his immediate attention. Gesticulating wildly, he screamed, "Powell is the Chief of the Seminole."

"He is?" said Graham, unmoved.

"That man is a criminal. He threw his knife at me. He has killed Charlie Ematha! I'm sure it was him that raided Clinch's plantation."

"It probably was," answered Graham. He had hated the sordid deal that made the six Seminole maidens into slaves. "That's probably why Donnelly is offering odds that you won't live past Christmas," he added, thoroughly enjoying the moment.

Thompson was frantic. "What are you going to do about it?"

Graham turned his back on him. He had taken several steps before Thompson caught up with him and tapped him on the shoulder. Graham turned back around. "I don't have the men to spare," replied Graham, shrugging his shoulders.

"General Clinch will see things differently when I tell him," threatened Thompson.

"You're going to ride out to the general's plantation? You're a brave man," said Graham, amused at this threat. Then he turned his back on Thompson so as not to laugh in his face.

Thompson stormed back to his office.

Standing outside on the steps, Donnelly took money from a soldier, then recorded his bet on the Thompson lottery in his black book.

That night, over Wild Cat's objections, Billy sought out Hadjo. He left his rifle and knife behind, believing that Hadjo wouldn't kill an unarmed Seminole. What a strange twist of fate, thought Billy, that he should first take away the man's fiancée, and then kill his father.

He found Hadjo sitting on a boulder alongside the river, looking at the moon's reflection on the water.

"I remember how I felt when my own father didn't return. And then, when a soldier shot my mother, I wanted to kill him," said Billy as he came up behind Hadjo.

Hadjo stood up and turned around. He put his hand on his knife. The two men stared at one another.

"Everyone will understand if you kill me," said Billy.

"I do not hold you responsible for my father's death," said Hadjo dully. "It was the white man. Being forced to accommodate them killed him, as surely as if they pulled the trigger."

"And Morning Dew?" asked Billy, seeing that Hadjo still had his hand on his knife. "Do you blame me for losing her?"

"Many white men will die before that score is settled," said Hadjo.

Billy gave an exaggerated sigh of relief. "Then you're not planning on killing me?" he said with a smile on his face. Hadjo removed his hand from his knife. "I promise you, Hadjo, there will be no more accommodations for the white man. From now on, only the arrow and tomahawk for them. Will you help us?" asked Billy.

"Kill white men?" asked Hadjo.

"There is more to it," said Billy.

"What do you want me to do?" asked Hadjo.

"Lead the men from your village as their warrior Chief," answered Billy.

"And take orders from you?" asked Hadjo, with a touch of trepidation in his voice.

"Together, we will win this war," said Billy enthusiastically.

"Osceola," said Hadjo, "I will lead my people and follow you." Then the two men shook hands.

2

The Maroons and Indians, women, children, men and boys, were taking in the harvest. Because the light was waning, torches illuminated what needed to be done. No one thought of rest. Any food they had must be protected. Their corn, wheat, sugar and beans would be stored deep in the Everglades, preserved and ready. With it, the Maroons and Indians could hold out indefinitely. The invading white army would be the one that would have to worry about eating. They would have extended supply lines that could easily be raided and cut off.

Those that were not harvesting were moving the Seminole and Maroon villages south into the Everglades, or were watching as sentries. Billy sat on his horse as his commands were carried out. Thanks to Abraham's foresight, the Seminole had already planted, deep in the Everglades, new fields of corn and wheat to be harvested next spring.

Morning Dew, recovering from her wounds, though still limping noticeably, joined Billy as he watched the nation packing and moving.

"I am staying with you," she announced.

"No. You must go where the white man cannot harm you."

"What can they do to me that they have not done?" asked Morning Dew bitterly.

She was right, and Billy knew it.

"I will never leave your side, never!" said Morning Dew. The two lovers hugged. It was what they both wanted: their fates sealed together, forever.

"Take me to the chickee," whispered Morning Dew in Billy's ear.

As they entered the hut, Morning Dew took off her top garment, revealing her firm breasts. Billy stroked her cheek with the back of his right hand. Then he gently placed both his hands on her shoulders. He moved his fingers down, caressing her breasts until he reached her nipples.

A shiver of excitement ran through her. Billy felt her nipples harden under his touch. They kissed. As they did, their mouths opened and they explored each other with their tongues.

Morning Dew reached down and felt Billy's sex through his buckskin pants. Then she slipped her hand inside his pants and felt his excitement. She dropped to her knees. As she did, she pulled down his pants revealing his engorged organ. She took hold of it with both her hands, and guided it into her mouth. She couldn't get enough of him as she tenderly sucked and licked him. He rocked back and forth in pleasure.

Then he raised her off her knees and kissed her passionately. Morning Dew removed her remaining garments and stood naked before Billy. He took her in his arms and gently laid her down upon the straw mattress. She spread her legs wide and Billy entered her.

Thus the lovers consummated their marriage. They repeated the act two more times and were lying in each other's arms when they heard Wild Cat announce himself. After entering, he bowed to Morning Dew, then addressed Billy with urgent news.

Two miles away Abraham sat in his chickee reading *The Iliad*, by Homer. Engrossed in a passage, he didn't look up or even acknowledge Billy when he entered. Billy blurted out, "The white army is approaching from two directions."

Abraham finished reading the passage, closed the book and looked up at Billy. "Did you know Drake really did finish his game of bowls on Plymouth Hoe before putting to sea and destroying the Spanish fleet?"

"I was brought up on the exploits of Bonnie Prince Charles," Billy said. "I have heard little of the English except their treachery."

"Then you'll know what to watch out for because the Americans are every bit as treacherous. Now, what news?"

"Wild Cat reports a cavalry unit with a cannon on the way from Fort Brooke, and a supply column is approaching from St. Augustine," said Billy.

A smile came over Abraham's face. "A supply column. How considerate of them," he thought out loud.

Alabama Jim entered Abraham's chickee and joined the two leaders. Billy nodded his hello, but Jim paid no attention to the gesture. By the look on his face, Abraham knew Jim was angry. Billy sensed he didn't belong in the middle of this confrontation and departed.

Abraham knew that anger could be a good thing in war. Alabama Jim's hatred would sustain him and his men. Yet his hatred could also tear their fragile alliance apart.

"Where are the boys?" demanded Jim, referring to the runaway slaves from Amelia's plantation.

"I took them home," said Abraham.

"You had no right!" Alabama Jim cried.

"We have to keep our word," replied Abraham calmly.

"You're no better than a white man."

Such insults didn't bother Abraham. "Fifty-five slaves are working on that plantation," he said. "In two years—"

"In two years they be free!" interrupted Alabama Jim, mimicking Abraham. "You believe that? In three hours we could slit her throat and have every one of those people back here."

"If you did that," explained Abraham, "the white army would not stop until it hung every one of us. We don't need to provoke them further. I made a deal and we will honor it."

"Yes, sir," said Jim calmly. His outward expression disguised the intense hatred he felt for Abraham. Everyone knew of the white woman who owned the plantation, whom Abraham protected. Now he'd even returned escaped slaves to her. Clearly, something needed to be done.

The supply column from St. Augustine moved slowly west. The two hundred enlisted men and officers, escorting ten wagons carrying ammunition and food stores for the coming campaign, were all very unhappy. Not only were they riding into hostile territory, they were moving at a snail's pace, which made them an easy target.

On the coast at St. Augustine the ocean breezes made the heat bearable, and kept the mosquitoes at bay. Yet now the road was winding through swampy lowlands. The soldiers, riding two abreast, felt as though they were descending into hell. Half of the men rode in front of the wagons; the others were close behind.

The road through the swamp became so narrow the legs of the soldiers riding side by side rubbed against one another. The soldiers looked about nervously, imagining all kinds of unspeakable terror awaiting them.

First Lieutenant Julian Rose, West Point '26, rode at the point, leading the column. Suddenly a crane took flight, in what appeared to be slow motion to the lieutenant. His hand moved to his rifle, but he thought better of it. Fresh fowl was always a welcome treat and it would be hard to miss this lumbering bird, but the shot might alarm those in the rear of the column.

It was late afternoon when the column reached a fifty-foot wooden bridge where the road was bisected by a swollen stream. As the first wagons crossed the bridge, the sounds of the crickets and bullfrogs almost obscured the noise of the wheels on the wooden slats.

In the swamp, Billy, Morning Dew and Abraham sat in a dugout canoe watching the progress of the supply column. Reeds and saw-grass were affixed to the sides of the canoe, camouflaging its presence. Nearby were ten more canoes, masked with vegetation. Each contained three of Billy's soldiers, two paddlers and a shooter.

Billy raised his right arm. Ten Indians, led by Wild Cat, aimed their rifles. He dropped his arm and his warriors fired into the soldiers bringing up the rear. Six cavalrymen fell from their horses.

The column ground to a halt. The Indians quickly paddled the canoes into the cover of the swamp. On the other side of the road were ten more canoes. In each, an Indian aimed and fired into the column. Five more soldiers fell dead.

First Lieutenant Rose attempted to ride back to the rear, but his path was blocked. He ordered the bugler to sound dismount. He motioned and a platoon of his men reluctantly plunged into the swamp to the right of the road. The remaining men followed him into the swamp to the left.

As Rose barked his orders, Wild Cat found him in his rifle sight and fired a ball into the lieutenant's forehead. Thus he became both the first hero and the first official casualty of the war.

Having fired at the rear of the column, the Indians paddled their canoes through the swamp to the front. The soldiers ordered into the swamp were firing wildly into the area that the Indians had already vacated. The officers in front urged the column to continue on.

As the first wagons traversed the bridge, Alligator and ten Indians fired. The two officers who had urged the column on fell dead. The other soldiers hurriedly dismounted and fired blindly into the swamp.

Under the bridge, Jumper and five Indians rose up out of their canoes and scaled the structure. As the lead wagon was crossing the bridge, Jumper confronted the driver and the soldier who was riding shotgun. He fired his pistol point-blank into the driver's chest. The man fell over, dead before he hit the ground. He turned to the terrified guard who leapt from the wagon before Jumper could plunge his knife into him. Jumper vaulted from the wagon and another Indian took his place, urging the team on across the bridge.

Three more wagons followed, each driven by Indians. Each contained ammunition to fight the American army. Equally important, the Seminole were denying the army these much-needed supplies.

Jumper had spent the morning wrapping cotton strips soaked in kerosene around his arrows. Now he removed the tinderbox from his pouch, held it next to an arrow, struck the flint against steel and the spark ignited the cotton. He drew his bow back and shot the flaming arrow into a wagon on the bridge. As it started to burn, he repeated the process and fired flaming arrows into all five of the remaining wagons. There would be no food or ammunition left behind for the white army.

First one, then a second wagon exploded, sending debris and body parts fifty feet into the air. Jumper was delighted with the fireworks display. He stood watching the explosions.

"Jumper!" called Billy, trying to get his attention over the noise. Jumper slowly turned and looked at Billy. He was grinning, proud of the part he had played. Billy waved for him to get moving, as a dozen soldiers were coming down the road. Jumper smiled and walked toward him. Then a bullet struck him, severing his spine.

"Jumper!" cried Billy. He started in his direction, but Abraham grabbed his arm. Billy tried to pull free.

"You can't help him," said Abraham.

Jumper found himself lying on the bridge. He tried, but he couldn't move his arms or legs. He looked up. Standing over him was the soldier who had shot him. He saw the soldier aim his rifle between his eyes. He saw the sun, he heard the sounds of the Everglades, the sounds he'd grown up with. Jumper smiled as the soldier pulled the trigger.

Two hundred yards down the road, fifty Seminoles, helped by Alabama Jim and a squad of Maroons, were removing the supplies from the wagons. They put them on the backs of the pack animals they'd brought along for this purpose, to be carried deep into the Everglades.

Lying in the wagons were a half dozen wounded soldiers, trembling in fear and unable to move. Hadjo decided to treat himself to the pleasure of killing each of them. He unsheathed his knife and cut the throat of the first soldier he came to. He watched as the blood spurted out of the man's carotid artery. He held his bloody knife up to the face of the second soldier. Hadjo smiled as he plunged it into the soldier's gut. He twisted it around and watched as the soldier writhed in pain before he died. The other wounded men all began screaming and pleading for mercy.

Drawn by the shrieks, Billy saw Hadjo executing the wounded. He came over and grabbed Hadjo's arm. "Let the wounded be," said Billy.

"All the whites must die," retorted Hadjo.

"These soldiers were only obeying orders," Billy said sternly.

"Then the other soldiers will know—if they obey, they will die," said Hadjo.

"No," ordered Billy.

Abraham had explained to Billy that they would need friends among the whites to win this war, and Billy told this to Hadjo. "Only by demonstrating that we are more civilized than they can we make these friends." Billy saw that his explanation did not have any effect.

Hadjo didn't care about public sentiment among the whites. He just wanted to kill them.

Billy had a thought. "There is one white man who needs killing."

Hadjo thought about it for a minute. "Thompson?" he asked.

"Yes," said Billy, "Thompson! I'll make sure he is saved for you."

3

Three days later, twenty-eight soldiers and officers limped back into St. Augustine. Without the supply wagons, there was no reason to push on to Fort King.

In the meantime the Seminole warriors returned to their village and held a subdued celebration. They'd lost Jumper and three others. As was the Seminole tradition, friends and relatives of the deceased commemorated their loved ones by recounting tales of their bravery around a community campfire.

"He gave new meaning to the term slow," laughed Wild Cat, as he spoke of Jumper. His name had been ironic, since he had never jumped to do his tasks.

"His laziness was legendary," concurred Alligator.

"Of course, when it came to fighting, he was a different man," reminded Wild Cat. "He was the first among us to attack the white army, and the first to die."

After other Indians took turns recounting the great victory from their own perspectives, the ceremony ended. Billy's thoughts turned to the intruders coming from the south. Going inside Abraham's chickee, Billy shared his vision for the war. He saw it as a game of chess. Florida was the chessboard and Billy knew his first six moves. Already he'd captured a year's supplies. Next he would surprise and destroy the army coming from the south; then he would wait for the army coming from the north. He would lure that army into the Everglades, deeper and deeper, cut off their supplies, then annihilate them.

Abraham was proud of his protégé. "Just remember, that our men are not replaceable. They have an infinite supply of men, weapons and resources. We only have our will to resist. The best we can work toward is a negotiated settlement, in which they let us stay."

Billy understood. Yet he proclaimed, "We have to bloody their noses every time they stick them in Florida."

"We need our story to be told," Abraham wished out loud. Billy didn't understand. Abraham explained that the citizens of New York and Boston and Philadelphia would take offense at paying for a slaving expedition, for that's what this was, a glorified slaving and land-stealing expedition financed by the government of the United States.

Abraham's voice rang with emotion. Billy was surprised. Abraham was always so calm. Billy just stared at him.

"But first," continued Abraham, "you are right—we have to bloody their nose." Abraham smiled and was again the picture of cold calculation.

Giving orders had become second nature to Billy. It was as though his entire life until now was preparation for this. He told Abraham, "I want you to take your army and harass the militia at Clinch's plantation. I don't want them marching on us while I take my army south."

"No," said Abraham. Billy was taken aback. "It must remain an

Indian war," said Abraham, reminding Billy of the other major tenet of their strategy. "They'll never negotiate with us, but they'll negotiate with you. Better that my troops protect your flank, the women, children and the supplies. Agreed?"

Billy swallowed and then nodded. He hadn't given thought to the matter of negotiations and wasn't at all certain he agreed with Abraham's strategy. This was a matter to which he'd have to give more thought. For now, though, he nodded and agreed.

When dawn broke, the Maroon cavalrymen had already fed and watered their horses and prepared their traveling gear. Each had a rifle, ammunition and five days' rations of dried meat and rice. There was a buzz of excitement as never before. The war had begun, and white men had been killed.

The entire army had assembled at the training site. All were present except those on perimeter guard duty. These guards were covertly posted in trees north, south, east and west of the Maroon camp. All day and night other soldiers would make their way from one post to the next. Sometimes they would go clockwise circling the camp, sometimes counterclockwise, never falling into any discernible pattern.

Abraham assembled the entire community. His words were brief and to the point. "Jamima will be in charge until my return. Prepare the home guard. You're on alert until Alabama Jim or I return." Alert meant that half the population would be at arms, posted throughout the village. The other half would go about gathering the remaining crops.

Alabama Jim had been expecting to lead the soldiers in annihilating the white army. He envisioned attacking the plantations and killing every white in Florida. He licked his lips at the thought.

Abraham turned to Alabama Jim, standing at the head of the army. The orders, given for all to hear, were, "Cover the Seminoles' flank to be sure there are no surprises."

This didn't sit right with Jim. "Yes, sir. Anything else, sir?" he answered in an overly subservient tone.

That alerted Abraham. He looked at Jim as if he'd just read his thoughts. "If we start killing the white women and children, we'll become a threat and they'll swarm on us like locusts."

"Yes sir, I understand, sir."

Martens was standing at attention in the ranks. He had wanted to ride with the troops, though he couldn't ride a horse very well. He could barely shoot his rifle straight. Yet he knew from Abraham's talks how important the home guard was to the community's safety.

"Martens, report to the south guard post. You're on perimeter patrol until tomorrow morning," barked Alabama Jim.

Martens fell out of the ranks. He felt honored that he'd been singled out to jog to the south post, two miles outside the village. Then he would patrol the perimeter between posts all night.

Delores was also standing at attention in Jamima's platoon. When she heard Alabama Jim's order to Martens, she felt only dread. She was certain that meant that he would be paying her a visit.

Alabama Jim mounted his horse and rode to the head of the cavalry. The rest of the troops were dismissed. Everyone hurried about their assignments. Before leaving for the perimeter, Martens sought out Delores. They hugged. Martens could see she was visibly shaken.

"There's nothing to fear. It's only guard duty," he reassured her.

She couldn't tell him that her fears had nothing to do with Martens walking the perimeter of the camp all night. Maybe it would be all right. After all, Alabama Jim had left with the horse soldiers.

Little baby Powell had just fallen asleep, but Delores lay there, waiting. She knew he'd come. Outside, she heard, "Midnight and all is well" in the distance. The night watch was making his rounds through Freedom Land.

Soon after, Alabama Jim entered her chickee. The fact that Delores insisted that she was his daughter didn't enter his mind. He was too aroused by the prospect of raping her again.

Delores' eyes were closed, but she was only feigning sleep. Jim placed his hand over her mouth so she wouldn't scream when he woke her. She opened her eyes and lay perfectly still. Jim got on top of her with his hand still over her mouth.

Delores reached for the knife she had placed alongside her bed for just this occasion. In one motion she brought her arm down hard, stabbing Alabama Jim. He'd moved an instant before she struck, so instead of penetrating his heart she only sliced into his left arm.

"Bitch!" muttered Alabama Jim. He grabbed the knife from Delores' hand.

Delores let out a scream that was muffled, as Jim's hand still covered her mouth.

"Shut up," he said. He punched her hard with his free hand, bloodying her nose.

Jim tore off his sleeve and wrapped his wound.

Baby Powell began screaming, and Jim moved toward him. Delores feared he would kill her baby, and she called out to Jim. She knew she had to do something, anything. She spread her legs wide open. Jim turned back to her. With his wrapped arm still dripping blood, Jim took the opportunity to mount her and thrust himself hard into her.

When Delores screamed, Jim took a handful of her blanket and shoved it into her mouth. Delores gagged on the blanket. She couldn't get any air because her nose was broken and bloodied from his blow. Jim kept riding her. Her struggles to push him off her were in vain. Delores lapsed into unconsciousness. Jim kept thrusting as the baby cried. When it was over, Jim rose up off her.

Only then did he notice that she was lifeless. He thought about it for a long minute. Then he took Delores's limp body and placed it under the blanket in the bed.

He placed another piece of his torn shirt over the wound on his left arm. Then he looked outside the chickee, saw no one, and made his exit into the night.

Jim was still angry. She'd hurt him, and in response got just what she deserved.

Five miles out of camp at the edge of a small clearing, Alabama Jim raised his arm, wheeled his horse around and addressed the eighty members of his company. "Why should we cover the rear of the Indians?" he asked them. "Their Chiefs made a deal to sell us back to the whites!"

The men weren't sure how to react. A few agreed with Jim and voiced their support, yet John Horse pointed out, "That was before Osceola."

Alabama Jim glared at the man. Then he turned to the others. "Thirty miles from here is a sugar plantation where our brothers toil in the fields, chained and whipped. I say we ride to free them."

There was a roar of overwhelming support from the troop, men shouting their agreement and exhilaration at the opportunity to free slaves.

Suddenly John Horse discharged his rifle in the air. All eyes turned to him. "Abraham's our leader. His orders—"

"Abraham doesn't want us to fight," shouted Jim, interrupting John with a disdain he usually reserved for nonblacks. "He doesn't want us to free slaves. He is not fit to command! Who will ride with me?" he asked. "Who wants a chance to kill the men that want to enslave us?"

Jean Paul LaBasque was the third generation of a family growing sugar cane in the Americas. His grandfather and father before him had raised the crop in Louisiana, but Jean Paul realized that the Florida climate and soil were much more conducive to the crop, and slave labor was readily available. This presented a bit of a dilemma. Jean Paul himself was a republican at heart. He openly admired the French Revolution, and its insistence on the rights of man.

Duncan Clinch presented his new neighbor with a proposal that allowed Jean Paul to produce the necessary bushels of sugar cane and not own any slaves. Major Clinch would lease the labor force to Jean Paul in return for a percentage of what the crop brought at market the following season. Clinch persuasively argued that he was bearing as much or more risk than Jean Paul, and that Jean would not own slaves. Jean would only need to feed and house the labor force and the overseer. Clinch pointed out that LaBasque could make sure they were well fed and housed. Clinch would handle the delivery and sale of the sugar cane, and exact his 25 percent off the top.

It wasn't until Abraham arrived on his doorstep years later that Jean acknowledged that his workers were still slaves. Abraham presented him with the opportunity to free the slaves working the plantation. Jean could harvest two more crops and then convert to paying his laborers, or he could go back to New Orleans with his family. When Abraham explained that the alternative was death, Jean quickly signed.

LaBasque's plantation residence was of modest size compared to others in the South. It was a two-story wood-framed house, painted pristine white with blue trim. A white picket fence surrounded it, and the tricolor of the French Revolution flew from the white flagpole in front.

On the last day of his life, Jean Paul enjoyed a breakfast of crepes topped with buttermilk pudding. As he dined, his slaves toiled in the already hot sun.

Unbeknownst to him, Alabama Jim's troops stood at the edge of the nearby woods waiting for their signal. Jim gave a war whoop, and the Maroons charged forward through the cane fields. The slaves stopped what they were doing and dropped the tools they were holding. Some stood in their tracks, others began to run toward the main house, convinced the world was coming to an end.

The overseer, George Farrier, wasn't a harsh man. He didn't even have a whip. Since the agreement with Abraham, the work had improved, and punishment was not needed.

George was dozing peacefully on horseback under a tree when he saw slaves running toward him. He looked up and saw Alabama Jim bearing down on him. He immediately turned, whipped his horse and galloped toward the main residence. Alabama Jim overtook the man and knocked him from his horse with a vicious swipe of his rifle. When George tried to get up, he was lassoed from behind, and fell backward as a Maroon dragged him through the cane field behind his horse.

As the black soldiers approached, Jean didn't understand. He stood up on the veranda. He raised his arms and called for calm. "There is obviously some mistake," said Jean. "Abraham assured me there would be no violence if I granted these people their freedom."

As he spoke, the bruised, barely breathing body of George was dragged in front of him. Jean was stunned as one of the Maroons dismounted and walked over to George. Raising his head, he swiftly cut George's throat.

All civility left Jean as he dashed for the house. He bolted the large front door behind him. Forty Maroons lined up outside. On command they raised their rifles and fired a volley into the house. Then Jim nodded his head, and a platoon of Maroons broke down the door.

Jean stood in the foyer, pointing his pistol at the intruders. "Stop, or I will shoot," he warned. The ten Maroons entering the house stopped for an instant. When they saw that he was alone, they rushed him. Jean fired, felling one of the Maroons before he was overwhelmed and stabbed multiple times. He lay on the floor bleeding to death as they dragged his wife and children from the house.

When they came out on the porch, they were greeted by the sight of George Farrier hanging upside down, his blood drained before them. The Maroons descended upon the family with machetes and began hacking away. They continued their hacking until each of the family was chopped to pieces, bathed in their own blood.

All of the slaves stood outside watching. "You are free. We welcome you to join us in our war of liberation," announced Alabama Jim.

Several of the slaves, and most of the house servants, stood crying over their slain masters. They had been treated fairly and knew they would be freed in another year. The field hands unfamiliar with their former master's republican sentiments felt no remorse. They stepped forward gleefully and volunteered to join the crusade.

Alabama Jim supervised the looting. He let each of his men take whatever they wanted. When everyone was finished, Jim and his men set both the main residence and the sugar cane fields aflame. It looked like hell on earth as the flames jumped into the afternoon sky. There was mass celebration among the army. They had never before been allowed to loot and pillage. When they came upon Jean's wine collection, Alabama Jim democratically passed the bottles around so that all of his army shared in the prize. Soon, unaccustomed to drink, many were reveling in a drunken frenzy, calling for more white blood.

John Horse took the opportunity to sneak away and head back to Abraham as quickly as possible.

Alabama Jim didn't notice him missing at first. When he did, he reasoned that pursuing him would be a waste. After all, he had the army under his command. Now that he had given them a taste of white blood, he assumed they felt like he did. He was certain he would have their loyalty when the inevitable confrontation occurred. He needed only to kill Abraham.

With his ranks swollen by the new recruits, Alabama Jim led his army, carrying their booty, toward the next plantation.

4

There was no snow, but the wind and the moisture it carried made the temperature feel a lot colder than it was. Strange, Wiley Thompson thought, in Florida the thermometer rarely dropped below the mid-forties, yet he was shivering.

As he took his morning constitutional, he admired the Christmas decorations around the fort. They made him nostalgic for other places and times. Ten years ago, when he was in Boston, he'd been married to an attractive woman of some standing. They'd strolled the Common together, arm in arm, looking in the little shops. How he missed his Margaret, who'd died in childbirth along with his infant son.

"Don't do anything stupid. I'm holding a lot of money that says you won't live through tomorrow," shouted Donnelly at Thompson as he walked the fort parade grounds.

It wasn't until Donnelly called out to him in his mocking tone that Thompson was reminded of where he was. Donnelly loathed Thompson, with his upper-crust manner, and his condescending tone. It'd almost be worth losing a hundred dollars, thought Donnelly, to see Thompson's scalp hanging in the forest.

Thompson entered the building he shared with Donnelly. He glared at the man. There was no love lost on Thompson's part either. He could not believe he was reduced to sharing his office, his building and his existence with the likes of trash like Donnelly.

Lieutenant Ronald Bosworth entered the store. He had graduated second in his class from West Point in 1830. Fort King was his first assignment in a war zone. Bosworth had already cultivated the favor of General Duncan Clinch. The general was impressed with his ambition and knew he could rely upon this officer to carry out his orders. Bosworth had come to buy a gift to bring with him to the general's Christmas party. He selected the finest bottle of whiskey available, and paid the two-dollar cost with recently minted silver coins he'd brought with him.

Thompson asked Bosworth about the festivities. "When are you going out to the general's party?"

Bosworth picked up his bottle and walked toward the door. "Right now."

"Wait. You mind if I ride out with you?" asked Thompson.

Bosworth thought the whole thing ridiculous, a government official sequestering himself inside a fort because a renegade had threatened retribution. "I don't know if I want to ride with you," said Bosworth, playing along with the local joke. Thompson's face drooped. Then Bosworth smiled at him and waved for him to come along. Thompson looked over at Donnelly and glared as he put on his overcoat.

Bosworth and Thompson rode out of the fort. They hadn't ridden a hundred yards when they were confronted by Hadjo. He maneuvered his horse to block their path. Bosworth raised his hand in a gesture of peace. "Greetings. . . ."

In a blur of motion Hadjo raised and fired the rifle he was holding. Bosworth toppled from his horse. Lying there on the ground, he looked up. There must be a mistake. He wasn't sure what had happened, but he couldn't focus. He didn't see Thompson turn and ride toward the fort. He didn't see Hadjo run him down, knock him from his horse and then jump on him. Hadjo took particular pleasure in opening up Thompson's midsection with his knife. He pulled out Thompson's intestines, mounted his horse and rode in a circle holding onto Thompson's innards. Thompson screamed as Hadjo strung out sixty feet of his intestines along the forest floor.

The gate to the fort was hastily closed as gunshots rang out in the direction of Hadjo. Ignoring them, Hadjo dismounted. He stood over Thompson, who was writhing in pain. He smiled as he dropped to a knee, took his knife and held it in front of Thompson's face.

"You remember, Thompson? I promised, if Morning Dew was harmed." Hadjo then cut along Thompson's forehead, pulled off his scalp and held it in front of Thompson for him to see. This was not as a trophy. Hadjo then proceeded to open Thompson's pants, exposing his genitals. Hadjo sliced them off and laid the pieces by Thompson's side.

Taking his revenge on Thompson was exhilarating for Hadjo. It momentarily quelled the constant rant of the demons in his head saying, "What kind of man are you who does not stand by his bride-to-be or his father?" When these feelings of shame returned, Hadjo realized that the only way he could absolve his dishonor was by killing more white men.

Before dawn, Billy and Morning Dew led two hundred warriors south to intercept the column from Fort Brooke. They had traveled less than a mile when Abraham appeared and joined Billy at the head of his warriors. "You're going with me?" inquired Billy.

"The outcome of this battle affects my people," answered Abraham.

That morning as they rode south in the cool, damp north-Florida air, Billy began sweating and shivering. He coughed hard, from deep inside his lungs. He put his hand on his chest as he coughed a second time. Abraham watched him, concerned. Billy wasn't from Florida. Abraham knew well that visitors were susceptible to sicknesses that didn't affect the natives. It was probably malaria, or maybe the quinsy.

The scouts had been watching Major Dade's army since it left Fort Brooke. Billy knew exactly where they were. Each day a scout would ride out and meet another scout twenty-five miles to the north. That scout would in turn ride and meet another twenty-five miles to the north. It was the system the Pony Express used years later. Each scout would return to his position the next day. Within one day Abraham and Billy knew the progress and numbers of the invaders.

The dog barked excitedly at the heels of Captain George Gardner's horse. Gardner urged his horse to a gallop. He was hoping to catch up with the company before sunset. He wished he'd left Fort Brooke with them. He didn't relish riding alone through Seminole territory. He was confident that Napoleon, his Irish terrier, would warn him of any trouble.

A third-generation Virginian, he was raised around horses and took great pride in his ability to ride, and when necessary, shoe, pull teeth and perform any of a dozen functions associated with horse husbandry.

Captain Gardner had stayed behind in Tampa because his wife was ill with quinsy. When he had received his marching orders, he had gone to the commander, Major Dade, for permission to stay with his very sick wife. It seemed to George that as soon as the troops pulled out, Emily got decidedly better. In actuality, she didn't want him to go. She'd had a foreboding feeling about the campaign. George promptly packed his gear and went after his company.

Major Francis Dade's column of regulars made its way north. As they exited the dense forest into an area of brush and pine trees, everyone was relieved. All along they had been worried about an ambush. Now, at least they'd be able to see their attackers.

As they approached a lake, Major Dade signaled for an advance guard to reconnoiter the area. Twelve men led by Lieutenant Harrison Gage, himself a recent officer, appointed from the ranks, trotted off and made their way around the perimeter of the lake.

Billy, Abraham, Morning Dew, Wild Cat and Alligator watched from the bush as the advance party rode by. Behind them, well camouflaged, were a hundred and ninety-six Seminole warriors, armed with U.S. Government-issue rifles, powder and shot courtesy of the supply train.

The main column approached. Riding at the head was Major Dade. Immediately behind him, holding the regimental colors, was private Ransom Clark. Bringing up the rear was Captain Gardner, with his dog bounding happily nearby.

"We're through the worst of the danger," shouted Dade to his men, loud enough so those troopers in the rear could hear him. "When we get to Fort King, you all get three days off for Christmas." This put a smile on every trooper's face.

Billy motioned with first his right and then his left arm, and the Indians behind him spread out. They each marked a target. The best shot among them was Wild Cat, although he was no match for Billy. Abraham quietly suggested to Billy, "The officers should be the first targets." Billy knew that already and was miffed that Abraham didn't think he did. His look told Abraham he was disappointed.

"Don't take it personally, Osceola. I have to make sure you do the right thing," explained Abraham.

Wild Cat took careful aim. As the major turned back around, Wild Cat's shot struck him in the temple, toppling him from his horse and killing him instantly.

That was the signal. A withering fire killed or maimed all of the

officers except Captain Gardner, and sixty of the one hundred enlisted soldiers in the first thirty seconds of the battle.

Lieutenant Gage, seeing the main force under fire, wheeled his
horse around and ordered his men to follow him. They rode directly
into a second ambush. Thirty Indians fired, killing ten of the twelve
men instantly. The other two turned their horses in an attempt to
ride off, but multiple bullets killed them and their horses.

Captain Gardner urged the cannon crew forward. He hoped to
form a defensive line behind the artillery and blast away at the yet-
unseen enemy. The five men assigned to the battery came forward
pulling the cannon. At the captain's command, they dismounted
and turned the cannon toward the forest.

Abraham noticed the cannon being positioned. He pointed it out
to Billy, who quickly signaled Alligator. Before the battle, Billy had
assigned Alligator the task of disposing of the artillery crew before
it could inflict any casualties.

Ten Indians descended upon the artillerymen before they could
load. They fired a volley, hitting three of the soldiers. Then they
threw down their rifles and sprinted toward the cannon. Captain
Gardner, armed with a pistol, saw the Indians coming, marked his
target and dropped Alligator with his first shot.

In an instant the Indians were upon them. Using knives and
tomahawks, the Indians made quick work of the five soldiers remaining. Captain Gardner, stabbed in the back and side, staggered
to the cannon. With his bayonet he destroyed the firing mechanism,
making sure that the Indians didn't capture it. Then everything began to spin around. He fell to the ground, thought of his sickly wife
and her pleas for him to stay, and said out loud, "You were right,
dear," as he died.

The Indians continued to fire on the shrinking group of soldiers.
If a soldier exposed himself, he was shot. The twenty-one surviving
soldiers crawled behind several fallen trees along the lake. They

pushed together more debris, dead wood and branches, and constructed a small three-cornered redoubt.

"Taking out the rest of this company would require a frontal assault and, in my opinion, it's not worth losing any warriors," said Abraham, addressing Billy.

"Soldiers, we do not want to kill you," shouted Billy to the survivors. "Throw down your arms and we will allow you to return to Fort Brooke."

"How do we know you won't kill us after we surrender?" shouted back Ransom Clark from behind the redoubt.

Billy rose up. He was wearing his father's red jacket and the white feather on his headband. "I'm Osceola, Chief of the Seminole. I give ye me word."

Billy was too much of a target for Clark to resist. He fired at him, hoping to kill the Chief and send the Indians into confusion. The bullet stuck the log in front of Billy, throwing up splinters.

Billy had his answer. The soldiers had their backs to the lake. They would not run out of water. They could hold out for days. From Billy's perspective the cannon could be very useful, as would the hundred rifles and ammunition. Then there was Alligator lying there halfway between the two factions.

Abraham saw that Billy was determined. He motioned for Wild Cat, Billy and Morning Dew to come closer.

"Osceola, have half your men pin them down with constant fire from both flanks. Then, on my signal, send your warriors crawling down the middle. Ten yards out, rise up and rush over the top. We should get there with sufficient numbers to overwhelm them."

Abraham sketched the plan out in the dirt. Billy understood that the one thing they could not replace was warriors. "The key is to keep them pinned down. When you charge, if they rise up to fire, your men have to shoot them," instructed Abraham.

Billy and Wild Cat nodded to show they understood. They gath-

ered the warriors and Billy explained the plan. Then he divided his
soldiers into three groups. Two groups left to take up positions on
each flank.

Billy motioned for his men to follow him. He would lead the
charge.

"No," cried Morning Dew.

"Me love, I am the leader of these men. I will not ask them to
do what I won't."

The Indians on the flanks began shooting. Some had climbed
trees so that they were able to shoot down into the soldiers, picking
them off.

Billy and his sixty followers crawled toward the soldiers' position.
They crawled past dead and dying soldiers groaning and begging
for help or to be put out of their misery. The Indians ignored them,
keeping their eyes trained straight ahead.

The flurry of bullets kept the surviving soldiers huddled behind
the barricade. Ten yards out Billy rose to a crouch and signaled for
the warriors on both sides of him to charge. The first wave of twenty
Indians sprinted to the barricade and jumped over it. With terrible
cries they fell upon the soldiers. When Billy arrived with the second
wave, all the soldiers except Private Ransom Clark were dead.

The Indians began celebrating with whoops and hollers. Billy
raised his rifle over his head to signal to Abraham and the others
that the battle was over. Spontaneous shouts of "Osceola" began to
ring out. That's when Billy noticed Clark lying nearby, wounded in
the arm and leg. He leaned over Clark. "If you had surrendered,
they'd be alive," said Billy, pointing to all the dead soldiers around
him. "We're going to let you live so you can tell the others: if you
fight us, you'll die."

His warriors were still shouting his name as Billy walked over to
where Alligator lay. Wild Cat was already kneeling beside him. Tears
welled up in both men's eyes.

Abraham accompanied Morning Dew across the battlefield. She threw her arms around Billy, and kissed him repeatedly as Abraham surveyed the carnage. Billy removed Morning Dew's arms from around his neck. "What's wrong?" asked Morning Dew. Billy pointed to Alligator.

"Congratulations, Chief, this is a great Seminole victory," said Abraham. Billy only nodded. He didn't feel like celebrating. Though he'd lost only three warriors while killing a hundred American soldiers and capturing their arms and ammunition, his friend Alligator was dead. Billy motioned and six Seminole came over. They lifted Alligator to carry him back for a proper burial.

Gardner's dog stood over his master's body barking, trying to summon him back from the dead. Wild Cat came over, knelt in front of the dog, and gave it a piece of dried jerky. Then Wild Cat stood and beckoned the dog, and he came.

In the meantime, Abraham walked to the cannon. Closer inspection revealed that the firing mechanism was destroyed. Abraham thought to himself that the officer lying dead beside the cannon had done his job. Too bad a good soldier had to die for this. Abraham suggested to Billy that they dump the cannon into the lake so that the white army, who could repair it, wouldn't be able to use it.

Wild Cat brought over a document he had taken from Major Dade's body. Abraham sat down beside the cannon and examined it.

War Department Official Orders
December 5, 1835
Major Francis Dade

March your company immediately to Fort King. Upon arrival you will be under the command of General Duncan Clinch. Your company will join General Clinch's army and march on the Seminole village at Long Swamp.

When Abraham showed the orders to Billy, he recognized Clinch's name. He'd daydreamed years before about leading an army against the fat soldier who had attacked his mother's village, stolen their land, and sent her tribe west. Wasn't he also responsible for enslaving Morning Dew?

Billy looked about. His warriors were busy stripping the dead American soldiers of everything of value. At that moment, Billy put his personal sorrow aside. "Seminole warriors, come to me," he shouted, while motioning with his arms for everyone to come closer. His warriors stopped what they were doing and gathered around him.

"My fellow Seminole, today we have won a great victory," began Billy. The warriors surrounding him shouted, "Ho to Osceola," in acknowledgment of the triumph. "But it is only the beginning," yelled Billy, silencing his followers. "Even as we stand here another white army, twenty times larger than this one, marches on our village. Many, perhaps all of us will perish in the coming struggle. If there are any among us who would prefer to gather their families and seek sanctuary in Arkansas, I will understand."

"No," shouted Morning Dew, "we fight with you." His men echoed her words, shouting, "We fight." Then, in unison, they began chanting, "Ho to Chief Osceola."

5

Seventy miles to the northwest, at Freedom Land, Jamima assembled the remainder of the population on the training field for roll call and assignments. Young Garcia stood there proudly with a musket resting on his shoulder. Jamima noticed that Delores was conspicuously absent.

After roll call, Jamima and her son went to Delores' chickee. She hadn't reported for her duties, and Jamima would have no slacking off, even if she'd recently given birth.

Standing outside her chickee, Jamima could hear the baby crying. "Delores, Delores!" she called. Still she only heard the sobs of baby Powell. "Maybe she's not there," thought Jamima as she entered the chickee.

She saw that Delores was lying under her blanket. She was strangely still. Jamima pulled back the blanket and gasped. She turned to her son. "Get out now!" When Garcia hesitated, she raised her voice, screaming, "Get out!"

The baby's wail reminded Jamima of her other pressing responsibility. She turned and picked up the child and held him close. She felt his warmth against the chill running through her body. Still holding baby Powell, Jamima investigated Delores' bruised face. She looked into her open eyes, fixed with the vacant stare of the dead. Looking downward, Jamima noticed dried semen around her vagina, and the blood on her knife beside the bed.

Martens had spent the night on guard duty marching between posts, and he was exhausted. He staggered into his chickee and saw Jamima holding his baby. He didn't understand the grim look on her face. He looked down and saw Delores. Then he saw the blood and the vacant stare.

"I'm sorry, Martens," said Jamima. "She's dead. She's been violated."

Martens began screaming. His shriek was heard throughout Freedom Land. He'd never experienced such agony, even from the savage whippings he'd suffered.

Among the population fear spread like a brushfire whipped by an ill wind. The people abandoned what they were doing and gathered outside Delores' chickee. Jamima handed Martens his son, and exited the hut.

"Back to your posts!" Jamima shouted at the top of her lungs. The people hesitated. Jamima understood that they knew something terrible had happened and wanted to know what, but she wasn't about to tell them that Delores had been murdered.

"Abraham's orders are to stay at your posts. The white man is coming!"

When her words didn't move the people, she took her son's musket out of his hand and raised it, pointing wildly at the crowd.

"I shoot anyone not at their post," Jamima cried. She swung her rifle around, pointing. "Hurry! The white man is coming."

At last, everyone shuffled away but Garcia, who stood there shaking. Jamima wondered if her son would ever be the same again.

She turned to Martens. "She was a fine women."

He stood there, openly sobbing. She put her arms around him, comforting him. "I know what it is like to lose your loved one. My own Garcia, the love of my life, he die in my arms."

"Who did this?" asked Martens, composing himself.

"Alabama Jim," said Jamima. Though she had no proof, she was certain that he was the one. She remembered how Jim had looked at Delores. She knew he was capable of cold-blooded murder.

"I will kill him," cried Martens.

"No," barked Jamima. "You will care for your child and join the harvest." She added in a dangerous undertone. "I will kill Jim."

The two-hundred-man Seminole army led by Billy, with Morning Dew at his side, arrived at Freedom Land. They had an additional fifty-five horses, ninety rifles, ammunition and Gardner's dog.

Though news of the victory over their common enemy spread, there was no celebration. A dark cloud hung over the residents. Never before had one of their own been murdered.

Soon after, John Horse rode into the village. His horse was lathered and panting from exhaustion. He dismounted and hurried over. Looking up at the still-mounted Abraham, John Horse pointed north.

"Alabama Jim is making his own war on the plantations," said John Horse, speaking between deep breaths.

"And the owners?" asked Abraham.

"Butchered. All the whites and their families," reported John Horse.

Abraham was furious. By murdering whites, Alabama Jim would

muster public opinion in the United States against the cause.

Then Abraham noticed Jamima standing in front of him, waiting to speak. He looked at her.

"That not all Jim do. He murder Delores," said Jamima.

Abraham's anger turned to shock. He knew what he must do. He had to stop Jim. Yet he also knew that the white army would be marching on Long Swamp, and he was needed at Freedom Land to organize the evacuation of the village.

"Gather the army," said Abraham to John Horse and Jamima.

Billy walked his horse over to Abraham. "Are you going to tell me?" asked Billy.

"Alabama Jim has taken the Maroon cavalry to make his own war," said Abraham, leaving out any reference to murder.

This was disconcerting news. Billy was counting on Abraham's cavalry. How could Abraham's soldiers be mutinying?

Billy coughed hard. "Maybe you better go and get your army back," he suggested.

Abraham didn't like his tone of voice, or his sarcastic suggestion.

"Do you know the story of Icarus?" asked Abraham.

"Can't say I do," answered Billy.

"Icarus learned to fly by making wings of feathers and fastening them to his arms with wax. He thought himself invincible. Daedalus, his father, warned him, don't fly too close to the sun. He didn't heed his father's warning. The wax melted, he lost his feathers, and he fell to earth."

"What's that got to do with me?" asked Billy.

"You think you're invincible, but you're not. You need to take care of that cough, or Morning Dew will be a widow and the Seminole will be without a leader."

"I'm fine," snapped Billy.

Abraham noticed his pale complexion and beads of sweat on his forehead. "No, you have the quinsy. I've seen it before. You need quinine."

Morning Dew was alarmed. She had known something was wrong, and now Abraham put a name on it.

"What does he do for quinsy?" asked Morning Dew.

"Quinine," answered Abraham, "but there is no cure. Maybe John the Baptist can help."

Ignoring him, Billy turned to his followers. He raised his right arm and shouted, "Let's go home." The Seminole army headed out of Freedom Land toward their village, three miles away.

Abraham hurried to his chickee. He needed a bath and a fresh change of clothes. He would have preferred to fill his tub with hot water and relax in it, but there was no time. Instead he undressed and wiped himself clean using a pan of fresh stream water and a bar of soap.

Abraham was wearing only pants and toweling himself off when Jamima entered. "I want to do something for the cause. I will kill Alabama Jim," she announced.

As he put on a clean shirt, Abraham shook his head. He would hear none of it. "No, I need you here."

"The people do not listen to me. Let me go, I kill him. I should have killed him when he kill Willie."

"That may be, but you're not going after him," said Abraham. "We need to bring the army back. Can you do that? No," said Abraham, answering his own question. "And the harvest?"

"The harvest is done," said Jamima, "so I can accompany you."

"I am going after Jim alone. When I find him, I will kill him," said Abraham, very matter-of-factly.

The next morning was overcast and windy. Abraham stood before the people, who were gathered in a tight circle. Delores' body, wrapped in a cotton cloth, lay at his feet. Martens held his baby son as tears streamed down his cheeks.

Abraham raised his arms to the sky. "We give our sister Delores to you, Lord," he began. "It is not our place to judge or even understand your ways, O Lord, but it is our place to fight for our God-given rights of life, liberty and the pursuit of happiness." Abraham looked around the gathering, to make sure they understood.

"All of us," he continued, "every man, woman and child must do their part if we are to prevail in our desperate struggle. Let us not mourn further, but let us celebrate her brave life by living our lives and fighting for our freedom, as Delores would have. We will start by burning Freedom Land to the ground."

There was a collective gasp among the populace.

"We are not giving up," clarified Abraham. "On the contrary, we will give no comfort to the enemy. The fire will be Delores' funeral pyre. Then we will poison the wells and march our families to our new home deep in the Everglades." He pointed around the village. "Now, everyone go to your house and gather up your important belongings, but only what you can carry. Then report to the training field with your weapons. There we will go over your assignments for the emigration. Jamima is my second in command. Honor her word as you do mine. John Horse and Martens will be her lieutenants."

Martens was surprised to hear his name. Even a bigger shock was that he was to be Jamima's lieutenant. He would've liked to share this honor with Delores. Their desperate flight to freedom had been at her instigation. Her faith had sustained them in their darkest hour. "Dear God, care for her," said Martens. "She believe in you with all her heart. Welcome her and care for her."

Under Abraham's command were three hundred eleven armed men and thirty-nine women, less the eighty traveling with Alabama Jim. It was understood that the other women and children, numbering over four hundred, would join in any battle before allowing themselves to be returned to slavery.

The entire population gathered. With them were their rifles and meager belongings. It had been a while since Abraham had reviewed

his troops personally. He had left that job to Alabama Jim, his mu-
tinous commander.

Abraham drilled them all afternoon. He divided them into
groups. He took the first two rows of twenty-five soldiers and led
them out to the field.

"Load," barked Abraham. The Maroon soldiers in the first row
dropped to one knee and shoved the powder and shot down into
the barrel with the plunger, then removed the plunger and cocked
the rifles. The soldiers behind them took three steps forward
through the space in between each of their loading comrades, and
aimed their rifles at the targets posted on the trees twenty yards
away.

"Fire!" shouted Abraham. Each of his soldiers pulled the trigger,
sending twenty-five balls into the targets affixed to the oak trees.

Immediately after firing they dropped to one knee to reload while
the soldiers behind them rose up and stepped forward between
them, aimed their rifles and fired on Abraham's next command.

Abraham reviewed his troops this way, fifty at a time. He watched
as they loaded and fired their rifles, making certain that every
weapon was in working order.

Next he ordered all of his soldiers into the field at the same time.
He put them in five rows of fifty. Each row was assigned an officer.
He put Martens in charge of the third row.

"I'm a lieutenant, Delores," said Martens under his breath as he
took his position at the head of the row.

Abraham's instructions were for each of the rows of soldiers to
step forward past the other four and fire, immediately drop to a
knee and reload, then stand and step forward and fire again, all in
thirty seconds. The entire exercise would be repeated ten times.
Running like a well-oiled machine, each row of the Maroon army
would be able to shoot every ten seconds, pouring almost three
hundred rounds a minute into an opposing force.

"Take a knee," ordered Abraham after the training session. His entire army dropped down and relaxed. "There is no army capable of withstanding that firepower if everyone does their part. In a battle, if your neighbor is hit and falls, leave him until the order is given to cease firing. You should not abandon your position in the line even if I am wounded or killed. Don't expect your friends or relatives to help you if you are wounded during the battle. Does everyone understand?"

The entire army answered Abraham with a chorus of "yes."

"If everyone does their part, we will prevail," said Abraham.

6

The mood in the Seminole Village was in sharp contrast to that in Freedom Land. As Billy and his warriors entered cheers rang out for the conquering army. Word of the victory had arrived before them. The entire population turned out. There was mass jubilation. They hadn't lost their lands. The white man had been soundly defeated, and their leader exuded a confidence that was contagious.

When the cheering diminished, Hadjo greeted Billy by handing him a piece of Thompson's scalp.

"Wiley Thompson!" announced Billy as he held the bloody remnant for all to see. The cheers and shouts of "Death to the white man" began again. Only Micanopy was conspicuously absent, preferring to stay in his chickee. He could not bring himself to face Billy and congratulate him on the victory; a victory that Micanopy still believed could only lead to the tribe's destruction.

That night Wild Cat mourned Alligator. They'd grown up together, hunted together and fought side by side. Around the camp-fire Wild Cat told the people how Alligator had ignored danger to make sure the white man's cannon didn't inflict any casualties on the Indians. As Billy listened, Morning Dew snuggled closer to him, glad that he was not a casualty.

In addition to Alligator, there were three others dead among the Seminole in what came to be known to the Americans as "the Dade Massacre."

The next morning Billy, Wild Cat and fifty warriors rode the three miles to Freedom Land. They saw the entire village in ashes, still smoldering from the self-started blaze. The population was gathered on the training field. Billy dismounted and walked over to Abraham.

"Burn your village and poison your wells, Chief," said Abraham as he greeted Billy.

"That's uncalled for, don't you think?" said Billy. "The white army will never reach here."

"Don't you remember what I said about Icarus?" said Abraham. He thought of all the overconfident generals whose mistakes he'd studied, going back to the Romans and their pursuit of Spartacus during a similar slave revolt two thousand years before.

"Our only chance," he explained, "is to pursue a strategy of total war. We can survive in the swamp without the village and the wells. The white man can't."

Billy knew that was true, but he wasn't ready to cut short the Seminole celebration and have the people burn their homes. There was still time before implementing this drastic measure.

"I have a plan," said Billy. "But I need you to support it with a company of your soldiers."

Abraham remained silent as he listened to Billy's plan.

"In other words," said Abraham when Billy was finished, "you are going to take your queen out and move her around in front of the Americans in the hope they follow her back into your trap?"

"Yes," answered Billy.

"Do you think exposing your queen is risky?" asked Abraham.

"I didn't realize that you played chess," said Billy.

"I've dabbled at it as a young man with General Hampton," said Abraham.

"Then you must know in order to achieve a quick checkmate, you need to take risks," said Billy.

"You fancy yourself quite the strategist," remarked Abraham with more than a touch of sarcasm in his voice.

"Good enough to best you," challenged Billy. "Shall we play and agree to use the winner's strategy?"

Beads of sweat appeared on his forehead. He wiped the moisture with his shirtsleeve, then ran both hands through his long hair, dampening it and pushing it straight back.

Behind him, scattered throughout the grassy meadow, his Seminole warriors lounged about in various states of repose, rifles at their side. Several interacted with their Maroon counterparts, renewing old acquaintance and trading sugar cane leaves, which they had in abundance, for tobacco. For the most part the army of Indians and the army of black men were separated, each behind their own leader, watching this strange contest between them.

Wild Cat was one of several Seminole who had wagered their sugar cane on the outcome. He stood directly behind Billy, who was sitting on a woven cotton blanket ornately decorated with multi-colored images of conquistadors slaughtering Indians. The blanket and many of the shirts worn by the Seminole had been obtained from Cuban traders in return for alligator hides. Abraham sat on the grass facing him. Between them was a tree stump on which sat a board with black and white figurines. John Horse stood behind Abraham, watching intently, though he didn't begin to understand what he was seeing. A huge oak tree provided shade for both con-testants and their immediate entourages.

"You're risking everything," chided Abraham.

"I don't view it that way," answered Billy.

"They advance, we retreat. They retreat, we stay put, and we live to fight another day," said Abraham, expounding his philosophy of combat against the numerically superior white army.

"That's what this contest is about, isn't it, whose strategy we follow?"

"Wait for them to come to you," implored Abraham.

"Advice from a commander whose cavalry has mutinied," retorted the Chief.

The comment angered Abraham, but he tempered his outward reaction. He knew Billy was right.

"I'll bring the Americans to me where and when I want them, and then I'll destroy their army," said Billy matter-of-factly. Then he smiled at Abraham and made his move, maneuvering the white bishop to cut off the black king's retreat.

"Check . . . mate," he said, pronouncing each word slowly and deliberately.

He reached and tipped over Abraham's black king with his index finger.

"Ho to Chief Osceola," cried Wild Cat when he realized he'd won. He raised his fist and then two-stepped about in a victory dance, before collecting a handful of tobacco from Abraham's lieutenant, John Horse.

Billy stood up and stretched. He then adjusted his white cotton headband and placed the eagle feather through the back of his long blond hair. A gentle breeze blew through the meadow, refreshing all except Billy. Suddenly he was chilled. He reached down to the blanket for his father's red officer's tunic and put it on.

"Congratulations," said Abraham, looking up at his adversary.

"I'm only going to borrow forty of your men. The rest can stay and protect the evacuation," Billy said, thinking he was being a gracious winner. "Now, hadn't you better be going if you're to bring back the rest of your army?" The question sounded more like an order.

Abraham rose to his feet. He turned to address his stunned followers. Never before had they seen anyone best Abraham at anything. "While I am gone, this army is under the command of Chief Osceola," he announced. He turned to his second in command. "Jamima, you are in charge of the evacuation. Lead the women and children south to Lake Okeechobee. I'll join you when I return with the cavalry." Jamima nodded proudly, relishing the responsibility. "If I don't return," said Abraham, almost as an afterthought, "I want you to kill Alabama Jim when he shows up."

Abraham walked to his horse and mounted. He dug his heels into the horse's sides and trotted off to the north.

Wild Cat was standing under the oak tree, puffing on a makeshift pipe, inhaling the precious tobacco he'd won, when he heard the Chief order, "Gather all of the men, Seminole and Maroon."

Billy placed the chess pieces and board into a burlap sack, then stepped up onto the tree stump. He motioned for his followers to gather in a semicircle facing him. When that was done, everyone grew quiet.

"Abraham is a good man," began the Chief. "His advice to me was to keep his army out of sight, as your presence will offend the whites. I say, if your black skin outrages these invaders, let us flaunt it, together, for he who fights with me is my brother, and I will not forsake my brothers."

The Seminole warriors vocalized their agreement by letting out war whoops. The Maroons were even louder, screaming, "Kill the white man!"

"Abraham says we are outnumbered, twenty of them for each one of us. Is not each one of us a match for twenty of these . . . slave masters?"

"Yes!" shouted the men of the two armies in unison.

"I say, the fewer of us the greater the glory."

The Seminole warriors raised their tomahawks and war clubs in the air and let out war cries. The Maroons lifted their muskets and fired in the air. The chief looked at his black allies.

"Was there ever a more just cause," continued Osceola, "than free men fighting against those who would enslave them?"

"No!" shouted the men.

"Was there ever a more corrupt cause than slavery or stealing other people's land?"

"No!" screamed the soldiers.

"Abraham says this is not about honor or glory, this is about survival. And Abraham is a good man. Yet I say, if it is a sin to covet honor, I am a most offending soul." Billy repeated the words he'd set to memory so long ago. "I would rather die here and now fighting these white devils than live as a slave."

Cheers rang out.

"And you, good men, both red and black, with strong limbs and stout hearts, standing before me this day, let us swear together that as long as one of us breathes, we will fight for our own and our brothers' freedom."

"I swear!" rang out the gathered voices.

"Osceola! Osceola!" shouted Wild Cat, leading a chant that echoed throughout the meadow.

The chief stood basking in his reception, content that he had inspired his soldiers. He didn't notice that Morning Dew and John the Baptist had ridden into the camp.

"Look at you, Billy Powell! You're sick," said Morning Dew. "Get down from there!"

When Billy climbed down off the stump, she took the blanket he'd been sitting on and wrapped it around her shivering husband. "Who's going to lead these men when the fever comes back? You?"

"Yes, my love, me." "She's so beautiful when she's angry," thought

Billy. He gently stroked her cheek. "This bud of love has proven a beautiful flower," he said softly.

"You and your father's words," she said, not moved. "What about me? I'm not ready to become a widow because you're too busy making war to care for yourself."

Standing beside Morning Dew was John the Baptist.

"Billy, John can heal you," she said excitedly.

"Heal me?" said Billy. "There's nothing wrong with me."

John put his hand on Billy's forehead and then raised one of his eyebrows, exposing the white of his eye. Billy had too much respect for him to resist his probing.

"You are suffering from the walking fever. But I can cure you." He handed Billy a bowl of broth. Billy just looked at the wooden bowl, full of a milky mixture of herbs. "I'll prepare it for you every day for the next two weeks while you rest here. After that you will be cured," John said.

"That's not possible," said Billy. "In two weeks we would be overrun."

Morning Dew's mouth dropped and her expression took a desperate turn. "You must," she demanded. "John the Baptist says you will die if you don't."

Billy looked at John, who nodded his head in agreement. He thought to himself, "I'll take the medicine while I conduct the campaign," and drank the potion.

"Now get to bed and rest," said John. "I will bring you a fresh dose tomorrow."

As dawn broke, all that remained of Freedom Land was a landscape of still-smoldering timbers where the thriving community had stood. Jamima supervised as soldiers loaded the youngest children and the infirm onto the fifty remaining horses, so as not to slow the emigration. They all knew what would happen if the white army arrived and they were still there.

Traveling south, the emigrants entered a pine forest. The trail was clearly marked and the trees offered shade from the hot Florida sun. Jamima walked among the slower-moving women and children, and constantly cajoled them to walk at a more rapid pace. Everyone carried their rifles loaded and ready. Garcia walked alongside Jamima. Despite his protests, she made him carry her loaded rifle, as Jamima was concerned that Alabama Jim might show up with his followers.

Just before midday the pine forest gave way to a sea of saw grass. Several women sat down in the last of the shade to eat. "Get up! Eat as you walk," barked Jamima.

Their destination was Lake Okeechobee, ninety miles to the south. While the Seminole people stayed in their village, the Maroons traveled thirty miles the first day. Jamima was satisfied with the progress. The next three days would be more difficult as the forest gave way to lowland marsh covered with a sea of elephant grass. There was an old Indian trail through it, but in many places the tribe would have to walk single file over the damp ground, slowing the pace considerably.

That morning in the Seminole village at Long Swamp, Billy rose early. He got out of bed and dressed, putting on his father's signature red tunic. He wanted to be conspicuous.

"You can't go," said Morning Dew. "You promised to stay in bed and let John the Baptist treat you."

"I made no such promise, my sweet," said Billy.

She was crestfallen to hear this but knew Billy would do what he wanted. She rushed out of the chickee, and a minute later returned with the healer.

"Give me a week's measure of the potion," said Billy to John the Baptist, trying to compromise.

"I cannot," said the shaman. "It needs to be prepared fresh daily from herbs I pick in the forest. Also, it must be combined with absolute bed rest to be effective."

"Well," said Billy, "I have a white man's disease and I guess I will have to find white man's medicine. After the war John can heal me," he said, turning back to his wife.

"No!" cried Morning Dew.

"My love, I am the leader of our people. I must put their welfare first. Besides," said Billy, "I feel very well today."

"It won't last," said the healer.

When Wild Cat appeared, Billy instructed him to gather all the warriors, and to send a message to Hadjo to come with his followers.

Three hours later, Billy stood before the four hundred eighty-three warriors from the various communities, and the forty Maroons under his command. He ordered two hundred eighty-three of his soldiers to stay in reserve at Long Swamp and guard the women and children. Everybody wanted to ride with Billy, but he made sure those left behind understood the important job that they were doing. Then he rode off with one hundred ninety-seven others in the first stage of his plan.

That same morning, a soldier galloped toward the Clinch plantation. At the gate he saluted the sentries and then rode his horse right up to the house. He dismounted in a hurry and, at the top of his lungs, shouted for General Clinch.

The general came out of his residence, looking annoyed at the interruption.

"Urgent news, sir." Saluting, the soldier handed Clinch a note. Clinch read it, folded it and put it in his pocket. His face registered his discomposure. "Sir, can I trade my horse for a fresh mount to get back to the fort?"

"Yes," said General Clinch, "but I have more urgent business for you. Go to the stable, get a fresh mount, then ride to the outlying plantations to warn the civilians."

The soldier saluted and departed.

Clinch then addressed his second in command, Captain Drain. "Prepare this place for a siege. Thompson's dead, and Dade's entire command has been massacred."

The captain saluted and went back to the barracks to turn out the guard.

Clinch stared into the distance for a long moment. Things were not turning out the way he had envisioned. On the other hand, Clinch was not one to dwell on bad news. "There is always a silver lining," he thought, "and if this is what it takes to awaken Washington, so be it."

7

Winter came early to Washington, D.C. By the New Year it had already snowed three times. Secretary of War Lewis Cass was presiding over a meeting that had started two hours late because of the difficulty negotiating the frozen streets.

Cass, a career bureaucrat, was seated behind his desk. A portrait of President Andrew Jackson in military uniform stared down at the participants from the wall behind him. Seated in front of Cass in a rough semicircle were a number of politicians and military representatives including Territory of Florida Governor Eaton; Congressman Reilly; the commander in chief of the Florida militia, Major General Richard K. Call; Quartermaster General of the Army Thomas Sidney Jesup; and Senator Stanton Beamish, a large, florid man with a dry tongue and a deceptively languid air.

Cass, having himself been recently called on the carpet by the commander in chief, addressed the meeting. "The President wants

to know why General Clinch is doing so little to contain these outrages, and why the Indians aren't being punished for their depre-
dations."

"I assure you, Mr. Secretary, sir, General Clinch is doing the best
he can with severely limited resources," said Congressman Reilly,
doing his best to defend the general.

Cass looked at the report on his desk. "Am I reading this correctly? The entire United States sugar-growing industry has been
wiped out?" he asked, not hiding his incredulity.

The details were fresh in Reilly's mind. "From the St. Johns River
to below St. Augustine, Mr. Secretary, consider this a formal request
for additional troops, and not ten-week volunteers, but the regular
army. Mr. Secretary, we are at war in Florida," he said. "We need
the proper resources."

General Jesup had heard all this before and wasn't surprised. He
rose to speak. "Gentlemen, may I make a suggestion that would
terminate these hostilities at a stroke?"

All heads turned to him. There was a long moment of silence.
General Jesup waited for effect. As a soldier, he was used to his
subordinates hanging on his every word. He drew a deep breath.
"Gentlemen, have the President rescind the Indian Removal Act and
allow the Seminole to stay where they are, within a defined reservation, on land they can cultivate. They're not normally warlike;
they're farmers and herdsmen."

There was another long silence while this outrageous remark was
digested. "I can tell you all," said Secretary Cass, not hiding his
displeasure with General Jesup's suggestion, "howsoever these matters are conducted, the President will not view with any favor a
reversal of policies he has so clearly formulated and defined."

General Jesup had known politicians long enough to expect the
secretary to take offense at reversing public policy. "Then prepare
yourselves, gentlemen, for what suggests itself to me will be long
and costly hostilities."

Planters and tenant farmers streamed into Fort King. Amelia, accompanied by Henry, drove her buckboard through the newly completed gates. There were over a thousand people inside the fort, ten times as many as before. Panic was in the air. People bustled about looking for a place to bed down. In one corner of the fort, a tent dealer was doing a brisk business. Wherever there was space, a tent went up and a settler claimed that area as his.

Amelia and Henry stood in a line at Donnelly's Pantry. After Thompson's demise, Donnelly took over the entire space, and promptly named it after himself. The line of customers extended out the door and onto the parade ground. She had never seen anything like this before. The line slowly made its way inside the store. When it was finally her turn she and Henry stepped up to the counter. She smiled at Donnelly, who all but ignored her charm. "May I have ten pounds of sugar, ten pounds of flour and two pounds of coffee?" requested Amelia.

"That will be, let's see, forty dollars for the sugar, twenty dollars for the flour and forty for the coffee; one hundred dollars altogether," said Donnelly.

"Did you say forty dollars for the sugar?" asked Amelia, looking at Donnelly in disbelief.

"Yes, ma'am," said Donnelly, "four dollars a pound for sugar, two dollars a pound for flour and twenty dollars a pound for coffee."

"Those items are less than ten cents a pound," said Amelia, outraged.

"Go elsewhere," said Donnelly, looking over her shoulder at the line of customers clamoring for his goods.

"You know that is quite impossible," said Amelia.

"If you don't want it, the people behind you will take it," said Donnelly impatiently, as he had no time for small talk. With the war, he would be rich in a matter of months.

"You, sir, are a profiteer," said Amelia, "and in a war zone, profiteers should be hung." With that, she turned her back on Donnelly. "Come Henry, we are leaving." She and Henry walked out the door and climbed up on her buckboard.

She shook her reins and clucked to the team. The wagon moved briskly through the crowded parade ground. As she was exiting the fort, a guard stopped her by grabbing the reins of her team. "Whoa, you can't be in that big of a hurry to lose that pretty head of hair," said the soldier.

Amelia, still outraged by her conversation with Donnelly, reached for her buggy whip. As she raised it to strike the soldier, she heard:

"Drop the reins, soldier, and get back to your post!"

The soldier saluted and hurriedly backed away from the wagon.

Amelia looked over. A lieutenant was standing beside her, flicking a polite salute. "Lieutenant Stanton Graham at your service, ma'am."

"Amelia Herbert Hampton, Lieutenant. Thank you."

Graham dropped his salute.

"Oh yes, ma'am, I know who you are. Everyone knows who you are," he said with a blush. "I consider it an honor to be of service, ma'am."

Amelia's carriage raised a cloud of dust as it rolled up the road adjacent to the Hampton Court plantation. On a small rise overlooking the grounds, Amelia pulled the horses to a stop. A stone memorial stood on a low hill near the roadside.

Henry got down to help Amelia alight. She took a few steps toward the monument, stopped and turned back to look at the view across to the house. Henry followed her gaze and looked back again at the monument. "So much has happened since he died," she said.

Henry took his hat off and nodded in agreement.

"Henry, when the time comes, I mean, when I leave here, what will you do? Will you go to Abraham in the south? Is that what you want?"

"I may have to," said Henry, ill at ease. He was not accustomed to having personal conversations with Amelia. He knew her to be a good woman, but still his words didn't come easily. "What we want and what we do, that's for the good Lord."

"You'll be free. That means you will have a choice," said Amelia, probing him further.

"Yes, Miss Amelia. You don't know what it means to us, you giving us our freedom. Seeing my family free in my lifetime."

"Well? Where will you go?" asked Amelia.

Henry said nothing for a moment. He looked at the monument, then back at the landscape. "In my heart, Miss Amelia?"

Amelia nodded.

"In my heart, it's wherever we have to go to live free, together as a family, all of us, my brothers and sisters and the children. Be good if it could be near here."

Amelia looked from Henry to the monument and back at Henry, who took it as his cue.

"And when we die, someone will know we were here. The general understood."

Amelia was surprised. She'd never heard Henry refer to her late husband. "Did he?" she asked.

"He knows you won't forget," said Henry.

"Or forget you, Henry," said Amelia. She shivered slightly and pulled her shawl tighter. "Let's go home please, Henry."

In the distance a cloud of dust indicated a large party of riders traveling fast. A group of Seminole warriors led by Billy Powell approached. Amelia and Henry quickly climbed aboard the buckboard and set off at a gallop for the gates to the house.

As the buckboard carrying Amelia passed some field hands, Henry called out to a young slave picking cotton. "Bring everyone in. Hurry!"

The boy saw the Indians coming and sprinted into the field, hollering for all of the slaves to come to the house.

Two hundred Seminole warriors, wearing war paint, led by Billy and Morning Dew, rode toward the plantation. At the gate, Billy raised his arm, then pointed along the stone wall. Most of the Seminole warriors dismounted and positioned themselves behind the wall, using it as cover against any possible army patrols. Then Billy led Morning Dew, followed by ten warriors, through the gate and up the red brick road. He halted before Amelia, who was standing on the steps at the entrance of her home.

Amelia stood proud. Henry stood next to her. Slaves had armed themselves with household and gardening instruments: axes, knives and staves. They surrounded Amelia, protecting her. They glared at the intruders. Ruth, exiting the house, pushed through the crowd to join Amelia and Henry.

Billy started to swing out of the saddle.

"I have not invited you to dismount," said Amelia, sounding ever so cool and firm.

Billy, one leg out of the stirrup, brought his leg back up and remounted. "Aye, how rude of me. Billy Powell, son of William Powell, late of the Ninth Regiment of Foot, son of Jasmine, great-grandson of Angus McQueen," he said, turning on the charm.

Amelia was astounded. "I have heard of you," she said, "but I didn't realize you were from Scotland."

"Nay," said Billy, "my dear departed father was."

Amelia looked at this band of Indians in a whole new light. She noticed Morning Dew. "And who is this beautiful maiden?"

"Morning Dew, my bride," said Billy proudly.

"She's lovely. Please, join me for tea," said Amelia, motioning toward the veranda.

Billy dismounted. He understood immediately why Abraham was taken with this woman. Ruth looked at Amelia as if she'd lost her mind, but she turned and went into the house. The warriors and the servants continued to confront one another in frozen silence.

Morning Dew had remained sitting stoically on her horse. Amelia's charms had not melted her resistance. "Both of you," Amelia said. Morning Dew looked at Billy, who nodded. Only then did she dismount.

Amelia, followed by her two visitors, took a seat at a table on the porch. Ruth returned from the house, set a service for three and put down a steeping teapot. Amelia poured the tea into Billy and Morning Dew's cups, then her own.

She turned to Billy. "Why have you come here?"

"I'm told you have quinine," said Billy.

Amelia was immediately concerned. Quinine meant the quinsy, a form of malaria. It also meant a slow, uncomfortable death, as quinine only fought a delaying action. "Who is it for?" asked Amelia

"Me," replied Billy, very matter-of-factly.

Amelia stared at him. Then, reassuringly, to Ruth she said, "Please bring the medicine chest."

As Ruth hurried off, Morning Dew picked up the teapot. She admired the matching design on the cups, then was careful to return it to its original position.

Amelia noticed, and asked, "You like it?"

Morning Dew nodded.

"Take it with you," offered Amelia.

Morning Dew shook her head.

"Consider it a wedding present." Refusing to take no for an answer, Amelia poured out the remaining tea and wrapped the pot in a cloth napkin from the table. She handed it to Morning Dew, who looked at Billy. He nodded in approval.

Ruth returned with the medicine box, and then retreated. Amelia opened the box, took out a bottle and handed it to Billy. He coughed, opened the bottle and took a swig. He recapped it and put it in his pocket.

There was nothing more to say. Morning Dew and Amelia nodded at one another. Billy and Morning Dew got up and walked down the steps, crossed to their horses and mounted.

"Thank you for your kindness," said Billy.

Amelia just smiled.

The contingent rode out of the gates. There they were joined by the remainder of Billy's army, and they proceeded to ride south. All was going as Billy had hoped. Yes, he needed quinine, but his plan, the reason he had brought his warriors out in broad daylight, was to entice the soldiers into chasing him.

Slowly, the slaves in front of the house dispersed. Amelia sat down on the porch. Ruth presented her with a small glass of brandy. Amelia sniffed it. "What a good idea," she said, thanking Ruth, then consumed the drink in one swallow.

Thirty minutes later forty cavalrymen, led by General Clinch, broke away from his main force of eight hundred militiamen and clattered up the driveway recently vacated by the Seminole.

"Miss Amelia, Miss Amelia!" called Duncan Clinch as he dismounted. "Miss Amelia!" he called again as he waddled up the steps of the house.

Amelia appeared. "General, is something amiss?" she asked, putting on a surprised look.

"We saw the savages. Are you all right?"

"As you see," said Amelia.

"Did they . . . ?" asked Clinch as he glanced around, puzzled. "Did they do any damage?"

"No," said Amelia.

"Did they take any slaves?" asked Clinch.

"No," said Amelia.

"Damn them. What did they want?" asked Clinch, frustration in his voice.

"I'm not sure," said Amelia. "One of them displayed particular interest in my crockery. Care to join me in a brandy?"

The general perked up at this suggestion. "Thank you, I believe I will."

Amelia handed the general the bottle of brandy and a glass. He quickly poured himself a drink and knocked it down.

He turned back to Amelia. "Miss Amelia, you were right when you said you don't belong out here. I can understand the attraction of Charleston. How much are you asking for your plantation?"

"Why, General, you do want my property," said Amelia. "To be fair to both of us, how about five times the bushel per acre return, plus five thousand for the house and barn."

Clinch was instantly reminded he could never get the best of Amelia Herbert Hampton. "And what does that come to?" asked Clinch, proceeding with caution.

"Fifty-five thousand, two hundred," answered Amelia, all business.

To the general the price sounded too good to be true. "That includes the slaves, of course."

"They are not included," said Amelia.

"You're taking them with you?" asked Clinch.

"What you do with your slaves is your business. My slaves are my business and in my care, just as they were my husband's," said Amelia, reminding Clinch that she was not to be trifled with.

"After all, General," said Amelia, batting her eyes at the potential buyer, "you'll have more than enough slaves when you recover all of those runaways."

"That I will," said Clinch. He had a broad smile on his face as he descended the stairs and rejoined the cavalry. A trooper put down a wooden step and gave Clinch a helping hand as the general stepped up onto his tall horse. Comfortable in the saddle, the general raised his right arm, and motioned for the troop to move out.

Clinch was jubilant. On the first day of the militia's march south, a band of Seminole, directly in front of him, was marking a clear path for his men to follow. There was only one thing bothering him. Why had they left Amelia's plantation alone? Was it that their former slave, Abraham, led the niggers? Perhaps one or more of her slaves were in league with them, giving them information. Clinch didn't imagine that Amelia herself might be involved with these insurrectionists.

Clinch ordered one of his sergeants to take twelve men and discreetly watch Hampton Court: the front, the back and the slave quarters. His orders were: "Notice who comes and goes, and if any nigger or Indian spies show up, capture them for questioning."

The army that Congressman Reilly helped fund through his emergency legislation gathered. Its mission was to avenge the murdered plantation owners, to enforce the treaty moving the Seminoles west, seize their lands, and to bring back any and all slaves.

On the first day heading south, the militia joined up with a force of seven hundred regular army soldiers led by Colonel Alexander Fanning and accompanied by General Jesup, the commander of the expedition. Together with twenty supply wagons the column was almost a half mile long. The general was pleased that their numbers were doubled. The band of Indians they were tracking was rumored to be five hundred strong.

From Fort King, Lieutenant Graham and his platoon were ordered to join up with the militia as it made its way south. In Graham's mind this was nothing more than a glorified slaving expedition and, as such, an affront to his sensibilities as a soldier.

When Graham's platoon joined the expedition, he found the soldiers singing the words to Francis Scott Key's poem, "The Star-Spangled Banner" to the tune of "Anacreon in Heaven," a popular barroom song. There was a joviality about the men that reminded Graham of soldiers on leave waiting their turn in a brothel. Having met and befriended their adversary, Billy Powell, Graham doubted the soldiers would be reveling for long.

At sunset, Graham stood supervising as his platoon dug latrines for the company. Three soldiers were putting up a tent for General Jesup when he motioned to Lieutenant Graham. Graham came over, saluted, and stood at attention in front of his commanding officer.

"Do you think you can find me a drink?" asked the general.

Graham was taken aback by the request. It seemed to Graham that half his waking hours were spent keeping his men from drinking. Of course, this was the commander. Graham looked at the general, who was preoccupied with his own thoughts. He saluted. When the general didn't return the salute, he left to fulfill the assignment.

Graham went to Private Charles Cobb, a man he knew was rarely without drink. Cobb was standing in the latrine pit digging while surreptitiously taking pulls on his flask. Graham ordered Cobb out of the hole. As Cobb stood rigid at attention, Graham took the flask from his back pocket. Without another word, Graham walked away.

"You can't take that, it's mine!" shouted Cobb.

Lieutenant Graham stopped in his tracks, turned and looked at him. "Seems to me you spent time on the log," said Graham, reminding Cobb of the price of drinking on duty. "Would you like to do so again?"

Cobb went back to digging the latrine without another word.

Graham returned to Jesup and stuck out the hand containing the flask. Jesup appreciated it with a salute, and then invited him to take a seat as he poured himself a drink. He needed one before conferring with his subordinates. Except for Colonel Fanning, he didn't have the slightest confidence in any of them.

He loathed the blustery General Duncan Clinch and, after seeing Major General Richard Call's Alabama militia, Jesup thought that Clinch might get his just deserts. He certainly couldn't count on General Rafael Hernandez or his Louisiana militia. He was a Spaniard leading a group of men who had only recently sworn allegiance to the United States. Only Colonel Alexander Fanning was a battle-tested veteran of the United States Army.

Jesup sensed this would be a hard campaign. Part of him was glad that he wouldn't be leading this army into battle. It was amateurish at best. The terrain was the ally of the enemy, unfamiliar and unforgiving. The foe would be determined, and who could blame them? Taking men back to slavery, stealing other men's land, it was a sour business. Jesup took a long pull on the drink.

Clinch and his fellow staff officers arrived while Jesup was in mid-swallow. Graham stood up, at attention. Jesup motioned for him to sit back down.

"You wanted to see us, General?" asked Clinch.

Jesup put down his drink. "Well, General," he said in an accusatory tone, "you wanted this war, you got it."

"And your idea, General?" answered Clinch in kind. "Give them land, let them farm, cede Florida, give the niggers a homeland? If you don't have the stomach to fight, resign your commission."

"I remind you, sir," said Jesup, indignantly, "you're addressing your superior and a general in the United States Army, not some political popinjay."

Jesup's words didn't bother Clinch. He was smug because he knew he would have the last laugh. His political influence in Washington had insured that.

Jesup took a minute to calm himself. Then he turned to his staff. "Gentlemen, these Seminoles must be brought to account. Persuade them, cajole them, bribe them. Take whatever steps you deem necessary to bring these proceedings to an early conclusion."

Jesup took another pull on the flask, emptying it. "General Hernandez," continued Jesup, "I want your cavalry to stay with the supply wagons. Those supplies must be protected at all costs." Jesup looked hard at the man until Hernandez saluted, signifying that he would obey.

"Where will you be, sir?" asked Colonel Fanning.

"Washington," answered General Jesup. "I've been recalled."

"Who will be in command, sir?" asked Fanning.

"General Clinch will be in overall command," said Jesup with much consternation.

"He's Georgia militia, sir," protested Colonel Fanning, "and—"

"I'm aware that he's Georgia militia," interrupted Jesup, "but those are my orders."

Congressman Reilly had maneuvered behind the scenes in Washington to make sure Clinch headed the expedition until General Zachary Taylor arrived with the regular army. Now, Clinch thought, the bleeding-heart Indian and nigger lovers wouldn't be able to interfere with what had to be done. Furthermore, Clinch would be in charge of all repatriated slaves, guaranteeing Reilly his share of the profits.

Clinch stood up and motioned with his hands for the banter to stop. "Relax, gentlemen," began Clinch in a very confident manner. "Rest assured, I will bring the savage to his knees in a most expeditious campaign. Then we will round up the niggers and go home."

On the second day of the march, insects in swarms descended on the men. It was as if a plague had set upon them. The men swatted with both hands, pulled their shirts up over their heads, waved their hats and cursed.

Late that afternoon it began to rain. First a drizzle, and then a downpour. The supply wagons became bogged down. Men who had been singing yesterday were standing ankle-deep in chilled water. It was a relief from the mosquitoes, but the prospect of sleeping on soaked ground was not appealing.

It rained all night. The army lost forty soldiers and militiamen to sickness, all suffering from the rot and various other conditions they contracted in the wet. Three of the twenty-eight supply wagons became stuck in the mud. Their wheels collapsed and the supplies of gunpowder were drenched and ruined.

Ahead of them, Billy waited. His scouts had broken branches off trees and hacked away growth so the army had a clearly marked trail to follow. His scouts told him the army was being commanded by the "fat general." Billy remembered him to be a coward. Billy also recognized by General Duncan Clinch's headlong pursuit that he was a very poor tactician. Billy was five moves ahead of him. Three more, and it was checkmate.

On the fifth day of the campaign the army's objective was to reach the Withlacoochee River. As yet no member of the army or its advance scouts had seen an Indian or escaped slave. What they had seen and followed was a clearly marked trail. They might not have been eager had they seen Wild Cat and five Seminole warriors marking the trail.

Clinch's map indicated that the main Seminole village was two miles south of the river. The trail they were following appeared to lead directly toward it. The late Wiley Thompson had sent a map by courier to the general. He'd procured it from an Indian he believed to be a member of Charlie Ematha's family, an enemy of Chief Osceola. Actually, the map had been drawn by Billy Powell and provided to Thompson by a member of Ematha's tribe who was fighting with him. Billy was making sure that his enemy would arrive on his preordained route.

"How far are we from the river?" Colonel Fanning asked the general.

"A half mile," said Clinch, looking up from consulting his map.

"Easy to ford, you say?" asked Fanning

"We'll hardly get our feet wet," assured Clinch.

Clinch was the only soldier mounted, so he wouldn't get his feet wet in any case, Fanning noticed. Realizing his cavalry would be useless in this terrain, Clinch had ordered his cavalry troopers to dismount and leave their horses with General Hernandez and his cavalry.

Fanning loathed Clinch. Having fought Indians on the western frontier, he'd been around commanders like Clinch. Mostly they got their men killed.

"March your men double-time to the river," ordered Clinch as he pointed south. Clinch was impatient to get on with the hostilities.

Fanning noticed, though, that the underbrush around the river was very thick, which would cause twisted ankles and cuts that could become infected. There was no reason to rush his soldiers through it. Then there was the distinct possibility of an ambush. No, he thought, he and his men would go forward one step at a time.

The half mile proved to be closer to two miles, and it took the army twenty-four hours to cover that distance. When they reached the Withlacoochee River, they found a twenty-yard-wide raging torrent. Clinch sat astride his horse and regarded it with dismay. His map indicated that it was a shallow riverbed. Behind him, his force of regulars and militia waited for orders.

"Shall we look for a crossing downriver, General?" asked Colonel Fanning.

"We'll cross here," the general decided abruptly. "They won't expect it."

Fanning was certain at that moment that Clinch had lost his mind. Then Clinch saw something and pointed. Fanning followed Clinch's gaze. Tied up on the opposite bank was a small boat.

"What luck," said Clinch. "God is on our side, Colonel."

"It might not be God's work, sir," said Fanning, who wasn't as sure. "It might be a trap set by the Indians."

Clinch looked at him with disdain, but it barely matched the contempt with which Fanning held Clinch. "You give them too much credit," said Clinch. "Send a volunteer to get the boat."

Fanning gave the order. Private Daniel Sagas of the Alabama militia came forward. He was a strong swimmer and proud of it.

Private Sagas stripped to the waist. Another soldier tied a rope around him while others pointed their rifles at the south bank to give him covering fire. He entered the water and swam across the fast-flowing current. His progress was slow and tortuous.

Sagas scrambled out of the water and examined the boat. It was big enough to carry eight men, but a bit battered. He climbed in, untied it from its mooring, took the rope from around his own body, secured it to a gunwale and waved. As his comrades on the north bank pulled the boat back across the river, Daniel bailed water with his hands.

Across the river Billy and Morning Dew, concealed well back from the south riverbank, watched the Americans on the north bank. Billy had covered every eventuality. His map indicated a shallow riverbed. When the rain came he knew he would need a boat.

"Maybe we should have left the boat on their side," suggested Morning Dew.

Billy shook his head. "A prize struggled for is a prize appreciated," said Billy, repeating a lesson his father had taught him years before.

Billy was not only five moves ahead of his adversary, he'd also planned and carried out his adversary's moves. His map, showing the "back way" to attack, was being followed. His father would be proud of him. Even though he was outnumbered as much as ten to one, or more, Billy was very confident. For one thing, sixty of his warriors had breech-loading rifles, which could fire three times as fast as the Americans' rifles, making his sixty men like one hundred eighty.

"Perhaps we should have left them a better boat," suggested Morning Dew.

"Why?" asked Billy.

"They may not use a boat that takes in water," said Morning Dew.

"Once the white man commits himself to a course of action, he finds it virtually impossible to change direction, especially this general," assured Billy.

"Perhaps all men are like that," suggested Morning Dew, not meaning to offend him.

Billy looked at her. "Am I like that?"

Morning Dew reassured Billy with a smile and a gentle hand on his shoulder.

"Abraham says that whites believe in their own superior judgment and invincibility. That's why they'll never negotiate with slaves. It puts them on their level," Billy said.

They moved away from their hiding place to inspect the trail they had left. It led to a hammock, a horseshoe-shaped open area with steep wooded sides. It was ideally suited for an ambush.

Hadjo and a dozen warriors from his tribe had cut a path through the tall grass for the soldiers to follow. It was here that Billy had decided to destroy the white army. They would be trapped without the possibility of reinforcements.

John Horse and forty Maroon scouts, as Abraham called them, arrived on horseback. Billy greeted them with a wave and a smile. He appreciated their support. Remembering Abraham's strategy, Billy detailed them to wait at the top of the hill out of sight of the advancing Americans. They would protect Billy's flank. He wouldn't use them in the coming battle unless absolutely necessary.

Hadjo made his way over to Billy. He could not bring himself to look at Morning Dew. At first it had been because he was repulsed by the rape. Now it was because he felt ashamed for not standing by her. Billy understood his discomfort.

"Take your warriors. Circle back to their supply wagons in the rear and destroy them," ordered Billy.

"I want to stay and kill white men," said Hadjo.

"It's more important that they not be able to keep fighting," said Billy.

"I will stay and kill white men, and then I will go," said Hadjo. Billy couldn't convince him to go. His alliance was a delicate one.

————

By mid-morning fifteen boatloads of soldiers had crossed the river. As the sixteenth made its way across, the soldiers, among them Colonel Fanning, bailed as they paddled. The boat reached the bank. They waded ashore, joining the 120-odd soldiers hiding behind whatever cover they could find.

Fanning couldn't see them, but he knew the Indians were there. He expected to be overwhelmed momentarily. Not wanting to infect his men with fear, he told them, "Keep a sharp eye."

Billy and Morning Dew watched the soldiers on the riverbank.

"How long?" asked Morning Dew.

"Soon," said Billy.

As the next boatload made its way across, Clinch spurred his horse and plunged him into the river, swimming alongside. The seventeen-hand gelding found it easier to carry the general in the water, and swam strongly toward the opposite bank. Dripping water, horse and rider emerged from the river. Clinch saw the soldiers and their commander. It looked to him as if his army was cowering.

"Colonel Fanning!" barked General Clinch, pointing at the soldiers. "I demand that these men form a column and move off in the direction of the Indians."

Fanning didn't move, and taking his cue, neither did any of his men.

"Hurry, before we lose the element of surprise," implored Clinch.

This comment earned him only a cynical stare from the combat-tested veteran. "Shouldn't we wait for the rest of the company?" suggested Fanning, looking up at the general from his hiding place.

"No," Clinch shouted. "We must move. . . . Move out!"

The soldiers slowly rose to their feet. They malingered and bunched up beside the trail. Nobody wanted to go first and be a target. General Clinch, the only man mounted, conspicuously brought up the rear. Colonel Fanning was a few paces ahead of him.

Lieutenant Graham emerged from the next boatload and ran up. "General Clinch," he cried, trying to get the general's attention.

"What?" said Clinch, very annoyed at Fanning's insubordination. "The Alabama militia isn't crossing, sir," said Graham.

Clinch turned and looked at him for the first time. "Why not?" he asked.

"They've stacked their arms, sir," explained Graham.

"Colonel Fanning!" bellowed the general.

"What is it, General? Have we lost the element of surprise?" asked Fanning insultingly.

The insult went over Clinch's head as he answered, "Call's not crossing."

Clinch turned back to Lieutenant Graham. "Go back there and tell him it's an order. If he doesn't obey it, he and his entire militia will be court-martialed!"

"Yes, sir," said Graham. He sprinted to the river, got into the empty boat and rowed it back across.

Clinch again gave the order to move out. He spurred his horse forward. Directly in front of him, Sergeant Paisley's platoon was huddled behind tree stumps, fallen logs and their own backpacks.

"You there, Sergeant—get those men moving or I'll take your stripes," threatened Clinch. Sergeant Paisley reluctantly rose and urged his platoon to move forward. Buck private Charles Webb was the last man to rise.

Seminole warriors waited for the signal to attack. Each of the two hundred men marked one of the soldiers in his rifle sights. Billy had hoped to be able to lure at least three hundred soldiers across the river before he gave the signal. However, the white army was moving at such a snail's pace that Billy decided to go with his alternate plan. He would destroy these soldiers and then, when the army approached again, he'd withdraw, circle around the body of the army and attack them while they were retreating to replenish their destroyed supplies.

Graham pulled himself the last few yards across the river, jumped out of the boat, splashed up the bank and ran toward General Richard Call. "The general is waiting for you to cross," said Graham between deep breaths.

Call was sitting on a log smoking a cigar. All around him his men were sprawled on the ground. Some were smoking, some were drinking from bottles and flasks. They had stacked their rifles in a dozen places.

"That's impossible," explained Call. He motioned for Graham to look at his men. "These men signed on for ten weeks. Their tour of duty expires at midnight. By the time I get all my men across, it'll be dark. I'd just have to ferry them all the way back again," explained Call.

"It's an order, sir, backed by the threat of court-martial!" said Graham.

Across the river Sergeant Paisley was doing his best to drive his men forward. "Get moving, you miserable bunch of dog shit," barked Paisley.

Reluctantly they moved forward. "I said move," he shouted, and the soldiers picked up the pace. They looked from side to side and up into the trees, expecting the worst, each soldier hoping he'd be able to dive for cover.

First Billy heard the voice and, recognizing it, he spotted the stout sergeant bullying his men forward. Here was the man who had beaten him unconscious. He was an easy target, and Billy marked him. From behind every tree and rock a rifle-wielding Seminole marked a target in the meadow below.

Billy fired the first shot, sending a bullet into Paisley's stomach. Paisley dropped his weapon and fell to his knees, clutching the wound. Paisley could languish for days before succumbing. There was no reprieve.

Following Billy's lead, the rest of the Seminole poured a deadly fire into the slowly advancing soldiers from two sides. Forty-one fell dead from the first volley, and thirty more were wounded. Charles Webb threw himself down at the first sound of gunfire. He lay there completely still as soldiers screamed and fell all around him.

Clinch's horse reared, and the three bullets aimed at the general struck the gelding. Miraculously the fat general was able to escape injury as the horse fell. He found himself on the ground with bullets peppering the ground around him as he huddled behind his dead horse. The withering fire from the Seminoles continued down on the exposed, defenseless army. There was no cover except behind dead or dying comrades.

Across the river, Graham heard the firing. "Sir, I beg you," he said, imploring General Call.

"If they need to fall back to the river, we'll give them covering fire," conceded Call.

Graham didn't waste any more words. He turned, ran back to the river, dove in and swam. When he sloshed out of the river, the sound of gunfire was loud and continuous. He hurried toward the path.

When Graham reached the hammock, he was taken aback by the number of dead and dying troops. The few unscathed soldiers fired blindly at the unseen Seminoles.

Clinch remained cowering behind his fallen horse. Fanning and Graham crawled over to him on their stomachs.

"General, we must retreat," implored Colonel Fanning.

He looked at Graham, soaking wet, lying flat against the ground behind him and asked, "Where's Call?"

"Guarding the north bank, sir," said Graham.

"Against what?" screamed Clinch.

Bullets continued to rain down from the Seminole positions. A ball struck Graham in the arm, just below his shoulder. "Damn it!" cursed Graham under his breath. He put his hand over the wound to stop the bleeding and assess the damage. He was glad to feel that the bone wasn't broken. Lying on his back, he wrapped a cloth around the wound using his opposite hand, then pulled it tight with his teeth.

Colonel Fanning saw his lieutenant whirling away from the shot. "We can't remain in this position, General," he shouted.

"Battles aren't won by retreating," snorted Clinch.

"Then I suggest we redeploy to the river, sir," said Colonel Fanning.

Bullets continued to pepper the ground around the general's dead horse.

In the trees above the hammock, Billy moved back and forth among his warriors, encouraging them, praising them, instructing them. "Mark your targets," he shouted. "Don't waste bullets."

The few surviving soldiers were doing their best to stay down and out of sight, or they were feigning death so as not to be shot at. The Seminoles were waiting. When someone moved, twenty rifles would fire in that direction. Hadjo and his fifteen followers moved along the ridge toward the river. They positioned themselves so that they had a clear shot at anyone seeking cover on the river's edge, or arriving or leaving on a raft.

"Sound the recall," shouted Clinch. The bugler lying a few yards ahead of the general put the horn to his lips and, without rising off his back, blew the command. Ten soldiers abandoned their weapons and raced toward the river, leaving scores of their wounded companions who were screaming and begging not to be left behind.

The ten soldiers ran right into Hadjo and his followers' line of fire. Hadjo smiled as the easy targets came into view. He fired and his men followed suit. Four of the soldiers dropped, hit by multiple bullets. The six survivors, including Charles Webb, reached the river and jumped in, then crawled up against the bank for cover. None of the six men could swim, or they would have continued across the river to safety. Pressed against the bank, the men were terrified at their prospects: either be eaten by the alligators inhabiting the river, or shot by the Seminole controlling the land.

Billy led a dozen warriors and they joined Hadjo. "Our mission rests with you," said Billy. "Take your men and destroy their supplies and we've got them. Take no unnecessary risks. We can't afford to lose even one warrior."

"I want to stay here and kill the whites as they cross the river," said Hadjo.

"You're my best warrior," said Billy. "I know that with you in charge, it will be done." Hadjo looked at Billy and saw that he was sincere in his remark.

"To the horses, men," ordered Hadjo, and fifteen of his followers withdrew to the place where their steeds were tethered.

Standing by their own horses were John Horse and the forty Maroon scouts. They had watched the killing from above and wished they could join in. John Horse assured them their opportunity would come soon enough.

Hadjo and his raiding party mounted and rode parallel to the river for three miles upstream. There they found a shallow crossing just before a small waterfall. They plunged their horses in and walked the animals across the shoulder-deep river. Once across, they made their way north through the thick forest.

On the north bank of the river, Major General Richard Call ordered his men to set to work. He supervised the construction of a huge raft, which was quickly improvised from the surrounding trees. It took less than three hours to complete. Then twenty soldiers carried it to the north bank and deposited it into the river with a splash. General Call leapt aboard.

"Who's with me, boys?" hollered Call. Forty men came forward, but the raft had standing room for only twenty. The nearest twenty joined Call and scrambled aboard. They poled themselves across the river.

The raft beached on the south bank. The first one out of the raft was Daniel Sagas. He took three steps before he noticed the other soldiers cowering behind the bank. Two Seminole marked him and fired. Lying there in the high grass Daniel wasn't sure how he got there. He heard the screams and moans of men around him. He heard an officer say, "This one's dead." He knew they were talking about him. He tried to say he wasn't dead, but couldn't speak.

He remembered the poster. *Alabama Militia mobilizing to march into Florida, $10 a month plus a share in any niggers captured and sold at auction.*

At the riverbank the surviving soldiers were spread out, lying flat, as there was very little cover. Mosquitoes swarmed around everyone. The men feared moving in order to swat them. A few of the soldiers cursed under their breath.

"General Clinch," shouted General Call from his position, squatting behind one of the few logs.

"You are a day late, sir!"

"They might have attacked our rear," retorted Call.

"You stayed there because you and your militia operate on a farmer's almanac," bellowed back Clinch.

"Your remarks, sir, excite my mirth," retorted Call at the top of his lungs.

Clinch and Call glared in each other's direction, though neither could see the other's face.

The moans and screams of the wounded pleading for help were the background noise to the generals' repartee.

Lieutenant Graham crawled over to Clinch. "Sir, the men. We must do something," urged Graham.

For the first time Clinch became aware of the chorus of moans and cries coming from his exposed wounded. "What do you suggest, Lieutenant?" asked the general.

"Ask for terms," said Graham.

"I will not," barked Clinch. Then he adjusted his tone and asked, "What are our alternatives, Lieutenant?"

"The wounded will all die. They'll kill us or wait for us to starve or die from the fever."

———

It was late afternoon when Graham waved a white flag of truce from his position behind a log. When he was sure the Indian marksmen saw it, he stood up holding it. Then he slowly advanced into the hammock. He walked past the dead and dying soldiers.

He called out, "Osceola! Osceola!" No less then forty Seminole had Graham in their sights. Wild Cat recognized the lieutenant and told those around him not to fire.

Billy walked down the sloping tree-lined rise toward Graham. They met at the bottom of the hill. It had begun to drizzle. Graham's arm was bound and in a sling. The two men smiled wistfully at each other.

"How is Morning Dew?" Graham inquired.

"Lovely as a summer's day," answered Billy.

"Will you allow us to bury our dead and tend to our wounded?" asked Graham.

"That depends," said Billy. "What do we get?"

"Peace," answered Graham.

"Peace?" questioned Billy.

"I've been instructed to ask you for terms and end the war. Will you sit down with the generals and discuss terms?" asked Graham.

Billy was elated but kept his face blank. "Throw your weapons in the river," ordered Billy.

"The general won't do that," protested Graham. "Your men could walk down and slaughter us."

Billy raised his eyebrows and looked at Graham. "We could do that now."

"Yes, you could," said Graham. "Agreed, no arms on this side of the river."

"Care for your wounded. Bury your dead," answered Billy. "We'll meet tomorrow morning where you're pinned down."

As Billy walked back toward his men, scattered cheers rang out among the victorious Seminole.

"Ho to Chief Osceola," shouted Wild Cat, encouraging the others to join in the praise. Soon all the Seminoles chanted in unison, "Osceola! Osceola!"

Billy walked to the center of the battlefield. He stood proud over the legion of dead and dying American soldiers. The thunderous cheers rang down from the woods above the hammock. He basked in the adulation.

Billy walked up the hill to where Morning Dew stood. He drew her to him. "This is the happiest day of my life, and all because of you."

"You are a true Seminole leader," said Morning Dew. They hugged.

As darkness fell, Hadjo and his followers exited the forest. To the east they could see the glow from the fires of Hernandez's cavalry and the supply wagons. It was an overcast night. The thick clouds prevented the moon from illuminating the area at all. When they were close, they took cover in the pitch black and waited.

At four A.M., fifteen warriors gathered three hundred yards north of the supply wagons. General Hernandez had concentrated his pickets a hundred yards in front of the wagons, but only to the south. He reasoned that any incursions would come from where the fighting was concentrated.

One warrior stayed behind to hold all of the horses. The other fourteen crawled closer. Each was armed with a bow and five arrows wrapped with kerosene-treated cotton. The wagons were bunched together in a semicircle of six wagons, three deep, for protection.

At twenty yards, the Seminole were within easy bowshot of the wagons. Hadjo signaled by striking the flint against the steel of his tinderbox, lighting a flame to his arrow. Simultaneously each warrior lit a flame to their arrows and shot them into the supply wagons. Within a minute each of the Indians had fired all five arrows.

First came shouts and screams from the soldiers sleeping in and underneath the wagons, who awakened to find themselves engulfed in flames. Within a few minutes the wagons were fifteen skeletons contributing to a raging inferno. Shots rang out but the sentries were firing blindly into the night. General Hernandez arrived and ran between the wagons, shouting for his men to douse them with water. By the time a water brigade was organized, however, it was too late. The army had lost its entire supply of fresh food, water and ammunition.

Hadjo and his warriors had already mounted and were riding west when they heard three huge explosions as powder kegs detonated. Hadjo was pleased. He'd carried out his assignment exactly as it was planned. None of his warriors received even a scratch, and hearing their screams, he imagined that many white soldiers had died. They circled back into the forest and headed south.

The other Seminole slept lying in among the trees. Billy, though, had the sweats again. First he felt chilled, and then he felt hot. In the midst of a fitful sleep, he dreamed of Chief William MacIntosh. He saw the chief sitting with his white friends, the governor of Georgia and the fat general. He saw the chief sign a document. As he signed, he saw the chief plunge his own knife into his heart. As blood spurted out, Billy watched helplessly. Finally he was able to scream.

Morning Dew was startled by Billy's frightened wail.

"You're fine now. I'm here," soothed Morning Dew as she hugged him. Billy was disoriented and in a cold sweat.

"You had a bad dream," explained Morning Dew. "Billy, promise me after the surrender you will go to John the Baptist and get healed."

"I promise," said Billy without further protest. He reached into his pouch for the quinine and drank the remainder, then threw the bottle aside. Needing to speak, he turned back to Morning Dew.

"My adopted father, Chief MacIntosh, was tricked into giving what remained of the tribe's land to the fat general."

Morning Dew snuggled closer and hugged Billy. "That's when you left?" asked Morning Dew.

"No, not then," said Billy. "I was accused by John MacIntosh of killing his father, which was absurd. None of the tribe believed that."

"So what happened?" inquired Morning Dew.

"It was the day I won my wool shirt and leggings," said Billy proudly. "A trading post on wheels came through the village. I noticed a carved chess set among the wares. The proprietor let me know right off it wasn't for sale. He asked, 'What would a half-breed do with it?'

"I told him, 'I can learn to play,'" said Billy. "'And then I can play with you.'"

"But you knew how to play," said Morning Dew naively. "You told me your father taught you."

Billy just stared at her, waiting for her to figure out that he had been baiting the man.

"Oh, I see," said Morning Dew.

"The man couldn't believe I could learn, let alone best him. White man's arrogance," explained Billy. "'Show me what the pieces do and I'll play with you,' is what I said.

"'What would we play for?' he asked me.

"I pointed to this wool shirt and a pair of buckskin leggings.

"'They're very expensive. What will you put up?' he asked. He was licking his lips at the prospect.

"'My mother's musket,' I said."

"Billy, it wasn't yours," scolded Morning Dew.

"He knew the musket was worth many times the shirt. I imagined my father was watching. In only ten moves the man was mated." Billy smiled as he described his triumph.

"I was wearing my new outfit when I stopped and took a last look at the ruins of the cabin my father built. I was reflecting on him and thanking him for the skill that allowed me this victory. I didn't notice John MacIntosh, Little Crow and Ned Smith until I heard, 'White dog!' "

Remembering the insult, the fight that followed and, most importantly, how his mother risked her life on his behalf, Billy told Morning Dew the whole story of how he came to leave the tribe. His mother's gift to him of his father's tunic, the last remnant of her marriage, touched her heart. Billy's anger at his treatment by MacIntosh, Little Crow and the others had truly taken second place to the preservation of the tunic.

It was almost dawn when Billy finished his story.

"Are you going to make peace with the fat general that degraded me and tricked Chief MacIntosh?" asked Morning Dew.

"There was bad blood on both sides," answered Billy.

"Now you sound like my father," said Morning Dew.

Billy thought about what she said. He did sound like Micanopy. Had he come full circle?

"I wish my mother was here," said Billy, abruptly changing the subject. "It would be a glorious moment for her, meeting you, seeing this," he said as he allowed himself the luxury of that daydream.

"Suppose something happens to you?" asked Morning Dew, bringing Billy back to the moment.

"What, me love?" answered Billy as he drew her close to him.

"Suppose they kill you," said Morning Dew.

"Kill me?" repeated Billy. "They've surrendered."

"Please, don't go alone," implored Morning Dew. She helped Billy out of his father's tunic.

"What are you doing?" asked Billy.

"We can't have the conquering hero looking ragged," said Morning Dew. She took out a needle and thread, and began repairing Billy's buttons.

"How long have you had that?" asked Billy.

"Can't a girl have any secrets?" asked Morning Dew as she smiled at him. Then she took a cloth and polished the buttons. Billy just sat there transfixed, watching her. When she was finished, she held up the coat for his approval.

Then they heard the three faint explosions. Billy knew it meant Hadjo was successful. He kissed Morning Dew and under their blanket they fell into lovemaking.

8

Looking down from the trees on both sides of the killing field, the Seminole watched as soldiers carried out the last of the wounded and laid out the dead for burial. Then the soldiers stacked their rifles in piles. Private Charles Webb stood there holding a large white cloth attached to a wooden stick. He waved it every few minutes, as if to remind the Indians not to kill him. The warriors kept their rifles trained on the soldiers.

At the top of the rise Hadjo stood with his followers, arguing with Billy Powell.

"They can't defend themselves. Their supplies are gone. Kill them all," said Hadjo. "Look at them down there, helpless. You think they wouldn't shoot us if the situation were reversed?" asked Hadjo.

"That's a flag of truce," reminded Billy, pointing at Charles Webb. "Abraham says we need the support of the American people. If we dishonor the truce there may never be peace. We have an opportunity to end it," explained Billy. "Yes, we're at their throats, and now we can dictate terms."

"You can't talk to white men," reminded Hadjo. "They only understand killing."

"Kill them," shouted the warriors behind Hadjo.

"We can only win a negotiated peace," said Billy, doing his best to explain his understanding of the situation.

"My people will have no part of this," answered Hadjo.

"If we make peace, and you keep killing, it will cause the war to continue," said Billy.

"Are the whites going to leave our land?" asked Hadjo rhetorically. Before Billy could answer, Hadjo said, "No."

"Those will be the terms for peace," said Billy.

"Regardless of what they promise, they will never leave," said Hadjo, "and we will keep killing white men." Hearing his words, his followers again shouted, "Kill the white men."

"That is your choice," said Billy, realizing he wasn't getting anywhere.

"You're a fool," said Hadjo, looking at Billy. With that, Hadjo and his followers stormed off.

With the sun high in the sky, Billy donned his father's sewn and polished coat, preparing to go down the hill and meet the American generals. He took Morning Dew's advice and invited all of the warriors to share in their triumph. Wild Cat and seventy-eight others accepted. The remainder of the Seminole were of a mind like Hadjo. They didn't trust the white man and wanted no part of any peace discussions.

Morning Dew stood to the side, and Billy walked over to her. He didn't want to go with her unhappy.

"Please, wait for Abraham to return," begged Morning Dew.

"He may not return for many days," said Billy.

"Then I'll go with you," Morning Dew demanded.

"No," said Billy, equally adamant. "The whites are provoked by dark skin."

Beyond the river, General Hernandez was upset. His sole mission had been to protect the supplies, and there in front of him were the still-smoldering burned-out shells of eighteen supply wagons. Miraculously, though several were severely burned, none of his men were killed, but neither were any of the Indians. No doubt, Hernandez thought, his superiors would think he didn't put up a fight.

Sitting on a chair assessing his possibilities, Hernandez gave a thought to taking his men and clearing out, heading back to Louisiana, rather than face his failings. That's when he saw the reinforcements on the horizon.

What he saw were two thousand regular army soldiers commanded by General Zachary Taylor, and led by a group of ten Creek and Osage Indian mercenaries. Taylor was recognizable by his protruding nose, which rivaled that of President Andrew Jackson, his signature white straw hat, and the old work overalls that he insisted on wearing. He had an aversion to uniforms.

General Taylor's resemblance to Jackson ended with the nose. Though both were generals, Taylor was a squat man with legs so short he needed to step up onto a wooden box carried by his aide in order to mount his horse, whereas Jackson was a tall, striking figure of a man. Though both Southerners, Taylor had northern sensibilities. He was adamantly opposed to the spread of slavery. Incongruously, he'd been put in command of this slaving expedition.

The chief scout was an Osage Indian named Tracks on the Moon. He had the reputation of being able to track any man or beast over any terrain. With him were Ned Smith and John MacIntosh. Times had been hard in Arkansas, and like many reservation Indians, they had jumped at the chance to scout for the U.S. Army. They felt no kinship to other tribes. When they were informed it was the infamous Billy Powell they were tracking, they relished the idea.

While General Hernandez was explaining to General Taylor how he'd lost the supplies, Tracks on the Moon noticed the trail left by Hadjo and his raiding party. Hernandez had no way of seeing, let alone following, the trail of Hadjo and his raiders. But there it was, plain as the sun in the sky for the Osage mercenary. Tracks on the Moon walked his horse a hundred yards to the west while looking down at the ground. He called out, and the other Indians joined him. He pointed out the tracks.

Saluting his senior, Hernandez asked, "General, can I borrow your scouts? They've picked up the trail of the raiders." General Taylor agreed to lend three of his scouts.

"Mount up," shouted Hernandez to his two hundred troopers. He had no thought of desertion now. The reinforcements had arrived with more supplies, and he was fresh on the trail of the bandits. Hernandez knew the Seminole would not be expecting him to follow. His two hundred militiamen, led by the three Indians, began following the trail.

Billy walked down the hill, followed by Wild Cat and the warriors. They made their way to the riverbank. The unarmed soldiers stared as their well-dressed adversaries strolled proudly into their encampment.

Wild Cat and the warriors stood to one side, forming a semicircle behind Billy. Each had a rifle at his side.

Billy sat down opposite Generals Call and Clinch, Lieutenant Graham and Colonel Fanning. Between them was a crude table made of the remains of the raft. It was covered by a cloth.

"Chief," said General Call, "my men are unarmed and yours are standing here with arms bristling. Would you have your warriors lay down their arms while we talk? My men fear yours will open fire."

Billy looked at the unarmed soldiers sitting on the riverbank behind the generals. He turned and motioned for his men to lay their rifles down on the ground beside them. They did so reluctantly, not trusting the white men. Then Billy turned back to his adversaries and began the negotiations.

General Clinch held up his hand and pointed at Billy. "Before we begin, I just want to say for the record that I knew this young man for twenty years. He is fair-minded and principled."

Billy was surprised by the compliment, but knew the fat general to be a dangerous, deceitful adversary.

"Withdraw your troops from Florida, and give me guarantees that you won't come back, and the war will be over," said Billy.

"We paid for this land," said General Call, interjecting.

"You stole the land," said Billy.

"Your Chiefs agreed," said Call.

"What choice did they have?" asked Billy.

"While we're discussing broken agreements," answered Clinch, "let me remind you a pledge was given to return our slaves."

"We don't recognize slavery. Any man, woman or child residing in Florida is free," announced Billy.

"Florida is part of the United States," answered Clinch with a decided emphasis on the first syllable, "and a slave state. You are stepping way beyond your authority. Dictating terms to the United States of America. Well I never—"

"My authority," interrupted Billy indignantly. "Don't push your luck, Clinch. It's through my authority that all of you are still living." Billy realized then that there was no dealing with General Clinch. Hadjo was right. The only thing he understood was killing.

Suddenly Wild Cat saw Hernandez's cavalry approaching. "Osceola, Osceola, look!" he called out.

Billy looked in time to notice the cavalry. They rode in past graves being dug and wounded being tended to, and stopped in front of the table where the parlay was in progress.

Billy looked at the Indian scouts leading them. They were

adorned in Creek markings. As Billy stared, it came to him. John MacIntosh was riding with the American cavalry. Dread came over Billy as he looked up at his old nemesis.

Hernandez dismounted, drew his pistol, and pointed it at Billy. "Powell, known as Osceola, Chief of the Seminole Nation, I am placing you under arrest." His two hundred soldiers drew their weapons and surrounded the Seminole warriors behind Billy with cocked rifles.

Billy didn't move. His men, with their rifles lying on the ground, were helpless. There was a moment of frozen silence.

"General?" said Colonel Fanning, questioning the order.

"Sir, they're here under a white flag," said Lieutenant Graham as he rose and approached the general.

"Silence," demanded General Hernandez. Looking at the soldiers under Clinch's command, Hernandez ordered, "Pick up their weapons."

"Nobody move," said Colonel Fanning, countermanding the order.

Hernandez swung his pistol around and aimed it at Fanning. "If you don't obey my order, I'll shoot you," he said. Then reiterating his order, he said, "Place these Indians under arrest."

"Nobody move. These men are under my protection," said Lieutenant Graham.

"I am a general, Lieutenant," said Hernandez. "My orders will be carried out, or my men will kill all of you."

Colonel Fanning turned his back on the general, walked down by the river and sat down, feeling disgusted.

"You dishonor every American soldier, General, by this treachery," said Graham, looking at Hernandez.

"One more word from you, Lieutenant, and you'll find yourself under arrest. Either you do your duty or face a field court-martial and a firing squad."

The soldiers still hesitated, however, knowing this was wrong.

Finally Clinch rose from the table. He walked over to Hernandez, stuck out his arm and shook Hernandez's hand.

"Well done, General!" said Clinch, congratulating him. "You've executed a brilliant maneuver, and I will see that you are amply rewarded."

Hernandez saluted Clinch. "Thank you, sir." Hernandez had gone from goat, losing all the supplies entrusted in his care, to hero. He'd captured the enemy and effectively ended the resistance. He sat on his steed, upright and proud.

Billy turned to Wild Cat. "I'm sorry. I failed you," said Billy, uttering his first words since his capture softly, almost under his breath.

"No," said Wild Cat, "you did not fail us. The white men lied, as they always do."

Fanning's soldiers collected the weapons. As soldiers put chains on Billy's arms and legs, he gazed up at MacIntosh. "Are ye proud, betraying your own kind for this scum?" baited Billy. "I guess the apple doesn't fall far from the tree, does it, John?"

John MacIntosh stared stonily at Billy. This was too much for him to take. He climbed down from his horse, and as he stepped toward Billy, he unsheathed his knife.

Billy braced himself for the attack. Though shackled, he lifted his arms and the chain that ran between them. Approaching Billy, MacIntosh held up the knife for Billy to see the instrument of his death. John MacIntosh smiled as he drew his arm back to plunge it into Billy's midsection.

Wild Cat grabbed hold of MacIntosh's arm as he brought it forward. The two men stood face-to-face, Wild Cat holding MacIntosh's knife arm with his own left hand, MacIntosh holding Wild Cat's right arm with his left. Each held the other's arm in a desperate test of strength for control of the knife.

The other Seminole took a step toward the nearest soldier. Lieutenant Graham fired a shot in the air to prevent what he believed would become a massacre of his now unarmed adversaries.

The soldiers trained their rifles on the Indians. Everyone froze but Wild Cat and John MacIntosh, whose desperate contest continued. There was an eerie silence as the two men fell to the ground locked in their dire embrace. They rolled over, MacIntosh landing on top, Wild Cat still grasping MacIntosh's knife arm. As MacIntosh pushed it down, close to Wild Cat's throat, Wild Cat brought his right leg up and over MacIntosh's head, flipping him off and over backward. Wild Cat leapt to his feet.

MacIntosh was disoriented. Looking first to his left, then to his right, he was greeted by Wild Cat's hard kick under his chin. MacIntosh staggered three steps backward from the blow, but held on to the knife. Wild Cat pressed his attack. Grasping MacIntosh's arm, he pushed it back, then brought it forward hard, plunging the knife into MacIntosh's lower back. The two men's eyes were less than an inch apart as Wild Cat twisted his adversary's arm, causing the knife to rupture organs and arteries. As MacIntosh's strength dissipated, Wild Cat released his grip, allowing John MacIntosh to fall to the ground and roll over in his final death throes.

Wild Cat stood there, exhausted. Tracks on the Moon had watched the events but did nothing other than turn his horse around and trot off. He'd had little use for the man. He wasn't a particularly good tracker, and Moon found him to be even worse company.

Ned Smith, though, took his rifle and aimed it at Wild Cat. Lieutenant Graham stepped in between Wild Cat and Ned Smith's line of fire.

"Hang him," ordered General Clinch.

"No," shouted Lieutenant Graham. "This man is a prisoner of war. He was defending himself. You can't hang him without a trial."

"Hang him!" said General Hernandez, reiterating his superior's order.

"These are prisoners, sir," said Graham.

"Sir, can I take my cavalry and round up the niggers, sir?" asked Hernandez.

"You say General Taylor has arrived with his army?"

"Yes sir, only twenty miles north of here," said Hernandez. "Because of the terrain, they can't bring the supply wagons any closer."

"Very well, take these prisoners to St. Augustine," ordered Clinch.

Hernandez's expression faded to disappointment, and Clinch saw this. "General, I have a very important mission for you. I want you to chair a military court and hang them all," ordered Clinch. "Then you can join Taylor's army. We'll come back with numbers and round up every nigger in Florida."

"Yes, sir," said Hernandez. He saluted General Clinch and turned smartly on his heel.

As Hernandez strode away, Lieutenant Graham stood beside Colonel Fanning. "Whichever way you look at it, it's treachery," said Graham. "Jesup gave the orders. He made it plain he didn't give a damn."

"Hernandez wanted to show what a loyal American he is and make up for his blunder," said Colonel Fanning.

"I blame Jesup," said Graham. "I hope he has to answer for this."

"Lieutenant Graham," said Clinch, "you need a lesson in obeying orders. You and your men are now assigned to General Taylor."

Soon General Hernandez and his army were moving east. In their midst were the captured Seminoles, roped together by the neck. Only Chief Osceola was shackled with chains. Hernandez was taking no chances that his prize captive might escape.

9

Amelia Hampton had decided to spend her Sunday going through her enormous wardrobe and culling out-of-fashion outfits that she would have no use for in Charleston.

She sat in her bedroom on a straight-backed dressing chair, one she often used to apply the final touches of her makeup. Scattered on the bed in front of her were dozens of her dresses and various skirts and blouses. Amelia was supervising as Ruth and Mandy, a sixteen-year-old house slave, took her clothes from the closets. Amelia intended to give her slaves the clothes that she no longer wanted.

"No, no, that is the pile for keeping," instructed Amelia, pointing to a formal outfit that she still planned on wearing in Charleston. "I hardly think you would have use for a ball gown!" Still, the younger girl ran her hands over the silk dress. She'd never felt anything like it.

Outside, Clinch's soldiers watching Amelia's plantation saw what looked to them like a horde of armed niggers approaching on horseback. They scrambled to their mounts and rode hard toward Auld Lang Syne, concerned only that the niggers didn't see and pursue them. Abraham was hiding directly in the path of the fleeing soldiers. He was forced to wait until they were out of sight.

Alabama Jim's cavalry, its ranks swollen to half again as large with freed slaves and horses liberated on their crusade north, resembled an angry mob. He led them through the front gates of Hampton Court. They went directly to the stables. Jim pointed and a group of his Maroon soldiers led the horses from the barn, then set it on fire.

Next they went to the slave quarters. Amelia gave the slaves Sunday off, so most were relaxing in and around their quarters. Alabama Jim watched as his men drove the slaves out of their huts, then set the huts on fire. All the while they cried, "You're free. You're free." Instead of embracing their liberators, Amelia's slaves ran from them in terror.

Inside Amelia's bedroom, the giggling stopped when the cries were heard. Amelia went to the window and saw a plume of smoke rising into the air. "The stables!" she screamed. Ruth and Mandy rushed first to the window, and then followed Amelia downstairs, squealing in frightened excitement.

Amelia came onto the veranda and found Henry already there. Other slaves gathered nearby. Alabama Jim, followed by his troops, rode up and dismounted with a harsh scowl. Amelia remained outwardly calm as she looked down at Alabama Jim. "You have no quarrel here," she said.

Alabama Jim laughed savagely. "No quarrel! You hear that? We have no quarrel!" he boomed in his most theatrical manner, playing for his troops. "The woman is right," he continued darkly. "When we leave here, there will be nothing left to quarrel about."

Jim walked up the steps and stopped in front of Amelia. He stroked the side of her face and ran his fingers through her hair.

Amelia slapped him hard across the face. Without hesitating Alabama Jim struck Amelia with the back of his hand. The force of the blow knocked her down.

Henry picked up a rake and swung it. Jim deflected the blow, then struck with his tomahawk at the side of Henry's neck, sending blood gushing out of an opened artery, which killed him instantly.

Amelia's slaves were all stunned. Henry, the father figure to every slave at Hampton Court, lay on the veranda in a pool of his own blood. Amelia crawled over and cuddled his broken body. She instantly was bathed in his blood. Ruth looked down at her husband, and shrieked in pain.

"Destroy this place. Burn it!" Alabama Jim commanded his followers. He watched as the Maroons ran about, shouting as they began looting Hampton Court.

Reaching down, he lifted Amelia up by the hair. He held her close to him and became so intoxicated with the thought of taking his pleasure, he didn't notice the sudden silence. The Maroons' shouting had stopped. The slaves had stopped their crying.

Abraham galloped past the burning barn and slave quarters to the foot of the steps and swiftly dismounted. He sprang up the steps to the veranda. His authority was immediate and complete.

Seeing him, Alabama Jim released Amelia. She crumpled to the ground next to Henry. Abraham and Alabama Jim stood staring at one another. Then Abraham turned to his soldiers. "While you are slaughtering women and children, your own families are defenseless! I am ordering you to mount up now!"

That's when Abraham saw Henry. Stunned, he asked, "Who did this?" But no response was needed. Abraham launched himself at Alabama Jim, punching him hard up under the jaw. The blow knocked Jim from his feet. He quickly rose and swung his tomahawk at Abraham's head, barely missing as Abraham ducked. The veranda cleared instantly.

Alabama Jim circled, tomahawk in hand, looking to strike a fatal blow at the unarmed Abraham. "You going to kill me now, Jim? Your actions already killed these people's dream," said Abraham, pointing to the Maroons.

"You're the one that betrayed us," said Jim. "You're the one that made deals with the white man, and you're the one that's going to die."

"Here," cried Amelia as she tossed Abraham a machete. Alabama Jim wielded his tomahawk and swung again at Abraham. Abraham blocked the blow with the machete, then punched Jim with his other hand. Jim stumbled backward, falling.

"What's the matter, Jim?" baited Abraham. "Not used to fighting an armed opponent?"

Jim raised himself up, pulled a knife from his belt and held it in his free hand. Circling Abraham, he brandished his tomahawk and knife. Abraham put both hands on the machete and raised it over his head. He stepped forward, thrusting again and again. Jim blocked the first blow with his tomahawk, the second with his knife. As Abraham stepped forward again, Jim kicked him behind the ankle, tripping him.

As Abraham sprawled to the ground, Alabama Jim stepped forward and swung his tomahawk, attempting to split open Abraham's skull. Abraham yanked his head to the side, avoiding the blow, and then plunged the machete into Jim's exposed middle. Alabama Jim's blood poured all over Abraham's arms as he held onto the machete. Then Jim raised himself up off the machete. He dropped his weapons and stood there, holding his wound, staring at Abraham. Then his knees buckled and he fell to the ground, dead.

Henry's death was the final reminder to Abraham that he'd made a terrible mistake when he put Alabama Jim in a position of authority. He hoped that it wasn't too late to return with the Maroon cavalry and save the day.

Exhausted, Abraham looked out at the Maroons. Words weren't necessary. They carefully placed the stolen belongings they were holding on the ground. Then they went to their horses, mounted up and formed a line. The freed slaves traveling with the Maroons took their cue and did the same.

Across the grounds, the stable and slave quarters burned. Abraham looked to Amelia's slaves, standing there stunned. He saw Henry's sons and called to them. "Elijah, Joseph! Put a bucket brigade together and douse those flames."

The boys reacted immediately, and in another minute a line of slaves had formed from the well to the barn and slave quarters, passing buckets of water between them.

Ruth cuddled Henry's body as Abraham lifted Amelia into his arms. She placed her head on his chest. Standing over Henry and Ruth, they both began to cry. Tears continued to run down Abraham's cheeks as he carried Amelia into the house.

He gently laid her on the sofa in the study. She clung to him, refusing to let go. "Don't leave me! Please!" she cried, pleading between tears.

"You'll be safe now," said Abraham soothingly.

"Stay with me," begged Amelia.

Abraham wanted to stay. He wanted to hold Amelia and make passionate love to her. He wanted to release the twenty-five years of pent-up passion he felt for her. Yet how could he delay here with the white army marching on Freedom Land?

"We both have to go. You'll be fine. Besides, I need your help in Charleston," said Abraham in a calm, collected tone.

"I'll help you," whispered Amelia, with all her heart. She managed a smile. For a moment it seemed Abraham was going to simply walk out. Suddenly he clasped Amelia in his arms. They embraced. Then he gently laid her onto the sofa and walked out without looking back.

10

The forced march to St. Augustine took three days. The Seminole were compelled to walk for twenty hours and sleep for only four. Fortunately, all of the Indians were in very good condition. This was not true of their leader. Billy was coughing and sweating all during the march. His health deteriorated in direct proportion to his state of mind. When they arrived at their destination, Billy was very weak and in a deep depression, although none of the Seminoles blamed him for the treachery.

The only building large enough to house all the captives until their trial was a warehouse used to store cotton. It had a large wooden door on a rolling hinge that allowed it to slide open. At gunpoint, the eighty Indians were forced to empty the bales of cotton onto wagons outside. Then they were herded into the warehouse. The large door was closed and bolted from the outside.

The room was dark and damp. There was only one small window

ten feet above the ground, so very little light came in. The Indians were given a large barrel of ground corn grits and a dozen small bowls. As the Seminoles gathered around the barrel, Wild Cat scooped out twelve bowls full and handed them to a dozen comrades. When they had finished eating, they brought the bowls back, and twelve more Indians ate. In an hour all of the Seminoles except Billy had eaten. Wild Cat took the last bowlful for Billy and knelt down beside him. Although Billy hadn't eaten in three days, he had no appetite.

"Eat!" demanded Wild Cat. Billy just looked at him with a blank stare. "Please," implored Wild Cat, taking a different tack. Billy reluctantly put a handful of ground corn in his mouth, chewed and swallowed. When Wild Cat offered more, Billy waved it off.

In one corner several Seminoles tried digging under the wall, using the bowls as shovels. All they accomplished was to produce a loud scraping, as the warehouse was constructed on top of a slab of bedrock. Outside, the guards heard them, banged their rifle butts against the wall of the warehouse, and laughed among themselves at the futility of the Indians' actions. The Seminoles were soon forced to urinate and defecate in that same corner. The air in the warehouse took on a decidedly foul odor.

General Hernandez scheduled the military trial of the captured renegades and their leader, Billy Powell, to commence immediately. The charges were that the Seminoles had killed United States Army personnel, stolen property, including weapons and supplies, harbored fugitives, including escaped slaves, and conspired to commit high treason against the republic. Five officers would hear evidence presented by Angus McClane, a civilian special prosecutor. McClane was a St. Augustine attorney with political aspirations, and his expectation was to parlay a conviction and mass hanging into the Florida governorship.

Hernandez's problem was that there was no lawyer available to defend the Seminoles. In the name of expediency, Hernandez appointed McClane's junior associate, twenty-three-year-old William Dawson. He was only a law clerk, and he didn't want to be charged with the responsibility for defending these men. However, after it was explained that his representation would be better than none at all, he reluctantly agreed. As for preparation, he was told he would hear the government's case the next day and formulate his defense based upon it. The trial would start promptly at nine A.M.

As the sun set, Billy squatted in a corner coughing. He was very weak. Wild Cat, his constant attendant, took his own shirt off and curled it up into a pillow. Then he eased Billy down, trying to make him as comfortable as possible. Billy lay back staring up at the ceiling. Suddenly he noticed that the roof was made of wooden planks. He lay there staring, transfixed in thought. As the last rays of daylight came through the small window, a new vitality seemed to take over Billy. Mustering his strength, he sat up.

"Men, we are getting out tonight," called out Billy to his fellow Seminoles.

"Osceola, close your eyes. You need to rest," said Wild Cat, thinking Billy delirious.

"Listen to me," implored Billy. He weakly pulled Wild Cat closer to hear his barely audible instructions. Soon Wild Cat was nodding eagerly.

Fifteen minutes later, an Indian stood on another Indian's shoulders and looked through the small high window to watch for the guards. Meanwhile, Billy supervised the construction of a human pyramid, eight men wide at the base. Six men climbed up on their shoulders, and then four more climbed on top of them.

Wild Cat climbed up the bodies to the top and began to work on loosening one of the planks. Gradually he pushed one free. The space was just large enough for a man to squeeze through.

Ten soldiers were on guard duty outside the bolted door of the warehouse. Forty soldiers patrolled the perimeter of the compound unaware of the happenings on the roof.

One by one the Seminoles climbed up the bodies of their comrades and exited through the gap. Once outside, each man lay flat against the roof. When there were no longer enough men remaining to be climbed over, an Indian was held by his ankles and lowered through the hole. Inside the prison, at ground level, another Indian would cup his hands, and then boost a comrade up into the waiting hands. Once their hands grasped, the Indians on the roof pulled their companion up through the hole. At four in the morning, three hours after the escape began, and less than two hours before dawn and certain exposure, only Wild Cat and Billy were left inside.

Billy sat down heavily, drained of strength. He gestured to Wild Cat, pointing upward. "Go and fight."

Wild Cat shook his head, refusing to leave Billy.

"Wild Cat, listen to me," said Billy. "I'm too weak."

"No!" said Wild Cat adamantly, in a hushed tone.

"Tell Abraham I flew too close to the sun."

Wild Cat didn't know what to make of the statement.

"Listen to me, Wild Cat. Hadjo should lead you. The white man will never fool him."

"No!" repeated Wild Cat.

"Listen," beseeched Billy. "Go, then come back and get me out."

This finally appeased Wild Cat, and he nodded. Billy struggled to his feet. He clasped his hands together for Wild Cat to step on. Wild Cat hugged Billy. Then he placed his foot in Billy's entwined hands. The two friends looked at each other.

"Tell Morning Dew I love her," said Billy.

He used the last of his strength to boost Wild Cat up to the hands hanging down from the roof. The entire warehouse was empty except for Billy as he crumpled to the ground.

Wild Cat looked down at the solitary figure. He knew what he had to do. He would avenge this treachery.

The forty-man squad patrolling the perimeter of the compound walked by the warehouse, unaware that seventy-nine Seminoles were lying flat against the roof. When the nearest sentries turned the corner, Wild Cat led the escaping Seminoles down the wall, across the cleared space and out into the nearby forest.

"Where is Osceola?" asked a Seminole warrior.

"He was too sick," answered Wild Cat.

"We must go back and get Osceola," said another Seminole, when he realized his leader was absent.

"No," said Wild Cat. "It was his decision to remain. He asked that we first defend our families against the white army, then come back and get him."

"But he'll be dead by then," protested the warrior.

"He is the Chief, and this is his order," said Wild Cat.

Wild Cat didn't need to urge anyone on. As tired as they were from their three-day march, the exhilaration of escape and the fresh air of freedom gave them renewed energy.

Fifty soldiers stood with rifles cocked as the door to the warehouse was unbolted. Behind them another fifty soldiers waited in reserve in the event the Seminole prisoners tried to make a break. Two soldiers carried in the bucket of ground corn that was breakfast for the eighty captives. Entering the dark, foul-smelling prison, the soldiers could not believe their eyes. Only Chief Osceola remained in the dimness.

The alarm was sounded throughout the compound, waking General Hernandez from a sound sleep. Coming out onto the veranda of the guest house dressed only in his robe, Hernandez was incensed when he heard of the escape. "Bring me the captain of the guard," he shouted. Immediately the captain appeared on the porch. He stood at attention. Hernandez slapped him across the face, hard. "You are demoted to private."

Hernandez was slightly relieved when he inspected the warehouse and found Chief Osceola lying in the corner, ill. Everyone knew Osceola was the mastermind of the resistance. Without his leadership the other Seminole wouldn't be difficult to round up. Still, he wanted to take no chances. Fearful that the Indians or niggers would be coming back, he ordered that Chief Osceola be transported north to Charleston for safekeeping until the military could reconvene his trial.

Hernandez then ordered a member of his militia to ride to General Taylor, alert him of the escape, and advise him to have Tracks on the Moon follow the escaping Seminoles' trail. "I'm certain it will lead to the rest of the savages and possibly even the niggers," wrote Hernandez in the dispatch to General Taylor.

The rest of the militia was put on heightened alert. If the Indians came back to free their Chief, the militia would be waiting.

The escaping Seminoles knew they would be pursued. Fortunately for them, General Hernandez had his company of cavalry ring the area surrounding Osceola's makeshift prison rather then chase them. He was convinced that they would be back to free their Chief.

As the Indians ran along a shallow ravine, Captain Gardner's dog jumped out in front of them and began barking, happy to see his new master, Wild Cat. Wild Cat stopped in his tracks, petted the animal and smiled.

"What are you doing here, boy? You come to rescue me?" asked Wild Cat.

"No," said Martens. "We came."

Wild Cat looked up as Martens and twenty-five Maroons stepped out of the bush. Each was armed with a Spanish breech-loading rifle, and a tomahawk and knife in his belt.

Wild Cat glanced over Martens' shoulder at the Maroon soldiers. Each of them looked determined to carry out their mission despite the heavy odds.

"I believe you'd've done it," said Wild Cat, heartened by his allies' presence. "The Spanish general's cavalry will be along soon," he cautioned.

"We know," said Martens. "There's also a white army; thousands of men marching south to take us back to slavery."

The American army, guided by Tracks on the Moon, followed the Seminole migration. This time the Seminole didn't intentionally leave a well-marked trial. They didn't need to, as the migration of over a thousand Maroon and Seminole men, women and children walking through a sea of saw grass had left a trail not unlike a herd of buffalo.

As Moon followed, showing General Taylor's army the way south toward Lake Okeechobee, he kept expecting to see evidence of the Indians doubling back to ambush them, but to his surprise it merely led onward.

The Maroon scouts were well aware of the lumbering American army's march south. It was Abraham's decision not to harass them, but to let them march unopposed deeper and deeper into Florida, stretching their supply lines and bolstering their false sense of confidence.

Dawn rose on a tranquil scene. A sea of green and gray blades of saw grass as high as eight feet in places flowed and ebbed with the soft morning breeze, blending in with the sky at the distant horizon. Beneath the saw grass the earth was muck, sometimes solidly packed, but in most other places a man would sink in knee-deep and a wagon wheel would disappear completely.

The Seminole people were scattered over almost a mile of this marsh. Each found a firm hammock on which to rest and spend the night after five grueling days of their forced retreat. They had been traveling twenty miles a day, a remarkable feat considering the migration included women, children, infants, toddlers and old men. Each had been carrying their meager belongings and a week's ration of dried meat and corn cakes, while battling the heat and powerful rays of the subtropical sun.

Hadjo led fifteen of his warriors through the ranks of the Seminole people, camped inside this grass prairie. Several carried freshly killed deer. They had stalked and killed them before daybreak in this rich marsh. They used their bows so as not to waste precious ammunition or alert the Americans to their whereabouts.

Smoke rose from the kettles boiling soup made from snakes, frogs, turtles and other kinds of reptiles that the Seminole children could catch. Hadjo and his warriors checked on the widows, orphans and infirm, leaving the fresh meat where they deemed necessary even before visiting their own families. There was no formal ceremony, but the Seminole tribe now looked to Hadjo as their leader to fill the vacuum left by Osceola's capture.

Micanopy, sitting beside his daughter, stood up and looked out over the throngs of what once had been his people. To Micanopy they would always be his people.

"If they listened to me, all of this could have been prevented," said Micanopy to no one in particular as he agonized, expecting the worst. Suddenly he had a revelation. "It may not be too late," he said, turning to his daughter. "With your help maybe I can save us."

Looking up at her father from her plate of fried corn meal, Morning Dew spat a pebblelike hard kernel of corn, as if to get the bad taste of her father's remark out of her mouth.

"Who left you in charge?" she seethed, dropping her plate and rising to look her father in the eye.

"I am trying to help our people," answered Micanopy passionately.

"Are you saying that my husband is dead?" asked Morning Dew.

"What do we do if he is dead?" asked Micanopy.

"I'll tell you what we are not going to do. We are not going to betray all he fought for," said Morning Dew. "One word out of you, and I'll kill you."

Micanopy looked into his daughter's eyes and knew she meant it. He sat back down. Morning Dew looked off in the distance, worried. Much as she made a conscious effort to believe that Billy was all right, her fears for his safety intensified.

There was no escaping the sun. Soon it would be high in the sky, and the comfort afforded by the early morning would evaporate with the dew. At any moment they would break camp and continue south. One more day of traveling and they would reach the shelter afforded by the thick wooded trees around Lake Okeechobee.

After waiting three days for the Seminole to return, General Hernandez realized they wouldn't be coming back to rescue their leader. He hoped to make up for the escape by somehow repeating his earlier success. Pushing his soldiers hard for six days and nights, he caught up with General Taylor's army marching south. Though they traveled over a hundred miles through the heart of Seminole territory, they had not seen even one Indian.

The army, despite the clear trail, had been slowed by poisoned wells, torrential rain, bogged-down wagons, humidity, and swarming mosquitoes.

When they reached the sea of saw grass, the Indians' trail led right through it. There was no way to go around it as it stretched as far as the eye could see in every direction. If they went east or west to avoid it, there was no telling how far they would have to go and whether they would be able to pick up the Indians' trail again.

"If they can cross it, we can," said General Taylor to Lieutenant Graham as he looked out at the waving sea of saw grass.

"I'm not sure it's a good idea, sir," said Graham.

"Poppycock," said General Taylor in response to Graham's reservations.

The mile-long column of soldiers, horses, wagons and artillery pieces entered the marsh. Within one hour, three wagons sank wheel-deep in the bog. Despite the efforts of twenty soldiers pushing and pulling, they could not free them. General Taylor ordered the remaining fifteen wagons to turn around and wait at the northern edge. A mile farther in, the two cannons were stuck in the mire. "Lieutenant, destroy the firing mechanisms and abandon the cannons," said General Taylor.

"Sir, it is not too late to turn back," said Graham.

"Artillery pieces are not necessary in battling the Seminole," said Taylor. "We are chasing a decimated group of Indians who have lost their leader. We must follow and capture them before they have a chance to disperse throughout Florida."

Graham knew that this was pure folly. Yes, the Indians were without Billy Powell, but the Seminole and their Negro allies were a formidable foe. "They'd already ambushed and destroyed Dade's command. True, this army was thirty times larger than Dade's," thought Graham, "but to take them on out here could lead to a disaster of epic proportions."

Fifty-two miles to the south, Lake Okeechobee covered seven hundred square miles of central Florida. Though nowhere more than fifteen feet deep, the huge freshwater lake dominated the central Florida landscape. Water from the lake flowed south through the Everglades to the Gulf of Mexico. The lake teemed with bass and catfish, making ideal fishing grounds for the Seminole and Maroons.

On Abraham's command all of the Maroon women and children, over five hundred in number, gathered in a large field by the lakeshore. The Maroon army was there as well, having accompanied their families south.

Jamima and Garcia passed out the two hundred remaining muskets to the Maroon women and children. They were familiar with these weapons, having been drilled repeatedly by Abraham. Even the younger children, boys not yet eight years old, were adept at loading.

Abraham believed in being prepared for every foreseeable obstacle. Previously, he had drilled his army during a torrential downpour. Not certain when the attack would come, Abraham did not rule out a nighttime strike by his adversary. Thus Abraham insisted that his army train in the dark.

Just before midnight, with the thick moisture-laden clouds hanging low and no stars visible, the Seminole women and children arrived, escorted by Hadjo and the remains of the Seminole army. They were surprised to see the Maroons, in full battle dress, being drilled by Abraham.

Abraham ordered everyone to remain at their battle stations while he had a word with Hadjo. After the brief conversation, Abraham ascertained that the Americans were at least a day behind. He then dismissed everyone with instructions to reconvene at dawn. The Maroons—soldiers, women and children—flopped down to rest until dawn. They were exhausted and wet from their own sweat, caused by the humidity and the light, misting rain they'd trained through. Mixed in among them were the Seminole women and children and two hundred twelve Seminole men. Hardly the professional army that Billy Powell envisioned when he plotted his plan for a quick victory over the Americans.

As dawn broke, Abraham ordered his lieutenants, Jamima and John Horse, to a conference at his command post, a U.S. Army-issue chair and canvas half tent taken in a recent supply raid. He laid out his plan for the coming battle. "You both know what I expect of you and those under your command," he said. He rose from his chair, took a rifle and fired it into the air. He wanted everyone assembled before him. "Gather around, people," shouted Abraham. "Hear my words. You all know that the white man is coming," he began. "We are outnumbered, but we are fighting a tired, hungry army which does not need a lot of discouragement to quit. I have a plan for the coming battle. If you follow it and do your part, we will win. It is particularly important that you act with courage at the start of the battle. I want all of you to stop a moment and look inside yourselves. Be thankful for the freedom that we have had. Then ask yourself what sacrifice you are willing to make to ensure your family's continued freedom. As long as one of you survives, free, we win. If all of us die fighting for our freedom, we win. It is only when we choose slavery to keep on living that we have betrayed ourselves and our cause."

The wind was blowing from the east. It was a sea breeze and all that Abraham hoped for. Looking up at the sky, Abraham was confident from the lack of clouds that the weather would hold.

The preparation for the battle was going forward. As instructed, John Horse and ten of his soldiers poured all of the remaining coal oil used for lamps onto the grass in a line going north and south fifty yards east of Abraham's projected defensive line. Then they sprinkled gunpowder into the mix. When they were done, John Horse stationed two of his soldiers at the entrance to the saw grass to warn when the Americans approached. Abraham chose this location because the American army exiting the marsh would enter his trap, or be forced to retreat back into the swamp.

"Preparations complete, sir," said John Horse as he arrived in front of Abraham.

Abraham nodded at his commander. "Form up!" shouted John Horse. His company of Maroons formed ranks. They assembled in the rows of a well-disciplined army.

"Form up," shouted Jamima, and the ten women and forty men in her command, including her son Garcia, fell into rows of five.

Behind Abraham two hundred Maroon soldiers took up their position facing the same hundred-yard corridor. These soldiers would be the anvil. John Horse and Jamima's soldiers would be the hammer. When the American army arrived in between, they would be flattened.

The Seminole warriors watched the preparation, weapons in hand, wondering if there was a place for them. Hadjo walked over and stood before Abraham. "Why is it, Abraham, that my warriors are not a part of your defense?" asked Hadjo.

"In a battle, everyone must follow orders. If someone shoots too soon, or doesn't protect the position assigned, all could be lost," said Abraham.

"You think we are cowards?" asked Hadjo.

"No one is questioning your courage," said Abraham. "In the past, though, you have shown a reluctance to obey orders you did not agree with. I cannot afford to have even one man act on his own."

Just then they heard, "They're coming! They're coming!" shouted by the two soldiers John Horse had stationed at the edge of the saw grass.

Yet emerging from the path was not the American army but Martens leading the twenty-four Maroon scouts, followed by Wild Cat and the rest of the escaped Seminoles.

Cheers rang out from the women who were cautiously watching from behind Abraham's soldiers. Everyone thought they'd seen the last of Osceola's brave soldiers. What a lift it provided, thought Abraham, when they most needed it.

Morning Dew led the women rushing through Abraham's defensive line, running to greet their loved ones. She spotted Wild Cat and cried out to him. Her heart was racing as she ran to him.

"I'm sorry," he said sorrowfully. "Osceola was sick. He remained behind, so that I could escape."

All the joy left Morning Dew. Abraham, following closely behind her, greeted Wild Cat with a smile. "Where is Osceola?" he asked.

"We'll have to go back and get him out," said Wild Cat.

"Did everyone else escape?" asked Abraham.

"Yes, and we're ready to fight," said Wild Cat.

Abraham turned to Morning Dew. "At least he's alive," he said, comforting her.

"I have to go to him. I need a horse," said Morning Dew. There were eighty horses belonging to his cavalry tied up near the women beside the lake.

"You can't," said Wild Cat. "Not now, anyway. There is a huge army right behind us."

"I'm going," insisted Morning Dew.

Hadjo, who had been watching, walked over to Micanopy. "You cannot let your daughter make this journey."

"She is very capable," said Micanopy. "Besides, if she stays here, chances are the Americans will kill her or make her a slave."

Hadjo knew this was true. He picked out a fresh horse, saddled it and walked the animal over to Morning Dew. Abraham handed her money, almost five hundred dollars.

"Ride due east to the Atlantic Ocean. Then make your way north. In St. Augustine hire a boat to take you to Charleston. It shouldn't cost more than a hundred dollars. In Charleston find Amelia Hampton, and she will help you." Morning Dew remembered Amelia and her kindness.

Hadjo gave her a leg up as she mounted the buckskin gelding. "Thank you, Hadjo," she said. A single tear dropped from her eyes. Hadjo reached up and grasped her arm in support. How he wished things had turned out differently! Then he handed her a musket. She laid the weapon across the horse's withers.

Micanopy stood watching. Morning Dew steered the horse over to her father, and looked down at him. At that moment he was certain that he'd been proved right by the events that were unfolding before him. The white man was attacking. The Seminoles would be no more. If the whites didn't kill them all here, they'd come back again and again until the last Seminole was shot down or sold into slavery.

"Here is your chance to show your people how a Chief fights," said Morning Dew, "and how a Chief dies. Good-bye, Father." She clucked to her horse to get him started.

"You're wrong," shouted Micanopy at his daughter. "I always put our people's welfare first." Morning Dew did not turn back to acknowledge her father. "Do you hear me?" shouted Micanopy, even more loudly as his daughter rode away.

"You will fight here?" said Wild Cat to Abraham, breaking the uneasy silence following the scene they had all witnessed.

"In the first instance," said Abraham.

"You know how we were captured," said Wild Cat. "We need rifles to pay back that treachery."

"Behind us the women have two hundred loaded rifles and ammunition," said Abraham. "Have each of your men take a rifle, plus powder and shot for a hundred rounds."

Wild Cat grinned, then ran with the seventy-eight other Seminole to where the Maroon women were loading.

Hadjo came to stand with Abraham. "We will obey your orders, Abraham," said Hadjo. Abraham smiled, nodded, and took a step to the side, making a place for Hadjo. Two more Seminoles joined them and the Maroon line spread apart to make room. Others followed this example in groups of four or five until all of the Seminoles melded with the Maroons.

Three hours later the advance guard of General Zachary Taylor's army, led by Tracks on the Moon, emerged from the sea of saw grass. Moon spotted the combination of oil and gunpowder on the ground. "We cannot follow this trail any longer."

Abraham saw the Indian tracker and knew he had to act. Immediately he ordered fifty of the two hundred men with him to rise up and show themselves without their rifles.

General Taylor, accompanied by Lieutenant Graham, galloped up to the front. "Well, that's a sight for sore eyes," said General Taylor to Graham as he looked out at the black men with their arms in the air, standing a hundred yards away.

"Don't shoot, masser, don't shoot!" shouted Abraham.

"Mercy, masser!" shouted the others in a show of submission.

"Hold your fire, men," ordered the general.

Graham looked at Tracks on the Moon. The scout shook his head, then said, "It is a trap."

Seeing that the Negroes were asking for quarter, General Taylor ignored Tracks on the Moon's warning. The Indian abruptly turned his horse around and retreated. He would not become part of the slaughter. He passed the rows of infantry, each with a trumpeter and flag holder, giving more of the appearance of an Independence Day parade than an army going into battle.

"Sir, the scout thinks it's a trap," cautioned Graham.

"Look for yourself," said General Taylor, annoyed. Then he ordered his infantry to advance. Row after row, ten soldiers in each, moved forward holding their rifles at waist level with fixed bayonets. As the first ranks approached them, Abraham and his men still stood with their arms in the air, crying, "Mercy, masser! Don't shoot, don't shoot!"

When the infantry front was thirty yards away, Abraham and his fifty soldiers suddenly dropped to the ground. Seventy-five Maroon soldiers, rifles cocked and targets marked, stood up, and fired into the advancing army, felling all twenty soldiers in the first two rows, and killing soldiers as far back as the fifth row. Then the line of Maroons dropped to a knee to reload. Seventy-five Seminole behind them took a step forward, past the comrades on their knees loading, and fired, felling another thirty soldiers.

Taylor, incensed by the treachery, screamed to his men, "Return fire!" Then his emotions got the better of his judgment. He decided to overwhelm the Negroes with sheer numbers. "Sound the charge," he ordered his bugler.

Waves of infantry marched forward in double time. On the right flank John Horse and fifty Maroons rose up and fired, felling a swath of the charging soldiers. As the fifty Maroons dropped to a knee to reload, Jamima and her troops stepped past them and fired.

Deadly fire was pouring forth in front of and to the right flank of the advancing American army. Only to their left were they free from the hail of bullets coming at them.

Watching from astride his horse at the edge of the saw grass, General Taylor realized that he was in danger of suffering a crushing defeat. He wished he could bring his cannon to dislodge the entrenched enemy. His army had suffered over a hundred casualties in the first five minutes of battle with the Negroes. Yet he had over two thousand more infantrymen behind him, all clamoring to go into battle. He had to bring his advantage to bear. "Lieutenant Graham," shouted Taylor, "ride back and expedite those troops forward."

Graham turned his horse and laid his spurs into its flanks, sending it toward the rear at a full gallop. Meanwhile, General Taylor rode his horse back and forth at the edge of the saw grass. He called out orders. "C Company, assault the line in front! D Company, attack the flank!" The bugler blew the charge again. "Let's go, men!" shouted a sergeant as fresh soldiers ran at Abraham's lines, stepping over their fallen comrades.

Soldiers who had been lying on the battlefield, feigning death, rose up and charged with the new assault. As they advanced, murderous fire continued to pour into each line, killing and maiming dozens of soldiers. Before they got within twenty yards, less than fifty of the five hundred men were still moving toward the Maroon and Indian riflemen.

General Taylor frantically waved his arms, pointing at the Maroon lines as he ordered two more companies forward.

Seeing the onslaught coming, Abraham set the oil and powder ablaze, creating a wall of fire to the left of the American army. With the wind out of the east, the fire quickly moved toward the infantry's position. The men on the battlefield, convinced they had walked into hell, stopped in their tracks, threw their rifles down, and ran from whence they came.

General Hernandez and his cavalry moved up from the rear past the cowering and retreating infantrymen. Here, he saw, was his opportunity to turn defeat into victory, and once more be the hero.

As the bugler blew the call to charge once again, Hernandez led his cavalry down the middle of the lines and straight at the Maroons' main force. As Hernandez charged, General Taylor rode his horse back and forth urging his infantrymen to dig in and concentrate all of their fire into the two Maroon positions.

Suddenly hundreds of rounds were pouring into the Maroon positions. Men fell all around Abraham. "Everyone on the ground!" he shouted, and those not hit dropped down next to their wounded and dead comrades. Wild Cat was squatting beside Abraham when he peeked out and saw Hernandez. He quickly reloaded, then rose up to take careful aim at him. Bullets whizzed all around Wild Cat, but he took steady aim and fired. Hernandez fell from his horse, dead. "That's for you, Billy," said Wild Cat.

Abraham stood erect and aimed into the cavalry charge.

"Everyone up!" he shouted, and all the others in his line followed suit.

"Just the horses!" shouted Abraham. Everyone fired into the charging cavalry. Horses on the dead run fell, some cartwheeling, tossing their riders in every direction, causing the horses behind them to fall over them. The charge was stopped in a tangle of dead horses and men.

The trooper carrying the standard dropped the colors. He made a futile effort to retrieve them, then turned and sent his horse into full retreat. Suddenly all of the soldiers in the field abandoned their arms and ran back toward the sea of saw grass. Those in the rear saw them coming.

"Stand fast!" shouted General Taylor, but his soldiers kept running. He quickly saw he would soon be all alone, and he urged his horse into retreat.

The remnant of General Taylor's army would retreat north for five days and nights until they were safely out of Florida.

11

It didn't hurt Amelia Herbert Hampton's standing and popularity in Charleston social circles to be housing the foremost celebrity to visit the city in a decade. Everyone wanted to meet him. There were dozens of luncheon and dinner invitations that she graciously turned down. She wanted to present Billy, but in a dignified fashion. If she were still at Hampton Court, with its banquet room and staff of house slaves, she would have staged a proper event. In her three-story brick townhouse, located on fashionable King Street, she could barely seat twenty. Having freed her slaves, she had no staff for formal entertaining. Then she hit upon the idea of using the Charleston Opera House. Chief Osceola might enjoy the spectacle and pageantry of the opera, and his wife most certainly would. Amelia believed all women appreciated beauty.

Amelia had caused a sensation by arranging for the *Charleston Post* to print the story of Billy's capture, vilifying General Jesup and honoring the noble savage who had spared the American army, but who had paid the price for their treachery. The story was picked up by the *National Intelligencer*. Americans up and down the East Coast were calling for Billy's release.

The public clamor became so great, politicians in Washington, specifically the opposition to President Jackson, demanded the Chief's release. When it became known that he was suffering from a serious illness, Billy was paroled to Amelia's custody to recover his health.

Amelia made arrangements to attend the Charleston Opera House premier of *Fidelio* by Ludwig van Beethoven. All of Charleston society would be there. Unfortunately, on the day of the performance, Billy was ill with fever and the shakes. Amelia brought him more quinine. Morning Dew wrapped him in a blanket and bolstered him with hot tea. She had wished a hundred times that John the Baptist was there. He would have a cure for this affliction ravaging Billy.

As evening approached, Billy was still very weak. "I'm too ill, love," he said from his bed, as Morning Dew attempted to help him dress.

"Chief, it's important for your cause," began Amelia. "I mean, our cause," she corrected herself. "You should meet or at least be seen by Charleston society."

She could see he wasn't moved. "Look upon this as an important battle," said Amelia, mustering all of her considerable persuasive powers. "Do you think Washington felt like getting out of his warm bed, crossing the Delaware and surprising the Hessians? No! He was ill, too, but he went, and the rest is history."

"Bring me my tunic," demanded Billy, delighted by this idea. "I'm going to take Charleston!"

Amelia was proud of herself. She'd invented this chapter in American history, but it had motivated Billy, and that's what mattered.

She brought out a cream-colored silk creation, fresh off the boat from Paris. She held the dress up against Morning Dew. With her skin color and tone, Amelia knew Morning Dew would be ravishing. Morning Dew protested, of course, but Billy insisted, reminding her, "It's for the cause of our freedom, love."

Amelia and her special guests, Billy and Morning Dew, arrived shortly before the second act began. As they made their way to her private box, the audience gave the stately couple a standing ovation.

The curtain rose, and Act II began. On stage, Florestan lay on the floor of a dungeon. He was heavily chained, and weak from starvation. It was his resistance to tyranny that had brought him here.

Billy and Morning Dew watched, transfixed. Though unable to understand the language, they knew there was a familiarity in the story line. Amelia could see that the couple were agitated as they watched the drama.

"Don't worry," whispered Amelia, leaning over toward the couple, "love and justice triumph in the end."

On stage, Florestan became delirious. He thought he saw his wife, in the form of an angel, watching over him, ready to lead him to the peace and the freedom of heaven.

As they watched, Morning Dew took Billy's hand. A tear ran down his cheek. Amelia took her handkerchief and handed it to Morning Dew. As she wiped Billy's face, he squeezed his bride's hand, ever appreciative of her love and loyalty.

Billy stood regally near his bedroom window, basking in the afternoon light. He was wearing the ornate trappings of someone's idea of what an Indian Chief would wear. George Catlin stood beside his easel, hoping to capture on canvas the spirit of the Chief for posterity.

"I'd rather be remembered wearing a kilt in the pattern of McQueen," protested Billy. As he took his brush to the canvas, George Catlin looked at him and smiled at his suggestion.

Through the open window, Billy heard music coming from King Street. Looking down from the third-floor window, Billy saw General Taylor and his staff trot by on horseback, followed by color bearers, a military marching band, and over a thousand infantry men. A reserved crowd of civilian onlookers watched as the army marched south.

"It's another final victory parade," said the painter, rolling his eyes. "Second one this year," he explained, with more than a touch of sarcasm.

Seeing the aghast look on Billy's face, Catlin clarified that. "Since there were huge casualties on our side, the army assumed there were at least as many Seminoles killed. That being the case, they reasoned the Seminole population had been wiped out."

"That's not true," protested Billy.

"You're preaching to the converted, son," said the artist.

Billy backed away from the window. He was in a cold sweat, having mustered all of his strength to stand there and pose.

Morning Dew rose from her chair next to the bed. She didn't hide the fact that she was very annoyed. "That's enough. He needs to be in bed."

She helped Billy take off the outfit, and then she tucked him into a four-poster bed. George Catlin cleaned his brush and laid it down. It had been very slow going for the portrait artist. It seemed that every time he got started he had to stop because of distractions like the parade or Billy's deteriorating condition.

As the artist was about to leave, Amelia Hampton entered, accompanied by the recently promoted Captain Graham in full dress uniform. Graham removed his hat. He noticed the easel and looked at the developing portrait. He turned back to Catlin and nodded his head in approval. He approached the bed and greeted Morning Dew, who was too annoyed to return the greeting. Billy smiled at the unexpected visitor.

"My company was marching in the victory parade," said Graham, "when I bumped into Miss Hampton. I had to see you. I hope you don't mind." He saw the quizzical look on Billy's face when he said victory parade. "Your side is winning," continued Graham. "The army abandoned Fort King and withdrew from Florida." He saw the blank stare on Billy's face.

"What about the victory parade?" uttered Billy weakly, still trying to understand.

"Yes, a victory parade," repeated Graham sarcastically. "One more such victory," he added, "would be all any nation could stand."

"Considering the magnitude of the victory," added Amelia facetiously, "they'll probably rename the towns in Florida after our illustrious military leaders."

Billy closed his eyes momentarily.

"Billy," called Amelia to get his attention. He opened his eyes and looked at her. "This letter was brought to me by..." Amelia searched for words to explain the slave who had handed her this letter, "special courier." She handed Billy the sealed envelope. "It's from Abraham."

Lying in bed, Billy fumbled with the envelope. Amelia took it from him, removed the letter and handed it back. As he read the words, Billy could almost hear Abraham speaking.

My Dear Friend,

May God speed your recovery. As it is unlikely we will see each other any time soon, it is important that you know how we feel about you. As long as my people live, they will speak your name. Their children will hear your story and their children's children will sing your praises. Your courage would have made your father, and your mother, proud. You will serve as a shining example wherever people fight for their freedom. Your selfless actions have enabled us to continue our struggle for freedom. We will never surrender.

—Forever in your debt,
Abraham.

Postscript,
I am writing at the behest of the Seminole and Maroon people and myself.

A smile came over Billy's face. "Graham, see if you can get someone to take a bet," he said, mustering all his strength to speak.

"A bet?" questioned Graham as he leaned closer to hear his weakened voice.

"Yes," said Billy. "I want to bet that a hundred years from now there will still be Seminole in Florida."

Graham patted Billy's shoulder reassuringly. "Of course there will be."

Billy looked at Morning Dew. He smiled, then closed his eyes. Then, opening them again, Billy looked up from his bed and saw his father standing there, straight and erect, wearing his red officer's tunic, brass buttons shimmering in the sunlight.

"Where'd you come from?" asked a very surprised Billy.

"I've always been here," said the major in his familiar Scottish brogue.

Billy climbed out of bed and stood at attention, much as he did the last time he saw him, during the attack on their village so many years ago.

"You must know that I lost my command," stated Billy, ashamed.

"I know that you're a hero," said the major, "and in a few short years achieved more than I did in a lifetime of service to the Crown."

"But I lost everything. I was arrogant, and as a result, I disgraced our name," said Billy.

"Wrong again," said the major. "You conducted a brilliant campaign. Yet, ironically, your victories didn't do as much for your cause as your deceitful capture."

Billy didn't understand. His father held up a copy of the *National Intelligencer*. The headline read, *Slaving expedition exposed. Congress cuts off funding. Jesup condemned for capture of Chief Osceola.*

"You won," said the major. "Your people, black and red, have stayed on the land, and the ones that did go to Arkansas took their Maroon allies with them. No one was returned to slavery."

Billy was stunned.

Then, as the happy news sank in, the major barked an order. "Follow me."

"Where are we going?" asked Billy.

"You'll see," said his father.

They walked side by side. There she was, Jasmine Powell, his mother, arms outstretched. Billy broke away from his father and ran into her arms. They hugged. Billy kissed her on the cheek. Tears welled up in both their eyes.

Billy turned to his father. "What about Morning Dew?"

"She'll be along," said the major.

Morning Dew, Amelia and Captain Graham looked down at the now-delirious Billy.

"What does he mean, 'What about Morning Dew?' Who's he talking to?" asked Graham.

"To whoever has come to take him to the spirit world," said Morning Dew, fighting back her tears.

Amelia put a comforting arm around Morning Dew's shoulder.

12

A month later Amelia was back in South Georgia. As was the custom, the distinctive ring of a high C note, made by a silver knife tapped against fine crystal, sounded three times. The guests, seventeen members of the South Georgia Cotton Planters Association, quieted. Their host was General Duncan Clinch.

A formally dressed house slave poured the 1824 Napoleon Brandy into the general's glass. He held it up for the toast. His guests did the same. "Ladies and gentlemen," said Clinch, "first let us toast Amelia Herbert Hampton, whose late husband was a charter member."

Everyone raised their glass and followed Clinch's lead. "To the fairest among us," said Clinch, before downing the drink. "Though she no longer resides among us, Miss Hampton traveled from Charleston on the recently completed railroad line to attend our annual meeting, at my behest. I wanted to show her that it is finally safe to be a cotton planter in South Georgia."

There was polite applause. Amelia smiled. All of the guests were aware of her harrowing escape from the hands of the renegade niggers. What they were not aware of was that she had taken this opportunity to rendezvous with Abraham.

"Rather than bore you with more long-winded speeches before dinner," said the general, "sit back now and enjoy the delicate treat of pheasant under glass which my chef has prepared for the occasion."

All of the guests knew that at Auld Lang Syne they were certain to get a first-class dinner, equal to the finest restaurants in Charleston, New York, or even Paris.

After another minute, though, no one came out of the kitchen. The general called over his wine servant. "Go to the kitchen and hurry things along. My guests are waiting."

The wine steward did as he was instructed and entered the large swinging door at the far end of the room. Thirty seconds later the wine steward exited the swinging door and walked directly over to General Clinch.

"Well?" demanded the general, sternly.

"They are all gone, sir," said the steward with just a touch of pride.

"What?" bellowed the general.

"The kitchen is empty, sir," repeated the steward.

The guests talked among themselves of this embarrassment, except for Amelia Hampton who, despite biting her cheek, began laughing.

The moon was behind low clouds as Martens led eight escaping slaves, still dressed in their white kitchen attire, away from the house and around the edge of a cotton field. A rider galloped by on the adjacent road. Martens held up his hand, and everyone crouched low. The slaves were nervous. As they squatted on the edge of the field, Martens heard echoes of what now seemed like another lifetime.

"This talk of Abraham and the promised land sounds like Bible talk to me," said one of the runaways.

"It's not Bible talk," was Martens' impassioned answer. "Freedom Land was real. I was there. One day, with your help, we will build it again."

Then, after looking all around, he raised his arm in a gesture for those with him to follow. "Come on," implored Martens, when the runaways hesitated.

Nearby, from astride his horse, Abraham watched the escape. He kept playing the scene of his rendezvous with Amelia over and over again in his mind. He had met her on the road. He had entered her luxury carriage. She pulled the curtains closed, and reached for him. "Make love to me," she said. He took her in his arms and kissed her passionately. As he touched her silky skin, he memorized every part of her.

Afterward, Amelia whispered in his ear, "Let's go away so we can be together."

"Where would we go?" asked Abraham, absently stroking her hair.

"Paris," said Amelia, without hesitating. "After all, your command of the French language is perfect. And when I introduce you as the general who beat the French army in Haiti, and the man who founded Freedom Land, the Parisians will love you."

Abraham smiled. "You think so? What would I do all day?"

"You could write your memoir. Call it *Up from Slavery*," Amelia said. She moved around in his arms to face him. She wanted to see his reaction. The look in his eyes was so loving, she thought. Then she saw the tear slide down his cheek.

"What would I do with the four-hundred families in my charge who are scattered throughout the Everglades?" he asked.

"But it's so dangerous now," Amelia said, as she drew him to her and hugged him tighter, terrified that she would never see him again. "You've already done so much."

Abraham gently untwined her so they could take a long last look at one another. Both knew that Paris would never happen. Then he kissed her gently on the forehead and exited the carriage.

"Abraham," called Martens. "Abraham," he said again, trying to get his attention. "We got to go." Abraham came back from his thoughts. He took one last look at the house in the distance. Amelia was in there. Then he looked down from his horse at the eight runaway slaves. He turned the animal around, and led the travelers south.

AUTHOR'S NOTE

The war lasted seven years. It cost the United States forty million dollars. Fifteen hundred American soldiers were officially reported killed or missing, though the actual casualties were at least triple that number.

Osceola was honored in every major newspaper of the time. His portrait, painted by George Catlin, hangs in the Smithsonian.

General Jesup, vilified by those same newspapers, spent the remainder of his career apologizing for capturing Osceola under a flag of truce.

The Seminole and their Maroon allies never surrendered. No Maroon was ever returned to slavery. Their descendants live free in Florida and Arkansas to this day.